GOING

FOR

A BEER

GOING

FOR

A BEER

selected
short fictions

ROBERT COOVER

Introduction by T.C. Boyle

W. W. NORTON & COMPANY
Independent Publishers Since 1923
New York | London

Copyright © 2018 by Robert Coover
Introduction copyright © 2018 by T.C. Boyle

For information about permission to reproduce selections from this book, write to Permissions, W. W. Norton & Company, Inc., 500 Fifth Avenue, New York, NY 10110

For information about special discounts for bulk purchases, please contact W. W. Norton Special Sales at specialsales@wwnorton.com or 800-233-4830

Manufacturing by LSC Communications, Harrisonburg
Book design by Chris Welch
Production manager: Beth Steidle

Library of Congress Cataloging-in-Publication Data

Names: Coover, Robert, author. | Boyle, T. Coraghessan, writer of introduction.
Title: Going for a beer : selected short fictions / Robert Coover ;
introduction by T.C. Boyle.
Description: First edition. | New York : W. W. Norton & Company, 2018.
Identifiers: LCCN 2017051773 | ISBN 9780393608465 (hardcover)
Classification: LCC PS3553.O633 A6 2018 | DDC 813/.54—dc23
LC record available at https://lccn.loc.gov/2017051773

W. W. Norton & Company, Inc., 500 Fifth Avenue, New York, N.Y. 10110
www.wwnorton.com

W. W. Norton & Company Ltd., 15 Carlisle Street, London W1D 3BS

1 2 3 4 5 6 7 8 9 0

For You, QBSP

Once, some time ago and in a distant land, I met a young maiden, known to her tribe as the Virgin of the Post, and she gave to me, amid prurient and mysterious ceremonies, a golden ring. Perhaps it was a local custom, a greeting of sorts. Or perhaps a message, an invitation, a mission even. Some peculiar Moorish device of transport and return. Wand-scabbard. Open-sesame. Who can say? It bears on one edge an indecipherable legend, a single cleft rune, not unlike the maiden's own vanished birthmark, and I am inclined to believe that portentous inscrutability may in fact be the point of it all. Now, to that Virgin, I offer these apprentice calculations of my own, invented under the influence of her gifts, begging her to remember the Wisdom of the Beast: "If I carry the poison in my head, in my tail which I bite with rage lies the remedy."

—from the original jacket flap copy for *Pricksongs & Descants*, 1969

CONTENTS

INTRODUCTION

by T.C. Boyle

In the beginning was the word, and rightly so: the world is constructed of stories, supported by stories, inhabited by stories. We get up in the morning, go for a beer, tumble into bed at night, and before we know it our lives have blinked out and we are none the wiser as to the essential story, the only one that matters: the story of what we are doing here on this mysterious planet. In its place—and as a buffer against the nullity of the universe stripped bare—we have created an elaborate and self-reflexive mythos to comfort and provoke us. From the earliest moments of consciousness we are bathed in words and we grow to batten on them and eventually manipulate them ourselves in the most deeply rooted incantatory way, *Humpty Dumpty had a great fall, You must remember this,* the Pied Piper of Hamelin, Goldilocks and the Three Bears, Jesus and God and Noah and the Virgin Birth, Aesop, *sour grapes,* the Invasion of the Martians, *But grandmother, what big teeth you have!*

Robert Coover isn't so much interested in decoding the ur-stories of Western civilization in the way of Jung and his archetypes or codifying them as Calvino did in *Fiabe italiane*, his magisterial compendium of Italian folktales, but rather employing them in the spirit of Borges or Asturias, by way of extracting their magic in order to make more and livelier magic from them. Coover's stories, and this is the case with nearly all the thirty selected here, exist in a cascading present-tense now that hurtles the reader through a shifting series of narrative choices mimicking the potentialities flooding the writer's psyche in the moment of composition. Thus, a story like "The Magic Poker," in which the idyll of a summer's day on a sunlit isle is repeatedly deconstructed and restored by the Prospero figure who creates it and imposes his own Caliban on the nubile sisters who come innocently to enjoy it. Or Coover's recasting of the Grimm Brothers' "Hansel and Gretel" in "The Gingerbread House," which similarly shuffles incident and perspective to oppose innocence and darkness, the door of the magical house "shining like a ruby, like hard cherry candy, and pulsing softly, radiantly. Yes, marvelous! delicious! insuperable! but beyond: what is that sound of black rags flapping?" That, of course, is the sound of experience, the sound of the three bears abjuring the niceties of civilization and reverting to, well, bears, it's the gargle in the throat of the dead queen, the mortal gasp of the eviscerated fox in "Aesop's Forest," the ending the fables subliminally promise but don't dare deliver.

So too with "The Babysitter," Coover's best-known story, in which the perspective shifts through a series of often conflicting incidents and points of view ("narrative slices," as William Gass has it, "that we might scoop . . . up and reshuffle, altering not the elements but the order or the rules of play"). Is the babysitter alive and well? Has the husband returned to rape her? Has the baby drowned in the tub? The result is a hilarious and subversive take on the conventional portrayal of the middle-class family and its mores, ending with two opposing possibilities: in the first, all is well, the children asleep and the dishes done; in the second, the housewife is informed, "Your children are murdered, your husband gone, a corpse in your bathtub, and your house is wrecked." This is most definitely not the American family we thought we knew, the family of the sitcom, the magazine spread, the stories we've placidly absorbed throughout our lives.

As time goes on, these received stories become dulled by repetition, fixed, ossified, while the authority of the storyteller reigns absolute ("Once upon a time, this was how it was"), trivializing the content and vitiating the form. Coover's transformations offer a sly counterpoint. They tell us this is how it is, or might be, or will be, or can't be, the story alive and evolving on the page, open-ended, sans predetermined outcome, as in "The Goldilocks Variations": "He dreams of happy endings, but the story he is in, which is every creature's story, must do without. Raising voices against it is of no avail. The consequence is a despair that invites the very ending one is seeking in vain to avoid." In the same way, the narrator of "Beginnings" ventures forth from his island to the shore, where people tell him stories, "astounding him with their fearless capacity for denouement." Beginnings and endings: there's no end to them.

Coover's first collection, *Pricksongs & Descants*, contains a book within a book, "Seven Exemplary Fictions," dedicated to Cervantes, whose example, as innovator and rejecter of "exhausted art forms," serves as his inspiration. In the *Prólogo* to this volume, Coover sets forth the aesthetic vision that will shape his work throughout his career, from the stories collected here to his novels and novellas as well: "The novelist uses familiar mythic or historical forms to combat the content of those forms and to conduct the reader . . . to the real, away from mystification to clarification, away from magic to maturity, away from mystery to revelation." Precisely. This is the method, this is the rationale. Though only one of the "Seven Exemplary Fictions" appears here—"The Brother," the first story in this collection—it underscores the point and serves as a gateway to all that follow.

The brother delivers his tale in a breathless unpunctuated monologue employing a sort of aw-shucks rural American dialect that disarms the reader into accepting—and sympathizing with—his version of events. Each reader will have a moment of epiphany, the key turning in the lock of the myth, as he or she realizes just whose brother the brother is and that his story is foreordained in the foundational mythology of Western civilization, the Bible. We wish him well, we root for him, but we know he doesn't have a chance (in hell—or, more to the point, in heaven). In the original, Noah has his orders from the very highest authority—humanity is a disappointment, a failed experiment, and God, the original God, the God of *my God* and *thank God* and *God what a mess*, has decided to start again, no exceptions. One wonders: Was all of humanity equally depraved? Did everyone, even someone as demonstrably good and kind and loving as our narrator, deserve his fate? Well, yes, of course he did—it says so right in the Good Book. The genius here—and this is one of the touchstone stories of our time— is in the way Coover reshuffles the deck and allows the reader to move "away from mystification to clarification," and see the story in a whole new light that calls that very authorial authority into question.

These are unexpected stories, bawdy, outrageous and lyrical by turns, and if Little Red Riding Hood, the Invisible Man, and the Phantom of the Opera take it on the nose, so much the better. The stories that sustain us, that have crusted around us, grown barnacles and descending layers of clinging oysters, exist not merely as cultural props but as clues to the mystery of life and civilization. We need them scraped clean and re-propped, with every possible hole poked through them so we can see the light for what it is. Robert Coover has been doing that for us for the past half century and more, and we can only be very, very thankful. These are the best of his stories, the oysters that are growing in fresh new beds and regenerating their pearls over and over again. Relish them.

GOING

FOR

A BEER

THE BROTHER

(1962)

right there right there in the middle of the damn field he says he wants to put that thing together him and his buggy ideas and so me I says "how the hell you gonna get it down to the water?" but he just focuses me out sweepin the blue his eyes rollin like they do when he gets het on some new lunatic notion and he says not to worry none about that just would I help him for God's sake and because he don't know how he can get it done in time otherwise and though you'd have to be loonier than him to say yes I says I will of course I always would crazy as my brother is I've done little else since I was born and my wife she says "I can't figure it out I can't see why you always have to be babyin that old fool he ain't never done nothin for you God knows and you got enough to do here fields need plowin it's a bad enough year already my God and now that red-eyed brother of yours wingin around like a damn cloud and not knowin what in the world he's doin buildin a damn boat in the country my God what next? you're a damn fool I tell you" but packs me some sandwiches just the same and some sandwiches for my brother Lord knows *his* wife don't have no truck with him no more says he can go starve for all she cares she's fed up ever since the time he made her sit out on a hillside for three whole days rain and everything because he said she'd see God and she didn't see nothin and in fact she like to die from hunger nothin but berries and his boys too they ain't so bright neither but at least they come to help him out with his damn boat so it ain't just the two of us thank God for *that* and it ain't no goddamn fishin boat he wants to put up neither in fact it's the biggest damn thing I ever heard of and for weeks *weeks* I'm tellin you we ain't doin nothin but cuttin down pine trees and haulin them out to his field which is really pretty high up a hill and my God *that's* work lemme tell you and my wife she sighs and says I am really crazy *r-e-a-l-l-y* crazy and her four months with a child and tryin to do my work and hers too and still when I come home from haulin timbers around all day she's got enough left to rub my shoulders and the small of my back and fix a hot meal her long black hair pulled to a knot behind her head and hangin marvelously down her back her eyes gentle but very tired my God and I says to my brother I says "look I got a lotta work to do buddy you'll have to finish this idiot thing yourself I wanna help you all I can you know that but" and he looks off and he says "it don't matter none your work" and I says "the hell it don't how you think me and my wife we're gonna eat I mean where do you think this food comes from you been puttin away man? you can't eat this goddamn boat out here ready to rot in that bastard sun" and he just sighs long and says "no it just don't matter" and he sits him down on a rock kinda tired like and stares off and looks like he might even for God's sake cry and so

I go back to bringin wood up to him and he's already started on
the keel and frame God knows how *he* ever found out to build a
damn boat lost in *his* fog where he is Lord he was twenty when
I was born and the first thing I remember was havin to lead
him around so he didn't get kicked by a damn mule him who
couldn't never do nothin in a normal way just a huge oversize
fuzzyface boy so anyway I take to gettin up a few hours earlier
ever day to do my farmin my wife apt to lose the baby if she
should keep pullin around like she was doin then I go to work
on the boat until sundown and on and on the days hot and dry
and my wife keepin good food in me or else I'd of dropped sure
and no matter what I say to try and get out of it my brother he
says "you come and help now the rest don't matter" and we just
keep hammerin away and my God the damn thing is big enough
for a hundred people and at least I think at *least* it's a place to
live and not too bad at that at least it's good for somethin but my
wife she just sighs and says no good will come of it and runs her
hands through my hair but she don't ask me to stop helpin no
more because she knows it won't do no good and she's kinda
turned into herself now these days and gettin herself all ready
and still we keep workin on that damn thing that damn boat
and the days pass and my brother he says we gotta work harder
we ain't got much time and from time to time he gets a coupla
neighbors to come over and give a hand them sucked in by the
size and the novelty of the thing makin jokes some but they
don't stay around more than a day or two and they go away
shakin their heads and swearin under their breath and disgusted they got weaseled into the thing in the first place and
me I only get about half my place planted and see to my stock
as much as I can my wife she takes more care of them than I

can but at least we won't starve we say if we just get some rain
and finally we get the damn thing done all finished by God and
we cover it in and out with pitch and put a kinda fancy roof on
it and I come home on that last day and I ain't never goin back
ain't *never* gonna let him talk me into nothin again and I'm all
smellin of tar and my wife she cries and cries and I says to her
not to worry no more I'll be home all the time and me I'm cryin
a little too though she don't notice just thinkin how she's had it
so lonely and hard and all and for one whole day I just sleep the
whole damn day and the rest of the week I work around the
farm and one day I get an idea and I go over to my brother's
place and get some pieces of wood left over and whaddaya know?
they are all livin on that damn boat there in the middle of
nowhere him and his boys and some women and my brother's
wife she's there too but she's madder than hell and carpin at
him to get outa that damn boat and come home and he says
she's got just one more day and then he's gonna drug her on the
boat but he don't say it like a threat or nothin more like a fact a
plain fact tomorrow he's gonna drug her on the boat well I ain't
one to get mixed up in domestic quarrels God knows so I grab
up the wood and beat it back to my farm and that evenin I make
a little cradle a kinda fancy one with little animal figures cut in
it and polished down and after supper I give it to my wife as a
surprise and she cries and cries and holds me tight and says
don't never go away again and stay close by her and all and I feel
so damn good and warm about it all and glad the boat thing is
over and we get out a little wine and we decide the baby's name
is gonna be either Nathaniel or Anna and so we drink an extra
cup to Nathaniel's health and we laugh and we sigh and drink
one to Anna and my wife she gently fingers the little animal

figures and says they're beautiful and really they ain't I ain't much good at that sorta thing but I know what she means and then she says "where did you get the wood?" and I says "it's left over from the boat" and she don't say nothin for a moment and then she says "you been over there again today?" and I says "yes just to get the wood" and she says "what's he doin now he's got the boat done?" and I says "funny thing they're all livin in the damn thing all except the old lady she's over there hollerin at him how he's gettin senile and where does he think he's sailin to and how if he ain't afraid of runnin into a octypuss on the way he oughta get back home and him sayin she's a nut there ain't no water and her sayin that's what *she's* been tellin *him* for six months" and my wife she laughs and it's the happiest laugh I've heard from her in half a year and I laugh and we both have another cup of wine and my wife she says "so he's just livin on that big thing all by hisself?" and I says "no he's got his boys on there and some young women who are maybe wives of the boys or somethin I don't know I ain't never seen them before and all kindsa damn animals and birds and things I ain't never seen the likes" and my wife she says "animals? what animals?" and I says "oh all kinds I don't know a whole damn menagerie all clutterin and stinkin up the boat *God* what a mess" and my wife laughs again and she's a little silly with the wine and she says "I bet he ain't got no pigs" and "oh yes I seen them" I says and we laugh thinkin about pigs rootin around in that big tub and she says "I bet he ain't got no jackdaws" and I says "yes I seen a couple of them too or mostly I heard them you couldn't hardly hear nothin else" and we laugh again thinkin about them crows and his old lady and the pigs and all and my wife she says "*I* know what he ain't got I bet he ain't got no lice" and we both laugh like crazy and when I can I says "oh yes he does less he's took a bath" and we both laugh till we're cryin and we finish off the wine and my wife says "look now I *know* what he ain't got he ain't got no termites" and I says "you're right I don't recollect no termites maybe we oughta make him a present" and my wife she holds me close quiet all of a sudden and says "he's really movin Nathaniel's really movin" and she puts my hand down on her round belly and the little fella is kickin up a terrific storm and I says kinda anxious "does it hurt? do you think that——?" and "no" she says "it's good" she says and so I says with my hand on her belly "here's to you Nathaniel" and we drain what's left in the bottom of our cups and the next day we wake up in each other's arms and it's rainin and *thank God* we say and since it's rainin real good we stay inside and do things around the place and we're happy because the rain has come just in time and in the evenin things smell green and fresh and delicious and it's still rainin a little but not too hard so I decide to take a walk and I wander over by my brother's place thinkin I'll ask him if he'd like to take on some pet termites to go with his collection and there by God is his wife on the boat and I don't know if he drug her on or if she just finally come by herself but she ain't sayin nothin which is damn unusual and the boys they ain't sayin nothin neither and my brother he ain't sayin nothin they're just all standin up there on top and gazin off and I holler up at them "nice rain ain't it?" and my brother he looks down at me standin there in the rain and still he don't say nothin but he raises his hand kinda funny like and then puts it back on the rail and I decide not to say nothin about the termites and it's startin to rain a little harder again so I turn away and go back home and I tell my wife about what happened and my wife she just laughs and says "they're *all* crazy he's finally got them *all* crazy" and she's cooked me up a special pastry with fresh meat and so we forget about them but by God the next day the rain's still comin down harder than ever and water's beginnin to stand around in places and after a week of rain I can see the crops is pretty well ruined and I'm havin trouble keepin my stock fed and my wife she's cryin and talkin about our bad luck that we might as well of built a damn boat as plant all them crops and still we don't figure things out I mean it just don't come to our minds not even when the rain keeps spillin down like a ocean dumped upsidedown and now water is beginnin to stand around in big pools really big ones and water up to the ankles around the house and leakin in and pretty soon the whole damn house is gettin fulla water and I keep sayin maybe we oughta go use my brother's boat till this blows over but my wife she says "never" and then she starts in cryin again so finally I says to her I says "we can't be so proud I'll go ask him" and so I set out in the storm and I can't hardly see where I'm goin and I slip up to my neck in places and finally I get to where the boat is and I holler up and my brother he comes out and he looks down at where I am and he don't say nothin that bastard he just looks at me and I shout up at him I says "hey is it all right for me and my wife to come over until this thing blows over?" and still he don't say a damn word he just raises his hand in that same sillyass way and I holler "hey you stupid sonuvabitch I'm soakin wet god-damn it and my house is fulla water and my wife she's about to have a kid and she's apt to get sick all wet and cold to the bone and all I'm askin you—" and right then right while I'm still talkin he turns around and he goes back in the boat and I can't hardly believe it me his brother but he don't come back out and

I push up under the boat and I beat on it with my fists and scream at him and call him ever name I can think up and I shout for his boys and for his wife and for anybody inside and nobody comes out "God*damn* you" I cry out at the top of my lungs and half sobbin and sick and then feelin too beat out to do anythin more I turn around and head back for home but the rain is thunderin down like mad now and in places I gotta swim and I can't make it no further and I recollect a hill nearby and I head for it and when I get to it I climb up on top of it and it feels good to be on land again even if it is soggy and greasy and I vomit and retch there awhile and move further up and the next thing I know I'm wakin up the rain still in my face and the water halfway up the hill toward me and I look out and I can see my brother's boat is floatin and I wave at it but I don't see nobody wave back and then I quick look out towards my own place and all I can see is the top of it and of a sudden I'm scared scared about my wife and I go tearin for the house swimmin most all the way and cryin and shoutin and the rain still comin down like crazy and so now well now I'm back here on the hill again what little there is left of it and I'm figurin maybe I got a day left if the rain keeps comin and it don't show no signs of stoppin and I can't see my brother's boat no more gone just water how *how* did he know? that bastard and yet I gotta hand it to him it's not hard to see who's crazy around here I can't see my house no more I just left my wife inside where I found her I couldn't hardly stand to look at her the way she was

THE ELEVATOR

(1966)

1

Every morning without exception and without so much as reflecting upon it, Martin takes the self-service elevator to the fourteenth floor, where he works. He will do so today. When he first arrives, however, he finds the lobby empty, the old building still possessed of its feinting shadows and silences, desolate though mutely expectant, and he wonders if today it might not turn out differently.

It is 7:30 A.M.: Martin is early and therefore has the elevator entirely to himself. He steps inside: this tight cell! he thinks with a kind of unsettling shock, and confronts the panel of numbered buttons. One to fourteen, plus "B" for basement. Impulsively, he presses the "B"—seven years and yet to visit the basement! He snorts at his timidity.

After a silent moment, the doors rumble shut. All night alert waiting for this moment! The elevator sinks slowly into the earth. The stale gloomy odors of the old building having aroused in him an unreasonable sense of dread and loss, Martin imagines suddenly he is descending into hell. *Tra la perduta gente*, yes! A mild shudder shakes him. Yet, Martin decides firmly, would that it were so. The old carrier halts with a quiver. The automatic doors yawn open. Nothing, only a basement. It is empty and nearly dark. It is silent and meaningless.

Martin smiles inwardly at himself, presses the number "14." "Come on, old Charon," he declaims broadly, "Hell's the other way!"

2

Martin waited miserably for the stench of intestinal gas to reach his nostrils. Always the same. He supposed it was Carruther, but he could never prove it. Not so much as a telltale squeak. But it was Carruther who always led them, and though the other faces changed, Carruther was always among them.

They were seven in the elevator: six men and the young girl who operated it. The girl did not participate. She was surely offended, but she never gave a hint of it. She possessed a surface detachment that not even Carruther's crude proposals could penetrate. Much less did she involve herself in the coarse interplay of men. Yet certainly, Martin supposed, they were a torment to her.

And, yes, he was right—there it was, faint at first, almost sweet, then slowly thickening, sickening, crowding up on him—

"Hey! Who fahred thet shot?" cried Carruther, starting it.

"Mart fahred-it!" came the inexorable reply. And then the crush of loud laughter.

"*What!* Is that Martin fartin' again?" bellowed another, as their toothy thicklipped howling congealed around him.

"Aw *please*, Mart! *don't fart!*" cried yet another. It would go on until they left the elevator. The elevator was small: their laughter packed it, jammed at the walls. "Have a heart, Mart! don't *part* that fart!"

It's not me, *it's not me*, Martin insisted. But only to himself. It was no use. It was fate. Fate and Carruther. (More laughter, more brute jabs.) A couple of times he had protested. "Aw, Marty, you're just modest!" Carruther had thundered. Booming voice, big man. Martin hated him.

One by one, the other men filed out of the elevator at different floors, holding their noses. "Old farty Marty!" they would shout to anyone they met on their way out, and it always got a laugh, up and down the floor. The air cleared slightly each time the door opened.

In the end, Martin was always left alone with the girl who operated the elevator. His floor, the fourteenth, was the top one. When it all began, long ago, he had attempted apologetic glances toward the girl on exiting, but she had always turned her shoulder to him. Maybe she thought he was making a play for her. Finally he was forced to adopt the custom of simply ducking out as quickly as possible. She would in any case assume his guilt.

Of course, there was an answer to Carruther. Yes, Martin knew it, had rehearsed it countless times. The only way to meet that man was on his home ground. And he'd do it, too. When the time came.

3

Martin is alone on the elevator with the operator, a young girl. She is neither slender nor plump, but fills charmingly her orchid-colored uniform. Martin greets her in his usual friendly manner and she returns his greeting with a smile. Their eyes meet momentarily. Hers are brown.

When Martin enters the elevator, there are actually several other people crowded in, but as the elevator climbs through the musky old building, the others, singly or in groups, step out. Finally, Martin is left alone with the girl who operates the elevator. She grasps the lever, leans against it, and the cage sighs upward. He speaks to her, makes a lighthearted joke about elevators. She laughs and

Alone on the elevator with the girl, Martin thinks: if this elevator should crash, I would sacrifice my life to save her. Her back is straight and subtle. Her orchid uniform skirt is tight, tucks tautly under her blossoming hips, describes a kind of cavity there. Perhaps it is night. Her calves are muscular and strong. She grasps the lever.

The girl and Martin are alone on the elevator, which is rising. He concentrates on her round hips until she is forced to turn and look at him. His gaze coolly courses her belly, her pinched and belted waist, past her taut breasts, meets her excited stare. She breathes deeply, her lips parted. They embrace. Her breasts plunge softly against him. Her mouth is sweet. Martin has forgotten whether the elevator is climbing or not.

4

Perhaps Martin will meet Death on the elevator. Yes, going out for lunch one afternoon. Or to the drugstore for cigarettes. He will press the button in the hall on the fourteenth floor, the doors will open, a dark smile will beckon. The shaft is deep. It is dark and silent. Martin will recognize Death by His silence. He will not protest.

He *will* protest! oh God! no matter what the

the sense of emptiness underneath breath lurching out

The shaft is long and narrow. The shaft is dark.

He will not protest.

5

Martin, as always and without so much as reflecting upon it, takes the self-service elevator to the fourteenth floor, where he works. He is early, but only by a few minutes. Five others join him, greetings are exchanged. Though tempted, he is not able to risk the "B," but presses the "14" instead. Seven years!

As the automatic doors press together and the elevator begins its slow complaining ascent, Martin muses absently on the categories. This small room, so commonplace and so compressed, he observes with a certain melancholic satisfaction, this elevator contains them all: space, time, cause, motion, magnitude, class. Left to our own devices, we would probably discover them. The other passengers chatter with self-righteous smiles (after all, they are on time) about the weather, the elections, the work that awaits them today. They stand, apparently motionless, yet moving. Motion: perhaps that's all there is to it after all. Motion and the medium. Energy and weighted particles. Force and matter. The image grips him purely. Ascent and the passive reorganization of atoms.

At the seventh floor, the elevator stops and a woman departs it. Only a trace of her perfume remains. Martin alone remarks—to himself, of course—her absence, as the climb begins again.

Reduced by one. But the totality of the universe is suffused: each man contains all of it, loss is inconceivable. Yet, if that is so—and a tremor shudders coolly through Martin's body— then the totality is as nothing. Martin gazes around at his four remaining fellow passengers, a flush of compassion washing in behind the tremor. One must always be alert to the possibility of action, he reminds himself. But none apparently need him. If he could do the work for them today, give them the grace of a day's contemplation . . .

The elevator halts, suspended and vibrant, at the tenth floor. Two men leave. Two more intermediate stops, and Martin is alone. He has seen them safely through. Although caged as ever in his inexorable melancholy, Martin nonetheless smiles as he steps out of the self-service elevator on the fourteenth floor. "I am pleased to participate," he announces in full voice. But, as the elevator doors close behind him and he hears the voided descent, he wonders: Wherein now is the elevator's totality?

6

The cable snaps at the thirteenth floor. There is a moment's deadly motionlessness—then a sudden breathless plunge! The girl, terrified, turns to Martin. They are alone. Though inside his heart is bursting its chambers in terror, he remains out-wardly composed. "I think it is safer lying on your back," he says. He squats to the floor, but the girl remains transfixed with shock. Her thighs are round and sleek under the orchid skirt, and in the shadowed— "Come," he says. "You may lie on me. My body will absorb part of the impact." Her hair caresses his cheek, her buttocks press like a sponge into his groin. In love, moved by his sacrifice, she weeps. To calm her, he clasps her heaving abdomen, strokes her soothingly. The elevator whistles as it drops.

7

Martin worked late in the office, clearing up the things that needed to be done before the next day, routine matters, yet part of the uninterrupted necessity that governed his daily life. Not a large office, Martin's, though he needed no larger, essentially neat except for the modest clutter on top of his desk. The room was equipped only with that desk and a couple of chairs, book-cases lining one wall, calendar posted on another. The overhead lamp was off, the only light in the office being provided by the fluorescent lamp on Martin's desk.

Martin signed one last form, sighed, smiled. He retrieved a cigarette, half-burned but still lit, from the ashtray, drew heavily on it, then, as he exhaled with another prolonged sigh, doubled the butt firmly in the black bowl of the ashtray. Still extinguishing it, twisting it among the heap of crumpled filters in the ashtray, he glanced idly at his watch. He was astonished to discover that the watch said twelve-thirty—and had stopped! Already after midnight!

He jumped up, rolled down his sleeves, buttoned them, whipped his suit jacket off the back of his chair, shoved his arms into it. Bad enough twelve-thirty—but my God! how much *later* was it? The jacket still only three-quarters of the way up his back, tie askew, he hastily stacked the loose papers on his desk and switched off the lamp. He stumbled through the dark room out into the hallway, lit by one dull yellow bulb, pulled his office door to behind him. The thick solid catch knocked hollowly in the vacant corridor.

He buttoned his shirt collar, straightened his tie and the collar of his jacket, which was doubled under on his right shoulder, as he hurried down the passageway past the other closed office doors of the fourteenth floor to the self-service elevator, his heels hammering away the stillness on the marble floor. He trembled, inexplicably. The profound silence of the old building disturbed him. Relax, he urged himself; we'll know what time it is soon enough. He pushed the button for the elevator, but nothing happened. Don't tell me I have to walk down! he muttered bitterly to himself. He poked the button again, harder, and this time he heard below a solemn rumble, a muffled thump, and an indistinct grinding plaint that grieved progressively nearer. It stopped and the doors of the elevator opened to receive him. Entering, Martin felt a sudden need to glance back over his shoulder, but he suppressed it.

Once inside, he punched the number "1" button on the self-service panel. The doors closed, but the elevator, instead of descending, continued to climb. Goddamn this old wreck! Martin swore irritably, and he jiggled the "1" button over and over. Just this night! The elevator stopped, the doors opened, Martin stepped out. Later, he wondered why he had done so. The doors slid shut behind him, he heard the elevator descend, its amused rumble fading distantly. Although here it was utterly dark, shapes seemed to form. Though he could see nothing distinctly, he was fully aware that he was not alone. His hand fumbled on the wall for the elevator button. Cold wind gnawed at his ankles, the back of his neck. Fool! wretched fool! he wept, there *is* no fifteenth floor! Pressed himself against the wall, couldn't

find the button, couldn't even find the elevator door, and even
the very wall was only

8

Carruther's big voice boomed in the small cage.

"Mart fahred-it!' came the certain reply. The five men
laughed. Martin flushed. The girl feigned indifference. The
fetor of fart vapours reeked in the tight elevator.

"Martin, damn it, cut the fartin'!"

Martin fixed his cool gaze on them. "Carruther fucks his
mother," he said firmly. Carruther hit him full in the face, his
glasses splintered and fell, Martin staggered back against the
wall. He waited for the second blow, but it didn't come. Someone
elbowed him, and he slipped to the floor. He knelt there, weeping softly, searched with his hands for his glasses. Martin tasted
the blood from his nose, trickling into his mouth. He couldn't
find the glasses, couldn't even see.

"Look out, baby!" Carruther thundered. "Farty Marty's jist
tryin' to git a free peek up at your pretty drawers!" Crash of
laughter. Martin felt the girl shrink from him.

9

Her soft belly presses like a sponge into his groin. No, safer on
your back, love, he thinks, but pushes the thought away. She
weeps in terror, presses her hot wet mouth against his. To calm
her, he clasps her soft buttocks, strokes them soothingly. So sudden is the plunge, they seem suspended in air. She has removed
her skirt. How will it feel? he wonders.

10

Martin, without so much as reflecting on it, automatically takes the self-service elevator to the fourteenth floor, where he works. The systematizing, that's what's wrong, he concludes, that's what cracks them up. He is late, but only by a few minutes. Seven others join him, anxious, sweating. They glance nervously at their watches. None of them presses the "B" button. Civilities are hurriedly interchanged.

Their foolish anxiety seeps out like a bad spirit, enters Martin. He finds himself looking often at his watch, grows impatient with the elevator. Take it easy, he cautions himself. Their blank faces oppress him. Bleak. Haunted. Tyrannized by their own arbitrary regimentation of time. Torture self-imposed, yet in all probability inescapable. The elevator halts jerkily at the third floor, quivering their sallow face-flesh. They frown. No one has pushed the three. A woman enters. They all nod, harrumph, make jittery little hand motions to incite the door to close. They are all more or less aware of the woman (she has delayed them, damn her!), but only Martin truly remarks— to himself—her whole presence, as the elevator resumes its upward struggle. The accretion of tragedy. It goes on, ever giving birth to itself. Up and down, up and down. Where will it end? he wonders. Her perfume floats gloomily in the stale air. These deformed browbeaten mind-animals. Suffering and insufferable. Up and down. He closes his eyes. One by one, they leave him.

He arrives, alone, at the fourteenth floor. He steps out of the old elevator, stares back into its spent emptiness. There, only there, is peace, he concludes wearily. The elevator doors press shut.

11

Here on this elevator, my elevator, created by me, moved by me, doomed by me, I, Martin, proclaim my omnipotence! In the end, doom touches all! MY doom! I impose it! TREMBLE!

12

The elevator shrieks insanely as it drops. Their naked bellies slap together, hands grasp, her vaginal mouth closes spongelike on his rigid organ. Their lips lock, tongues knot. The bodies: how will they find them? Inwardly, he laughs. He thrusts up off the plummeting floor. Her eyes are brown and, with tears, love him.

13

But—ah!—the doomed, old man, the DOOMED! What are they to us, to ME? ALL! We, I love! Let their flesh sag and dewlaps tremble, let their odors offend, let their cruelty mutilate, their stupidity enchain—but let them laugh, father! FOREVER! let them cry!

14

but hey! theres this guy see he gets on the goddamn elevator and its famous how hes got him a doodang about five feet long Im not kiddin you none five feet and he gets on the— yeah! can you imagine a bastard like that boardin a friggin pubic I mean public elevator? hoohah! no I dont know his

name Mert I think or Mort but the crux is he is possessed
of this motherin digit biggern ole Rahab see—do with it?
I dont know I think he wraps it around his leg or carries
it over his shoulder or somethin jee*zuss!* What a problem!
why I bet hes *killt* more poor bawdies than I ever dipped my
poor worm in! once he was even a—listen! Carruther tells
this as the goddamn truth I mean he *respects* that bastard—
he was even one a them jackoff gods I forget how you call
them over there with them Eyetalians after the big war see
them dumb types when they seen him furl out this here
five foot hose of his one day—he was just tryin to get the
goddamn knots out Carruther says—why they thought he
musta been a goddamn jackoff god or somethin and wanted
to like employ him or whatever you do with a god and well
Mort he figgered it to be a not so miserable occupation dont
you know better anyhow than oildrillin with it in Arabia
or stoppin holes in Dutch dikes like hes been doin so the
bastard he stays on there a time and them little quiff there
in that Eyetalian place they grease him up with hogfat or
olive oil and all workin together like vested virgins they
pull him off out there in the fields and spray the crops and
well Mort he says *he* says it's the closest hes ever got to the
real mccoy jeezuss! hes worth a thousand laughs! and they
bring him all the old aunts and grannies and he splits them
open a kinda stupendous euthanasia for the old ladies and
he blesses all their friggin procreations with a swat of his
doodang and even does a little welldiggin on the side but
he gets in trouble with the Roman churchers on accounta
not bein circumcised and they wanta whack it off but Mort
says no and they cant get close to him with so prodigious a

batterin ram as hes got so they work a few miracles on him and wrinkle up his old pud with holy water and heat up his semen so it burns up the fields and even one day ignites a goddamn volcano and *jeezuss!* He wastes no time throwin that thing over his shoulder and hightailin it *outa* there I can tell you! but now like Im sayin them pastoral days is dead and gone and hes goin up and down in elevators like the rest of us and so here he is boardin the damn cage and theys a bunch of us bastards clownin around with the little piece who operates that deathtrap kinda brushin her swell butt like a occasional accident and sweet jeezus her gettin fidgety and hot and half fightin us off and half pullin us on and playin with that lever *zoom!* wingin up through that scraper and just then ole Carruther jeezuss he really breaks you up sometimes that crazy bastard he hefts up her little purple skirt and whaddaya know! the little quiff aint wearin no skivvies! its somethin *beautiful* man I mean a sweet cleft peach right outa some foreign orchard and poor ole Mort he is kinda part gigglin and part hurtin and for a minute the rest of us dont see the pointa the whole agitation but then that there incredible thing suddenly pops up quivery right under his chin like the friggin eye of god for crissake and then theres this big wild rip and man! it rears up and splits outa there like a goddamn redwood topplin *gawdamighty!* and knocks old Carruther *kapow!* right to the deck! his best buddy and that poor little cunt she takes one glim of that impossible rod wheelin around in there and whammin the walls and she faints dead away and *jeeezusss!* she tumbles right on that elevator lever and man! I thought for a minute we was *all* dead

15

They plunge, their damp bodies fused, pounding furiously, in terror, in joy, the impact is

I, Martin, proclaim against all dooms
the indestructible seed

Martin does not take the self-service elevator to the fourteenth floor, as is his custom, but, reflecting upon it for once and out of a strange premonition, determines instead to walk the fourteen flights. Halfway up, he hears the elevator hurtle by him and then the splintering crash from below. He hesitates, poised on the stair. Inscrutable is the word he finally settles upon. He pronounces it aloud, smiles faintly, sadly, somewhat wearily, then continues his tedious climb, pausing from time to time to stare back down the stairs behind him.

THE WAYFARER

(1968)

I came upon him on the road. I pulled over, stepped out, walked directly over to him where he sat. On an old milestone. His long tangled beard was a yellowish gray, his eyes dull with the dust of the road. His clothes were all of a color and smelled of mildew. He was not a sympathetic figure, but what could I do?

I stood for a while in front of him, hands on hips, but he paid me no heed. I thought: at least he will stand. He did not. I scuffed up a little dust between us with the toe of my boot. The dust settled or disappeared into his collection of it. But still, he stared obliviously. Vacantly. Perhaps (I thought): mindlessly. Yet I could be sure he was alive, for he sighed deeply from time to time. He is afraid to acknowledge me, I reasoned. It may or may not have been the case, but it served, for the time being, as a useful premise. The sun was hot, the air dry. It was silent, except for the traffic.

I cleared my throat, shifted my feet, made a large business of extracting my memo-book from my breast pocket, tapped my pencil on it loudly. I was determined to perform my function in the matter, without regard to how disagreeable it might prove to be. Others passed on the road. They proffered smiles of commiseration, which I returned with a pleasant nod. The wayfarer wore a floppy black hat. Tufts of yellow-gray hair poked out of the holes in it like dead wheat. No doubt, it swarmed. Still, he would not look at me.

Finally, I squatted and interposed my face in the path of his stare. Slowly—painfully, it would seem—his eyes focused on mine. They seemed to brighten momentarily, but I am not sure why. It could have been joy as easily as rage, or it could have been fear. Only that: his eyes brightened; his face remained slack and inexpressive. And it was not a glow, nothing that could be graphed, it was just a briefest spark, a glimmer. Then dull again. Filmy as though with a kind of mucus smeared over. And he lost the focus. I don't know whether or not in that instant of perception he noticed my badge. I wished at the time that he would, then there could be no further ambiguities. But I frankly doubted that he did. He has traveled far, I thought.

I had begun with the supposition that he feared me. It is generally a safe supposition. Now I found myself beset with doubt. It could have been impatience, I reasoned, or anger—or even: *contempt!* The thought, unwonted, jolted me. I sat back in the dust. I felt peculiarly light, baseless. I studied my memo-book. It was blank! my God! *it was blank!* Urgently, I wrote something in it. There! Not so bad now. I began to recover. Once again, I supposed it was fear. I was able to do that. I stood, brushed the dust off my trousers, then squatted down once again. And now: with a certain self-assurance. Duty, a proper sense of it, is our best teacher: my catechism was coming back to me. He would enjoy no further advantages.

I asked him about himself, received no answers. I recorded his silence in my book. I wrote the word *aphonia*, then erased it. True, I could have determined the matter, a mere palpation of the neck cords, but the prospect of dipping my fingers into the cavities behind that moldy beard revolted me, and the question, after all, was not of primary concern. Moreover, a second method then occurred to me: if I could provoke a sound out of him, any sound, it would prove that the vocal mechanism was still intact. Of course, if he uttered no sound, it would not establish that he was mute, but I felt confident I could provoke a sound and have an end to the problem.

I unstrapped my rifle from my back and poked the barrel under his nose. His gaze floated unimpeded down the barrel through my chest and out into indeterminate space. I asked him his name. I asked him the President's name. I asked him my name. I reminded him of the gravity of his violation and of my own unlimited powers. I asked him what day it was. I asked him what place it was. He was adamant. I lowered the barrel and punched it into his chest. The barrel thumped in the thick coats he wore and something cracked, but he said nothing. Not so much as a whisper. He did not even wince. I was becoming angry. Inwardly, I cautioned myself. And still that old man refused—I say *refused*, although it may not have been a question of volition; in fact, it *was* not, *could not have been*—to look at me. I lowered the barrel and punched it into his groin. I might as well have been poking a pillow. He seemed utterly unaware of my attentions.

I stood impatiently. I knew, of course, that much was at stake.

How could I help but know it? Those passing were now less sympathetic, more curious, more—yes: more reproving. I felt the sweat under my collar. I loosened my tie. I shouted down at him. I ordered him to stand. I ordered him to lie down. I shook the rifle in front of his nose. I ordered him to remove his hat. I fired a shot over his head. I kicked dust into his face. I stomped down on his old papery shoes with my boots. I ordered him to look at me. I ordered him to lift one finger. *He would not even lift one finger!* I screamed at him. I broke his nose with my rifle butt. But still he sat, sat on that old milestone, sat and stared. I was so furious I could have wept.

I would try a new tack. I knelt down in front of him. I intruded once more in the line—if so vague a thing could be called that—of his gaze. I bared my teeth. I ordered him to sit. I ordered him to stare vacantly. I ordered him not, under threat of death, to focus his eyes. I ordered the blood to flow from his pulpy nose. He obeyed. Or, rather: he remained exactly as he was before. I was hardly gratified. I had anticipated a certain satisfaction, a partial restoration of my confidence, but I was disappointed. In fact, I felt more frustrated than ever. I no longer looked at those passing. I knew their reproachful eyes were on me. My back sweat from the intensity of their derision.

I set my teeth. It was time. I told him if he did not speak, I would carry out my orders and execute him on the spot. My orders, to be precise, did not specify this place, but on the other hand they did not exclude it, and if he would not move, what choice did I have? Even as I asked him to speak, I knew he would not. Even while I was forming and emitting the very words, I already was contemplating the old dilemma. If I shot him in the chest, there was a fair chance I would miss or only

graze the heart. He would die slowly. It could take several days.
I am more humane than to take pleasure in that thought. On
the other hand, if I shot him in the head, he would surely die
instantly, but it would make a mess of his countenance. I do
not enjoy the sight of mutilated heads. I do not. I have often
thought, myself, when the time came, I would rather receive it
in the chest. The chest seems to me farther away than the head.
In fact, I could almost enjoy dying, allowed the slow dreamy
regard of my chest distantly fountaining blood. Contrarily, the
thought of the swift hard knock in the skull is an eternal torment to me. Given these considerations, I shot him in the chest.

As I had feared, he did not die immediately. He did not even,
for the moment, alter either his expression or his posture. His
coats were thick and many. I could see the holes drilled by the
rifle shells, but I saw no blood. What could that mean? I was
shaken by a sudden violent fever of impatience. Only by strenuous self-control was I able to restrain myself from tearing his
clothes off to inspect the wound. I thought: if I don't see blood
immediately, *I shall lose it again!* I was trembling. I wiped my
mouth with the back of my hand. Then, slowly, a dark stain
began to appear in the tatters. In the nick of time! It spread. I
sighed. I sat back and lay the rifle across my knees. Now there
was only to wait. I glanced toward the road from time to time
and accepted without ceremony the commendatory nods.

The stain enlarged. It would not take long. I sat and waited.
His coats were soon soaked and the blood dripped down the
milestone between his legs. Suddenly, his eyes fixed on mine.
His lips worked, his teeth chewed his beard. I wished he would
end it quickly. I even considered firing a second shot through
his head. And then he spoke. He spoke rapidly, desperately, with

neither punctuation nor sentence structure. Just a ceaseless eruption of obtuse language. He spoke of constellations, bone structures, mythologies, and love. He spoke of belief and lymph nodes, of excavations, categories, and prophecies. Faster and faster he spoke. His eyes gleamed. Harmonics! Foliations! Etymology! Impulses! Suffering! His voice rose to a shriek. Immateriality patricide ideations heatstroke virtue predication—I grew annoyed and shot him in the head. At last, with this, he fell.

My job was done. As I had feared, he was a mess. I turned my back to him, strapped my rifle securely on my back, reknotted my tie. I successfully put his present condition out of my mind, reconstructing my earlier view of him still whole. It was little better, I admit, but it was the first essential step toward forgetting him altogether. In the patrol car, I called in details of the incident and ordered the deposition squad to the scene. I drove a little farther down the road, parked, jotted down the vital data in my memo-book. I would make the full report out later, back at the station. I noted the exact time.

This done, I returned the memo-book to my breast pocket, leaned back, and stared absently out the window. I was restless. My mind was not yet entirely free of the old man. At times, he would loom in my inner eye larger than the very landscape. I supposed that this was due to my having stooped down to his level: my motives had been commendable, of course, but the consequences of such a gesture, if practiced habitually, could well prove disastrous. I would avoid it in the future. The rifle jammed against my spine. I slid down farther to relieve the obtrusion, resting my head against the back of the seat. I watched the traffic. Gradually, I became absorbed in it. Uniformly it flowed, quietly, possessed of its own unbroken grace and precision. There was a variety in detail, but the stream itself was one. One. The thought warmed me. It flowed away and away and the unpleasant images that had troubled my mind flowed away with it. At last, I sat up, started the motor, and entered the flow itself. I felt calm and happy. A participant. I enjoy my work.

THE HAT ACT

(1968)

In the middle of the stage: a plain table.

A man enters, dressed as a magician with black cape and black silk hat. Doffs hat in wide sweep to audience, bows elegantly.

Applause.

He displays inside of hat. It is empty. He thumps it. It is clearly empty. Places hat on table, brim up. Extends both hands over hat, tugs back sleeves exposing wrists, snaps fingers. Reaches in, extracts a rabbit.

Applause.

Pitches rabbit into wings. Snaps fingers over hat again, reaches in, extracts a dove.

Applause.

Pitches dove into wings. Snaps fingers over hat, reaches in, extracts another rabbit. No applause. Stuffs rabbit hurriedly back in hat, snaps fingers, reaches in, extracts another hat, precisely like the one from which it came.

Applause.

Places second hat alongside first one. Snaps fingers over new hat, withdraws a third hat, exactly like the first two.

Light applause.

Snaps fingers over third hat, withdraws a fourth hat, again identical. No applause. Does not snap fingers. Peers into fourth hat, extracts a fifth one. In fifth, he finds a sixth. Rabbit appears in third hat. Magician extracts seventh hat from sixth. Third hat rabbit withdraws a second rabbit from first hat. Magician withdraws eighth hat from seventh, ninth from eighth, as rabbits extract other rabbits from other hats. Rabbits and hats are everywhere. Stage is one mad turmoil of hats and rabbits.

Laughter and applause.

Frantically, magician gathers up hats and stuffs them into each other, bowing, smiling at audience, pitching rabbits three and four at a time into wings, smiling, bowing. It is a desperate struggle. At first, it is difficult to be sure he is stuffing hats and pitching rabbits faster than they are reappearing. Bows, stuffs, pitches, smiles, perspires.

Laughter mounts.

Slowly the confusion diminishes. Now there is one small pile of hats and rabbits. Now there are no rabbits. At last there are only two hats. Magician, perspiring from overexertion, gasping for breath, staggers to table with two hats.

Light applause, laughter.

Magician, mopping brow with silk handkerchief, stares in perplexity at two remaining hats. Pockets handkerchief. Peers into one hat, then into other. Attempts tentatively to stuff first into second, but in vain. Attempts to fit second into first, but also without success. Smiles weakly at audience. No applause. Drops first hat to floor, leaps on it until crushed. Wads crushed hat in fist, attempts once more to stuff it into second hat. Still, it will not fit.

Light booing, impatient applause.

Trembling with anxiety, magician presses out first hat, places it brim up on table, crushes second hat on floor. Wads second hat, tries desperately to jam it into first hat. No, it will not fit. Turns irritably to pitch second hat into wings.

Loud booing.

Freezes. Pales. Returns to table with both hats, first in fair condition brim up, second still in a crumpled wad. Faces hats in defeat. Bows head as though to weep silently.

Hissing and booing.

Smile suddenly lights magician's face. He smoothes out second hat and places it firmly on his head, leaving first hat bottomside-up on table. Crawls up on table and disappears feet first into hat.

Surprised applause.

Moments later, magician's feet poke up out of hat on table, then legs, then torso. Last part to emerge is magician's head, which, when lifted from table, brings first hat with it. Magician doffs first hat to audience, shows it is empty. Second hat has disappeared. Bows deeply.

Enthusiastic and prolonged applause, cheers.

Magician returns hat to head, thumps it, steps behind table. Without removing hat, reaches up, snaps fingers, extracts rabbit from top of hat.

Applause.

Pitches rabbit into wings. Snaps fingers, withdraws dove from top of hat.

Sprinkling of applause.

Pitches dove into wings. Snaps fingers, extracts lovely assistant from top of hat.

Astonished but enthusiastic applause and whistles.

Lovely assistant wears high feathery green hat, tight green halter, little green shorts, black net stockings, high green heels. Smiles coyly at whistles and applause, scampers bouncily offstage.

Whistling and shouting, applause.

Magician attempts to remove hat, but it appears to be stuck. Twists and writhes in struggle with stuck hat.

Mild laughter.

Struggle continues. Contortions. Grimaces.

Laughter.

Finally, magician requests two volunteers from audience. Two large brawny men enter stage from audience, smiling awkwardly.

Light applause and laughter.

One large man grasps hat, other clutches magician's legs. They pull cautiously. The hat does not come off. They pull harder. Still, it is stuck. They tug now with great effort, their heavy faces reddening, their thick neck muscles taut and throbbing. Magician's neck stretches, snaps in two: POP! Large men tumble apart, rolling to opposite sides of stage, one with body, other with hat containing magician's severed head.

Screams of terror.

Two large men stand, stare aghast at handiwork, clutch mouths.

Shrieks and screams.

Decapitated body stands.

Shrieks and screams.

Zipper in front of decapitated body opens, magician emerges. He is as before, wearing same black cape and same black silk hat. Pitches deflated decapitated body into wings. Pitches hat and head into wings. Two large men sigh with immense relief, shake heads as though completely baffled, smile faintly, return to audience. Magician doffs hat and bows.

Wild applause, shouts, cheers.

Lovely assistant, still in green costume, enters, carrying glass of water.

Applause and whistling.

Lovely assistant acknowledges whistling with coy smile, sets glass of water on table, stands dutifully by. Magician hands her his hat, orders her by gesture to eat it.

Whistling continues.

Lovely assistant smiles, bites into hat, chews slowly.

Laughter and much whistling.

She washes down each bite of hat with water from glass she has
brought in. Hat at last is entirely consumed, except for narrow
silk band left on table. Sighs, pats slender exposed tummy.

Laughter and applause, excited whistling.

Magician invites young country boy in audience to come to
stage. Young country boy steps forward shyly, stumbling clumsily over own big feet. Appears confused and utterly abashed.

Loud laughter and catcalls.

Young country boy stands with one foot on top of other, staring
down redfaced at his hands, twisting nervously in front of him.

Laughter and catcalls increase.

Lovely assistant sidles up to boy, embraces him in motherly
fashion. Boy ducks head away, steps first on one foot, then on
other, wrings hands.

More laughter and catcalls, whistles.

Lovely assistant winks broadly at audience, kisses young country boy on cheek. Boy jumps as though scalded, trips over own
feet, and falls to floor.

Thundering laughter.

Lovely assistant helps boy to his feet, lifting him under armpits. Boy, ticklish, struggles and giggles helplessly.

Laughter (as before).

Magician raps table with knuckles. Lovely assistant releases hysterical country boy, returns smiling to table. Boy resumes awkward stance, wipes his runny nose with back of his hand, sniffles.

Mild laughter and applause.

Magician hands lovely assistant narrow silk band of hat she has eaten. She stuffs band into her mouth, chews thoughtfully, swallows with some difficulty, shudders. She drinks from glass. Laughter and shouting have fallen away to expectant hush. Magician grasps nape of lovely assistant's neck, forces her head with its feathered hat down between her stockinged knees. He releases grip and her head springs back to upright position. Magician repeats action slowly. Then repeats action rapidly four or five times. Looks inquiringly at lovely assistant. Her face is flushed from exertion. She meditates, then shakes head: no. Magician again forces her head to her knees, releases grip, allowing head to snap back to upright position. Repeats this two or three times. Looks inquiringly at lovely assistant. She smiles and nods. Magician drags abashed young country boy over behind lovely assistant and invites him to reach into lovely assistant's tight green shorts. Young country boy is flustered beyond belief.

Loud laughter and whistling resumes.

Young country boy, in desperation, tries to escape. Magician captures him and drags him once more behind lovely assistant.

Laughter etc. (as before).

Magician grasps country boy's arm and thrusts it forcibly into lovely assistant's shorts. Young country boy wets pants.

Hysterical laughter and catcalls.

Lovely assistant grimaces once. Magician, smiling, releases grip on agonizingly embarrassed country boy. Boy withdraws hand. In it, he finds he is holding magician's original black silk hat, entirely whole, narrow silk band and all.

Wild applause and footstamping, laughter and cheers.

Magician winks broadly at audience, silencing them momentarily, invites young country boy to don hat. Boy ducks head shyly. Magician insists. Timidly, grinning foolishly, country boy lifts hat to head. Water spills out, runs down over his head, and soaks young country boy

Laughter, applause, wild catcalls.

Young country boy, utterly humiliated, drops hat and turns to run offstage, but lovely assistant is standing on his foot. He trips and falls to his face.

Laughter etc. (as before).

Country boy crawls abjectly offstage on his stomach. Magician, laughing heartily with audience, pitches lovely assistant into wings, picks up hat from floor. Brushes hat on sleeve, thumps it two or three times, returns it with elegant flourish to his head.

Appreciative applause.

Magician steps behind table. Carefully brushes off one space on table. Blows away dust. Reaches for hat. But again, it seems to be stuck. Struggles feverishly with hat.

Mild laughter.

Requests volunteers. Same two large men as before enter. One quickly grasps hat, other grasps magician's legs. They tug furiously, but in vain.

Laughter and applause.

First large man grabs magician's head under jaw. Magician appears to be protesting. Second large man wraps magician's legs around his waist. Both pull apart with terrific strain, their faces reddening, the veins in their temples throbbing. Magician's tongue protrudes, hands flutter hopelessly.

Laughter and applause.

Magician's neck stretches. But it does not snap. It is now several feet long. Two large men strain mightily.

Laughter and applause.

Magician's eyes pop like bubbles from their sockets.

Laughter and applause.

Neck snaps at last. Large men tumble head over heels with respective bloody burdens to opposite sides of stage. Expectant amused hush falls over audience. First large man scrambles to his feet, pitches head and hat into wings, rushes to assist second large man. Together they unzip decapitated body. Lovely assistant emerges.

Surprised laughter and enthusiastic applause, whistling.

Lovely assistant pitches deflated decapitated body into wings. Large men ogle her and make mildly obscene gestures for audience.

Mounting laughter and friendly catcalls.

Lovely assistant invites one of two large men to reach inside her tight green shorts.

Wild whistling.

Both large men jump forward eagerly, tripping over each other and tumbling to floor in angry heap. Lovely assistant winks broadly at audience.

Derisive catcalls.

Both men stand, face each other, furious. First large man spits at second. Second pushes first. First returns push, toppling second to floor. Second leaps to feet, smashes first in nose. First reels, wipes blood from nose, drives fist into second's abdomen.

Loud cheers.

Second weaves confusedly, crumples miserably to floor clutching abdomen. First kicks second brutally in face.

Cheers and mild laughter.

Second staggers blindly to feet, face a mutilated mess. First smashes second back against wall, knees him in groin. Second doubles over, blinded with pain. First clips second with heel of hand behind ear. Second crumples to floor, dead.

Prolonged cheering and applause.

First large man acknowledges applause with self-conscious bow. Flexes knuckles. Lovely assistant approaches first large man, embraces him in motherly fashion, winks broadly at audience.

Prolonged applause and whistling.

Large man grins and embraces lovely assistant in unmotherly fashion, as she makes faces of mock astonishment for audience.

Shouting and laughter, wild whistling.

Lovely assistant frees self from large man, turns plump hind-quarters to him, and bends over, her hands on her knees, her shapely legs straight. Large man grins at audience, pats lovely assistant's green-clad rear.

Wild shouting etc. (as before).

Large man reaches inside lovely assistant's tight green shorts, rolls his eyes, and grins obscenely. She grimaces and wiggles rear briefly.

Wild shouting etc. (as before).

Large man withdraws hand from inside lovely assistant's shorts, extracting magician in black cape and black silk hat.

Thunder of astonished applause.

Magician bows deeply, doffing hat to audience.

Prolonged enthusiastic applause, cheering.

Magician pitches lovely assistant and first large man into wings. Inspects second large man, lying dead on stage. Unzips him and young country boy emerges, flushed and embarrassed. Young country boy creeps abjectly offstage on stomach.

Laughter and catcalls, more applause.

Magician pitches deflated corpse of second large man into wings. Lovely assistant reenters, smiling, dressed as before in high feathery hat, tight green halter, green shorts, net stockings, high heels.

Applause and whistling.

Magician displays inside of hat to audience as lovely assistant points to magician. He thumps hat two or three times. It is empty. Places hat on table, and invites lovely assistant to enter it. She does so.

Vigorous applause.

Once she has entirely disappeared, magician extends both hands over hat, tugs back sleeves exposing wrists, snaps fingers. Reaches in, extracts one green high-heeled shoe.

Applause.

Pitches shoe into wings. Snaps fingers over hat again. Reaches in, withdraws a second shoe.

Applause.

Pitches shoe into wings. Snaps finger over hat. Reaches in, withdraws one long net stocking.

Applause and scattered whistling.

Pitches stocking into wings. Snaps fingers over hat. Reaches in, extracts a second black net stocking.

Applause and scattered whistling.

Pitches stocking into wings. Snaps fingers over hat. Reaches in, pulls out high feathery hat.

Increased applause and whistling, rhythmic stamping of feet.

Pitches hat into wings. Snaps fingers over hat. Reaches in, fumbles briefly.

Light laughter.

Withdraws green halter, displays it with grand flourish.

Enthusiastic applause, shouting, whistling, stamping of feet.

Pitches halter into wings. Snaps fingers over hat. Reaches in, fumbles. Distant absorbed gaze.

Burst of laughter.

Withdraws green shorts, displays them with elegant flourish.

Tremendous crash of applause and cheering, whistling.

Pitches green shorts into wings. Snaps fingers over hat. Reaches in. Prolonged fumbling. Sound of a slap. Withdraws hand hastily, a look of astonished pain on his face. Peers inside.

Laughter.

Head of lovely assistant pops out of hat, pouting indignantly.

Laughter and applause.

With difficulty, she extracts one arm from hat, then other arm. Pressing hands down against hat brim, she wriggles and twists until one naked breast pops out of hat.

Applause and wild whistling.

The other breast: POP!

More applause and whistling.

She wriggles free to the waist. She grunts and struggles, but is unable to free her hips. She looks pathetically, but uncertainly at magician. He tugs and pulls but she seems firmly stuck.

Laughter.

He grasps lovely assistant under armpits and plants feet against hat brim. Strains. In vain.

Laughter.

Thrusts lovely assistant forcibly back into hat. Fumbles again. Loud slap.

Laughter increases.

Magician returns slap soundly.

Laughter ceases abruptly, some scattered booing.

Magician reaches into hat, withdraws one unstockinged leg. He reaches in again, pulls out one arm. He tugs on arm and leg, but for all his effort cannot extract the remainder.

Scattered booing, some whistling.

Magician glances uneasily at audience, stuffs arm and leg back into hat. He is perspiring. Fumbles inside hat. Withdraws nude hindquarters of lovely assistant.

Burst of cheers and wild whistling.

Smiles uncomfortably at audience. Tugs desperately on plump hindquarters, but rest will not follow.

Whistling diminishes, increased booing.

Jams hindquarters back into hat, mops brow with silk handkerchief.

Loud unfriendly booing.

Pockets handkerchief. Is becoming rather frantic. Grasps hat and thumps it vigorously, shakes it. Places it once more on table, brim up. Closes eyes as though in incantations, hands extended over hat. Snaps fingers several times, reaches in tenuously.

Fumbles. Loud slap. Withdraws hand hastily in angry astonishment. Grasps hat. Gritting teeth, infuriated, hurls hat to floor,
leaps on it with both feet. Something crunches. Hideous piercing shriek.

Screams and shouts.

Magician, aghast, picks up hat, stares into it. Pales.

Violent screaming and shouting.

Magician gingerly sets hat on floor, and kneels, utterly appalled
and grief-stricken, in front of it. Weeps silently.

Weeping, moaning, shouting.

Magician huddles miserably over crushed hat, weeping convulsively. First large man and young country boy enter timidly,
soberly, from wings. They are pale and frightened. They peer
uneasily into hat. They start back in horror. They clutch their
mouths, turn away, and vomit.

Weeping, shouting, vomiting, accusations of murder.

Large man and country boy tie up magician, drag him away.

Weeping, retching.

Large man and country boy return, lift crushed hat gingerly, and
trembling uncontrollably, carry it at arm's length into wings.

Momentary increase of weeping, retching, moaning, then dying away of sound to silence.

Country boy creeps onto stage, alone, sets up placard against table and facing audience, then creeps abjectly away.

THIS ACT IS CONCLUDED
THE MANAGENENT REGRETS THERE
WILL BE NO REFUND

THE GINGERBREAD HOUSE

(1969)

1

A pine forest in the midafternoon. Two children follow an old man, dropping breadcrumbs, singing nursery tunes. Dense earthy greens seep into the darkening distance, flecked and streaked with filtered sunlight. Spots of red, violet, pale blue, gold, burnt orange. The girl carries a basket for gathering flowers. The boy is occupied with the crumbs. Their song tells of God's care for little ones.

2

Poverty and resignation weigh on the old man. His cloth jacket is patched and threadbare, sunbleached white over the shoulders, worn through on the elbows. His feet do not lift, but shuffle through the dust. White hair. Parched skin. Secret forces of despair and guilt seem to pull him earthward.

3

The girl plucks a flower. The boy watches curiously. The old man stares impatiently into the forest's depths, where night seems already to crouch. The girl's apron is a bright orange, the gay color of freshly picked tangerines, and is stitched happily with blues and reds and greens; but her dress is simple and brown, tattered at the hem, and her feet are bare. Birds accompany the children in their singing and butterflies decorate the forest spaces.

4

The boy's gesture is furtive. His right hand trails behind him, letting a crumb fall. His face is half-turned toward his hand, but his eyes remain watchfully fixed on the old man's feet ahead. The old man wears heavy mud-spattered shoes, high-topped and leather-thonged. Like the old man's own skin, the shoes are dry and cracked and furrowed with wrinkles. The boy's pants are a bluish-brown, ragged at the cuffs, his jacket a faded red. He, like the girl, is barefoot.

5

The children sing nursery songs about May baskets and gingerbread houses and a saint who ate his own fleas. Perhaps they sing to lighten their young hearts, for puce wisps of dusk now coil through the trunks and branches of the thickening forest. Or perhaps they sing to conceal the boy's subterfuge. More likely, they sing for no reason at all, a thoughtless childish habit. To hear themselves. Or to admire their memories. Or to entertain the old man. To fill the silence. Conceal their thoughts. Their expectations.

6

The boy's hand and wrist, thrusting from the outgrown jacket (the faded red cuff is not a cuff at all, but the torn limits merely, the ragged edge of the soft worn sleeve), are tanned, a little soiled, childish. The fingers are short and plump, the palm soft, the wrist small. Three fingers curl under, holding back crumbs, kneading them, coaxing them into position, while the index finger and thumb flick them sparingly, one by one, to the ground, playing with them a moment, balling them, pinching them as if for luck or pleasure, before letting them go.

7

The old man's pale blue eyes float damply in deep dark pouches, half-shrouded by heavy upper lids and beetled over by shaggy white brows. Deep creases fan out from the moist corners, angle down past the nose, score the tanned cheeks and pinch the mouth. The old man's gaze is straight ahead, but at what? Perhaps at nothing. Some invisible destination. Some irrecoverable point of departure. One thing can be said about the eyes: they are tired. Whether they have seen too much or too little, they betray no will to see yet more.

8

The witch is wrapped in a tortured whirl of black rags. Her long face is drawn and livid, and her eyes glow like burning coals. Her

angular body twists this way and that, flapping the black rags—
flecks of blue and amethyst wink and flash in the black tangle. Her
gnarled blue hands snatch greedily at space, shred her clothes, claw
cruelly at her face and throat. She cackles silently, then suddenly
screeches madly, seizes a passing dove, and tears its heart out.

9

The girl, younger than the boy, skips blithely down the forest path,
her blonde curls flowing freely. Her brown dress is coarse and plain,
but her apron is gay and white petticoats wink from beneath the
tattered hem. Her skin is fresh and pink and soft, her knees and
elbows dimpled, her cheeks rosy. Her young gaze flicks airily from
flower to flower, bird to bird, tree to tree, from the boy to the old
man, from the green grass to the encroaching darkness, and all of it
seems to delight her equally. Her basket is full to overflowing. Does
she even know the boy is dropping crumbs? or where the old man
is leading them? Of course, but it's nothing! A game!

10

There is, in the forest, even now, a sunny place, with mintdrop
trees and cotton candy bushes, an air as fresh and heady as lemonade. Rivulets of honey flow over gumdrop pebbles, and lollypops grow wild as daisies. This is the place of the gingerbread
house. Children come here, but, they say, none leave.

11

The dove is a soft lustrous white, head high, breast filled, tip
of the tail less than a feather's thickness off the ground. From

above, it would be seen against the pale path—a mixture of umbers and grays and the sharp brown strokes of pine needles—but from its own level, in profile, its pure whiteness is set off glowingly against the obscure mallows and distant moss greens of the forest. Only its small beak moves. Around a breadcrumb.

12

The song is about a great king who won many battles, but the girl sings alone. The old man has turned back, gazes curiously but dispassionately now at the boy. The boy, too, has turned, no longer furtive, hand poised but no crumb dropping from his fingertips. He stares back down the path by which they three have come, his mouth agape, his eyes startled. His left hand is raised, as if arrested a moment before striking out in protest. Doves are eating his breadcrumbs. His ruse has failed. Perhaps the old man, not so ignorant in such matters after all, has known all along it would. The girl sings of pretty things sold in the market.

13

So huddled over her prey is the witch that she seems nothing more than a pile of black rags heaped on a post. Her pale long-nailed hands are curled inward toward her breast, massaging the object, her head lower than her hunched shoulders, wan beaked nose poked in among the restless fingers. She pauses, cackling softly, peers left, then right, then lifts the heart before her eyes. The burnished heart of the dove glitters like a ruby, a polished cherry, a brilliant, heart-shaped bloodstone. It beats still. A soft radiant pulsing. The black bony shoulders of the witch quake with glee, with greed, with lust.

14

A wild blur of fluttering white: the dove's wings flapping! Hands clutch its body, its head, its throat, small hands with short plump fingers. Its wings flail against the dusky forest green, but it is forced down against the umber earth. The boy falls upon it, his hands bloodied by beak and claws.

15

The gingerbread house is approached by flagstones of variegated wafers, through a garden of candied fruits and all-day suckers in neat little rows.

16

No song now from the lips of the girl, but a cry of anguish. The basket of flowers is dropped, the kings and saints forgotten. She struggles with the boy for the bird. She kicks him, falls upon him, pulls his hair, tears at his red jacket. He huddles around the bird, trying to elbow free of the girl. Both children are weeping, the boy of anger and frustration, the girl of pain and pity and a bruised heart. Their legs entangle, their fists beat at each other, feathers fly.

17

The pale blue eyes of the old man stare not ahead, but down. The squint, the sorrow, the tedium are vanished; the eyes focus clearly. The deep creases fanning out from the damp corners pinch inward, a brief wince, as though at some inner hurt, some certain anguish, some old wisdom. He sighs.

18

The girl has captured the bird. The boy, small chest heaving, kneels in the path watching her, the anger largely drained out of him. His faded red jacket is torn; his pants are full of dust and pine needles. She has thrust the dove protectively beneath her skirt, and sits, knees apart, leaning over it, weeping softly. The old man stoops down, lifts her bright orange apron, her skirt, her petticoats. The boy turns away. The dove is nested in her small round thighs. It is dead.

19

Shadows have lengthened. Umbers and lavenders and greens have grayed. But the body of the dove glows yet in the gathering dusk. The whiteness of the ruffled breast seems to be fighting back against the threat of night. It is strewn with flowers, now beginning to wilt. The old man, the boy, and the girl have gone.

20

The beams of the gingerbread house are licorice sticks, cemented with taffy, weatherboarded with gingerbread, and coated with caramel. Peppermint-stick chimneys sprout randomly from its chocolate roof and its windows are laced with meringue. Oh, what a house! And the best thing of all is the door.

21

The forest is dense and deep. Branches reach forth like arms. Brown animals scurry. The boy makes no furtive gestures. The girl, carrying her flowerbasket, does not skip or sing. They walk, arms linked, eyes wide open and staring ahead into the forest. The old man plods on, leading the way, his heavy old leather-thonged shoes shuffling in the damp dust and undergrowth.

22

The old man's eyes, pale in the sunlight, now seem to glitter in the late twilight. Perhaps it is their wetness picking up the last flickering light of day. The squint has returned, but it is not the squint of weariness: resistance, rather. His mouth opens as though to speak, to rebuke, but his teeth are clenched. The witch twists and quivers, her black rags whirling, whipping, flapping. From her lean bosom, she withdraws the pulsing red heart of a dove. How it glows, how it rages, how it dances in the dusk! The old man now does not resist. Lust flattens his face and mists his old eyes, where glitter now reflections of the ruby heart. Grimacing, he plummets forward, covering the cackling witch, crashing through brambles that tear at his clothes.

23

A wild screech cleaves the silence of the dusky forest. Birds start up from branches and the undergrowth is alive with frightened animals. The old man stops short, one hand raised protectively in front of him, the other, as though part of the same instinct, reaching back to shield his children. Dropping her basket of flowers, the girl cries out in terror and springs forward into the old man's arms. The boy blanches, shivers as though a cold wind might be wetly wrapping his young body, but manfully holds his ground. Shapes seem to twist and coil, and vapors seep up from the forest floor. The girl whimpers and the old man holds her close.

24

The beds are simple but solid. The old man himself has made them. The sun is setting, the room is in shadows, the children tucked safely in. The old man tells them a story about a good fairy who granted a poor man three wishes. The wishes, he knows, were wasted, but so then is the story. He lengthens the tale with details about the good fairy, how sweet and kind and pretty she is, then lets the children complete the story with their own wishes, their own dreams. Below, a brutal demand is being forced upon him. Why must the goodness of all wishes come to nothing?

25

The flowerbasket lies, overturned, by the forest path, its wilting flowers strewn. Shadows darker than dried blood spread beneath its gaping mouth. The shadows are long, for night is falling.

26

The old man has fallen into the brambles. The children, weeping, help pull him free. He sits on the forest path staring at the boy and girl. It is as though he is unable to recognize them.

Their weeping dies away. They huddle more closely together, stare back at the old man. His face is scratched, his clothes torn. He is breathing irregularly.

27

The sun, the songs, the breadcrumbs, the dove, the overturned basket, the long passage toward night: where, the old man wonders, have all the good fairies gone? He leads the way, pushing back the branches. The children follow, silent and frightened.

28

The boy pales and his heart pounds, but manfully he holds his ground. The witch writhes, her black rags fluttering, licking at the twisted branches. With a soft seductive cackle, she holds before him the burnished cherry-red heart of a dove. The boy licks his lips. She steps back. The glowing heart pulses gently, evenly, excitingly.

29

The good fairy has sparkling blue eyes and golden hair, a soft sweet mouth and gentle hands that caress and soothe. Gossamer wings sprout from her smooth back; from her flawless chest two firm breasts with tips bright as rubies.

30

The witch, holding the flaming pulsing heart out to the boy, steps back into the dark forest. The boy, in hesitation, follows. Back. Back. Swollen eyes aglitter, the witch draws the ruby heart close to her dark lean breast, then past her shoulder and away from the boy. Transfixed, he follows it, brushing by her. The witch's gnarled and bluish fingers claw at his poor garments, his pale red jacket and bluish-brown pants, surprising his soft young flesh.

31

The old man's shoulders are bowed earthward, his face is lined with sorrow, his neck bent forward with resignation, but his eyes glow like burning coals. He clutches his shredded shirt to his throat, stares intensely at the boy. The boy stands alone and trembling on the path, staring into the forest's terrible darkness. Shapes whisper and coil. The boy licks his lips, steps forward. A terrible shriek shreds the forest hush. The old man grimaces, pushes the whimpering girl away, strikes the boy.

32

No more breadcrumbs, no more pebbles, no more songs or flowers. The slap echoes through the terrible forest, doubles back on its own echoes, folding finally into a sound not unlike a whispering cackle.

33

The girl, weeping, kisses the struck boy and presses him close, shielding him from the tormented old man. The old man, taken aback, reaches out uncertainly, gently touches the girl's frail shoulder. She shakes his hand off—nearly a shudder—and shrinks toward the boy. The boy squares his shoulders, color returning to his face. The familiar creases of age and despair crinkle again the old man's face. His pale blue eyes mist over. He looks away. He leaves the children by the last light of day.

34

But the door! The door is shaped like a heart and is as red as a cherry, always half-open, whether lit by sun or moon, is sweeter than a sugarplum, more enchanting than a peppermint stick. It is red as a poppy, red as an apple, red as a strawberry, red as a bloodstone, red as a rose. Oh, what a thing is the door of that house!

35

The children, alone in the strange black forest, huddle wretchedly under a great gnarled tree. Owls hoot and bats flick menacingly through the twisting branches. Strange shapes writhe and rustle before their weary eyes. They hold each other tight and, trembling, sing lullabies, but they are not reassured.

36

The old man trudges heavily out of the black forest. His way is marked, not by breadcrumbs, but by dead doves, ghostly white in the empty night.

37

The girl prepares a mattress of leaves and flowers and pine needles. The boy gathers branches to cover them, to hide them, to protect them. They make pillows of their poor garments.

Bats screech as they work and owls blink down on their bodies, ghostly white, young, trembling. They creep under the branches, disappearing into the darkness.

38

Gloomily, the old man sits in the dark room and stares at the empty beds. The good fairy, though a mystery of the night, effuses her surroundings with a lustrous radiance. Is it the natural glow of her small nimble body or perhaps the star at the tip of her wand? Who can tell? Her gossamer wings flutter rapidly, and she floats, ruby-tipped breasts downward, legs dangling and dimpled knees bent slightly, glowing buttocks arched up in defiance of the night. How good she is! In the black empty room, the old man sighs and uses up a wish: he wishes his poor children well.

39

The children are nearing the gingerbread house. Passing under mintdrop trees, sticking their fingers in the cotton candy bushes, sampling the air as heady as lemonade, they skip along singing nursery songs. Nonsense songs about dappled horses and the slaying of dragons. Counting songs and idle riddles. They cross over rivulets of honey on gumdrop pebbles, picking the lollypops that grow as wild as daffodils.

40

The witch flicks and flutters through the blackened forest, her livid face twisted with hatred, her inscrutable condition. Her eyes burn like glowing coals and her black rags flap loosely. Her gnarled hands claw greedily at the branches, tangle in the night's webs, dig into tree trunks until the sap flows beneath her nails. Below, the boy and girl sleep an exhausted sleep. One ghostly white leg, with dimpled knee and soft round thigh, thrusts out from under the blanket of branches.

41

But wish again! Flowers and butterflies. Dense earthy greens seeping into the distance, flecked and streaked with midafternoon sunlight. Two children following an old man. They drop breadcrumbs, sing nursery songs. The old man walks leadenly. The boy's gesture is furtive. The girl—but it's no use, the doves will come again, there are no reasonable wishes.

42

The children approach the gingerbread house through a garden of candied fruits and all-day suckers, hopping along on flagstones of variegated wafers. They sample the gingerbread weatherboarding with its caramel coating, lick at the meringue on the windowsills, kiss each other's sweetened lips. The boy climbs up on the chocolate roof to break off a peppermint-stick chimney, comes sliding down into a rainbarrel full of vanilla pudding. The girl, reaching out to catch him in his fall, slips on a sugarplum and tumbles into a sticky rock garden of candied chestnuts. Laughing gaily, they lick each other clean. And how grand is the red-and-white striped chimney the boy holds up for her! how bright! how sweet! But the door: here they pause and catch their breath. It is heart-shaped and bloodstone-red, its burnished surface gleaming in the sunlight. Oh, what a thing is that door! Shining like a ruby, like hard cherry candy, and pulsing softly, radiantly. Yes, marvelous! delicious! insuperable! but beyond: what is that sound of black rags flapping?

THE MAGIC POKER

(1969)

I wander the island, inventing it. I make a sun for it, and trees—pines and birch and dogwood and firs—and cause the water to lap the pebbles of its abandoned shores. This, and more: I deposit shadows and dampness, spin webs, and scatter ruins. Yes: ruins. A mansion and guest cabins and boat houses and docks. Terraces, too, and bath houses and even an observation tower. All gutted and window-busted and autographed and shat upon. I impose a hot midday silence, a profound and heavy stillness. But anything can happen.

This small and secretive bay, here just below what was once the caretaker's cabin and not far from the main boat house, probably once possessed its own system of docks, built out to protect boats from the big rocks along the shore. At least the refuse—the long bony planks of gray lumber heaped up at one end of the bay—would suggest that. But aside from the planks, the bay is now only a bay, shallow, floored with rocks and cans and bottles. Schools of silver fish, thin as fingernails, fog the bottom, and dragonflies dart and hover over its placid surface. The harsh snarl of the boat motor—for indeed a boat has been approaching, coming in off the lake into this small bay—breaks off abruptly, as the boat carves a long gentle arc through the bay, and slides, scraping bottom, toward a shallow pebbly corner. There are two girls in the boat.

Bedded deep in the grass, near the path up to the first guest cabin, lies a wrought-iron poker. It is long and slender with an intricately worked handle, and it is orange with rust. It lies shadowed, not by trees, but by the grass that has grown up wildly around it. I put it there.

The caretaker's son, left behind when the island was deserted, crouches naked in the brambly fringe of the forest overlooking the bay. He watches, scratching himself, as the boat scrapes to a stop and the girls stand—then he scampers through the trees and bushes to the guest cabin.

The girl standing forward—fashionbook-trim in tight gold pants, ruffled blouse, silk neckscarf—hesitates, makes one false start, then jumps from the boat, her sandaled heel catching the water's edge. She utters a short irritable cry, hops up on a rock, stumbles, lands finally in dry weeds on the other side. She turns her heel up and frowns down over her shoulder at it. Tiny muscles in front of her ears tense and ripple. She brushes anxiously at a thick black fly in front of her face, and asks peevishly: "What do I do *now*, Karen?"

I arrange the guest cabin. I rot the porch and tatter the screen door and infest the walls. I tear out the light switches, gut the mattresses, smash the windows, and shit on the bathroom floor. I rust the pipes, kick in the papered walls, unhinge doors. Really, there's nothing to it. In fact, it's a pleasure.

Once, earlier in this age, a family with great wealth purchased this entire island, here up on the border, and built on it all these houses, these cabins and the mansion up there on the promontory, and the boat house, docks, bath houses, observation tower. They tamed the island some, seeded lawn grass, contrived their own sewage system with indoor appurtenances, generated electricity for the rooms inside and for the japanese lanterns and postlamps without, and they came up here from time to time in the summers. They used to maintain a caretaker on the island year round, housed him in the cabin by the boat house, but then the patriarch of the family died, and the rest had other things to do. They stopped coming to the island and forgot about caretaking.

The one in gold pants watches as the girl still in the boat switches the motor into neutral and upends it, picks up a yellowish-gray rope from the bottom, and tosses it ashore to her. She reaches for it straight-armed, then shies from it, letting it fall to the ground. She takes it up with two fingers and a thumb and holds it out in front of her. The other girl, Karen (she wears a light yellow dress with a beige cardigan over it), pushes a toolkit under a seat, gazes thoughtfully about the boat, then jumps out. Her canvas shoes splash in the water's edge, but she pays no notice. She takes the rope from the girl in gold pants, loops it around a birch near the shore, smiles warmly, and then, with a nod, leads the way up the path.

At the main house, the mansion, there is a kind of veranda or terrace, a balcony of sorts, high out on the promontory, offering a spectacular view of the lake with its wide interconnected expanses of blue and its many islands. Poised there now, gazing thoughtfully out on that view, is a tall slender man, dressed in slacks, white turtleneck shirt, and navy-blue jacket, smoking a pipe, leaning against the stone parapet. Has he heard a boat come to the island? He is unsure. The sound of the motor seemed to diminish, to grow more distant, before it stopped. Yet, on water, especially around islands, one can never trust what he hears.

Also this, then: the mansion with its many rooms, its debris, its fireplace and wasps' nests, its musty basement, its grand hexagonal loggia and bright red doors. Though the two girls will not come here for a while—first, they have the guest cabin to explore, the poker to find—I have been busy. In the loggia, I have placed a green piano. I have pulled out its wires, chipped and yellowed its ivory keys, and cracked its green paint. I am nothing if not thorough, a real stickler for detail. I have dismembered the piano's pedals and dropped an old boot in its body (this, too, I've designed: it is horizontal and harp-shaped). The broken wires hang like rusted hairs.

The caretaker's son watches for their approach through a shattered window of the guest cabin. He is stout and hairy, muscular, dark, with short bowed legs and a rounded spiny back. The hair on his head is long, and a thin young beard sprouts on his chin and upper lip. His genitals hang thick and heavy and his buttocks are shaggy. His small eyes dart to and fro: where are they?

In the bay, the sun's light has been constant and oppressive; along the path, it is mottled and varied. Even in this variety, though, there is a kind of monotony, a determined patterning that wants a good wind. Through these patterns move the two girls, Karen long-striding with soft steps and expectant smile, the other girl hurrying behind, halting, hurrying again, slapping her arms, her legs, the back of her neck, cursing plaintively. Each time she passes between the two trees, the girl in pants stops, claws the space with her hands, runs through, but spiderwebs keep diving and tangling into her hair just the same.

Between two trees on the path, a large spider—black with a red heart on its abdomen—weaves an intricate web. The girl stops short, terrified. Nimbly, the shiny black creature works, as though spelling out some terrible message for her alone. How did Karen pass through here without brushing into it? The girl takes a step backward, holding her hands to her face. Which way around? To the left it is dark, to the right sunny: she chooses the sunny side and there, not far from the path, comes upon a wrought-iron poker, long and slender with an intricately worked handle. She bends low, her golden haunches gleaming over the grass: how beautiful it is! On a strange impulse, she kisses it—POOF! before her stands a tall slender man, handsome, dressed in dark slacks, white turtleneck shirt, and jacket, smoking a pipe. He smiles down at her. "Thank you," he says, and takes her hand.

Karen is some distance in front, almost out of sight, when the other girl discovers, bedded in the grass, a wrought-iron poker. Orange with rust, it is long and slender with an elaborate handle. She crouches to examine it, her haunches curving golden above the bluegreen grass, her long black hair drifting lightly down over her small shoulders and wafting in front of her fine-boned face. "Oh!" she says softly. "How strange! How beautiful!" Squeamishly, she touches it, grips it, picks it up, turns it over. Not so rusty on the underside—but bugs! *millions* of them! She drops the thing, shudders, stands, wipes her hand several times on her pants, shudders again. A few steps away, she pauses, glances back, then around at everything about her, concentrating, memorizing the place probably. She hurries on up the path and sees her sister already at the first guest cabin.

The girl in gold pants? yes. The other one, Karen? also. In fact, they are sisters. I have brought two sisters to this invented island, and shall, in time, send them home again. I have dressed them and may well choose to undress them. I have given one three marriages, the other none at all, nor is that the end of my beneficence and cruelty. It might even be argued that I have invented their common parents. No, I have not. We have options that may, I admit, seem strangely limited to some . . .

She crouches, haunches flexing golden above the bluegreen grass, and kisses the strange poker, kisses its handle and its long rusted shaft. Nothing. Only a harsh unpleasant taste. I am a fool, she thinks, a silly romantic fool. Yet why else has she been diverted to this small meadow? She kisses the tip—POOF! "Thank you," he says, smiling down at her. He bows to kiss her cheek and take her hand.

The guest cabin is built of rough-hewn logs, hardly the fruit of necessity, given the funds at hand, but probably it was thought

fashionable; proof of traffic with other cultures is adequately provided by its gabled roof and log columns. It is here, on the shaded
porch, where Karen is standing, waiting for her sister. Karen
waves when she sees her, ducking down there along the path; then
she turns and enters the cabin through the broken front door.

He knows that one. He's been there before. He crouches inside
the door, his hairy body tense. She enters, staring straight at
him. He grunts. She smiles, backing away. "Karen!" His small
eyes dart to the doorway, and he shrinks back into the shadows.

She kisses the rusted iron poker, kisses its ornate handle, its long
rusted shaft, kisses the tip. Nothing happens. Only a rotten taste
in her mouth. Something is wrong. "Karen!"

"Karen!" the girl in pants calls from outside the guest cabin.
"Karen, I just found the most beautiful thing!" The second
step of the porch is rotted away. She hops over it onto the porch,
drags open the tattered screen door. "Karen, I—*oh, good God!*
look what they've *done* to this house! Just *look!*" Karen, about
to enter the kitchen, turns back, smiling, as her sister surveys
the room: "The walls all smashed in, even the plugs in the wall
and the light switches pulled out! Think of it, Karen! They even
had electricity! Out here on this island, so far from everything
civilized! And, see, what beautiful paper they had on the walls!
And now just look at it! It's so—oh! what a dreadful beautiful
beastly thing all at once!"

But where is the caretaker's son? I don't know. He was here,
shrinking into the shadows, when Karen's sister entered. Yet,

though she catalogues the room's disrepair, there is no mention of the caretaker's son. This is awkward. Didn't I invent him myself, along with the girls and the man in the turtleneck shirt? Didn't I round his back and stunt his legs and cause the hair to hang between his buttocks? I don't know. The girls, yes, and the tall man in the shirt—to be sure, he's one of the first of my inventions. But the caretaker's son? To tell the truth, I sometimes wonder if it was not he who invented me . . .

The caretaker's son, genitals hanging hard and heavy, eyes aglitter, shrinks back into the shadows as the girl approaches, and then goes bounding silently into the empty rooms. Behind an unhinged door, he peeks stealthily at the declaiming girl in gold pants, then slips, almost instinctively, into the bathroom to hide. It was here, after all, where first they met.

Karen passes quietly through the house, as though familiar with it. In the kitchen, she picks up a chipped blue teakettle, peers inside. All rust. She thumps it, the sound is dull. She sets it on a bench in the sunlight. On all sides, there are broken things: rubble really. Windows gape, shards of glass in the edges pointing out the middle spaces. The mattresses on the floors have been slashed with knives. What little there is of wood is warped. The girl in the tight gold pants and silk neckscarf moves, chattering, in and out of rooms. She opens a white door, steps into a bathroom, steps quickly out again. "Judas God!" she gasps, clearly horrified. Karen turns, eyebrows raised in concern. "Don't go in there, Karen! *Don't go in there!*" She clutches one hand to her ruffled blouse. "About a hundred million people have gone to the *bath*room in there!" Exiting the bathroom behind her, a lone fly swims lazily past her elbow into the close warm air of the kitchen. It circles over a cracked table—the table bearing newspapers, shred of wallpaper, tin cans, a stiff black washcloth— then settles on a counter near a rusted pipeless sink. It chafes its rear legs, walks past the blue teakettle's shadow into a band of pure sunlight stretched out along the counter, and sits there.

The tall man stands, one foot up on the stone parapet, gazing out on the blue sunlit lake, drawing meditatively on his pipe. He has been deeply moved by the desolation of this island. And yet, it is only the desolation of artifact, is it not, the ruin of man's civilized arrogance, nature reclaiming her own. Even the willful mutilations: a kind of instinctive response to the futile artifices of imposed order, after all. But such reasoning does not appease him. Leaning against his raised knee, staring out upon the vast wilderness, hoping indeed he has heard a boat come here, he puffs vigorously on his pipe and affirms reason, man, order. Are we merely blind brutes loosed in a system of mindless energy, impotent, misdirected, and insolent? "No," he says aloud, "we are not."

She peeks into the bathroom; yes, he is in there, crouching obscurely, shaggily, but eyes aglitter, behind the stool. She hears his urgent grunt and smiles. "Oh, Karen!" cries the other girl from the rear of the house. "It's so very sad!" Hastily, Karen steps out into the hallway, eases the bathroom door shut, her heart pounding.

"Oh, Karen, it's so very sad!" That's the girl in the gold pants again, of course. Now she is gazing out a window. At: high weeds and grass, crowding young birches, red rattan chair with the seat smashed out, backdrop of gray-trunked pines. She is thinking of her three wrecked marriages, her affairs, and her desolation of spirit. The broken rattan chair somehow communicates to her a sensation of real physical pain. Where have all the Princes gone? she wonders. "I mean, it's not the ones who stole the things, you know, the scavengers. I've seen people in Paris and Mexico and Algiers, lots of places, scooping rotten oranges and fishheads out of the heaped-up gutters and eating them, and I didn't blame them, I didn't dis*like* them, I felt *sorry* for them. I even felt sorry for them if they were just doing it to be stealing something, to get something for nothing, even if they weren't hungry or anything. But it isn't the people who look for things they want or need or even don't need and take them, it's the people who just *destroy*, destroy because—God! Because they just *want* to destroy! Lust! That's all, Karen! See? Somebody just went around these rooms driving his fist in the walls because he had to hurt, it didn't matter who or what, or maybe he kicked them with his feet, and bashed the windows and ripped the curtains and then went to the *bath*room on it all! Oh my God! *Why?* Why would anybody want to *do* that?" The window in front of Karen (she has long since turned her back) is, but for one panel, still whole. In the excepted panel, the rupture in the glass is now spanned by a spiderweb more intricate than a butterfly's wing, than a system of stars, its silver paths seeming to imitate or perhaps merely to extend the delicate tracery of the fractured glass still surrounding the hole. It is a new web, for nothing has entered it yet to alter its original construction. Karen's hand reaches toward it, but then withdraws. "Karen, let's get out of here!"

The girls have gone. The caretaker's son bounds about the guest cabin, holding himself with one hand, smashing walls and busting windows with the other, grunting happily as he goes. He leaps up onto the kitchen counter, watches the two girls from the window, as they wind their way up to the main mansion, then squats joyfully over the blue teakettle, depositing . . . a love letter, so to speak.

A love letter! Wait a minute, this is getting out of hand! What happened to that poker, I was doing much better with the poker, I had something going there, archetypal and even maybe beautiful, a blend of eros and wisdom, sex and sensibility, music and myth. But what am I going to do with shit in a rusty teakettle? No, no, there's nothing to be gained by burdening our fabrications with impieties. Enough that the skin of the world is littered with our contentious artifice, lepered with the stigmata of human aggression and despair, without suffering our songs to be flatted by savagery. Back to the poker.

"Thank you," he says, smiling down at her, her haunches gleaming golden over the shadowed grass. "But, tell me, how did you know to kiss it?" "Call it woman's intuition," she replies, laughing lightly, and rises with an appreciative glance. "But the neglected state that it was in, it must have tasted simply dreadful," he apologizes, and kisses her gently on the check. "What momentary bitterness I might have suffered," she responds, "has been more than indemnified by the sweetness of your disenchantment." "My disenchantment? Oh no, my dear, there *are* no disenchantments, merely progressions and styles of possession. To exist is to be spell-bound." She collapses, marveling, at his feet.

Karen, alone on the path to the mansion, pauses. Where is her sister? Has something distracted her? Has she strayed? Perhaps she has gone on ahead. Well, it hardly matters, what can happen on a desolate island? they'll meet soon enough at the mansion. In fact, Karen isn't even thinking about her sister, she's staring silently, entranced, at a small green snake, stretched across the path. Is it dozing? Or simply unafraid? Maybe it's never seen a real person before, doesn't know what people can do. It's possible: few people come here now, and it looks like a very young snake. Slender, wriggly, green, and shiny. No, probably it's asleep. Smiling, Karen leaves the path, circling away from the snake so as not to disturb it. To the right of the path is a small clearing and the sun is hot there; to the left it is cool and shadowed in the gathering forest. Karen moves that way, in under the trees, picking the flowers that grow wildly here. Her cardigan catches on brambles and birch seedlings, so she pulls it off, tosses it loosely over her shoulder, hooked on one finger. She hears, not far away, a sound not unlike soft footfalls. Curious, she wanders that way to see who or what it is.

The path up to the main house, the mansion, is not even mottled, the sun does not reach back here at all, it is dark and damp-smelling, an ambience of mushrooms and crickets and fingery rustles and dead brown leaves never quite dry, or so it might seem to the girl in gold pants, were she to come this way. Where is she? His small eyes dart to and fro. Here, beside the path, trees have collapsed and rotted, seedlings and underbrush have sprung up, and lichens have crept softly over all surfaces, alive and dead. Strange creatures abide here.

"Call it woman's intuition," she says with a light laugh. He appraises her fineboned features, her delicate hands, her soft maidenly breasts under the ruffled blouse, her firm haunches gleaming golden over the shadowed grass. He pulls her gently to her feet, kisses her cheek. "You are enchantingly beautiful, my dear!" he whispers. "Wouldn't you like to lie with me here awhile?" "Of course," she replies, and kisses his cheek in return, "but these pants are an awful bother to remove, and my sister awaits us. Come! Let us go up to the mansion!"

A small green snake lies motionless across the path. The girl approaching does not see it, sees only the insects flicking damply, the girl in tight pants which are still golden here in the deep shadows. Her hand flutters ceaselessly before her face, it was surely the bugs that drove these people away from here finally, "Karen, is this the right way?," and she very nearly walks right on the snake, which has perhaps been dozing, but which now switches with a frantic whip of its shiny green tail off into the damp leaves. The girl starts at the sudden whirring shush at her feet, spins around clutching her hands to her upper arms, expecting the worst, but though staring wide-eyed right at the sound, she can see nothing. Why did she ever let her sister talk her into coming here? *"Karen!"* She runs, ignoring the webs now, right through all the gnats and flies, on up the path, crying out her sister's name.

The caretaker's son, poised gingerly on a moss-covered rock, peeking through thick branches, watches the girl come up the path. Karen watches the caretaker's son. From the rear, his prominent feature is his back, broad and rounded, humped almost, where tufts of dark hair sprout randomly. His head is just a small hairy lump beyond the mound of heavy back. His arms are as long as his legs are short, and the elbows, like the knees, turn outward. Thick hair grows between his buttocks and down his thighs. Smiling, she picks up a pebble to toss at him, but then she hears her sister call her name.

Leaning against his raised knee, smoking his pipe, the tall man on the parapet stares out on the wilderness, contemplating the island's ruin. Tress have collapsed upon one another, and vast areas of the island, once cleared and no doubt the stage for garden parties famous for miles around, are now virtually impassable. Brambles and bunchberries grow wildly amid saxifrage and shinleaf, and everything in sight is mottled with moss. Lichens: the symbiotic union, he recalls, of fungi and algae. He smiles and at the same moment, as though it has been brought into being by his smile, hears a voice on the garden path. A girl. How charming, he's to have company, after all! At least two, for he heard the voice on the path behind the mansion, and below him, slipping surefootedly through the trees and bushes, moves another creature in a yellow dress, carrying a beige sweater over her shoulder. She looks a little simple, not his type really, but then dissimilar organisms can, at times, enjoy mutually advantageous partnerships, can they not? He knocks the ashes from his pipe and refills the bowl.

At times, I forget that this arrangement is my own invention. I begin to think of the island as somehow real, its objects solid and intractable, its condition of ruin not so much an aesthetic design as an historical denouement. I find myself peering into

blue teakettles, batting at spiderwebs, and contemplating a
greenish-gray growth on the side of a stone parapet. I wonder
if others might wander here without my knowing it; I wonder
if I might die and the teakettle remain. "I have brought two
sisters to this invented island," I say. This is no extravagance. It
is indeed I who burdens them with curiosity and history, appetite and rhetoric. If they have names and griefs, I have provided
them. "In fact," I add, "without me they'd have no cunts." This
is not (I interrupt here to tell you that I have done all that I
shall do. I return here to bring you this news, since this seemed
as good a place as any. Though you have more to face, and even
more to suffer from me, this is in fact the last thing I shall say
to you. But can the end be in the middle? Yes, yes, it always is . . .)
meant to alarm, merely to make a truth manifest—yet *I* am
myself somewhat alarmed. It is one thing to discover the shag
of hair between my buttocks, quite another to find myself tugging the tight gold pants off Karen's sister. Or perhaps it is the
same thing, yet troubling in either case. Where does this illusion come from, this sensation of "hardness" in a blue teakettle
or an iron poker, golden haunches or a green piano?

In the hexagonal loggia of the mansion stands a grand piano,
painted bright green, though chipped and cracked now with
age and abuse. One can easily imagine a child at such a piano,
a piano so glad and ready, perhaps two children, and the sun
is shining—no, rather, there is a storm on the lake, the sky is
in a fury, all black and pitching, the children are inside here
out of the wind and storm, the little girl on the right, the boy
on the left, pushing at each other a bit, staking out property
lines on the keys, a grandmother, or perhaps just a lady, yet why

not a grandmother? sitting on a window-bench gazing out on the frothy blue-black lake, and the children are playing "Chopsticks," laughing, a little noisy surely, and the grandmother, or lady, looks over from time to time, forms a patient smile if they chance to glance up at her, then—well, but it's only a supposition, who knows whether there were children or if they cared a damn about a green piano even on a bad day, "Chopsticks" least of all? No, it's only a piece of fancy, the kind of fancy that is passing through the mind of the girl in gold pants who now reaches down, strikes a key. There is no sound, of course. The ivory is chipped and yellowed, the pedals dismembered, the wires torn out and hanging like rusted hairs. The girl wonders at her own unkemptness, feels a lock loose on her forehead, but there are no mirrors. Stolen or broken. She stares about her, nostalgically absorbed for some reason, at the elegantly timbered roof of the loggia, at the enormous stone fireplace, at the old shoe in the doorway, the wasps' nests over one broken-out window. She sighs, steps out on the terrace, steep and proud over the lake. "It's a sad place," she says aloud.

The tall man in the navy-blue jacket stands, one foot up on the stone parapet, gazing out on the blue sunlit lake, drawing meditatively on his pipe, while being sketched by the girl in the tight gold pants. "I somehow expected to find you here," she says. "I've been waiting for you," replies the man. Her three-quarters view of him from the rear allows her to include only the tip of his nose in her sketch, the edge of his pipebowl, the collar of his white turtleneck shirt. "I was afraid there might be others," she says. "Others?" "Yes. Children perhaps. Or somebody's grandmother. I saw so many names everywhere I went, on walls and

doors and trees and even scratched into that green piano." She
is carefully filling in on her sketch the dark contours of his
navy-blue jacket. "No," he says, "whoever they were, they left
here long ago." "It's a sad place," she says, "and all too much like
my own life." He nods. "You mean, the losing struggle against
inscrutable blind forces, young dreams brought to ruin?" "Yes,
something like that," she says. "And getting kicked in and gutted and shat upon." "Mmm." He straightens. "Just a moment,"
she says, and he resumes his pose. The girl has accomplished
a reasonable likeness of the tall man, except that his legs are
stubby (perhaps she failed to center her drawing properly, and
ran out of space at the bottom of the paper) and his buttocks are
bare and shaggy.

"It's a sad place," he says, contemplating the vast wilderness.
He turns to find her grinning and wiggling her ears at him.
"Karen, you're mocking me!" he complains, laughing. She
props one foot up on the stone parapet, leans against her leg,
sticks an iron poker between her teeth, and scowls out upon the
lake. "Come on! Stop it!" he laughs. She puffs on the iron poker,
blowing imaginary smokerings, then turns it into a walking
stick and hobbles about imitating an old granny chasing young
children. Next, she puts the poker to her shoulder like a rifle
and conducts an inspection of all the broken windows facing on
the terrace, scowling or weeping broadly before each one. The
man has slumped to the terrace floor, doubled up with laughter.
Suddenly, Karen discovers an unbroken window. She leaps up
and down, does a somersault, pirouettes, jumps up and clicks
her heels together. She points at it, kisses it, points again. "Yes,
yes!" the man laughs, "I see it, Karen!" She points to herself,

then at the window, to herself again. "You? You're like the window, Karen?" he asks, puzzled, but still laughing. She nods her head vigorously, thrusts the iron poker into his hands. It is dirty and rusty and he feels clumsy with the thing. "I don't understand . . ." She grabs it out of his hands and—*crash!*—drives it through the window. "Oh no, Karen! No, no . . . !"

"It's a sad place." Karen has joined her sister on the terrace, the balcony, and they gaze out at the lake, two girls alone on a desolate island. "Sad and yet all too right for me, I suppose. Oh, I don't regret any of it, Karen. No, I was wrong, wrong as always, but I don't regret it. It'd be silly to be all pinched and morbid about it, wouldn't it, Karen?" The girl, of course, is talking about the failure of her third marriage. "Things are done and they are undone and then we get ready to do them again." Karen looks at her shyly, then turns her gentle gaze back out across the lake, blue with a river's muted blue under this afternoon sun. "The sun!" the girl in gold pants exclaims, though it is not clear why she thought of it. She tries to explain that she is like the sun somehow, or the sun is like her, but she becomes confused. Finally, she interrupts herself to blurt out: "Oh, Karen! *I'm so miserable!*" Karen looks up anxiously: there are no tears in her sister's eyes, but she is biting down painfully on her lower lip. Karen offers a smile, a little awkward, not quite understanding perhaps, and finally her sister, eyes closing a moment, then fluttering open, smiles wanly in return. A moment of grace settles between them, but Karen turns her back on it clumsily.

"No, Karen! Please! Stop!" The man, collapsed to the terrace floor, has tears of laughter running down his cheeks. Karen has found an old shoe and is now holding it up at arm's length, making broad silent motions with her upper torso and free arm as though declaiming upon the sadness of the shoe. She sets the shoe on the terrace floor and squats down over it, covering it with the skirt of her yellow dress. "No, Karen! No!" She leaps up, whacks her heels together in midair, picks up the shoe and peers inside. A broad smile spreads across her face, and she does a little dance, holding the shoe aloft. With a little curtsy, she presents the shoe to the man. "No! Please!" Warily, but still laughing, he looks inside. "What's this? Oh no! A flower! Karen, this is too much!" She runs into the mansion, returns carrying the green piano on her back. She drops it so hard, one leg breaks off. She finds an iron poker, props the piano up with it, sits down on an imaginary stool to play. She lifts her hands high over her head, then comes driving down with extravagant magisterial gestures. The piano, of course, has been completely disemboweled, so no sounds emerge, but up and down the broken keyboard Karen's stubby fingers fly, arriving at last, with a crescendo of violent flourishes, at a grand climactic coda, which she delivers with such force as to buckle the two remaining legs of the piano and send it all crashing to the terrace floor. "No, Karen! Oh my God!" Out of the wreckage, a wild goose springs, honking in holy terror, and goes flapping out over the lake. Karen carries the piano back inside, there's a splintering crash, and she returns wielding the poker. "Careful!" She holds the poker up with two hands and does a little dance, toes turned outward, hippety-hopping about the terrace. She stops abruptly over the man, thrusts the poker in front of his nose, then slowly brings it to her own lips and kisses it. She makes a wry face. "Oh, Karen! Whoo! Please! You're killing me!" She kisses the handle, the shaft, the tip. She wrinkles her nose and shudders, lifts her skirt and wipes her tongue with it. She scowls at the poker. She takes a firm grip on the poking end and bats the handle a couple times against the stone parapet as though testing it. "Oh, Karen! Oh!" Then she lifts it high over her head and brings it down with all her might—WHAM!—POOF! it is the caretaker's son, yowling with pain. She lets go and spins away from him, as he strikes out at her in distress and fury. She tumbles into a corner of the terrace and cowers there, whimpering, pale and terrified, as the caretaker's son, breathing heavily, back stooped and buttocks tensed, circles her, prepared to spring. Suddenly, she dashes for the parapet and leaps over, the caretaker's son bounding after, and off they go, scrambling frantically through the trees and brambles, leaving the tall man in the white turtleneck shirt alone and limp from laughter on the terrace.

There is a storm on the lake. Two children play "Chopsticks" on the green piano. Their grandmother stirs the embers in the fireplace with an iron poker, then returns to her seat on the windowbench. The children glance over at her and she smiles at them. Suddenly a strange naked creature comes bounding into the loggia, grinning idiotically. The children and their grandmother scream with terror and race from the room and on out of the mansion, running for their lives. The visitor leaps up on the piano bench and squats there, staring quizzically at the ivory keys. He reaches for one and it sounds a note—he jerks his hand back in fright. He reaches for another—a different note. He brings his fist down—BLAM! Aha! Again: BLAM! Excitedly, he leaps up and down on the piano bench, banging his fists on the piano keyboard. He hops up on the piano, finds wires inside, and pulls them out. TWANG! TWANG! He holds his genitals with one hand and rips out the wires with the other, grunting with delight. Then he spies the iron poker. He grabs it up, admires it, then bounds joyfully around the room, smashing windows and wrecking furniture. The girl in gold pants enters and takes the poker away from him. "Lust! That's all it is!" she scolds. She whacks him on the nates with the poker, and yelping with pain and astonishment, he bounds away, leaping over the stone parapet, and slinks off through the brambly forest.

"Lust!" she says, "that's all it is!" Her sketch is nearly complete. "And they're not the worst ones. The worst ones are the ones who just let it happen. If they'd kept their caretaker here. . ." The man smiles. "There never was a caretaker," he explains. "Really? But I thought——!" "No," he says, "that's just a legend of the island." She seems taken aback by this new knowledge. "Then . . . then I don't understand . . ." He relights his pipe, wanders over to appraise her sketch. He laughs when he sees the shaggy buttocks. "Marvelous!" he exclaims, "but a poor likeness, I'm afraid! Look!" He lowers his dark slacks and shows her his hindend, smooth as marble and hairless as a movie starlet's. Her curiosity is caught, however, not by his barbered buttocks, but by the hair around his genitals: the tight neat curls fan out in both directions like the wings of an eagle, or a wild goose . . .

The two sisters return to the loggia, their visit nearly concluded, the one in gold pants still trying to explain about herself and the sun, about consuming herself with an outer fire, while harboring an icecold center within. Her gaze falls once more on the green piano. It is obvious she still has something more to say. But now as she declaims, she has less of an audience. Karen stands distractedly before the green piano. Haltingly, she lifts a finger, strikes a key. No note, only a dull thuck. Her sister reveals a new insight she has just obtained about it not being the people who steal or even those who wantonly destroy, but those who let it happen, who just don't give a proper damn. She provides instances. Once, Karen nods, but maybe only at something she has thought to herself. Her finger lifts, strikes. Thuck! Again. Thuck! Her whole arm drives the strong blunt finger. Thuck! Thuck! There is something genuinely beautiful about the girl in gold pants and silk neckscarf as she gestures and speaks. Her eyes are sorrowful and wise. Thuck! Karen strikes the key. Suddenly, her sister breaks off her message. "Oh, I'm sorry, Karen!" she says. She stares at the piano, then runs out of the room.

I am disappearing. You have no doubt noticed. Yes, and by some no doubt calculable formula of event and pagination. But before we drift apart to a distance beyond the reach of confessions (though I warn you: like Zeno's turtle, I am with you always), listen: it's just as I feared, my invented island is really taking its place in world geography. Why, this island sounds very much like the old Dahlberg place on Jackfish Island up on Rainy Lake, people say, and I wonder: can it be happening? Someone tells me: I understand somebody bought the place recently and plans to fix it up, maybe put a resort there or something. On *my* island? Extraordinary!—and yet it seems possible. I look on a map: yes, there's Rainy Lake, there's Jackfish Island. Who invented this map? Well, I must have, surely. And the Dahlbergs, too, of course, and the people who told me about them. Yes, and perhaps tomorrow I will invent Chicago and Jesus Christ and the history of the moon. Just as I have invented you, dear reader, while lying here in the afternoon sun, bedded deeply in the bluegreen grass like an old iron poker . . .

There is a storm on the lake and the water is frothy and black. The wind howls around the corner of the stone parapet and the pine trees shake and creak. The two children playing "Chopsticks" on the green piano are arguing about the jurisdiction of the bench and keyboard. "Come over here," their grandmother says from her seat by the window, "and I'll tell you the story of 'The Magic Poker' . . ."

Once upon a time, a family of wealthy Minnesotans bought an island on Rainy Lake up on the Canadian border. They built a home on it and guest cabins and boat houses and an observation tower. They installed an electric generator and a sewage system with indoor toilets, maintained a caretaker, and constructed docks and bath houses. Did they name it Jackfish Island, or did it bear that name when they bought it? The legend does not say, nor should it. What it does say, however, is that when the family abandoned the island, they left behind an iron poker, which, years later, on a visit to the island, a beautiful young girl, not quite a princess perhaps, yet altogether equal to the occasion, kissed. And when she did so, something quite extraordinary happened . . .

Once upon a time there was an island visited by ruin and inhabited by strange woodland creatures. Some thought it had once had a caretaker who had either died or found another job elsewhere. Others said, no, there was never a caretaker, that was only a childish legend. Others believed there was indeed a caretaker and he lived there yet and was in fact responsible for the island's tragic condition. All this is neither here nor there. What is certainly beyond dispute is that no one who visited the island, whether searching for its legendary Magic Poker or avenging the loss of a loved one, ever came back. Only their names were left, inscribed hastily on walls and ceilings and carved on trees.

Once upon a time, two sisters visited a desolate island. They walked its paths with their proclivities and scruples, dreaming their dreams and sorrowing their sorrows. They scared a snake and probably a bird or two, broke a few windows (there were few left to break), and gazed meditatively out upon the lake from the terrace of the main house. They wrote their names above the stone fireplace in the hexagonal loggia and shat in the soundbox of an old green piano. One of them did anyway; the other one couldn't get her pants down. On the island, they found a beautiful iron poker, and when they went home, they took it with them.

The girl in gold pants hastens out of the big house and down the dark path where earlier the snake slept and past the gutted guest cabin and on down the mottled path toward the boat. To either side of her, flies and bees mumble indolently under the summer sun. A small speckled frog who will not live out the day squats staring on a stone, burps, hops into a darkness. A white moth drifts silently into the web of a spider, flutters there awhile before his execution. Suddenly, there on the path mottled with sunlight, the girl stops short, her breath coming in short gasps, looking around her. Wasn't this——? Yes, yes, it is the place! A smile begins to form. And in fact, there it is! She waits for Karen.

Once upon a time there was a beautiful young Princess in tight gold pants, so very tight in fact that no one could remove them from her. Knights came from far and wide, and they huffed and they puffed, and they grunted and they groaned, but the pants would not come down. One rash Knight even went so far as to jam the blade of his sword down the front of the gold pants, striving to pry them from her, but he succeeded only in shattering his sword, much to his lifelong dismay and ignominy. The King at last delivered a Proclamation. "Whosoever shall succeed in pulling my daughter's pants down," he declared, "shall have her for his bride!" Since this was perhaps not the most tempting of trophies, the Princess having been married off three times already in previous competitions, the King added: "And moreover he shall have bestowed upon him the Magic Poker, whose powers and prodigies are well-known in the Kingdom!" "The Old Man's got his bloody cart before his horse," one Knight complained sourly to a companion upon hearing the Proclamation. "If I had the bloody Poker, you could damn well bet I'd have no trouble gettin' the bloody pants off her!" Now, it chanced that this heedless remark was overheard by a peculiar little gnome-like creature, huddling naked and unshaven in the brush alongside the road, and no sooner had the words been uttered than this strange fellow determined to steal the Magic Poker and win the beauty for himself. Such an enterprise might well have seemed impossible for even the most dauntless of Knights, much less for so hapless a creature as this poor naked brute with the shaggy loins, but the truth, always stranger than fiction, was that his father had once been the King's Official Caretaker, and the son had grown up among the mysteries and secret chambers of the Court. Imagine the entire Kingdom's astonishment, therefore, when, the very next day, the Caretaker's son appeared, squat, naked, and hirsute, before the King and with grunts and broad gestures made manifest his intention to quit the Princess of her pants and win the prizes for himself! "Indeed!" cried her father. The King's laughter boomed throughout the Palace, and all the Knights and Ladies joined in, creating the jolliest of uproars. "Bring my daughter here at once!" the King thundered, delighted by the droll spectacle. The Princess, amused, but at the same time somewhat afrighted of the strange little man, stepped timidly forward, her golden haunches gleaming in the bright lights of the Palace. The Caretaker's son promptly drew forth the Magic Poker, pointed it at the Princess, and—POOF!—the gold pants dropped—plop!—to the Palace floor. "Oh's!" and "Ah's!" of amazement and admiration rose up in excited chorus from the crowd of nobles attending this most extraordinary moment. Flushed, trembling, impatient, the Princess grasped the Magic Poker and kissed it—POOF!—a handsome Knight in shining armor of white and navy blue stood before her, smoking a pipe. He drew his sword and slew the Caretaker's son. Then, smiling at the maiden standing in her puddle of gold pants, he sheathed his sword, knocked the ashes from his pipe bowl, and knelt before the King. "Your Majesty," he said, "I have slain the monster and rescued your daughter!" "Not at all," replied the King gloomily. "You have made her a widow. Kiss the fool, my dear!" "No, please!" the Knight begged. "Stop!"

"Look, Karen, look! See what I found! Do you think we can take it? It doesn't hurt, does it, I mean, what with everything else—? It's just beautiful and I can scour off the rust and—?" Karen glances at the poker in the grass, shrugs, smiles in assent, turns to stride on down the rise toward the boat, a small white edge of which can be glimpsed through the trees, below, at the end of the path. "Karen—? Could you please—?" Karen turns around, gazes quizzically at her sister, head tilted to one side— then laughs, a low grunting sound, something like a half-gargle, walks back and picks up the poker, brushes off the insects with her hand. Her sister, delighted, reaches for it, but Karen grunts again, keeps it, carries it down to their boat. There, she washes it clean in the lake water, scrubbing it with sand. She dries it on her dress. "Don't get your dress dirty, Karen! It's rusty anyway. We'll clean it when we get home." Karen holds it between them a moment before tossing it into the boat, and they both smile to see it. Wet still, it glistens, sparkling with flecks of rainbow-colored light in the sunshine.

The tall man stands poised before her, smoking his pipe, one hand in the pocket of his navy-blue jacket. Besides the jacket, he wears only a white turtleneck shirt. The girl in gold pants is kissing him. From the tip of his crown to the least of his toes. Nothing happens. Only a bitter wild goose taste in the mouth. Something is wrong. "Karen!" Karen laughs, a low grunting sound, then takes hold of the man and lifts her skirts. "No, Karen! Please!" he cries, laughing. "Stop!" POOF! From her skirts, Karen withdraws a wrought-iron poker, long and slender with an intricately worked handle. "It's beautiful, Karen!" her sister exclaims and reaches for it. Karen grunts again, holds it up between them a moment, and they both smile to see it. It glistens in the sunshine, a handsome souvenir of a beautiful day.

Soon the bay is still again, the silver fish and the dragonflies are returned, and only the slightest murmur near the shore by the old waterlogged lumber betrays the recent disquiet. The boat is already far out on the lake, its stern confronting us in retreat. The family who prepared this island does not know the girls have been here, nor would it astonish them to hear of it. As a matter of fact, with that touch of the divinity common to the rich, they have probably forgotten why they built all the things on this island in the first place, or whatever possessed them seriously to concern themselves, to squander good hours, over the selection of this or that object to decorate the newly made spaces or to do the things that had usually to be done, over the selection of this or that iron poker, for example. The boat is almost out of sight, so distant in fact, it's no longer possible to see its occupants or even to know how many there are—all just a blurred speck on the bright sheen laid on the lake by the lowering sun. The lake is calm. Here, a few shadows lengthen, a frog dies, a strange creature lies slain, a tanager sings.

THE BABYSITTER

(1969)

S he arrives at 7:40, ten minutes late, but the children, Jimmy and Bitsy, are still eating supper, and their parents are not ready to go yet. From other rooms come the sounds of a baby screaming, water running, a television musical (no words: probably a dance number—patterns of gliding figures come to mind). Mrs. Tucker sweeps into the kitchen, fussing with her hair, and snatches a baby bottle full of milk out of a pan of warm water, rushes out again. "Harry!" she calls. "The babysitter's here already!"

○

That's My Desire? I'll Be Around? He smiles toothily, beckons faintly with his head, rubs his fast balding pate. Bewitched, maybe? Or, What's the Reason? He pulls on his shorts, gives his hips a slap. The baby goes silent in mid-scream. Isn't this the one who used their tub last time? Who's Sorry Now, that's it.

○

Jack is wandering around town, not knowing what to do. His girl-friend is babysitting at the Tuckers', and later, when she's got the kids in bed, maybe he'll drop over there. Sometimes he watches TV with her when she's babysitting, it's about the only chance he gets to make out a little since he doesn't own wheels, but they have to be careful because most people don't like their sitters to have boyfriends over. Just kissing her makes her nervous. She won't close her eyes because she has to be watching the door all the time. Married people really have it good, he thinks.

○

"Hi," the babysitter says to the children, and puts her books on top of the refrigerator. "What's for supper?" The little girl, Bitsy, only stares at her obliquely. She joins them at the end of the kitchen table. "I don't have to go to bed until nine," the boy announces flatly, and stuffs his mouth full of potato chips. The babysitter catches a glimpse of Mr. Tucker hurrying out of the bathroom in his underwear.

○

Her tummy. Under her arms. And her feet. Those are the best places. She'll spank him, she says sometimes. Let her.

○

That sweet odor that girls have. The softness of her blouse. He catches a glimpse of the gentle shadows amid her thighs, as she curls her legs up under her. He stares hard at her. He has a lot of meaning packed into that stare, but she's not even looking. She's popping her gum and watching television. She's sitting right there, inches away, soft, fragrant, and ready: but what's his next move? He notices his buddy Mark in the drugstore, playing the pinball machine, and joins him. "Hey, this mama's cold, Jack baby! She needs your touch!"

○

Mrs. Tucker appears at the kitchen doorway, holding a rolled-up diaper. "Now, don't just eat potato chips, Jimmy! See that he eats his hamburger, dear." She hurries away to the bathroom. The boy glares sullenly at the babysitter, silently daring her to carry out the order. "How about a little of that good hamburger now, Jimmy?" she says perfunctorily. He lets half of it drop to the floor. The baby is silent and a man is singing a love song on the TV. The children crunch chips.

○

He loves her. She loves him. They whirl airily, stirring a light breeze, through a magical landscape of rose and emerald and deep blue. Her light brown hair coils and wisps softly in the breeze, and the soft folds of her white gown tug at her body and then float away. He smiles in a pulsing crescendo of sincerity and song.

○

"You mean she's alone?" Mark asks. "Well, there's two or three kids," Jack says. He slides the coin in. There's a rumble of steel balls tumbling, lining up. He pushes a plunger with his thumb, and one ball pops up in place, hard and glittering with promise. His stare? to say he loves her. That he cares for her and would protect her, would shield her, if need be, with his own body. Grinning, he bends over the ball to take careful aim: he and Mark have studied this machine and have it figured out, but still it's not that easy to beat.

○

On the drive to the party, his mind is partly on the girl, partly on his own high-school days, long past. Sitting at the end of the kitchen table there with his children, she had seemed to be self-consciously arching her back, jutting her pert breasts, twitching her thighs: and for whom if not for him? So she'd seen him coming out of there, after all. He smiles. Yet what could he ever do about it? Those good times are gone, old man. He glances over at his wife, who, readjusting a garter, asks: "What do you think of our babysitter?"

○

He loves her. She loves him. And then the babies come. And dirty diapers and one goddamn meal after another. Dishes. Noise. Clutter. And fat. Not just tight, her girdle actually hurts. Somewhere recently she's read about women getting heart attacks or cancer or something from too-tight girdles. Dolly pulls the car door shut with a grunt, strangely irritated, not knowing why. Party mood. Why is her husband humming, "Who's Sorry Now?" Pulling out of the drive, she glances back at the lighted kitchen window. "What do you think of our babysitter?" she asks. While her husband stumbles all over himself trying to answer, she pulls a stocking tight, biting deeper with the garters.

○

"Stop it!" she laughs. Bitsy is pulling on her skirt and he is tick-ling her in the ribs. "Jimmy! Don't!" But she is laughing too much to stop him. He leaps on her, wrapping his legs around her waist, and they all fall to the carpet in front of the TV, where just now a man in a tuxedo and a little girl in a flouncy white dress are doing a tapdance together. The babysitter's blouse is pulling out of her skirt, showing a patch of bare tummy: the target. "I'll spank!"

○

Jack pushes the plunger, thrusting up a steel ball, and bends studiously over the machine. "You getting any off her?" Mark asks, and clears his throat, flicks ash from his cigarette. "Well, not exactly, not yet," Jack says, grinning awkwardly, but try-ing to suggest more than he admits to, and fires. He heaves his weight gently against the machine as the ball bounds off a rubber bumper. He can feel her warming up under his hands, the flippers suddenly coming alive, delicate rapid-fire patterns emerging in the flashing of the lights. 1000 WHEN LIT: *now!* "Got my hand on it, that's about all." Mark glances up from the machine, cigarette dangling from his lip. "Maybe you need some help," he suggests with a wry one-sided grin. "Like maybe together, man, we could do it."

○

She likes the big tub. She uses the Tuckers' bath salts, and loves to sink into the hot fragrant suds. She can stretch out, sub-merged, up to her chin. It gives her a good sleepy tingly feeling.

○

"What do you think of our babysitter?" Dolly asks, adjusting a garter. "Oh, I hardly noticed," he says. "Cute girl. She seems to get along fine with the kids. Why?" "I don't know." His wife tugs her skirt down, glances at a lighted window they are passing, adding: "I'm not sure I trust her completely, that's all. With the baby, I mean. She seems a little careless. And the other time, I'm almost sure she had a boyfriend over." He grins, claps one hand on his wife's broad gartered thigh. "What's wrong with that?" he asks. Still in anklets, too. Bare thighs, no girdles, nothing up there but a flimsy pair of panties and soft adolescent flesh. He's flooded with vague remembrances of football rallies and movie balconies.

○

How tiny and rubbery it is! she thinks, soaping between the boy's legs, giving him his bath. Just a funny jiggly little thing that looks like it shouldn't even be there at all. Is that what all the songs are about?

○

Jack watches Mark lunge and twist against the machine. Got her running now, racking them up. He's not too excited about the idea of Mark fooling around with his girlfriend, but Mark's a cooler operator than he is, and maybe, doing it together this once, he'd get over his own timidity. And if she didn't like it, there were other girls around. If Mark went too far, he could cut him off, too. He feels his shoulders tense: enough's enough, man . . . but sees the flesh, too. "Maybe I'll call her later," he says.

○

"Hey, Harry! Dolly! Glad you could make it!" "I hope we're not late." "No, no, you're one of the first, come on in! By golly, Dolly, you're looking younger every day! How do you do it? Give my wife your secret, will you?" He pats her on her girdled bottom behind Mr. Tucker's back, leads them in for drinks.

o

8:00. The babysitter runs water in the tub, combs her hair in front of the bathroom mirror. There's a western on television, so she lets Jimmy watch it while she gives Bitsy her bath. But Bitsy doesn't want a bath. She's angry and crying because she has to be first. The babysitter tells her if she'll take her bath quickly, she'll let her watch television while Jimmy takes his bath, but it does no good. The little girl fights to get out of the bathroom, and the babysitter has to squat with her back against the door and forcibly undress the child. There are better places to babysit. Both children mind badly, and then, sooner or later, the baby is sure to wake up for a diaper change and more bottle. The Tuckers do have a good color TV, though, and she hopes things will be settled down enough to catch the 8:30 program. She thrusts the child into the tub, but she's still screaming and thrashing around. "Stop it now, Bitsy, or you'll wake the baby!" "I have to go potty!" the child wails, switching tactics. The babysitter sighs, lifts the girl out of the tub and onto the toilet, getting her skirt and blouse all wet in the process. She glances at herself in the mirror. Before she knows it, the girl is off the seat and out of the bathroom. "Bitsy! Come back here!"

o

"Okay, that's enough!" Her skirt is ripped and she's flushed and crying. "Who says?" "I do, man!" The bastard goes for her, but he tackles him. They roll and tumble. Tables tip, lights topple, the TV crashes to the floor. He slams a hard right to the guy's gut, clips his chin with a rolling left.

○

"We hope it's a girl." That's hardly surprising, since they already have four boys. Dolly congratulates the woman like everybody else, but she doesn't envy her, not a bit. That's all she needs about now. She stares across the room at Harry, who is slapping backs and getting loud, as usual. He's spreading out through the middle, so why the hell does he have to complain about her all the time? "Dolly, you're looking younger every day!" was the nice greeting she got tonight. "What's your secret?" And Harry: "It's all those calories. She's getting back her baby fat." "Haw haw! Harry, have a heart!"

○

"Get her feet!" he hollers at Bitsy, his fingers in her ribs, running over her naked tummy, tangling in the underbrush of straps and strange clothing. "Get her shoes off!" He holds her pinned by pressing his head against her soft chest. "No! No, Jimmy! Bitsy, stop!" But though she kicks and twists and rolls around, she doesn't get up, she can't get up, she's laughing too hard, and the shoes come off, and he grabs a stockinged foot and scratches the sole ruthlessly, and she raises up her legs, trying to pitch him off, she's wild, boy, but he hangs on, and she's laughing, and on the screen there's a rattle of hooves, and he and Bitsy are rolling around and around on the floor in a crazy rodeo of long bucking legs.

○

He slips the coin in. There's a metallic fall and a sharp click as the dial tone begins. "I hope the Tuckers have gone," he says. "Don't worry, they're at our place," Mark says. "They're always the first ones to come and the last ones to go home. My old man's always bitching about them." Jack laughs nervously and dials the number. "Tell her we're coming over to protect her from getting raped," Mark suggests, and lights a cigarette. Jack grins, leaning casually against the door jamb of the phonebooth, chewing gum, one hand in his pocket. He's really pretty uneasy, though. He has the feeling he's somehow messing up a good thing.

○

Bitsy runs naked into the livingroom, keeping a hassock between herself and the babysitter. "Bitsy . . . !" the babysitter threatens. Artificial reds and greens and purples flicker over the child's wet body, as hooves clatter, guns crackle, and stagecoach wheels thunder over rutted terrain. "Get outa the way, Bitsy!" the boy complains. "I can't see!" Bitsy streaks past and the babysitter chases, cornering the girl in the back bedroom. Bitsy throws something that hits her softly in the face: a pair of men's undershorts. She grabs the girl scampering by, carries her struggling to the bathroom, and with a smart crack on her glistening bottom, pops her back into the tub. In spite, Bitsy peepees in the bathwater.

○

Mr. Tucker stirs a little water into his bourbon and kids with his host and another man, just arrived, about their golf games. They set up a match for the weekend, a threesome looking for a fourth. Holding his drink in his right hand, Mr. Tucker swings his left through the motion of a tee-shot. "You'll have to give me a stroke a hole," he says. "I'll give you a stroke!" says his host: "Bend over!" Laughing, the other man asks: "Where's your boy Mark tonight?" "I don't know," replies the host, gathering up a trayful of drinks. Then he adds in a low growl: "Out chasing tail probably." They chuckle loosely at that, then shrug in commiseration and return to the livingroom to join their women.

○

Shades pulled. Door locked. Watching the TV. Under a blanket maybe. Yes, that's right, under a blanket. Her eyes close when he kisses her. Her breasts, under both their hands, are soft and yielding.

○

A hard blow to the belly. The face. The dark beardy one staggers. The lean-jawed sheriff moves in, but gets a spurred boot in his face. The dark one hurls himself forward, drives his shoulder into the sheriff's hard midriff, her own tummy tightens, withstands, as the sheriff smashes the dark man's nose, slams him up against a wall, slugs him again! and again! The dark man grunts rhythmically, backs off, then plunges suicidally forward—her own knees draw up protectively—the sheriff staggers! caught low! but instead of following through, the other man steps back—a pistol! the dark one has a pistol! the sheriff draws! shoots from the hip! explosions! She clutches her hands between her thighs—no! the sheriff spins! wounded! The dark man hesitates, aims, her legs stiffen toward the set, the sheriff rolls desperately in the straw, fires: dead! the dark man is dead! groans, crumples, his pistol drooping in his collapsing hand, dropping, he drops. The sheriff, spent, nicked, watches weakly from the floor where he lies. Oh, to be whole! to be good and strong and right! To embrace and be embraced by harmony and wholeness! The sheriff, drawing himself painfully up on one elbow, rubs his bruised mouth with the back of his other hand.

○

"Well, we just sorta thought we'd drop over," he says, and winks broadly at Mark. "Who's we?" "Oh, me and Mark here." "Tell her, good thing like her, gotta pass it around," whispers Mark, dragging on his smoke, then flicking the butt over under the pinball machine. "What's that?" she asks. "Oh Mark and I were just saying, like two's company, three's an orgy," Jack says, and winks again. She giggles. "Oh, Jack!" Behind her, he can hear shouts and gunfire. "Well, okay, for just a little while, if you'll both be good." Way to go, man.

○

Probably some damn kid over there right now. Wrestling around on the couch in front of his TV. Maybe he should drop back to the house. Just to check. None of that stuff, she was there to do a job! Park the car a couple doors down, slip in the front door before she knows it. He sees the disarray of clothing, the young thighs exposed to the flickering television light, hears his baby crying. "Hey, what's going on here! Get outa here, son, before I call the police!" Of course, they haven't really been doing anything. They probably don't even know how. He stares benignly down upon the girl, her skirt rumpled loosely around her thighs. Flushed, frightened, yet excited, she stares back at him. He smiles. His finger touches a knee, approaches the hem. Another couple arrives. Filling up here with people. He wouldn't be missed. Just slip out, stop back casually to pick up something or other he forgot, never mind what. He remembers that the other time they had this babysitter, she took a bath in their house. She had a date afterwards, and she'd just come from cheerleading practice or something. Aspirin maybe. Just drop quietly and casually into the bathroom to pick up some aspirin. "Oh, excuse me, dear! I only . . . !" She gazes back at him, astonished, yet strangely moved. Her soft wet breasts rise and fall in the water, and her tummy looks pale and ripply. He recalls that her pubic hairs, left in the tub, were brown. Light brown.

○

She's no more than stepped into the tub for a quick bath, when Jimmy announces from outside the door that he has to go to the bathroom. She sighs: just an excuse, she knows. "You'll have to wait." The little nuisance. "I can't wait." "Okay, then come ahead, I'm taking a bath." She supposes that will stop him, but it doesn't. In he comes. She slides down into the suds until she's eye-level with the edge of the tub. He hesitates. "Go ahead, if you have to," she says, a little awkwardly, "but I'm not getting out." "Don't look," he says. She: "I will if I want to."

○

She's crying. Mark is rubbing his jaw where he's just slugged him. A lamp lies shattered. "Enough's enough, Mark! Now get outa here!" Her skirt is ripped to the waist, her bare hip bruised. Her panties lie on the floor like a broken balloon. Later, he'll wash her wounds, help her dress, he'll take care of her. Pity washes through him, giving him a sudden hard-on. Mark laughs at it, pointing. Jack crouches, waiting, ready for anything.

○

Laughing, they roll and tumble. Their little hands are all over her, digging and pinching. She struggles to her hands and knees, but Bitsy leaps astride her neck, bowing her head to the carpet. "Spank her, Jimmy!" His swats sting: is her skirt up? The phone rings. "The cavalry to the rescue!" she laughs, and throws them off to go answer.

○

Kissing Mark, her eyes closed, her hips nudge toward Jack. He stares at the TV screen, unsure of himself, one hand slipping cautiously under her skirt. Her hand touches his arm as though to resist, then brushes on by to rub his leg. This blanket they're under was a good idea. "Hi! This is Jack!"

○

Bitsy's out and the water's running. "Come on, Jimmy, your turn!" Last time, he told her he took his own baths, but she came in anyway. "I'm not gonna take a bath," he announces, eyes glued on the set. He readies for the struggle. "But I've already run your water. Come on, Jimmy, please!" He shakes his head. She can't make him, he's sure he's as strong as she is. She sighs. "Well, it's up to you. I'll use the water myself then," she says. He waits until he's pretty sure she's not going to change her mind, then sneaks in and peeks through the keyhole in the bathroom door: just in time to see her big bottom as she bends over to stir in the bubblebath. Then she disappears. Trying to see as far down as the keyhole will allow, he bumps his head on the knob. "Jimmy, is that you?" "I—I have to go to the bath- room!" he stammers.

○

Not actually in the tub, just getting in. One foot on the mat, the other in the water. Bent over slightly, buttocks flexed, teats swaying, holding on to the edge of the tub. "Oh, excuse me! I only wanted . . . !" He passes over her astonishment, the awk- ward excuses, moves quickly to the part where he reaches out to—"What on earth are you doing, Harry?" his wife asks, star- ing at his hand. His host, passing, laughs. "He's practicing his swing for Sunday, Dolly, but it's not going to do him a damn bit of good!" Mr. Tucker laughs, sweeps his right hand on through the air as though lifting a seven-iron shot onto the green. He makes a *dok!* sound with his tongue. "In there!"

○

"No, Jack, I don't think you'd better." "Well, we just called, we just, uh, thought we'd, you know, stop by for a minute, watch television for thirty minutes, or, or something." "Who's we?" "Well, Mark's here, I'm with him, and he said he'd like to, you know, like if it's all right, just—" "Well, it's *not* all right. The Tuckers said no." "Yeah, but if we only—" "And they seemed awfully suspicious about last time." "Why? We didn't—I mean,

I just thought—" "No, Jack, and that's period." She hangs up. She returns to the TV, but the commercial is on. Anyway, she's missed most of the show. She decides maybe she'll take a quick bath. Jack might come by anyway, it'd make her mad, that'd be the end as far as he was concerned, but if he should, she doesn't want to be all sweaty. And besides, she likes the big tub the Tuckers have.

○

He is self-conscious and stands with his back to her, his little neck flushed. It takes him forever to get started, and when it finally does come, it's just a tiny trickle. "See, it was just an excuse," she scolds, but she's giggling inwardly at the boy's embarrassment. "You're just a nuisance, Jimmy." At the door, his hand on the knob, he hesitates, staring timidly down on his shoes. "Jimmy?" She peeks at him over the edge of the tub, trying to keep a straight face, as he sneaks a nervous glance back over his shoulder. "As long as you bothered me," she says, "you might as well soap my back."

○

"The aspirin . . ." They embrace. She huddles in his arms like a child. Lovingly, paternally, knowledgeably, he wraps her nakedness. How compact, how tight and small her body is! Kissing her ear, he stares down past her rump at the still clear water. "I'll join you," he whispers hoarsely.

○

She picks up the shorts Bitsy threw at her. Men's underwear. She holds them in front of her, looks at herself in the bedroom mirror. About twenty sizes too big for her, of course. She runs her hand inside the opening in front, pulls out her thumb. How funny it must feel!

○

"Well, man, I say we just go rape her," Mark says flatly, and swings his weight against the pinball machine. "Uff! Ahh! Get in there, you mother! Look at that! Hah! Man, I'm gonna turn this baby over!" Jack is embarrassed about the phone conversation. Mark just snorted in disgust when he hung up. He cracks down hard on his gum, angry that he's such a chicken. "Well, I'm game if you are," he says coldly.

○

8:30. "Okay, come on, Jimmy, it's time." He ignores her. The western gives way to a spy show. Bitsy, in pajamas, pads into the livingroom. "No, Bitsy, it's time to go to bed." "You said I could watch!" the girl whines, and starts to throw another tantrum. "But you were too slow and it's late. Jimmy, you get in that bathroom, and right now!" Jimmy stares sullenly at the set, unmoving. The babysitter tries to catch the opening scene of the television program so she can follow it later, since Jimmy gives himself his own baths. When the commercial interrupts, she turns off the sound, stands in front of the screen. "Okay, into the tub, Jimmy Tucker, or I'll take you in there and give you your bath myself!" "Just try it," he says, "and see what happens."

○

They stand outside, in the dark, crouched in the bushes, peeking in. She's on the floor, playing with the kids. Too early. They seem to be tickling her. She gets to her hands and knees, but the little girl leaps on her head, pressing her face to the floor. There's an obvious target, and the little boy proceeds to beat on it. "Hey, look at the kid go!" whispers Mark, laughing and snapping his fingers softly. Jack feels uneasy out here. Too many neighbors, too many cars going by, too many people in the world. That little boy in there is one up on him, though: he's never thought about tickling her as a starter.

○

His little hand, clutching the bar of soap, lathers shyly a narrow space between her shoulderblades. She is doubled forward against her knees, buried in rich suds, peeking at him over the edge of her shoulder. The soap slithers out of his grip and plunks into the water. "I . . . I dropped the soap," he whispers. She: "Find it."

○

"I dream of Jeannie with the light brown pubic hair!" "Harry! Stop that! You're drunk!" But they're laughing, they're all laughing, damn! he's feeling pretty goddamn good at that, and now he just knows he needs that aspirin. Watching her there, her thighs spread for him, on the couch, in the tub, hell, on the kitchen table for that matter, he tees off on Number Nine, and— *whap!*—swats his host's wife on the bottom. "Hole in one!" he shouts. "Harry!" Why can't his goddamn wife Dolly ever get happy-drunk instead of sour-drunk all the time? "Gonna be tough Sunday, old buddy!" "You're pretty tough right now, Harry," says his host.

○

The babysitter lunges forward, grabs the boy by the arms and hauls him off the couch, pulling two cushions with him, and drags him toward the bathroom. He lashes out, knocking over an endtable full of magazines and ashtrays. "You leave my brother alone!" Bitsy cries and grabs the sitter around the waist. Jimmy jumps on her and down they all go. On the silent screen, there's a fade-in to a dark passageway in an old apartment building in some foreign country. She kicks out and somebody falls between her legs. Somebody else is sitting on her face. "Jimmy! Stop that!" the babysitter laughs, her voice muffled.

○

She's watching television. All alone. It seems like a good time to go in. Just remember: really, no matter what she says, she wants it. They're standing in the bushes, trying to get up the nerve. "We'll tell her to be good," Mark whispers, "and if she's not good, we'll spank her." Jack giggles softly, but his knees are weak. She stands. They freeze. She looks right at them. "She can't see us," Mark whispers tensely. "Is she coming out?" "No," says Mark, "she's going into—that must be the bathroom!" Jack takes a deep breath, his heart pounding. "Hey, is there a window back there?" Mark asks.

○

The phone rings. She leaves the tub, wrapped in a towel. Bitsy gives a tug on the towel. "Hey, Jimmy, get the towel!" she squeals. "Now stop that, Bitsy!" the babysitter hisses, but too late: with one hand on the phone, the other isn't enough to hang on to the towel. Her sudden nakedness awes them and it takes them a moment to remember about tickling her. By then, she's in the towel again. "I hope you got a good look," she says angrily. She feels chilled and oddly a little frightened. "Hello?" No answer. She glances at the window—is somebody out there? Something, she saw something, and a rustling—footsteps?

○

"Okay, I don't care, Jimmy, don't take a bath," she says irritably. Her blouse is pulled out and wrinkled, her hair is all mussed, and she feels sweaty. There's about a million things she'd rather be doing than babysitting with these two. Three: at least the baby's sleeping. She knocks on the overturned endtable for luck, rights it, replaces the magazines and ashtrays. The one thing that really makes her sick is a dirty diaper. "Just go on to bed." "I don't have to go to bed until nine," he reminds her. Really, she couldn't care less. She turns up the volume on the TV, settles down on the couch, poking her blouse back into her skirt, pushing her hair out of her eyes. Jimmy and Bitsy watch from the floor. Maybe, once they're in bed, she'll take a quick bath. She wishes Jack would come by. The man, no doubt the spy, is following a woman, but she doesn't know why. The woman passes another man. Something seems to happen, but it's not clear what. She's probably already missed too much. The phone rings.

○

Mark is kissing her. Jack is under the blanket, easing her panties down over her squirming hips. Her hand is in his pants, pulling it out, pulling it toward her, pulling it hard. She knew just where it was! Mark is stripping, too. God, it's really happening! he thinks with a kind of pious joy, and notices the open door. "Hey! What's going on here?"

○

He soaps her back, smooth and slippery under his hand. She
is doubled over, against her knees, between his legs. Her light
brown hair, reaching to her gleaming shoulders, is wet at the
edges. The soap slips, falls between his legs. He fishes for it,
finds it, slips it behind him. "Help me find it," he whispers in
her ear. "Sure, Harry," says his host, going around behind him.
"What'd you lose?"

○

Soon be nine, time to pack the kids off to bed. She clears the table,
dumps paper plates and leftover hamburgers into the garbage,
puts glasses and silverware into the sink, and the mayonnaise,
mustard, and ketchup in the refrigerator. Neither child has eaten
much supper finally, mostly potato chips and ice cream, but it's
really not her problem. She glances at the books on the refrigerator. Not much chance she'll get to them, she's already pretty
worn out. Maybe she'd feel better if she had a quick bath. She
runs water into the tub, tosses in bubblebath salts, undresses.
Before pushing down her panties, she stares for a moment at the
smooth silken panel across her tummy, fingers the place where
the opening would be if there were one. Then she steps quickly
out of them, feeling somehow ashamed, unhooks her brassiere.
She weighs her breasts in the palms of her hands, watching herself in the bathroom mirror, where, in the open window behind
her, she sees a face. She screams.

○

She screams: "Jimmy! Give me that!" "What's the matter?"
asks Jack on the other end. "Jimmy! Give me my towel! Right

now!" "Hello? Hey, are you still there?" "I'm sorry, Jack," she says, panting. "You caught me in the tub. I'm just wrapped in a towel and these silly kids grabbed it away!" "Gee, I wish I'd been there!" "Jack—!" "To protect you, I mean." "Oh, sure," she says, giggling. "Well, what do you think, can I come over and watch TV with you?" "Well, not right this minute," she says. He laughs lightly. He feels very cool. "Jack?" "Yeah?" "Jack, I . . . I think there's somebody outside the window!"

○

She carries him, fighting all the way, to the tub, Bitsy pummeling her in the back and kicking her ankles. She can't hang on to him and undress him at the same time. "I'll throw you in, clothes and all, Jimmy Tucker!" she gasps. "You better not!" he cries. She sits on the toilet seat, locks her legs around him, whips his shirt up over his head before he knows what's happening. The pants are easier. Like all little boys his age, he has almost no hips at all. He hangs on desperately to his underpants, but when she succeeds in snapping these down out of his grip, too, he gives up, starts to bawl, and beats her wildly in the face with his fists. She ducks her head, laughing hysterically, oddly entranced by the spectacle of that pale little thing down there, bobbing and bouncing rubberily about with the boy's helpless fury and anguish.

○

"Aspirin? Whaddaya want aspirin for, Harry? I'm sure they got aspirin here, if you—" "Did I say aspirin? I meant, uh, my glasses. And, you know, I thought, well, I'd sorta check to see if everything was okay at home." Why the hell is it his mouth feels like it's got about six sets of teeth packed in there, and a tongue the size of that liverwurst his host's wife is passing around? "Whaddaya want your glasses for, Harry? I don't understand you at all!" "Aw, well, honey, I was feeling kind of dizzy or something, and I thought—" "Dizzy is right. If you want to check on the kids, why don't you just call on the phone?"

○

They can tell she's naked and about to get into the tub, but the bathroom window is frosted glass, and they can't see anything clearly. "I got an idea," Mark whispers. "One of us goes and calls her on the phone, and the other watches when she comes out." "Okay, but who calls?" "Both of us, we'll do it twice. Or more."

○

Down forbidden alleys. Into secret passageways. Unlocking the world's terrible secrets. Sudden shocks: a trapdoor! a fall! or the stunning report of a rifle shot, the *whaaii-ii-iing!* of the bullet biting concrete by your ear! Careful! Then edge forward once more, avoiding the light, inch at a time, now a quick dash for an open doorway—*look out!* there's a knife! a struggle! no! the long blade glistens! jerks! thrusts! *stabbed!* No, no, it missed! The assailant's down, yes! the spy's on top, pinning him, a terrific thrashing about, the spy rips off the assailant's mask: a *woman!*

○

Fumbling behind her, she finds it, wraps her hand around it, tugs. "Oh!" she gasps, pulling her hand back quickly, her ears turning crimson. "I . . . I thought it was the soap!" He squeezes her close between his thighs, pulls her back toward him, one hand sliding down her tummy between her legs. I Dream of Jeannie— "I have to go to the bathroom!" says someone outside the door.

○

She's combing her hair in the bathroom when the phone rings. She hurries to answer it before it wakes the baby. "Hello, Tuckers." There's no answer. "Hello?" A soft click. Strange. She feels suddenly alone in the big house, and goes in to watch TV with the children.

○

"Stop it!" she screams. "Please, stop!" She's on her hands and knees, trying to get up, but they're too strong for her. Mark holds her head down. "Now, baby, we're gonna teach you how to be a nice girl," he says coldly, and nods at Jack. When she's doubled over like that, her skirt rides up her thighs to the leg bands of her panties. "C'mon, man, go! This baby's cold! She needs your touch!"

○

Parks the car a couple blocks away. Slips up to the house, glances in his window. Just like he's expected. Her blouse is off and the kid's shirt is unbuttoned. He watches, while slowly, clumsily, childishly, they fumble with each other's clothes. My God, it takes them forever. "Some party!" "You said it!" When they're more or less naked, he walks in. "Hey! What's going on here?" They go white as bleu cheese. Haw haw! "What's the little thing you got sticking out there, boy?" "Harry, behave yourself!" No, he doesn't let the kid get dressed, he sends him home bareassed.

"Bareassed!" He drinks to that. "Promises, promises," says his host's wife. "I'll mail you your clothes, son!" He gazes down on the naked little girl on his couch. "Looks like you and me, we got a little secret to keep, honey," he says coolly. "Less you wanna go home the same way your boyfriend did!" He chuckles at his easy wit, leans down over her, and unbuckles his belt. "Might as well make it two secrets, right?" "What in God's name are you talking about, Harry?" He staggers out of there, drink in hand, and goes to look for his car.

o

"Hey! What's going on here?" They huddle half-naked under the blanket, caught utterly unawares. On television: the clickety-click of frightened running feet on foreign pavements. Jack is fumbling for his shorts, tangled somehow around his ankles. The blanket is snatched away. "On your feet there!" Mr. Tucker, Mrs. Tucker, Mark's mom and dad, the police, the neighbors, everybody comes crowding in. Hopelessly, he has a terrific erection. So hard it hurts. Everybody stares down at it.

o

Bitsy's sleeping on the floor. The babysitter is taking a bath. For more than an hour now, he's had to use the bathroom. He doesn't know how much longer he can wait. Finally, he goes to knock on the bathroom door. "I have to use the bathroom." "Well, come ahead, if you have to." "Not while you're in there." She sighs loudly. "Okay, okay, just a minute," she says, "but you're a real nuisance, Jimmy!" He's holding on, pinching it as tight as he can. "*Hurry!*" He holds his breath, squeezing shut his eyes. No. Too late. At last, she opens the door. "Jimmy!" "I *told* you to hurry!" he sobs. She drags him into the bathroom and pulls his pants down.

○

He arrives just in time to see her emerge from the bathroom, wrapped in a towel, to answer the phone. His two kids sneak up behind her and pull the towel away. She's trying to hang on to the phone and get the towel back at the same time. It's quite a picture. She's got a sweet ass. Standing there in the bushes, pawing himself with one hand, he lifts his glass with the other and toasts her sweet ass, which his son now swats. Haw haw, maybe that boy's gonna shape up, after all.

○

They're in the bushes, arguing about their next move, when she comes out of the bathroom, wrapped in a towel. They can hear the baby crying. Then it stops. They see her running, naked, back to the bathroom like she's scared or something. "I'm going in after her, man, whether you're with me or not!" Mark whispers, and he starts out of the bushes. But just then, a light comes sweeping up through the yard, as a car swings in the drive. They hit the dirt, hearts pounding. "Is it the cops?" "I don't know!" "Do you think they saw us?" "Sshh!" A man comes staggering up the walk from the drive, a drink in his hand, stumbles on in the kitchen door and then straight into the bathroom. "It's Mr. Tucker!" Mark whispers. A scream. "Let's get outa here, man!"

○

9:00. Having missed most of the spy show anyway and having little else to do, the babysitter has washed the dishes and cleaned the kitchen up a little. The books on the refrigerator remind her of her better intentions, but she decides that first she'll see what's next on TV. In the livingroom, she finds little Bitsy sound asleep on the floor. She lifts her gently, carries her into her bed, and tucks her in. "Okay, Jimmy, it's nine o'clock, I've let you stay up, now be a good boy." Sullenly, his sleepy eyes glued still to the set, the boy backs out of the room toward his bedroom. A drama comes on. She switches channels. A ballgame and a murder mystery. She switches back to the drama. It's a love story of some kind. A man married to an aging invalid wife, but in love with a younger girl. "Use the bathroom and brush your teeth before going to bed, Jimmy!" she calls, but as quickly regrets it, for she hears the baby stir in its crib.

o

Two of them are talking about mothers they've salted away in rest homes. Oh boy, that's just wonderful, this is one helluva party. She leaves them to use the john, takes advantage of the retreat to ease her girdle down awhile, get a few good deep breaths. She has this picture of her three kids carting her off to a rest home. In a wheelbarrow. That sure is something to look forward to, all right. When she pulls her girdle back up, she can't seem to squeeze into it. The host looks in. "Hey, Dolly, are you all right?" "Yeah, I just can't get into my damn girdle, that's all." "Here, let me help."

o

She pulls them on, over her own, standing in front of the bedroom mirror, holding her skirt bundled up around the waist. About twenty sizes too big for her, of course. She pulls them tight from behind, runs her hand inside the opening in front, pulls out her thumb. "And what a good boy am I!" She giggles: how funny it must feel! Then, in the mirror, she sees him: in the doorway behind her, sullenly watching. "Jimmy! You're supposed to be in bed!" "Those are my daddy's!" the boy says. "I'm gonna tell!"

○

"Jimmy!" She drags him into the bathroom and pulls his pants down. "Even your shoes are wet! Get them off!" She soaps up a warm washcloth she's had with her in the bathtub, scrubs him from the waist down with it. Bitsy stands in the doorway, staring. "Get out! Get out!" the boy screams at his sister. "Go back to bed, Bitsy. It's just an accident." "Get out!" The baby wakes and starts to howl.

○

The young lover feels sorry for her rival, the invalid wife; she believes the man has a duty toward the poor woman and insists she is willing to wait. But the man argues that he also has a duty toward himself: his life, too, is short, and he could not love his wife now even were she well. He embraces the young girl feverishly; she twists away in anguish. The door opens. They stand there grinning, looking devilish, but pretty silly at the same time. "Jack! I thought I told you not to come!" She's angry, but she's also glad in a way: she was beginning to feel a little too alone in the big house, with the children all sleeping. She should have taken that bath, after all. "We just came by to see if you were being a good girl," Jack says and blushes. The boys glance at each other nervously.

○

She's just sunk down into the tubful of warm fragrant suds, ready for a nice long soaking, when the phone rings. Wrapping a towel around her, she goes to answer: no one there. But now the baby's awake and bawling. She wonders if that's Jack bothering her all the time. If it is, brother, that's the end. Maybe it's the end anyway. She tries to calm the baby with the half-empty bottle, not wanting to change it until she's finished her bath. The bathroom's where the diapers go dirty, and they make it stink to high heaven. "Shush, shush!" she whispers, rocking the crib. The towel slips away, leaving an airy empty tingle up and down her backside. Even before she stoops for the towel, even before she turns around, she knows there's somebody behind her.

○

"We just came by to see if you were being a good girl," Jack says, grinning down at her. She's flushed and silent, her mouth half open. "Lean over," says Mark amiably. "We'll soap your back, as long as we're here." But she just huddles there, down in the suds, staring up at them with big eyes.

○

"Hey! What's going on here?" It's Mr. Tucker, stumbling through the door with a drink in his hand. She looks up from the TV. "What's the matter, Mr. Tucker?" "Oh, uh, I'm sorry, I got lost—no, I mean, I had to get some aspirin. Excuse me!" And he rushes past her into the bathroom, caroming off the livingroom door jamb on the way. The baby wakes.

○

"Okay, get off her, Mr. Tucker!" "Jack!" she cries, "what are *you* doing here?" He stares hard at them a moment: so that's where it goes. Then, as Mr. Tucker swings heavily off, he leans into the bastard with a hard right to the belly. Next thing he knows, though, he's got a face full of an old man's fist. He's not sure, as the lights go out, if that's his girlfriend screaming or the baby . . .

○

Her host pushes down on her fat fanny and tugs with all his might on her girdle, while she bawls on his shoulder: "I don't *wanna* go to a rest home!" "Now, now, take it easy, Dolly, nobody's gonna make you—" "Ouch! Hey, you're hurting!" "You should buy a bigger girdle, Dolly." "You're telling me?" Some other guy pokes his head in. "Whatsamatter? Dolly fall in?" "No, she fell out. Give me a hand."

○

By the time she's chased Jack and Mark out of there, she's lost track of the program she's been watching on television. There's another woman in the story now for some reason. That guy lives a very complicated life. Impatiently, she switches channels. She hates ballgames, so she settles for the murder mystery. She switches just in time, too: there's a dead man sprawled out on the floor of what looks like an office or a study or something. A heavyset detective gazes up from his crouch over the body: "He's been strangled." Maybe she'll take that bath, after all.

○

She drags him into the bathroom and pulls his pants down. She soaps up a warm washcloth she's had in the tub with her, but just as she reaches between his legs, it starts to spurt, spraying her arms and hands. "Oh, Jimmy! I thought you were done!" she cries, pulling him toward the toilet and aiming it into the bowl. How moist and rubbery it is! And you can turn it every which way. How funny it must feel!

○

"Stop it!" she screams. "Please stop!" She's on her hands and knees and Jack is holding her head down. "Now we're gonna teach you how to be a nice girl," Mark says and lifts her skirt. "Well, I'll be damned!" "What's the matter?" asks Jack, his heart pounding. "Look at this big pair of men's underpants she's got on!" "Those are my daddy's!" says Jimmy, watching them from the doorway. "I'm gonna tell!"

○

People are shooting at each other in the murder mystery, but she's so mixed up, she doesn't know which ones are the good guys. She switches back to the love story. Something seems to have happened, because now the man is kissing his invalid wife tenderly. Maybe she's finally dying. The baby wakes, begins to scream. Let it. She turns up the volume on the TV.

○

Leaning down over her, unbuckling his belt. It's all happening just like he's known it would. Beautiful! The kid is gone, though his pants, poor lad, remain. "Looks like you and me, we got a secret to keep, child!" But he's cramped on the couch and everything is too slippery and small. "Lift your legs up, honey. Put them around my back." But instead, she screams. He rolls off, crashing to the floor. There they all come, through the front door. On television, somebody is saying: "Am I a burden to you, darling?" "Dolly! My God! Dolly, I can explain . . . !"

○

The game of the night is Get Dolly Tucker Back in Her Girdle Again. They've got her down on her belly in the livingroom and the whole damn crowd is working on her. Several of them are stretching the girdle, while others try to jam the fat inside. "I think we made a couple inches on this side! Roll her over!" Harry?

○

She's just stepped into the tub, when the phone rings, waking the baby. She sinks down in the suds, trying not to hear. But that baby doesn't cry, it screams. Angrily, she wraps a towel around herself, stamps peevishly into the baby's room, just letting the phone jangle. She tosses the baby down on its back, unpins its diapers hastily, and gets yellowish baby stool all over her hands. Her towel drops away. She turns to find Jimmy staring at her like a little idiot. She slaps him in the face with her dirty hand, while the baby screams, the phone rings, and nagging voices argue on the TV. There are better things she might be doing.

○

What's happening? Now there's a young guy in it. Is he after the young girl or the old invalid? To tell the truth, it looks like he's after the same man the women are. In disgust, she switches channels. "The strangler again," growls the fat detective, hands on hips, staring down at the body of a half-naked girl. She's considering either switching back to the love story or taking a quick bath, when a hand suddenly clutches her mouth.

○

"You're both chicken," she says, staring up at them. "But what if Mr. Tucker comes home?" Mark asks nervously.

○

How did he get here? He's standing pissing in his own goddamn bathroom, his wife is still back at the party, the three of them are, like good kids, sitting in there in the livingroom watching TV. One of them is his host's boy Mark. "It's a good murder mystery, Mr. Tucker," Mark said, when he came staggering in on them a minute ago. "Sit still" he shouted, "I'm just home for a moment!" Then whump thump on into the bathroom. Long hike for a weewee, Mister. But something keeps bothering him. Then it hits him: the girl's panties, hanging like a broken balloon from the rabbit-ear antennae on the TV! He barges back in there, giving his shoulder a helluva crack on the livingroom door jamb on the way—but they're not hanging there any more. Maybe he's only imagined it. "Hey, Mr. Tucker," Mark says flatly. "Your fly's open."

○

The baby's dirty. Stinks to high heaven. She hurries back to the livingroom, hearing sirens and gunshots. The detective is crouched outside a house, peering in. Already, she's completely lost. The baby screams at the top of its lungs. She turns up the volume. But it's all confused. She hurries back in there, claps an angry hand to the baby's mouth. "Shut up!" she cries. She throws the baby down on its back, starts to unpin the diaper, as the baby tunes up again. The phone rings. She answers it, one eye on the TV. "*What?*" The baby cries so hard it starts to choke. Let it. "I said, hi, this is Jack!" Then it hits her: oh no! the diaper pin!

○

"The aspirin . . ." But she's already in the tub. Way down in the tub. Staring at him through the water. Her tummy looks pale and ripply. He hears sirens, people on the porch.

○

Jimmy gets up to go to the bathroom and gets his face slapped and smeared with baby poop. Then she hauls him off to the bathroom, yanks off his pajamas, and throws him into the tub. That's okay, but next she gets naked and acts like she's gonna get in the tub, too. The baby's screaming and the phone's ringing like crazy and in walks his dad. Saved! he thinks, but, no, his dad grabs him right back out of the tub and whales the dickens out of him, no questions asked, while she watches, then sends him—*whack!*—back to bed. So he's lying there, wet and dirty and naked and sore, and he still has to go to the bathroom, and outside his window he hears two older guys talking. "Listen, you know where to do it if we get her pinned?" "No! Don't you?"

○

"Yo ho heave ho! *Ugh!*" Dolly's on her back and they're working on the belly side. Somebody got the great idea of buttering her down first. Not to lose the ground they've gained, they've shot it inside with a basting syringe. But now suddenly there's this big tug-of-war under way between those who want to stuff her in and those who want to let her out. Something rips, but she feels better. The odor of hot butter makes her think of movie theaters and popcorn. "Hey, has anybody seen Harry?" she asks. "Where's Harry?"

o

Somebody's getting chased. She switches back to the love story, and now the man's back kissing the young lover again. What's going on? She gives it up, decides to take a quick bath. She's just stepping into the tub, one foot in, one foot out, when Mr. Tucker walks in. "Oh, excuse me! I only wanted some aspirin . . ." She grabs for a towel, but he yanks it away. "Now, that's not how it's supposed to happen, child," he scolds. "Please! Mr. Tucker . . . !" He embraces her savagely, his calloused old hands clutching roughly at her backside. "Mr. Tucker!" she cries, squirming. "Your wife called—!" He's pushing something between her legs, hurting her. She slips, they both slip—something cold and hard slams her in the back, cracks her skull, she seems to be sinking into a sea . . .

o

They've got her over the hassock, skirt up and pants down. "Give her a little lesson there, Jack baby!" The television lights flicker and flash over her glossy flesh. 1000 WHEN LIT. Whack! Slap! Bumper to bumper! He leans into her, feeling her come alive.

o

The phone rings, waking the baby. "Jack, is that you? Now, you listen to me—!" "No, dear, this is Mrs. Tucker. Isn't the

TV awfully loud?" "Oh, I'm sorry, Mrs. Tucker! I've been getting—" "I tried to call you before, but I couldn't hang on. To the phone, I mean. I'm sorry, dear." "Just a minute, Mrs. Tucker, the baby's—" "Honey, listen! Is Harry there? Is Mr. Tucker there, dear?"

○

"Stop it!" she screams and claps a hand over the baby's mouth. "Stop it! Stop it! *Stop it!*" Her other hand is full of baby stool and she's afraid she's going to be sick. The phone rings. "No!" she cries. She's hanging on to the baby, leaning woozily away, listening to the phone ring. "Okay, okay," she sighs, getting ahold of herself. But when she lets go of the baby, it isn't screaming any more. She shakes it. Oh no . . .

○

"Hello?" No answer. Strange. She hangs up and, wrapped only in a towel, stares out the window at the cold face staring in— she screams!

○

She screams, scaring the hell out of him. He leaps out of the tub, glances up at the window she's gaping at just in time to see two faces duck away, then slips on the bathroom tiles, and crashes to his ass, whacking his head on the sink on the way down. She stares down at him, trembling, a towel over her narrow shoulders. "Mr. Tucker! Mr. Tucker, are you alright . . . ?" Who's Sorry Now? Yessir, whose back is breaking with each . . . He stares up at the little tufted locus of all his woes, and passes out, dreaming of Jeannie . . .

○

The phone rings. "Dolly! It's for you!" "Hello?" "Hello, Mrs. Tucker?" "Yes, speaking." "Mrs. Tucker, this is the police calling . . ."

○

It's cramped and awkward and slippery, but he's pretty sure he got it in her, once anyway. When he gets the suds out of his eyes, he sees her staring up at them. Through the water. "Hey, Mark! Let her up!"

○

Down in the suds. Feeling sleepy. The phone rings, startling her. Wrapped in a towel, she goes to answer. "No, he's not here, Mrs. Tucker." Strange. Married people act pretty funny sometimes. The baby is awake and screaming. Dirty, a real mess. Oh boy, there's a lot of things she'd rather be doing than babysitting in this madhouse. She decides to wash the baby off in her own bathwater. She removes her towel, unplugs the tub, lowers the water level so the baby can sit. Glancing back over her shoulder, she sees Jimmy staring at her. "Go back to bed, Jimmy." "I have to go to the bathroom." "Good grief, Jimmy! It looks like you already have!" The phone rings. She doesn't bother with the towel—what can Jimmy see he hasn't already seen?—and goes to answer. "No, Jack, and that's final." Sirens, on the TV, as the police move in. But wasn't that the channel with the love story? Ambulance maybe. Get this over with so she can at least catch the news. "Get those wet pajamas off, Jimmy, and I'll find clean ones. Maybe you better get in the tub, too." "I think something's wrong with the baby," he says. "It's down in the water and it's not swimming or anything."

○

She's staring up at them from the rug. They slap her. Nothing happens. "You just tilted her, man!" Mark says softly. "We gotta get outa here!" Two little kids are standing wide-eyed in the doorway. Mark looks hard at Jack. "No, Mark, they're just little kids . . . !" "We gotta, man, or we're dead."

○

"Dolly! My God! Dolly, I can explain!" She glowers down at them, her ripped girdle around her ankles. "What the four of you are doing in the bathtub with *my* babysitter?" she says sourly. "I can hardly wait!"

○

Police sirens wail, lights flash. "I heard the scream!" somebody shouts. "There were two boys!" "I saw a man!" "She was running with the baby!" "My God!" somebody screams, "they're *all* dead!" Crowds come running. Spotlights probe the bushes.

○

"Harry, where the hell you been?" his wife whines, glaring blearily up at him from the carpet. "I can explain," he says. "Hey, whatsamatter, Harry?" his host asks, smeared with butter for some goddamn reason. "You look like you just seen a ghost!" Where did he leave his drink? Everybody's laughing, everybody except Dolly, whose cheeks are streaked with tears. "Hey, Harry, you won't let them take me to a rest home, will you, Harry?"

O

10:00. The dishes done, children to bed, her books read, she watches the news on television. Sleepy. The man's voice is gentle, soothing. She dozes—awakes with a start: a babysitter? Did the announcer say something about a babysitter?

O

"Just want to catch the weather," the host says, switching on the TV. Most of the guests are leaving, but the Tuckers stay to watch the news. As it comes on, the announcer is saying something about a babysitter. The host switches channels. "They got a better weatherman on four," he explains. "Wait!" says Mrs. Tucker. "There was something about a babysitter . . . !" The host switches back. "Details have not yet been released by the police," the announcer says. "Harry, maybe we'd better go . . ."

O

They stroll casually out of the drugstore, run into a buddy of theirs. "Hey! Did you hear about the babysitter?" the guy asks. Mark grunts, glances at Jack. "Got a smoke?" he asks the guy.

O

"I think I hear the baby screaming!" Mrs. Tucker cries, running across the lawn from the drive.

O

She wakes, startled, to find Mr. Tucker hovering over her. "I must have dozed off!" she exclaims. "Did you hear the news about the babysitter?" Mrs. Tucker asks. "Part of it," she says, rising. "Too bad wasn't it?" Mr. Tucker is watching the report of the ball scores and golf tournaments. "I'll drive you home in just a minute, dear," he says. "Why, how nice!" Mrs. Tucker exclaims from the kitchen. "The dishes are all done!"

○

"What can I say, Dolly?" the host says with a sigh, twisting the buttered strands of her ripped girdle between his fingers. "Your children are murdered, your husband gone, a corpse in your bathtub, and your house is wrecked. I'm sorry. But what can I say?" On the TV, the news is over, and they're selling aspirin. "Hell, *I* don't know," she says. "Let's see what's on the late late movie."

BEGINNINGS

(1972)

In order to get started, he went to live alone on an island and
shot himself. His blood, unable to resist a final joke, splattered the cabin wall in a pattern that read: It is important to
begin when everything is already over.

This maxim, published on the cabin wall between an out-
dated calendar and a freshwater fish chart, would have pleased
him. He had once begun a story about the raising of Lazarus,
in which Jesus, having had the dead man dragged from the
tomb and unwrapped, couldn't seem to get the hang of bringing him around. There was an awful stink, the Jews crowding
around were getting sick, and Jesus, sweating, was saying: Heh
heh, bear with me, folks! Won't be a minute! If I can just get it
started, the rest'll come easy!

This, then, was his problem: beginning. And having begun:
avoiding resolutions. Thus, there were worse jokes his blood
might have played on him. Its message might have read: All
beginnings imply an apocalypse. Perhaps, in fact, that's what it

did say, how was he to know? Pulling the trigger, he thought: This is working! I'm getting on!

It was comfortable, that cabin, roomy and clean-smelling, with walls of unvarnished Norway pine, Coleman lanterns for light, a wood cookstove, and a long pine table with a yellow checkered oilcloth he'd bought for it, big enough to eat on and write on at the same time. There was a bay out front with a small pier for the boat. He was alone on the island, except for a few squirrels, frogs, muskrats, the odd weasel, birds, porcupines. The nearest people were about a mile's boatride away.

He rarely needed these people, though sometimes he visited them when his imagination failed him or he ran out of peanutbutter. On these occasions, they often told him stories, astounding him with their fearless capacity for denouement, and he'd return to his island shaken, thinking: I'm the last man alive on earth! Once they told him about a man who had come to one of the islands to write, but on arriving had shot himself. Yes, he told them, that was me, and they noticed then that his head was coming apart, and on the wall was a message: You ain't seen nothin' yet, friends!

He once wrote a story about a man who was born at the age of thirtytwo with a self-destruct mechanism in his gonads, such that he could be sure of only one orgasm before he died. This man traveled all over the world, seeking out the perfect mate for this ultimate experience, but blew it one night in a wet dream on a jet flight over Bangkok. What was fascinating about this story was neither his travels nor his dream, but rather the peculiar physical appearance of a man kept so long in the womb. He had rather liked this story and stayed with it longer than most, but had had to abandon it finally when he'd heard about the new cults forming aboard jetliners.

Well, we've made a start, his blood said on the wall. Nothing else matters. The people who had come to identify the body crowded around, staring in disbelief. This is impossible, they cried. That story wasn't true, it was only a legend! They noticed that he'd left the coffeepot on the stove and it had boiled over. They pointed to it and said: Aha!, satisfying thereby their lust for motive, but they couldn't conceal a certain disappointment. They scratched about, however, and finally found enough pea-nutbutter for two sandwiches, though there wasn't any bread. Well, at least we haven't come for nothing, they said.

There was nothing primitive about this island. He had a shal-low bay to bathe in, a cabin to eat and sleep in and an outhouse to shit in, a chair to read in, wild blueberries for breakfast, saws and axes for cutting wood, a boat to go to town in, and he could write anywhere. If he subsisted largely on peanutbutter, that was his own fault, because he even had a gas refrigerator and stove. These he used as little as possible, though, because his principal hardship was exchanging used butane tanks for new in town, then singlehandedly dragging the loaded one back to the boat, later heaving it out of the boat and up the steep hill to the cabin, and finally setting it up in place and lighting it with-out blowing himself up.

As for the old wood cookstove, he loved it. When the lake was darkened by a storm, or at night, he could sit for hours in front of it, watching the flames, warming himself, brewing coffee, frying up feasts of fish and potatoes when he had them, imag-ining a life free of settings forth, and thus immortal. What lim-ited his use and diminished his enjoyment of the stove was the need to chop wood for it. He found it took about as long to burn the wood as it took to cut it. There seemed to lurk some kind

of unpleasant moral here, and it was this more than the hard
work, which in his womb-wrinkled condition he should have
welcomed, that made him use the cookstove less and less. He
would have abandoned it altogether, but for his insomnia. On
bad nights, he could stare at the flames, each one new, violent,
unique, and sooner or later all this variety would put him to
sleep.

An ordinary island then, with ordinary trees and bushes,
ordinary bugs, birds, and reptiles, ordinary lake water lapping
it about, yet even before pulling the trigger, he recognized that
there was something suspicious about it, as though it might
have been, like the air he breathed, just another metaphor. So
many otherwise solid and habitable islands had gone that way
in the past, it was a kind of pollution. Perhaps he should have
shot himself in the boat on the way to the island, spared the
world another bloody epigram and the island this transgression,
this erosion. It was Adam did the naming, why did Eve get all
the blame?

Because she was near at hand. This was her offense: affec-
tionate trespass. She wanted company. She couldn't leave well
enough alone, she had to turn up and tax his vocabulary. She
must have come there sometime between the pulling of the
trigger and the loosing of his blood and brains against the cabin
wall. He named her many times over, but never Eve, having
after all a certain integrity. What could he say in her behalf?
That she helped him drag the butane tanks up the hill. But
she helped him use them up faster, too, contaminating his days
with history.

Yet he was grateful, because he was able to throw away everything he had written before she had come there, and this altered

the fuel balance, permitting more fires in the cookstove. Also she was good at finding blueberries and cleaning fish, chopping off their heads like false starts. But she confused him by insisting she had been there first, he was the newcomer to the island, and she lifted her skirts to show him the missing rib. It was at this time that he began to suspect that he, not the island, was the metaphor. He began a story in which the first-person narrator was the story itself, he merely one of the characters, dead before the first paragraph was over.

He returned the rib to her and discovered it was more blessed to give than to receive, though this was not accomplished without some bloodletting. They found much peace and pleasure in this sharing of the rib, and called it fucking. Thus, he was still naming things. Perhaps because it rhymed with luck: fucking, they thought, was good for it, good for the raw nerve ends of his navel, too. I think this is the beginning of something, he said, as his hips bucked. Though they never let it get in the way of their struggles with one another, it always proved useful whenever they began to repeat themselves. It was almost like a place, somewhere to go when the island and his work became hostile and wounded him, an island within an island.

Small wonder, then, that he took to inventing stories in which time had a geography, like an island, place moved like the hands of a clock, and point of view was a kind of punctuation. He assigned numbers and symbols to death, love, characters, unexpected developments, transitions, then submitted them to the rhythms of numerologies. He invented a story with several narrators, each quoting the next, the last quoting the first and telling the story being told. He began another, added footnotes, subfootnotes to the footnotes, further footnotes to the subfootnotes, and so on to exhaustion, which came early: he still had something to learn about pacing himself.

The woman, like all women no doubt, was always the same woman and never the same woman twice. Sometimes she was pregnant, sometimes she was not. Sometimes she soaped him up when they bathed in the bay, and then they fucked in the water, or else on shore, under the trees, in the cabin, out in the woodpile, less often when she was pregnant. She did her best to hide the children from him for fear he'd eat them. Sometimes she was distracted and then he did eat them. He was always sorry about it afterwards, because he missed them and they gave him constipation for a week. In which case, she cared for him, scratched his head, gave him enemas, strewed the path to the outhouse with rose petals.

The outhouse was a short walk away from the cabin by the thick forest of pines, poplars, birch, and dogwood. It was strictly for the relief of mind or bowels, since it was their habit to pee wherever they were when the need hit them, except inside the cabin. Sometimes, at night, simply out the front door into the moonlight, hoping not to get bit by mosquitoes. Hoping did little good, they got bit anyway. This added a certain purpose and energy to their fucking, true, but did little to improve their technique. It was like the sting of conscience, teaching them to murder or be damned.

The children were less scrupulous about their toilet, with the result that the cabin often smelled worse than the outhouse. On such days, he would take the boat out on the lake and fish for walleyes and bass, pretending to be the Good Provider. He was not lucky at it, though, and hated taking the hook out, so sooner or later he'd go on into town and buy fish at the store.

The woman was always amazed at his luck in catching filleted fish. It's a parable, he explained, and put the gun to his head. Soon I'll be able to dispense with this gun altogether, he thought with his scattering brain. It's like taking a cathartic.

Sometimes he thought that might be the way to get started at last: with a cathartic. But what if the trouble was heartburn? For it was true, his writing was a vice and tended to alienate them. He found he did no writing at all while fucking, and vice versa. It could be even worse inbetweentimes, when he wasn't sure which he was doing, or should be doing. He ate better than when he lived alone, slept better, she even took to chopping the wood and dragging the butane tanks up by herself, he had all the time in the world, and yet if anything he was writing less. He used to spill beer, ashes, peanutbutter, kerosene into his typewriter, and hardly noticed; now she kept it clean for him, and it kept breaking down. Whenever an idea really gripped him, she would cry and accuse him of leaving the island; he'd apologize and take her for a ride in the boat, wondering where it was he'd been. She diapered the children in the climaxes of his stories, doing him a service, but she also borrowed his typing ribbon for a clothesline and mistook his story notes for a grocery list, nearly poisoning them all.

And yet, she was indispensable. When he complained about the suffering of the artist, she added more fruit to his diet, and in truth he suffered less. Alone, he used to sit in front of the cookstove and listen to the stillness beyond the flames; now there was her breathing. And who else was there to read to? He realized he had been writing so as to be able to sleep at night, but she could purge his guilt with a simple backrub, confirming his suspicion that it was nothing more than a cramp in the lumbar region. When he reasoned that perhaps he needed the writing, after all, to stay awake in the daytime, she sent the children in to play with him. He began a parody on Plato's cave parable, in which he celebrated, not the shadows, but the generosity of the wall.

Also, it became important to delay the climax. Thus, he got involved with spirals, revolutions, verb tenses, and game theory. There were puns that could make endings almost impossible, like certain very thick prophylactic devices. He started a story about a man who was granted a wish by a good fairy and who promptly blew the circuits by packing the universe out with good fairies. He applied Zeno's paradox to a suicide bullet, and kept it up all night. He invented a story about Noah in which the old man starts by making the door and the window, then can't figure out how to build the ark around them. God, too, is confused by this approach, but is too proud of his storied omniscience to admit it, and so provides dogmatic solutions which turn out to be self-contradictory. Many volumes of profound arguments ensue, explicating God's wit. Noah meanwhile builds himself a captain's cabin, complete with yellow oilcloth and Coleman lanterns, but God, annoyed by its pretensions, turns Noah into a pillar of peanutbutter and then invites the animals in, inventing the Eucharist. Enough of these false starts, these dead fish heads, he reasoned, taking his children down to the bay for an afternoon swim, and the flood will never come.

It was beautiful, that little bay, clean and quiet, cool, with only the occasional leech like a cautionary tale. Sometimes a turtle would swim in, looking for the old days. The woman would kneel on a flat rock at the lip of the bay like Psyche, washing out diapers, as though to impress upon him the inadequacy of his revisions. On sunny days, schools of tiny fish would arrive like visitors from the city, white and nervous, and birds would come down, looking for action. His children splashed at the edges, played in the sand, scrambled about in the boat, chased toads, cried when they got ants on them, peed on the bluebells and each other, ate mud. Now and then, one would drown or get carried off by the crabs, and he'd wonder: why do we go on making them if they're just going to quit on us? Oddly, neither the woman nor his balls ever seemed to ask that question, and he felt alienated. He contemplated a detective story, in which all the victims and suspects are murdered, as well as the detective and all those who come to investigate the murders of the detectives who came before. But he was an intransigent realist, and he knew, as he climbed up on the small pier, that he'd probably bog down in the research. He dove off, projecting out a multivolume work on the blessings of mortality to be entitled, *Adventures of a Mongoloid Idiot*, and struck his head on the bottom, thinking: all this from the pulling of one trigger!

The message on the bloodspattered wall was a learned discourse on the fortyseventh chromosome of mongoloid idiots, and its influence on the prime number theorem of imminent apocalypse. Was it enough to say that he'd shot himself because he'd let the coffee boil? Probably it was enough. He'd apparently run out of bread and had been eating his peanutbutter between manuscript pages. His typing ribbon was missing. First lines lay scattered like crumbs and ants were carrying them off. One of them read: In eternity, beginning is consummation.

Much of the island was unvisited, being too thickly overgrown with trees and brambles. You could sink up to your knees in pulp from the last era's forest. His children occasionally wandered off and never returned. Perhaps there were ogres. Probably not, for they'd have heard them snorting and farting on still nights. Sometimes they took the boat around the shore of the island, gathering bleached driftwood. One of these twisted shapes led him to a story about a monster that was devouring the earth in bits and drabs as though to simplify its categories, but he threw it away, recognizing it as genteel autobiography. On one corner of the island, amid tall reeds, herons nested. Their long graceful necks seemed to give them an overview that spared them the embarrassment of opening sallies. If my head was on a neck like that, he thought, I might not have to shoot it off.

The cabin itself sat in a small sunny clearing above the little bay, with a view out over the lake and other islands. Now and then, a boat passed distantly, put-putting along. He wondered about the people who used to tell him stories. They probably died when the bombs fell. Yes, some politician did it one morning in a fit of pique or boredom, blew the whole thing up. The earth was never revisited. In time, the sun burned out. The cooling planet shuddered out of orbit and became a meteor, disintegrating gradually in its fierce passage through eons. Nothing was ever known of man. He may as well have never existed. He liked to sit in a chair in front of the cabin in the warm sunshine, gazing out over the blue lake, contemplating the final devastation, and thinking: all right, what next? He could just imagine that politician, the last giant of his race, pushing the button and thinking: This is one day they won't soon forget!

He sat in the chair less often when the woman was on the island, for he seemed then to attract chores and children like flies. At such times, he would go up and sit among the spiders in the outhouse, contemplating his aesthetic, which seemed to have something to do with molten flats, hyperbole, and scare-crows. He wanted to write about Job's last years, after he'd got his wealth back, but lost his memory. He thought: the central theme should be stated in the title and then abandoned alto-gether. He had a story about a soldier who'd been in a foxhole for fifty years and who, having forgotten entirely who the enemy was or what his rifle was for, crawled out one day and got shot. He could call it: *Beginnings*. He planned to write about Colum-bus voyaging to the end of the world and, more or less abruptly, finding it. He imagined an Eden in which nothing grew, but always seemed about to. To keep Adam from starving, Eve turned herself into an apple, which quite willingly he ate, for-getting that without her he could never find his way out of the place. He shat and called the turd Unable, because this was his prerogative. He wiped his ass and, glancing at the paper before dropping it down the hole, saw that it read: Once upon a time they lived happily ever after. Maybe I've got cancer, he thought.

Though on still days the outhouse could be a little suffocat-ing, the smell was not really unpleasant. It was said that peo-ple who grew up in the days of outhouses often longed for that smell for the rest of their lives. The same could be said for piles of dead bodies, the important thing being the chlorinated lime. And to keep the door open.

Of course, that was an open invitation to bees and wasps. One thing leads to another, he thought, and that's how we keep mov-ing along. The blast of the gun, the crash in his skull, were already fading, shrinking into history, wouldn't hear them at all soon, feel them at all. Once, frantically shooing a yellowjacket out the door with a rolled-up manuscript, he hadn't noticed the wasp that had gone down the hole, while he'd bobbed up off it.

He sat down and then he noticed it. He yipped all the way down the path, through the cabin, and on down the hill to the bay, and what the woman, ever his best critic, said was: Hush, you'll wake the baby. After that, he always took a can of bugspray with him on trips to the outhouse, learning something as he squirted about the essential anality of the apocalyptic aesthetic.

At this time, he was also a great killer of flies. He carried a flyswatter around with him, indoors and out, and when he couldn't think how to start a story, he killed flies instead. There were a lot of first lines lying about, including a new one about an apostate priest in a sacred-fly cult who'd begun to question his faith during the ritual of Gathering at the Pig's Ass, but there were a lot more dead flies. It's too bad they're not edible, said the woman. She prepared him a fresh pot of coffee, then took the boat to town to have another baby and get some food.

He knew that what he was doing was good, because the flies were holding the earth together. He swatted them badminton-style, caught them on the hairline edge of sills and chair arms, laid jelly-blob traps for them and outscored that holy fiend the tailor, and always with a smiling self-righteous zeal: cleanliness is next to—WHAP!—godliness! He felt like Luther, his finger on the trigger, splattering dark ages against the cabin wall like brains. It's the beginning of something, he thought, wielding the fly-swatter like a pastoral staff. A disease perhaps. The coffee was boiling over on the stove when the woman returned. I think I missed my calling, he said. It's a boy, she replied, and opened her blouse to give it suck.

He understood there was nothing banal about giving birth, even to mongoloid idiots, and through the first half dozen or so, he suffered nearly as much as she did, or so he told himself, writing odes to navelstrings and the beauty of ripe watermelons to keep his mind off the unpleasant tearing sensation in his testicles. He began a story about a man who brings his wife to the hospital to have a child. They're both excited and very happy. The wife is led away by the doctor and the man enjoys a sympathetic and goodnatured exchange with the staff. The delivery seems to take longer than it ought, however, and he begins to worry. When he asks the staff about it, he gets odd evasive answers. Finally, in a panic, he goes in search of the doctor, finds him at a party, roaring drunk and smeared to the ears in blood. He realizes that in fact he's in some kind of nightclub, not a hospital at all. The doctor is a stand-up comedian, delivering a dirtymouth routine on the facts of life and using his wife's corpse as a prop. The worst part is that he can't help laughing. Ah, what shall we do with all these dead? he wondered. The island was becoming a goddamn necropolis.

He'd even managed to kill the snake and the frog, though the woman had spared them. It was as though they couldn't escape their natural instincts toward snakes, his panic, her affection. The frog was just one of those innocent bystanders who come along to thicken the plot, like himself or Jesus Christ. The woman was bathing in the bay, standing in the shallow water, haloed about with suds, just kissing the surface with her vulva, and he was on his way down the path with shampoo and towel to join her. There was a snake across the path and he stopped short, his heart racing. Its mouth was stretched around the bottom half of a frog. He could see the frog's heart pounding, in fact he could hardly see the frog for its thumping panic. He ran to the woodpile and grabbed up an axe. The woman, who had seen his heart pounding in his ears and eyes, came up to see what had frightened him. Her bottom half was dripping wet, and there was soapscum in her pubes. He was trembling as he crept up on the snake with the axe: he thought that the frog might be a decoy, a secret ally, that he was the one the snake was after. It's some kind of identity crisis, he realized. The frog's eyes blinked in the snake's maw. The woman kicked the snake gently. It disgorged the frog, feinted as though to strike, then suddenly was gone. Stupefied still, he hopped a few feet into the underbrush and began a story about the old serpent, left behind in Eden after the action had moved elsewhere, who comes on a frog, green as the New Testament, first one he's seen in years, swallows it, and dies of indigestion. She nudged him in the ass with her toe, but he only cowered there, his heart thumping in his ears. She saw that he was in trouble and went down to secure the boat against the coming storm.

It's always like this, he thought. You just get started and then the storm comes. He knew that if he wrote a story about the heath, after Lear, the Fool, Poor Tom and all the rest were dead and gone, just the heath, the storm raging on, phrases lying about like stones, metaphors growing like stunted bushes, it would be the most important story of his age, but he also knew the age would be over before he could ever begin. He no longer believed there would be any message on the cabin wall: let's have no illusions, he thought, about blood and brains. Outside, the wind was howling, the boat was bumping against the pier, and pine branches swept the cabin roof restlessly. They sat inside and played strip poker, starting naked so as not to delude themselves. He drew a pair of Queens and a King, but the woman beat him with a heart flush. Off with his head! she screamed. What have I got to lose? he said. The wind blew in and swept the cards away. In bed, their sheets flapped like sails.

He awoke the next morning, tangled in first lines like wrinkled sheets. The windows were smashed and birds lay about with broken necks. The woman was down at the bay, rinsing diapers, the children huddled about her like the sting of conscience. He went out to pee and saw that the boat had sunk. First lines lay all about like fallen trees, shattered and twisted. Columbus, his hips bucking, was voyaging to the end of the world, crying: This is working! I'm getting on! Jesus was raising mongoloid idiots from the grave like filleted fish, pretending to be the Good Provider. He half hoped that, as he peed, the boat would bob to the surface, but it just lay there on the bottom in a gray sullen stupor, only its gunwales showing like a line drawing for a suppository or a cathedral window. He felt as if he'd opened one too many holes in his body, and the wind had blown in and filled him with dead bees. It's time to leave the island, he told the woman. I've already packed, she said. We'll make a fresh start, he shouted, but she couldn't hear him because the children were crying. She was bailing the boat out with the diaper bucket. A fresh start!

But back in the cabin, the coffee was boiling over on the stove and he saw there was no bread for the peanutbutter. Everything seemed to be receding. They were back in the boat, and as they pulled away, the island suddenly sank into the lake and disappeared. Hey, look! he cried. You did that on purpose, the woman said. You always have to try to end it all! He had his reasons, but they didn't justify such devastation. Who was he to be the last giant of his race? Who was he to christen turds? So much for fresh starts. He might as well not have pulled the trigger in the first place. But it was done and that was an end to it. Or so it said on the cabin wall.

THE DEAD QUEEN

(1973)

The old Queen had a grin on her face when we buried her in the mountain, and I knew then that it was she who had composed this scene, as all before, she who had led us, revelers and initiates, to this cold and windy grave site, hers the design, ours the enactment, and I felt like the first man, destined to rise and fall, rise and fall, to the end of time. My father saw this, perhaps I was trembling, and as though to comfort me, said: No, it was a mere grimace, the contortions of pain, she had suffered greatly after all, torture often exposes the diabolic in the face of man, she was an ordinary woman, beautiful it is true, and shrewd, but she had risen above her merits, and falling, had lost her reason to rancor. We can learn even from the wretched, my son; her poor death and poorer life teach us to temper ambition with humility, and to ignore reflections as one ignores mortality. But I did not believe him, I could see for myself, did not even entirely trust him, this man who thought power a localized convention, magic a popular word for concealment, for though it made him a successful King, decisive and respected, the old Queen's grin mocked such simple faith and I was not consoled.

My young bride, her cheeks made rosy by the mountain air, smiled benignly through the last rites, just as she had laughed with open glee at her stepmother's terrible entertainment at our wedding feast the night before, her cheeks flushed then with wine. I tried to read her outrageous cheerfulness, tried to understand the merriment that such an awesome execution had provoked. At times, she seemed utterly heartless, this child, become the very evil she'd been saved from. Had all our watch-fulness been in vain, had that good and simple soul been enven-omed after all, was it she who'd invited her old tormentor to the ball, commissioned the iron slippers, drawn her vindictively into that ghastly dance? Or did she simply laugh as the righ-teous must to see the wicked fall? Perhaps her own release from death had quickened her heart, such that mere continuance now made her a little giddy. Or had she, absent, learned something of hell? How could I know? I could vouch for her hymen from this side, but worried that it had been probed from within. How she'd squealed to see the old Queen's flailing limbs, how she'd applauded the ringing of those flaming iron clogs against the marble floors! Yet, it was almost as though she were ignorant of the pain, of any cause or malice, ignorant of consequences— like a happy child at the circus, unaware of any skills or risks. Once, the poor woman had stumbled and sprawled, her skirts heaped up around her ears, and this had sprung a jubilant roar of laughter from the banqueters, but Snow White had only smiled expectantly, then clapped gaily as the guards set the dying Queen on her burning feet again. Now, as I stood there on the mountainside, watching my bride's black locks flow in the wintry wind and her young breasts fill with the rare air, she suddenly turned toward me, and seeing me stare so intensely, smiled happily and squeezed my hand. No, I thought, she's suffered no losses, in fact that's just the trouble, that hymen can never be broken, not even by me, not in a thousand nights, this is her gift and essence, and because of it, she can see neither fore nor aft, doesn't know there is a mirror on the wall. Perhaps it was this that had made the old Queen hate her so.

If hate was the word. Perhaps she'd loved her. Or more likely, she'd had no feelings toward her at all. She'd found her unconscious and so useful. Did Snow White really believe she was the fairest in the land? Perhaps she did, she had a gift for the absurd. And thereby her stepmother had hatched a plot, and the rest, as my father would say, is history. What a cruel irony, those redhot shoes! For it wasn't that sort of an itch that had driven the old Queen—what she had lusted for was a part in the story, immortality, her place in guarded time. To be the forgotten stepmother of a forgotten Princess was not enough. It was the mirror that had fucked her, fucked us all. And did she foresee those very boots, the dance, that last obscenity? No doubt. Or something much like them. Just as she foresaw the Hunter's duplicity, the Dwarfs' ancient hunger, my own weakness for romance. Even our names were lost, she'd transformed us into colors, simple proclivities, our faces were forever fixed and they weren't even our own!

I was made dizzy by these speculations. I felt the mountain would tip and spill us all to hell or worse. I clutched for my bride's hand, grabbed the nose of a Dwarf instead. He sneezed loudly. The mourners ducked their heads and tittered. Snow

White withdrew a lace kerchief from her sleeve and helped the Dwarf to blow his nose. My father frowned. I held my breath and stared at the dead Queen, masked to hide her eyes, which to what my father called a morbid imagination might seem to be winking, one open, the other squeezed shut. I thought: We've all been reduced to jesters, fools; tragedy she reserved for herself alone. This seemed true, but so profoundly true, it seemed false. I kept my feet apart and tried to think about the Queen's crimes. She had commissioned a child's death and eaten what she'd hoped was its heart. She'd reduced a Princess to a menial of menials, then sought to destroy her, body, mind, and soul. And, I thought, poisoned us all with pattern. Surely, she deserved to die.

In the end, in spite of everything, she'd been accepted as part of the family, spared the outcast's shame, shrouded simply in black and granted her rings and diadems. Only her feet had been left naked, terribly naked: stripped even of their nails and skin. They were raw and blistery, shriveling now and seeming to ooze. Her feet had become one with the glowing iron shoes, of course, the moment we'd forced them on her—what was her wild dance, after all, but a desperate effort to jump out of her own skin? She had not succeeded, but ultimately, once she had died and the shoes had cooled, this final freedom had been more or less granted her, there being no other way to get her feet out of the shoes except to peel them out. I had suggested—naively, it seemed—that the shoes be left on her, buried with her, and had been told that the feet of the wicked were past number, but the Blacksmith's art was rare and sacred. As my Princess and I groped about in our bridal chamber, fumbling darkly toward some new disclosure, I had wondered: Do such things happen at all weddings? We could hear them in the scullery, scraping the shoes out with picks and knives and rinsing them in acid.

What a night, our wedding night! A pity the old Queen had arrived so late, died so soon, missed our dedicated fulfillment of her comic design—or perhaps this, too, was part of her tragedy, the final touch to a life shaped by denial. Of course, it could be argued that she had courted reversals, much as a hero makes his own wars, that she had invented, then pursued the impossible, in order to push the possible beyond her reach, and thus had died, as so many have believed, of vanity, but never mind, the fact is, she was her own consummation, and we, in effect, had carried out—were still carrying out—our own ludicrous performances without an audience. Who could not laugh at us?

My sweetheart and I had sealed our commitment at high noon. My father had raised a cup to our good fortune, issued a stern proclamation against peddlers, bestowed happiness and property upon us and all our progeny, and the party had begun. Whole herds had been slaughtered for our tables. The vineyards of seven principalities had filled our casks. We had danced, sung, clung to one another, drunk, laughed, cheered, chanted the sun down. Bards had pilgrimaged from far and wide, come with their alien tongues to celebrate our union with pageants, prayers, and sacrifices. Not soon, they'd said, would this feast be forgotten. We'd exchanged epigrams and gallantries, whooped the old Queen through her death dance, toasted the fairies and offered them our firstborn. The Dwarfs had recited an ode in praise of clumsiness, though they'd forgotten some of the words and had got into a fight over which of them had dislodged the apple from Snow White's throat, and how, pushing each other into soup bowls and out of windows. They'd thrown cakes and

pies at each other for awhile, then had spilled wine on everybody, played tug-of-war with the Queen's carcass, regaled us
with ribald mimes of regicide and witch-baiting, and finally
had climaxed it all by buggering each other in a circle around
Snow White, while singing their gold-digging song. Snow
White had kissed them all fondly afterward, helped them up
with their breeches, brushed the crumbs from their beards, and
I'd wondered then about my own mother, who was she?—and
where was Snow White's father? Whose party was this? Why
was I so sober? Suddenly I'd found myself, minutes before midnight, troubled by many things: the true meaning of my bride's
name, her taste for luxury and collapse, the compulsions that
had led me to the mountain, the birdshit on the glass coffin
when I'd found her. Who *were* all these people, and why did
things happen as though they were necessary? Oh, I'd reveled
and worshipped with the rest of the party right to the twelfth
stroke, but I couldn't help thinking: We've been too rash, we're
being overtaken by something terrible, and who's to help us
now the old Queen's dead?

The hole in the mountain was dug. The Dwarfs stepped back
to admire their handiwork, tripped over their own beards, and
fell in a big heap. They scrambled clumsily to their feet, clout-
ing each other with their picks and shovels, wound up bowling
one another over like duckpins and went tumbling in a roly-poly
landslide down the mountain, grunting and whistling all the
way. While we waited for them to return, I wondered: Why
are we burying her in the mountain? We no longer believe in
underworlds nor place hope in moldering kings, still we stuff
them back into the earth's navel, as though anticipating some
future interest, much as we stuff our treasures in crypts, our

fiats in archives. Well, perhaps it had been her dying wish, I'm
not told everything, her final vanity. Perhaps she had wanted
to bring us back to this mountain, where her creation by my
chance passage had been accomplished, to confront us with our
own insignificance, our complaisant transience, the knowledge
that it was ended, the rest would be forgotten, our fates were not
sealed, merely eclipsed. She had eaten Snow White's heart in
order to randomize her attentions, deprive her of her center, and
now, like her victim and the bite of poison apple, she had vomited the heart up whole and undigested—but like the piece of
apple, it could never be restored to its old function, it had its own
life now, it would create its own circumambience, and we would
be as remote from this magic as those of a hundred generations
hence. Of course . . . it wasn't Snow White's heart she ate, no, it
was the heart of a boar, I was getting carried away, I was forgetting things. She'd sent that child of seven into the woods with a
restless lech, and he'd brought her back a boar's heart, as though
to say he repented of his irrational life and wished to die. But
then, perhaps that had been what she'd wanted, perhaps she had
ordered the boar's heart, or known anyway that would be the
Hunter's instinct, or perhaps there had been no Hunter at all,
perhaps it had been that master of disguises, the old Queen herself, it was possible, it was all possible. I was overswept by confusion and apprehension. I felt like I'd felt that morning, when
I'd awakened, spent, to find no blood on the nuptial linens.

   The wedding party had ended at midnight. A glass slipper
had been ceremoniously smashed on the last stroke of the hour,
and the nine of us—Snow White and I and, at her insistence,
my new brethren the seven Dwarfs—had paraded to the bridal
chamber. I had been too unsettled to argue, had walked down

the torchlit corridors through the music and applause as though in a trance, for I had fallen, moments before, into an untimely sobriety, had suddenly, as it were, become myself for the first time all day, indeed for the first time in my life, and at the expense of all I'd held real, my Princeship, my famous disenchantments, my bride, my songs, my family, had felt for a few frantic moments like a sun inside myself, about to be exposed and extinguished in a frozen void named Snow White. This man I'd called my father, I'd realized, was a perfect stranger, this palace a playhouse, these revelers the mocking eyes of a dying demiurge! Perhaps all bridegrooms suffer this. Though I'd carried my cock out proudly, as all Princes must, I'd not recognized it as my own when the citizenry in the corridors had knelt to honor it—not a mere ornament of office, I'd told myself, but the officer itself, I its loyal and dispensable retinue. Someone, as I'd passed, had bit it as though to test its readiness, and the pain had reached me like a garbled dispatch from the front line of battle: Victory is ours, alas, all is lost . . .

But once inside the nuptial chamber, the door clicking shut behind me, Snow White cuddling sleepily on my shoulder, the Dwarfs flinging off their clothes and fighting over the chamber pot, I'd returned from my extravagant vagrancy, cock and ceremony had become all mine again, and for some reason I hadn't felt all that grateful. Maybe, I'd thought, maybe I'm a little drunker than I think. I could not have hoped for a more opulent setting: the bed a deep heap of silken eiderdowns, the floors covered with the luxuriant skins of mountain goats, mirrors on all the walls, perfume burning in golden censers, flasks of wine and bowls of fruit on the marble tables, lutes and pipes scattered decorously about. In the morning, I'd vowed, I shall arise before daybreak and compose a new song for my bride to remember this night by. Gently then, sequentially, as though being watched and judged, as though preparing the verses for my song, I'd embraced and commenced to disrobe her. I'd thought: I should be more excited than this. The Dwarfs had seemed to pay us no attention, but I'd begun to resent them: if I failed, they'd pay! One of them had got his foot stuck in the chamber pot and was clumping about in a rage. Another had seemed to be humping a goatskin. I'd nuzzled in Snow White's black tresses, kissed her white throat, whence she'd vomited the fateful apple, and wondered: Why hadn't I been allowed to disenchant her with a kiss like everybody else? Of course, with the apple there, it might not have been all that pleasant . . .

Her nimble hands had unfastened my sashes and buckles with ease, stroked my back, teased my buttocks and balls, but my own fingers had got tangled in her laces. The Dwarfs had come to the rescue, and so had made me feel a fool again. Leave me alone! I'd cried. I can do it by myself! I'd realized then that Snow White had both her arms around my neck and the finger up my ass certainly wasn't my own. I'd gazed into the mirrors to see, for the first time, Snow White's paradigmatic beauty, but instead it had been the old Queen I'd seen there, flailing about madly in her redhot shoes. Maybe it had been the drinking, all the shocks, or some new trick of my brethren, or else the scraping of the shoes in the scullery that had made me imagine it, but whatever, I had panicked, had gone lurching about drunkenly, shaking off Dwarfs, shrouding all the mirrors with whatever had come to hand, smashing not a few of them, feeling the eyes close, the grimaces fade, the room darken: This night is *mine*! I'd cried, and covered the last of them.

We'd been plunged into night—I'd never known a dark so deep, nor felt so much alone. Snow White? Snow White! I'd heard her answer, thought I'd heard her, it was as though she'd called my name—I'd lunged forward, banged my knee on a marble table, cut my foot on broken glass. Snow White! I'd heard whispering, giggling, soft sighs. Come on, what're you doing? I've cut myself! Light a candle! I'd stumbled over someone's foot, run my elbow through a lute. I'd lain there thinking: Forget it, the state I'm in, I might as well wait until morning, why has my father let me suffer such debasement, it must be yet another of his moral lessons on the sources of a King's majesty. The strange sensation had come to me suddenly that this bride I now pursued did not even exist, was just something in *me*, something locked and frozen, waiting to be released, something lying dormant, like an accumulation of ancestral visions and vagaries seeking corporeity—but then I'd heard her struggling, gasping, whimpering. *Help me! Please*—! Those Dwarfs! I'd leaped up and charged into a bedpost. *I'm coming!* Those goddamn dirty Dwarfs! Ever since the day of Snow White's disenchantment, when I'd embraced them as brothers, I'd had uneasy suspicions about them I couldn't quite allow myself to admit, but now they'd burst explosively to the surface, in the dark I'd been able to see what I couldn't see in full daylight, from the first night she'd shared their seven beds, just a child, to the unspeakable things they were doing with her now beneath the eiderdowns, even their famous rescues had been nothing more than excuses to strip her, play with her, how many years had the old witch let them keep her? *Leave her alone! You hear?* I'd chased her voice, but the Dwarfs had kept shifting her about. They worked underground, it was easy for them, they were used to the dark. I'd kept pushing toward her muted voice, scrambling over goatskins and featherbedding, under bed and tables, through broken glass and squashed fruit, into closets, cracking my head on pillars and doorjambs, backing my bare nates into a hot oil lamp, recently extinguished. I'd tried to light it, but all the oil had been spilled. In fact, I was sitting in it.

But never mind, I'd begun to enjoy this, I was glad to have it out in the open, I could beat those Dwarfs at their own game, yes, I'd got a real sweat up, and an appetite, too: Whatever those freaks could do, I could do better! I'd brushed up against a couple of beards, grabbed them and knocked the heads together: *Hah!* There'd been the popping sound of something breaking, like a fruit bowl. I'd laughed aloud, crawled toward Snow White's soft cries over their bodies: they'd felt like goatskins. The spirit had begun to wax powerful within me, my foaming steed, as they say in the fairytales, was rampant, my noble lance was at the ready. Hardly before I'd realized I'd begun, I'd found myself plunging away in her wet and eager body, the piercing of her formidable hymen already just a memory, her sweet cry of pain mere history, as now she, panting, breathed my name: Charming! *Oh dear dear Charming!* She'd seemed to have a thousand hands, a mouth everywhere at once, a glowing furnace between her thrashing thighs, I'd sucked at her heaving breasts, groped in her leaping buttocks, we'd slithered and slid over and under one another, rolling about in the eiderdowns, thrice around the world we'd gone in a bucking frenzy of love and lubricity, seven times we'd died in each other, and as at last, in a state of delicious annihilation, I'd lost consciousness, my fading thoughts had been: Those damned Dwarfs are all right after all, they're all right . . .

And we'd awakened at dawn, alone, clasped in each other's arms, the bed unmussed and unbloodied, her hymen intact.

The Dwarfs had returned from their roll down the mountain, patched and bandaged and singing a lament for the death of the unconscious, and we prepared to enter the old Queen in her tomb. I gazed at her in the glass coffin, the coffin that had once contained my wife, and thought: If she wakes, she will stare at the glass and discover there her own absence. I was beginning to appreciate her subtlety, and so assumed that this, too, had been part of her artifice, a lingering hope for her own liberation, she'd used the mirror as a door, tried to. This was her Great Work, this her use of a Princess with hair as black as ebony, a skin as white as snow, lips as red as blood, this her use of miners of gold! Of course there were difficulties in such a perfect view of things, she was dead, for example, but one revelation was leading to another, and it came to me suddenly that maybe the old Queen had loved me, had died for me! I, too, was too prone to linger at still pools, to listen to the flattery of soothsayers, to organize my life and others' by threes and sevens—it was as if she'd lived this exemplary life, died this tragic death, to lead me away from the merely visible to vision, from the image to the imaged, from reflections to the projecting miracle itself, the heart, the pure snow white . . . !

One of the Dwarfs had been hopping about frantically, and now Snow White took him over behind a bush, but if this was meant to distract me, it did not succeed. The old Queen had me now, everything had fallen into place, I knew now the force that had driven her, that had freed me, freed us all, that we might live happily ever after, though we didn't deserve it, weren't even aware of how it had happened, yes, I knew her cause, knew her name—I wrenched open the coffin, threw myself upon her, and kissed her lips.

If I'd expected something, it did not occur. She did not return my kiss, did not even cease grinning. She stank and her blue mouth was cold and rubbery as a dead squid. I'd been wrong about her, wrong about everything . . .

The others had fallen back in horror and dismay. Snow White had fainted. Someone was vomiting. My father's eyes were full of tears and anger.

Though nauseated, I pitched forward and kissed her again, this time more out of pride and affection, than hope. I thought: It would've helped if the old clown had died with her mouth shut.

They tore me away from her body. It tumbled out of the coffin and, limbs awry, obstinately grinning, skidded a few feet down the mountainside. The flesh tore, but did not bleed. The mask fell away from her open eye, now milky white.

Please! I pleaded, though I no longer even hoped I was right. Let me try once more! Maybe a third time!

Guards restrained me. My father turned his back. The Dwarfs were reviving Snow White by fanning her skirts. The Queen's corpse was dumped hastily back into the coffin and quickly interred, everyone holding his nose. The last thing I saw were her skinned feet. I turned and walked down the mountain.

Thinking: If this is the price of beauty, it's too high. I was glad she was dead.

THE FALLGUY'S FAITH

(1976)

Falling from favor, or grace, some high artifice, down he dropped like a discredited predicate through what he called space (sometimes he called it time) and with an earsplitting crack splattered the base earth with his vital attributes. Oh, I've had a great fall, he thought as he lay there, numb with terror, trying desperately to pull himself together again. This time (or space) I've really done it! He had fallen before of course: short of expectations, into bad habits, out with his friends, upon evil days, foul of the law, in and out of love, down in the dumps—indeed, as though egged on by some malevolent metaphor generated by his own condition, he had *always* been falling, had he not?—but this was the most terrible fall of all. It was like the very fall of pride, of stars, of Babylon, of cradles and curtains and angels and rain, like the dread fall of silence, of sparrows, like the fall of doom. It was, in a word, as he knew now, surrendering to the verb of all flesh, the last fall (*his* last anyway: as for the chips, he sighed, releasing them, let them fall where they may)—yet why was it, he wanted to know, why was it that everything that had happened to him had seemed to have happened in language? Even this! Almost as though, without words for it, it might not have happened at all! Had he been nothing more, after all was said and done, than a paraphrastic curiosity, an idle trope, within some vast syntactical flaw of existence? Had he fallen, he worried as he closed his eyes for the last time and consigned his name to history (may it take it or leave it), his juices to the soil (was it soil?), *merely to have it said he had fallen?* Ah! tears tumbled down his cheeks, damply echoing thereby the greater fall, now so ancient that he himself was beginning to forget it (a farther fall perhaps than all the rest, this forgetting: a fall as it were within a fall), and it came to him in these fading moments that it could even be said that, born to fall, he had perhaps fallen simply to be born (birth being less than it was cracked up to be, to coin a phrase)! Yes, yes, it could be said, what can *not* be said, but he didn't quite believe it, didn't quite believe either that accidence held the world together. No, if he had faith in one thing, this fallguy (he came back to this now), it was this: in the beginning was the *gesture*, and that gesture was: he opened his mouth to say it aloud (to prove some point or other?), but too late—his face cracked into a crooked smile and the words died on his lips . . .

IN BED ONE NIGHT

(1980)

S o one night he comes in from using the bathroom takes off his clothes stretches scratches himself puts on his pajamas yawns sets the alarm turns down the sheets crawls into bed fumbles for the lightswitch above him bumps something soft with his elbow which turns out to be a pale whitehaired lady in a plain gray nightgown lying in bed beside him *wha—?!* he cries out in alarm and demanding an explanation is told she has been assigned to his bed by the social security it's the shortage she says the s's not coming out just right her teeth he sees now in a glass of water on the nighttable private beds are a luxury the world can no longer afford she explains adding that she hopes he won't kick during the night because of her brother who has only one leg is ailing poor soul and is sleeping at the foot of the bed (this is true he feels him there sees him knobby old gent in a cloth cap and long underwear one leg empty pinned up to the rear flap) all of which takes him by surprise and with a gasp he says so to which the old lady replies in her prim toothless way that yes yes life in the modern world what there is left of it is not always easy young man it's what they call the progress of civilized paradox she's heard about it on the television but at least at least he still has his own bed has he not he's after all luckier than most naming no names (she sighs) even if it is only a three-quarters and a bit tight for five and—*five!!* he cries rearing up in panic *five*—? and sure enough there they are two more three in fact how did he miss them before a skinny oriental huddling down behind the old lady dishwater hands shifty eyes antiseptic smell quivering taut as a mainspring and on this side just arriving a heavybellied worker in oily overalls staggering toward the bed with a fat woman tottering on stiletto heels huge butt squeezed shinily into a tight green dress hair undone eyes wet their faces smeared with sweat and paint and cockeyed the—look out!—both of them as they—*crash!*—hit the nighttable send it flying lamp waterglass teeth and all upsetting the old lady needless to say who goes crawling around on the splashed bed on her hands and knees looking for the teeth spluttering petulantly through her flabby lips that woman's not allowed here it's not fair they said five! the worker paying no mind or too drunk to hear hauling off his overalls kicking them aside his underwear belching growling pushing the woman toward the bed cracking her big ass soundly when she hesitates making her yelp with pain not here Duke not with that old lady watching shut up goddamn you I don't ask for much the old lady is complaining still scratching about for her dentures justice that's all a little respect dignity a dress rips the worker blows a beery fart it's a hard thing growing old but I don't ask for any prizes—pwitheth she says—and look at that chink Duke look at his goddamn eyes bug what's he staring at but the worker

just grunts irritably and shoves her roughly onto the bed and
onto its erstwhile owner now too overcome by the well-meant
outrages of a world turned to rubble and mercy even to move ah
me! all this order he thinks as the worker plummets down upon
them both like a felled tree and commences to fumble groggily
for the bawling fat woman's seat of bliss (he could show him
where it is but if he doesn't know how to ask politely then to hell
with him) all this desperate husbandry this tender regulation of
woe the whore on him weeping and groaning now ass high and
soft legs flailing believe me says the old lady crankily still on
her bony knees if I don't find my dentures there'll be the dickens
to pay I mean it—my denthyurth she says—it ain't fair complains the old man at the foot of the bed him having a woman
all to hisself that ain't square ignore them Albert says the old
lady don't encourage them she's not even supposed to be here I
know my rights insists the old man and gets a foot in the face
for them they's a law—*splut! kaff!*—he squawks disappearing
over the foot of the bed which is now rocking and creaking fear-
somely with the mighty thrashing about of the drunken lovers
linked up on top of what on a different occasion might loosely be
thought of as the host knocking his wind out whap whump oh⊤
Duke my god Duke gasp! Albert—? a sweet stink rising are you
all right Albert? and true the pounding friction wet and massive
giving him a certain local pleasure for all the burden of it but it
does not console him what can? sunk as he is in the dark corrup-
tions of nostalgia dreaming of the good old days get back up here
Albert you'll catch your death oh Christ Duke—slop! slap!—kill
that—*pant!*—kill that chink Duke break his fucking neck pop
his yellow eyes out yes alas those days of confusion profligacy
ruthless solitude tears come to his eyes just thinking about them

as the old man reappears at the foot crawling hand over hand the pin that was holding up his empty pantleg between his teeth the old lady remonstrating no violence now please the oriental crouching tremulous on the pillow by the headboard with a knife a gentle answer Albert turneth away—screams groans grunts the worker roaring in pain and rage oh my god Duke! but he wipes away the foolish tears angry with his own weakness forget those days they're gone and just as well he lectures himself as a pale woman enters with three runnynosed kids clinging to her limp skirts there's been some mistake but we're awfully tired sir just a little corner—? Yes forget those stupid times get some sleep and then tomorrow it's down to the social security for a new bed assignment a pretty lady maybe to hear his case Duke? report the losses tidy up wash the sheets out are you okay? say something Duke and lulled by the heavy rhythms of fucking and weeping the kids wrestling their mother whispering at them to settle down or the nice man will ask them to leave the old lady's gummy scolding he drifts off dreaming of a short queue happy accidents and wondering if he Duke? remembered to switch off the bathroom light *aack!* screw the cap back on the toothpaste *now* what have you done Albert oh no! *thwallowed the pin—?!*

THE TINKERER

(1981)

he took a chance and invented mind

set it walking around jumping up and down seeing what it
would do

if it could turn circles cut corners take steep hills how long before
it ran down

not long and it was stiff and jerky at first cutting corners that
weren't there and circling right into heavy traffic

or through plate glass windows over precipices not very promising other inventions had worked better: heart appetite the
city

whack bam sputter thud probably ought to shitcan this one he
thought

start over with something new like melody or force work with
what you know: the old rule

yet even as mind lunged and tottered through its catastrophes

even as it splattered against brick walls and found itself treading air a mile up in the sky clutching for the skyscraper ledge
or the edge of the cliff

there was something engaging about it something that made
him

keep watching

hard to put one's finger on it impossible in fact

at least while it was moving

but it was ah

well it was something *new*

yes it was different somehow it had a certain *style*

maybe I'm on to something after all he thought just a few simple adjustments

so he waited for it to run down screwed in number data recall
concept projection syntax wonder crossed a few wires and
wound it up again hoping for the best or at least a brief
entertainment

but

the results were much the same except that now it *ran* at the
walls *charged* the traffic and *leapt* off the precipices dropping
without so much as an endearing whistle

goddamn it

too late he realized that what he'd invented was not mind but
love and now he'd gone and blown it

always a tinkerer he rebuked himself can't ever leave well enough
   alone

he tried to get ahold of his invention take all that junk out but
   it was running amok

cars were crashing women screaming men were shinnying up
   lampposts the seats of their pants chewed away

children laughed and went to play with it it ate them up

his own wife fell down and frothed at the mouth

buildings toppled ships sank the fields turned brown the city
   fathers ugly

I'M NOT RESPONSIBLE! he cried as they came after him

but though the thing was still on a rampage and only he could fix it

they outlawed inventions and inventors ordered the tinkerer
   boiled in oil

so what could he do he broke away went underground

holing up in caves sewers abandoned farmhouses hollow trees

on the run just kidding himself he knew he couldn't get away

knew if the city fathers didn't get him his invention would

he could hear it whumping hugely around out there

wrecking the world

it would come crashing crazily in on him someday and tear him
   apart making him sorry he'd passed up that simple bath in
   the cauldron

no

not even his newest brainstorm could save him now could he
   finish it and he couldn't

but he went on anyway this tinkerer

frantically inventing serenity

and dreaming as he staggered through sleepless nights with his
   screwdriver safety pins and ball of twine

of a steadfast world free of slapdash and stumble

and the menace of misbegotten thingamajigs

YOU MUST REMEMBER THIS

(1985)

It is dark in Rick's apartment. Black leader dark, heavy and abstract, silent but for a faint hoarse crackle like a voiceless plaint, and brief as sleep. Then Rick opens the door and the light from the hall scissors in like a bellboy to open up space, deposit surfaces (there is a figure in the room), harbinger event (it is Ilsa). Rick follows, too preoccupied to notice: his café is closed, people have been shot, he has troubles. But then, with a stroke, he lights a small lamp (such a glow! The shadows retreat, *everything* retreats: where are the walls?) and there she is, facing him, holding open the drapery at the far window like the front of a nightgown, the light flickering upon her white but determined face like static. Rick pauses for a moment in astonishment. Ilsa lets the drapery and its implications drop, takes a step forward into the strangely fretted light, her eyes searching his.

"How did you get in?" he asks, though this is probably not the question on his mind.

"The stairs from the street."

This answer seems to please him. He knows how vulnerable he is, after all, it's the way he lives—his doors are open, his head is bare, his tuxedo jacket is snowy white—that's not important. What matters is that by such a reply a kind of destiny is being fulfilled. Sam has a song about it. "I told you this morning you'd come around," he says, curling his lips as if to advertise his appetite for punishment, "but this is a little ahead of schedule." She faces him squarely, broad-shouldered and narrow-hipped, a sash around her waist like a gun belt, something shiny in her tensed left hand. He raises both his own as if to show they are empty: "Well, won't you sit down?"

His offer, whether in mockery or no, releases her. Her shoulders dip in relief, her breasts; she sweeps forward (it is only a small purse she is carrying: a toothbrush perhaps, cosmetics, her hotel key), her face softening: "Richard!" He starts back in alarm, hands moving to his hips. "I had to see you!"

"So you use Richard again!" His snarling retreat throws up a barrier between them. She stops. He pushes his hands into his pockets as though to reach for the right riposte: "We're back in Paris!"

That probably wasn't it. Their song seems to be leaking into the room from somewhere out in the night, or perhaps it has been there all the time—Sam maybe, down in the darkened bar, sending out soft percussive warnings in the manner of his African race: "Think twice, boss. Hearts fulla passion, you c'n rely. Jealousy, boss, an' hate. Le's go fishin'. Sam."

"*Please!*" she begs, staring at him intently, but he remains unmoved:

"Your unexpected visit isn't connected by any chance with

the letters of transit?" He ducks his head, his upper lip swelling with bitterness and hurt. "It seems as long as I have those letters, I'll never be lonely."

Yet, needless to say, he will always be lonely—in fact, this is the confession ("You can ask any price you want," she is saying) only half-concealed in his muttered subjoinder: Rick Blaine is a loner, born and bred. Pity him. There is this lingering, almost primal image of him, sitting alone at a chessboard in his white tuxedo, smoking contemplatively in the midst of a raucous conniving crowd, a crowd he has himself assembled about him. He taps a pawn, moves a white knight, fondles a tall black queen while a sardonic smile plays on his lips. He seems to be toying, self-mockingly, with Fate itself, as indifferent toward Rick Blaine (never mind that he says—as he does now, turning away from her—that "*I'm* the only cause *I'm* interested in . . .") as toward the rest of the world. It's all shit, so who cares?

Ilsa is staring off into space, a space that a moment ago Rick filled. She seems to be thinking something out. The negotiations are going badly; perhaps it is this she is worried about. He has just refused her offer of "any price," ignored her ultimatum ("You *must* giff me those letters!"), sneered at her husband's heroism, and scoffed at the very cause that first brought them together in Paris. How could he do that? And now he has abruptly turned his back on her (does he think it was just sex? what has happened to him since then?) and walked away toward the balcony door, meaning, apparently, to turn her out. She takes a deep breath, presses her lips together, and, clutching her tiny purse with both hands, wheels about to pursue him: "Richard!" This has worked before, it works again: he turns to face her new approach: "We luffed each other once . . ." Her voice catches in her throat, tears come to her eyes. She is beautiful there in the slatted shadows, her hair loosening around her ears, eyes glittering, throat bare and vulnerable in the open V-neck of her ruffled blouse. She's a good dresser. Even that little purse she squeezes: so like the other one, so lovely, hidden away. She shakes her head slightly in wistful appeal: "If those days meant . . . anything at all to you . . ."

"I wouldn't bring up Paris if I were you," he says stonily. "It's poor salesmanship."

She gasps (*she* didn't bring it up: is he a madman?), tosses her head back: "Please! Please listen to me!" She closes her eyes, her lower lip pushed forward as though bruised. "If you knew what really happened, if you only knew the truth—!"

He stands over this display, impassive as a Moorish executioner (that's it! he's turning into one of these bloody Arabs, she thinks). "I wouldn't believe you, no matter what you told me," he says. In Ethiopia, after an attempt on the life of an Italian officer, he saw 1600 Ethiopians get rounded up one night and shot in reprisal. Many were friends of his. Or clients anyway. But somehow her deceit is worse. "You'd say anything now, to get what you want." Again he turns his back on her, strides away.

She stares at him in shocked silence, as though all that had happened eighteen months ago in Paris were flashing suddenly before her eyes, now made ugly by some terrible revelation. An exaggerated gasp escapes her like the breaking of wind: his head snaps up and he turns sharply to the right. She chases him, dogging his heels. "You want to feel sorry for yourself, don't you?" she cries and, surprised (he was just reaching for something on an ornamental table, the humidor perhaps), he turns back to her. "With so much at stake, all you can think off is your own feeling," she rails. Her lips are drawn back, her breathing labored, her eyes watering in anger and frustration. "One woman has hurt you, and you take your reffenge on the rest off the world!" She is choking, she can hardly speak. Her accent seems to have got worse. "You're a coward, und veakling, und—"

She gasps. What is she saying? He watches her, as though faintly amused. "No, Richard, I'm sorry!" Tears are flowing in earnest now: she's gone too far! This is the expression on her face. She's in a corner, struggling to get out. "I'm sorry, but—" She wipes the tears from her cheek, and calls once again on her husband, that great and courageous man whom they both admire, whom the whole world admires: "—you're our last hope! If you don't help us, Victor Laszlo will die in Casablanca!"

"What of it?" he says. He has been waiting for this opportunity. He plays with it now, stretching it out. He turns, reaches for a cigarette, his head haloed in the light from an arched doorway. "I'm gonna die in Casablanca. It's a good spot for it." This line is meant to be amusing, but Ilsa reacts with horror. Her eyes widen. She catches her breath, turns away. He lights up, pleased with himself, takes a practiced drag, blows smoke. "Now," he says, turning toward her, "if you'll—"

He pulls up short, squints: she has drawn a revolver on him. So much for toothbrushes and hotel keys. "All right. I tried to reason with you. I tried effrything. Now I want those letters." Distantly, a melodic line suggests a fight for love and glory, an ironic case of do or die. "Get them for me."

"I don't have to." He touches his jacket. "I got 'em right here."

"Put them on the table."

He smiles and shakes his head. "No." Smoke curls up from

the cigarette he is holding at his side like the steam that envel-
oped the five o'clock train to Marseilles. Her eyes fill with tears.
Even as she presses on ("For the last time . . . !"), she knows that
"no" is final. There is, behind his ironic smile, a profound sadness, the fatalistic survivor's wistful acknowledgment that, in
the end, the fundamental things apply. Time, going by, leaves
nothing behind, not even moments like this. "If Laszlo and
the cause mean so much," he says, taunting her with her own
uncertainties, "you won't stop at anything . . ."

He seems almost to recede. The cigarette disappears, the
smoke. His sorrow gives way to something not unlike eagerness.
"All right, I'll make it easier for you," he says, and walks toward
her. "Go ahead and shoot. You'll be doing me a favor."

She seems taken aback, her eyes damp, her lips swollen and
parted. Light licks at her face. He gazes steadily at her from his
superior moral position, smoke drifting up from his hand once
more, his white tuxedo pressed against the revolver barrel. Her
eyes close as the gun lowers, and she gasps his name: "Richard!" It is like an invocation. Or a profession of faith. "I tried
to stay away," she sighs. She opens her eyes, peers up at him in
abject surrender. A tear moves slowly down her cheek toward
the corner of her mouth like secret writing. "I thought I would
neffer see you again . . . that you were out off my life . . ." She
blinks, cries out faintly—"Oh!"—and (he seems moved at last,
his mask of disdain falling away like perspiration) turns away,
her head wrenched to one side as though in pain.

Stricken with sudden concern, or what looks like concern, he
steps up behind her, clasping her breasts with both hands, nuzzling in her hair. "The day you left Paris . . . !" she sobs, though
she seems unsure of herself. One of his hands is already down

between her legs, the other inside her blouse, pulling a breast
out of its brassiere cup. "If you only knew . . . what I . . ." He is
moaning, licking at one ear, the hand between her legs nearly
lifting her off the floor, his pelvis bumping at her buttocks. "Is
this . . . right?" she gasps.

"I—I don't know!" he groans, massaging her breast, the nip-
ple between two fingers. "I can't think!"

"But . . . you *must* think!" she cries, squirming her hips. Tears
are streaming down her cheeks now. "For . . . for . . ."

"What?" he gasps, tearing her blouse open, pulling on her
breast as though to drag it over her shoulder where he might
kiss it. Or eat it: he seems ravenous suddenly.

"I . . . I can't remember!" she sobs. She reaches behind to jerk
at his fly (what else is she to do, for the love of Jesus?), then rips
away her sash, unfastens her skirt, her fingers trembling.

"Holy shit!" he wheezes, pushing his hand inside her girdle
as her skirt falls. His cheeks too are wet with tears. "*Ilsa!*"

"*Richard!*"

They fall to the floor, grabbing and pulling at each other's
clothing. He's trying to get her bra off which is tangled up now
with her blouse, she's struggling with his belt, yanking at his
black pants, wrenching them open. Buttons fly, straps pop,
there's the soft unfocused rip of silk, the jingle of buckles and
falling coins, grunts, gasps, whimpers of desire. He strips the
tangled skein of underthings away (all these straps and stays—
how does she get in and out of this crazy elastic?); she works his
pants down past his bucking hips, fumbles with his shoes. "*Your
elbow—!*"

"*Mmmff!*"

"*Ah—!*"

She pulls his pants and boxer shorts off, crawls round and (he strokes her shimmering buttocks, swept by the light from the airport tower, watching her full breasts sway above him: it's all happening so fast, he'd like to slow it down, repeat some of the better bits—that view of her rippling haunches on her hands and knees just now, for example, like a 22, his lucky number—but there's a great urgency on them, they can't wait) straddles him, easing him into her like a train being guided into a station. *"I luff you, Richard!"* she declares breathlessly, though she seems to be speaking, eyes squeezed shut and breasts heaving, not to him but to the ceiling, if there is one up there. His eyes too are closed now, his hands gripping her soft hips, pulling her down, his breath coming in short anguished snorts, his face puffy and damp with tears. There is, as always, something deeply wounded and vulnerable about the expression on his battered face, framed there against his Persian carpet: Rick Blaine, a man annealed by loneliness and betrayal, but flawed— hopelessly, it seems—by hope itself. He is, in the tragic sense, a true revolutionary: his gaping mouth bespeaks this, the spittle in the corners of his lips, his eyes, open now and staring into some infinite distance not unlike the future, his knitted brow. He heaves upward, impaling her to the very core: *"Oh, Gott!"* she screams, her back arching, mouth agape as though to commence "La Marseillaise."

Now, for a moment, they pause, feeling themselves thus conjoined, his organ luxuriating in the warm tub of her vagina, her enflamed womb closing around his pulsing penis like a mother embracing a lost child. "If you only knew . . . ," she seems to say, though perhaps she has said this before and only now it can be heard. He fondles her breasts; she rips his shirt open,

strokes his chest, leans forward to kiss his lips, his nipples. This
is not Victor inside her with his long thin rapier, all too rare
in its embarrassed visits; this is not Yvonne with her cunning
professional muscles, her hollow airy hole. This is love in all
its clammy mystery, the ultimate connection, the squishy rub
of truth, flesh as a self-consuming message. This is necessity,
as in woman needs man, and man must have his mate. Even
their identities seem to be dissolving; they have to whisper each
other's name from time to time as though in recitative struggle
against some ultimate enchantment from which there might
be no return. Then slowly she begins to wriggle her hips above
him, he to meet her gentle undulations with counterthrusts
of his own. They hug each other close, panting, her breasts
smashed against him, moving only from the waist down. She
slides her thighs between his and squeezes his penis between
them, as though to conceal it there, an underground member on
the run, wounded but unbowed. He lifts his stockinged feet and
plants them behind her knees as though in stirrups, her buttocks above pinching and opening, pinching and opening like
a suction pump. And it is true about her vaunted radiance: she
seems almost to glow from within, her flexing cheeks haloed in
their own dazzling luster.

"It feels so good, Richard! In there . . . I've been so—*ah!*—so
lonely . . . !"

"Yeah, me too, kid. *Ngh!* Don't talk."

She slips her thighs back over his and draws them up beside
his waist like a child curling around her teddybear, knees
against his ribs, her fanny gently bobbing on its pike like a
mind caressing a cherished memory. He lies there passively
for a moment, stretched out, eyes closed, accepting this warm

rhythmical ablution as one might accept a nanny's teasing bath, a mother's care (a care, he's often said, denied him), in all its delicious innocence—or seemingly so: in fact, his whole body is faintly atremble, as though, with great difficulty, shedding the last of its pride and bitterness, its isolate neutrality. Then slowly his own hips begin to rock convulsively under hers, his knees to rise in involuntary surrender. She tongues his ear, her buttocks thumping more vigorously now, kisses his throat, his nose, his scarred lip, then rears up, arching her back, tossing her head back (her hair is looser now, wilder, a flush has crept into the distinctive pallor of her cheeks and throat, and what was before a fierce determination is now raw intensity, what vulnerability now a slack-jawed abandon), plunging him in more deeply than ever, his own buttocks bouncing up off the floor as though trying to take off like the next flight to Lisbon— "Gott in Himmel, *this is fonn!*" she cries. She reaches behind her back to clutch his testicles, he clasps her hand in both of his, his thighs spread, she falls forward, they roll over, he's pounding away now from above (he lacks her famous radiance: if anything his buttocks seem to suck in light, drawing a nostalgic murkiness around them like night fog, signaling a fundamental distance between them, and an irresistible attraction), she's clawing at his back under the white jacket, at his hips, his thighs, her voracious nether mouth leaping up at him from below and sliding back, over and over, like a frantic greased-pole climber. Faster and faster they slap their bodies together, submitting to this fierce rhythm as though to simplify themselves, emitting grunts and whinnies and help-less little farts, no longer Rick Blaine and Ilsa Lund, but some nameless conjunction somewhere between them, time, space, being itself getting redefined by the rapidly narrowing focus of their incandescent passion—then suddenly Rick rears back, his face seeming to puff out like a gourd, Ilsa cries out and kicks upward, crossing her ankles over Rick's clenched buttocks, for a moment they seem almost to float, suspended, unloosed from the earth's gravity, and then—*whumpf!*—they hit the floor again, their bodies continuing to hammer together, though less regularly, plunging, twitching, prolonging this exclamatory dialogue, drawing it out even as the intensity diminishes, even as it becomes more a declaration than a demand, more an inquiry than a declaration. Ilsa's feet uncross, slide slowly to the floor. "Fooff . . . *Gott!*" They lie there, cheek to cheek, clutching each other tightly, gasping for breath, their thighs quivering with the last involuntary spasms, the echoey reverberations, deep in their loins, of pleasure's fading blasts.

"Jesus," Rick wheezes, "I've been saving that one for a goddamn year and a half . . . !"

"It was the best fokk I effer haff," Ilsa replies with a tremulous sigh, and kisses his ear, runs her fingers in his hair. He starts to roll off her, but she clasps him closely: "No . . . wait . . . !" A deeper thicker pleasure, not so ecstatic, yet somehow more moving, seems to well up from far inside her to embrace the swollen visitor snuggled moistly in her womb, once a familiar friend, a comrade loved and trusted, now almost a stranger, like one resurrected from the dead.

"Ah—!" he gasps. God, it's almost like she's milking it! Then she lets go, surrounding him spongily with a kind of warm wet pulsating gratitude. "Ah . . ."

He lies there between Ilsa's damp silky thighs, feeling his weight thicken, his mind soften and spread. His will drains away as if it were some kind of morbid affection, lethargy overtaking

him like an invading army. Even his jaw goes slack, his fingers
(three sprawl idly on a dark-tipped breast) limp. He wears his
snowy white tuxedo jacket still, his shiny black socks, which,
together with the parentheses of Ilsa's white thighs, make his
melancholy buttocks—beaten in childhood, lashed at sea, run
lean in union skirmishes, sunburned in Ethiopia, and shot at
in Spain—look gloomier than ever, swarthy and self-pitying,
agape now with a kind of heroic sadness. A violent tenderness.
These buttocks are, it could be said, what the pose of isolation
looks like at its best: proud, bitter, mournful, and, as the prefect
of police might have put it, tremendously attractive. Though
his penis has slipped out of its vaginal pocket to lie limply like
a fat little toe against her slowly pursing lips, she clasps him
close still, clinging to something she cannot quite define, something like a spacious dream of freedom, or a monastery garden,
or the discovery of electricity. "Do you have a gramophone on,
Richard?"

"What—?!" Her question has startled him. His haunches
snap shut, his head rears up, snorting, he seems to be reaching
for the letters of transit. "Ah . . . no . . ." He relaxes again, letting
his weight fall back, though sliding one thigh over hers now,
stretching his arms out as though to unkink them, turning his
face away. His scrotum bulges up on her thigh like an emblem
of his inner serenity and generosity, all too often concealed,
much as an authentic decency might shine through a mask of
cynicism and despair. He takes a deep breath. (A kiss is just a
kiss is what the music is insinuating. A sigh . . .) "That's probably Sam . . ."

She sighs (. . . and so forth), gazing up at the ceiling above
her, patterned with overlapping circles of light from the room's

lamps and swept periodically by the wheeling airport beacon, coming and going impatiently, yet reliably, like desire itself. "He hates me, I think."

"Sam? No, he's a pal. What I think, he thinks."

"When we came into the bar last night, he started playing 'Luff for Sale.' Effryone turned and looked at me."

"It wasn't the song, sweetheart, it was the way you two were dressed. Nobody in Casablanca—"

"Then he tried to chase me away. He said I was bad luck to you." She can still see the way he rolled his white eyes at her, like some kind of crazy voodoo zombie.

Richard grunts ambiguously. "Maybe you should stop calling him 'boy.'"

Was that it? "But in all the moofies—" Well, a translation problem probably, a difficulty she has known often in her life. Language can sometimes be stiff as a board. Like what's under her now. She loves Richard's relaxed weight on her, the beat of his heart next to her breast, the soft lumpy pouch of his genitals squashed against her thigh, but the floor seems to be hardening under her like some kind of stern Calvinist rebuke and there is a disagreeable airy stickiness between her legs, now that he has slid away from there. "Do you haff a bidet, Richard?"

"Sure, kid." He slides to one side with a lazy grunt, rolls over. He's thinking vaguely about the pleasure he's just had, what it's likely to cost him (he doesn't care), and wondering where he'll find the strength to get up off his ass and go look for a cigarette. He stretches his shirttail down and wipes his crotch with it, nods back over the top of his head. "In there."

She is sitting up, peering between her spread legs. "I am afraid we haff stained your nice carpet, Richard."

"What of it? Put it down as a gesture to love. Want a drink?"

"Yes, that would be good." She leans over and kisses him, her face still flushed and eyes damp, but smiling now, then stands and gathers up an armload of tangled clothing. "Do I smell something burning?"

"What—?!" He rears up. "My goddamn cigarette! I musta dropped it on the couch!" He crawls over, brushes at it: it's gone out, but there's a big hole there now, dark-edged like ringworm. "Shit." He staggers to his feet, stumbles over to the humidor to light up a fresh smoke. Nothing's ever free, he thinks, feeling a bit light-headed. "What's your poison, kid?"

"I haff downstairs been drinking Cointreau," she calls out over the running water in the next room. He pours himself a large whiskey, tosses it down neat (light, sliding by, catches his furrowed brow as he tips his head back: what is wrong?), pours another, finds a decanter of Grand Marnier. She won't know the difference. In Paris she confused champagne with sparkling cider, ordered a Pommard thinking she was getting a rosé, drank gin because she couldn't taste it. He fits the half-burned cigarette between his lips, tucks a spare over his ear, then carries the drinks into the bathroom. She sits, straddling the bidet, churning water up between her legs like the wake of a pleasure boat. The beacon doesn't reach in here: it's as though he's stepped out of its line of sight, but that doesn't make him feel easier (something is nagging at him, has been for some time now). He holds the drink to her mouth for her, and she sips, looking mischievously up at him, one wet hand braced momentarily on his hipbone. Even in Paris she seemed to think drinking was naughtier than sex. Which made her on occasion something of a souse. She tips her chin, and he sets her drink down on the sink.

"I wish I didn't luff you so much," she says casually, licking her lips, and commences to work up a lather between her legs with a bar of soap.

"Listen, what did you mean," he asks around the cigarette (this is it, or part of it: he glances back over his shoulder apprehensively, as though to find some answer to his question staring him in the face—or what, from the rear, is passing for his face), "when you said, 'Is this right?' "

"When . . . ?"

"A while ago, when I grabbed your, you know—"

"Oh, I don't know, darling. Yust a strange feeling, I don't exactly remember." She spreads the suds up her smooth belly and down the insides of her thighs, runs the soap up under her behind. "Like things were happening too fast or something."

He takes a contemplative drag on the cigarette, flips the butt into the toilet. "Yeah, that's it." Smoke curls out his nostrils like balloons of speech in a comic strip. "*All* this seems strange somehow. Like something that shouldn't have—"

"Well, I *am* a married woman, Richard."

"I don't mean that." But maybe he does mean that. She's rinsing now, her breasts flopping gaily above her splashing, it's hard to keep his mind on things. But he's not only been pronging some other guy's wife, this is the wife of Victor Laszlo of the International Underground, one of his goddamn heroes. One of the world's. Does that matter? He shoves his free hand in a jacket pocket, having no other, tosses back the drink. "Anyway," he wheezes, "from what you tell me, you were married already when we met in Paris, so that's not—"

"Come here, Richard," Ilsa interrupts with gentle but firm Teutonic insistence. *Komm' hier.* His back straightens, his eyes narrow, and for a moment the old Rick Blaine returns, the lonely American warrior, incorruptible, melancholy, master of his own fate, beholden to no one—but then she reaches forward and, like destiny, takes a hand. "Don't try to escape," she murmurs, pulling him up to the bidet between her knees. "You will neffer succeed."

She continues to hold him with one hand (he is growing there, stretching and filling in her hand with soft warm pulsations, and more than anything else that has happened to her since she came to Casablanca, more even than Sam's song, it is this sensation that takes her back to their days in Paris: wherever they went, from the circus to the movies, from excursion boats to dancehalls, it swelled in her hand, just like this), while soaping him up with the other. "Why are you circumcised, Richard?" she asks, as the engorged head (when it flushes, it seems to flush blue) pushes out between her thumb and index finger. There was something he always said in Paris when it poked up at her like that. She peers wistfully at it, smiling to herself.

"My old man was a sawbones," he says, and takes a deep breath. He sets his empty glass down, reaches for the spare fag. It seems to have vanished. "He thought it was hygienic."

"Fictor still has his. Off course in Europe it is often important not to be mistaken for a Chew." She takes up the fragrant bar of soap (black market, the best, Ferrari gets it for him) and buffs the shaft with it, then thumbs the head with her sudsy hands as though, gently, trying to uncap it. The first day he met her, she opened his pants and jerked him off in his top-down convertible right under the Arc de Triomphe, then, almost without transition, or so it seemed to him, blew him spectacularly in the Bois de Boulogne. He remembers every detail, or anyway the best parts. And it was never—ever—any better than that. Until tonight.

She rinses the soap away, pours the rest of the Grand Marnier (she thinks: Cointreau) over his gleaming organ like a sort of libation, working the excess around as though lightly basting it (he thinks: priming it). A faint sad smile seems to be playing at the corners of her lips. "Say it once, Richard . . ."

"What—?"

She's smiling sweetly, but: is that a tear in her eye? "For old times' sake. Say it . . ."

"Ah." Yes, he'd forgotten. He's out of practice. He grunts, runs his hand down her damp cheek and behind her ear. "Here's lookin' at you, kid . . ."

She puckers her lips and kisses the tip, smiling cross-eyed at it, then, opening her mouth wide, takes it in, all of it at once. "Oh, Christ!" he groans, feeling himself awash in the thick muscular foam of her saliva, "I'm crazy about you, baby!"

"Mmmm!" she moans. He has said that to her before, more than once no doubt (she wraps her arms around his hips under the jacket and hugs him close), but the time she is thinking about was at the cinema one afternoon in Paris. They had gone to see an American detective movie that was popular at the time, but there was a newsreel on before showing the Nazi conquests that month of Copenhagen, Oslo, Luxembourg, Amsterdam, and Brussels. "The Fall of Five Capitals," it was called. And the scenes from Oslo, though brief, showing the Gestapo goose-stepping through the storied streets of her childhood filled her with such terror and nostalgia (something inside her was screaming, "Who *am* I?"), that she reached impulsively for Richard's hand, grabbing what Victor calls "the old fellow" instead. She started to pull her hand back, but he held it there, and the next thing she knew she had her head in his lap, weeping and sucking as though at her dead mother's breast, the terrible roar of the German blitzkrieg pounding in her ears, Richard kneading her nape as her father used to do before he died (and as Richard is doing now, his buttocks knotted up under her arms, his penis fluttering in her mouth like a frightened bird), the Frenchmen in the theater shouting out obscenities, her own heart pounding like cannon fire. "God! I'm crazy about you, baby!" Richard whinnied as he came (now, as his knees buckle against hers and her mouth fills with the shockingly familiar unfamiliarity of his spurting seed, it is just a desperate "Oh fuck! Don't let go . . . !"), and when she sat up, teary-eyed and drooling and gasping for breath (it is not all that easy to breathe now, as he clasps her face close to his hairy belly, whimpering gratefully, his body sagging, her mouth filling), what she saw on the screen were happy Germans, celebrating their victories, taking springtime strolls through overflowing flower and vegetable markets, going to the theater to see translations of Shakespeare, snapping photographs of their children. "Oh Gott," she sniffled then (now she swallows, sucks and swallows, as though to draw out from this almost impalpable essence some vast structure of recollection), "it's too much!" Whereupon the man behind them leaned over and said: "Then try mine, mademoiselle. As you can see, it is not so grand as your Nazi friend's, but here in France, we grow men not pricks!" Richard's French was terrible, but it was good enough to understand "your Nazi friend": he hadn't even put his penis back in his pants (now it slides greasily past her chin, flops down her chest, his buttocks in her hugging arms going soft as butter, like a delicious half-grasped memory losing its clear outlines, melting into mere sensation), but just leapt up and took a swing at the Frenchman. With that, the cinema broke into an uproar with everybody calling everyone else a fascist or a whore. They were thrown out of the theater of course, the police put Richard on their blacklist as an exhibitionist, and they never did get to see the detective movie. Ah well, they could laugh about it then . . .

He sits now on the front lip of the bidet, his knees knuckled under hers, shirttails in the water, his cheek fallen on her broad shoulder, arms loosely around her, feeling wonderfully unwound, mellow as an old tune (which is still there somewhere, moonlight and love songs, same old story—maybe it's coming up through the pipes), needing only a smoke to make things perfect. The one he stuck over his ear is floating in the scummy pool beneath them, he sees. Ilsa idly splashes his drooping organ as though christening it. Only one answer, she once said, peeling off that lovely satin gown of hers like a French letter, will take care of all our questions, and she was right. As always. He's the one who's made a balls-up of things with his complicated moral poses and insufferable pride—a diseased romantic, Louis once called him, and he didn't know the half of it. She's the only realist in town; he's got to start paying attention. Even now she's making sense: "My rump is getting dumb, Richard. Dry me off and let's go back in the other room."

But when he tries to stand, his knees feel like toothpaste, and he has to sit again. Right back in the bidet, as it turns out, dipping his ass like doughnuts in tea. She smiles understandingly, drapes a bath towel around her shoulders, pokes through the medicine cabinet until she finds a jar of Yvonne's cold cream, then takes him by the elbow. "Come on, Richard. You can do it, yust lean on me." Which reminds him (his mind at least is still working, more or less) of a night in Spain, halfway up (or down) Suicide Hill in the Jarama valley, a night he thought was to be his last, when he said that to someone, or someone said it to him. God, what if he'd got it shot off there? And missed this? An expression compounded of hope and anguish, skepticism and awe, crosses his weary face (thirty-eight at Christmas, if Strasser is right—oh mother of God, it *is* going by!), picked up by the wheeling airport beacon. She removes his dripping jacket, his shirt as well, and towels his behind before letting him collapse onto the couch, then crosses to the ornamental table for a cigarette from the humidor. She wears the towel like a cape, her haunches under it glittering as though sequined. She is, as always, a kind of walking light show, no less spectacular from the front as she turns back now toward the sofa, the nubbly texture of the towel contrasting subtly with the soft glow of her throat and breast, the sleek wet gleam of her belly.

She fits two cigarettes in her lips, lights them both (there's a bit of fumbling with the lighter, she's not very mechanical), and gazing soulfully down at Rick, passes him one of them. He grins. "Hey, where'd you learn that, kid?" She shrugs enigmatically, hands him the towel, and steps up between his knees. As he rubs her breasts, her belly, her thighs with the towel, the cigarette dangling in his lips, she gazes around at the chalky rough-plastered walls of his apartment, the Moorish furniture with its filigrees and inlaid patterns, the little bits of erotic art (there is a statue of a camel on the sideboard that looks like a man's wet penis on legs, and a strange nude statuette that might be a boy, or a girl, or something in between), the alabaster lamps and potted plants, those slatted wooden blinds, so exotic to her Northern eyes: he has style, she thinks, rubbing cold cream into her neck and shoulder with her free hand, he always did have . . .

She lifts one leg for him to dry and then the other, gasping inwardly (outwardly, she chokes and wheezes, having inhaled the cigarette by mistake: he stubs out his own with a sympathetic grin, takes what is left of hers) when he rubs the towel briskly between them, then she turns and bends over, bracing herself on the coffee table. Rick, the towel in his hands, pauses a moment, gazing thoughtfully through the drifting cigarette haze at these luminous buttocks, finding something almost otherworldly about them, like archways to heaven or an image of eternity. Has he seen them like this earlier tonight? Maybe, he can't remember. Certainly now he's able to savor the sight, no longer crazed by rut. They are, quite literally, a dream come true: he has whacked off to their memory so often during the last year and a half that it almost feels more appropriate to touch himself than this present manifestation. As he reaches toward them with the towel, he seems to be crossing some strange threshold, as though passing from one medium into another. He senses the supple buoyancy of them bouncing back against his hand as he wipes them, yet, though flesh, they remain somehow immaterial, untouchable even when touched, objects whose very presence is a kind of absence. If Rick Blaine were to believe in angels, Ilsa's transcendent bottom is what they would look like.

"Is this how you, uh, imagined things turning out tonight?" he asks around the butt, smoke curling out his nose like thought's reek. Her cheeks seem to pop alight like his Café Américain sign each time the airport beacon sweeps past, shifting slightly like a sequence of film frames. Time itself may be like that, he knows: not a ceaseless flow, but a rapid series of electrical leaps across tiny gaps between discontinuous bits. It's what he likes to call his link-and-claw theory of time, though of course the theory is not his . . .

"Well, it may not be perfect, Richard, but it is better than if I haff shot you, isn't it?"

"No, I meant . . ." Well, let it be. She's right, it beats eating a goddamn bullet. In fact it beats anything he can imagine. He douses his cigarette in the wet towel, tosses it aside, wraps his arms around her thighs and pulls her buttocks (he is still thinking about time as a pulsing sequence of film frames, and not so much about the frames, their useless dated content, as the gaps between: infinitesimally small when looked at two-dimensionally, yet in their third dimension as deep and mysterious as the cosmos) toward his face, pressing against them like a child trying to see through a foggy window. He kisses and nibbles at each fresh-washed cheek (and what if one were to slip *between* two of those frames? he wonders—), runs his tongue into (—where would he be then?) her anus, kneading the flesh on her pubic knoll between his fingers all the while like little lumps of stiff taffy. She raises one knee up onto the cushions, then the other, lowering her elbows to the floor (oh! she thinks as the blood rushes in two directions at once, spreading into her head and sex as though filling empty frames, her heart the gap between: what a strange dizzying dream time is!), thus lifting to his contemplative scrutiny what looks like a clinging sea anemone between her thighs, a thick woolly pod, a cloven chinchilla, open purse, split fruit. But it is not the appearance of it that moves him (except to the invention of these fanciful cata-

logues), it is the smell. It is this which catapults him suddenly
and wholly back to Paris, a Paris he'd lost until this moment
(she is not in Paris, she is in some vast dimensionless region
she associates with childhood, a nighttime glow in her mid-
summer room, featherbedding between her legs) but now has
back again. Now and for all time. As he runs his tongue up and
down the spongy groove, pinching the lips tenderly between
his tongue and stiff upper lip (an old war wound), feeling it
engorge, pulsate, almost pucker up to kiss him back, he seems to
see—as though it were fading in on the blank screen of her gently rolling bottom—that night at her apartment in Paris when
she first asked him to "Kiss me, Richard, here. My other mouth
wants to luff you, too . . ." He'd never done that before. He had
been all over the world, had fought in wars, battled cops, been
jailed and tortured, hid out in whorehouses, parachuted out of
airplanes, had eaten and drunk just about everything, had been
blown off the decks of ships, killed more men than he'd like
to count, and had banged every kind and color of woman on
earth, but he had never tasted one of these things before. Other
women had sucked him off, of course, before Ilsa nearly caused
him to wreck his car that day in the Bois de Boulogne, but he
had always thought of that as a service due him, something he'd
paid for in effect—he was the man, after all. But reciprocation,
sucking back—well, that always struck him as vaguely queer,
something guys, manly guys anyway, didn't do. That night,
though, he'd had a lot of champagne and he was—this was the
simple truth, and it was an experience as exotic to Rick Blaine
as the taste of a cunt—madly in love. He had been an unhappy
misfit all his life, at best a romantic drifter, at worst and in
the eyes of most a sleazy gunrunner and chickenshit merce-

nary (though God knows he'd hoped for more), a whoremon-
ger and brawler and miserable gutter drunk: nothing like Ilsa
Lund had ever happened to him, and he could hardly believe
it was happening to him that night. His immediate reaction—
he admits this, sucking greedily at it now (she is galloping her
father's horse through the woods of the north, canopy-dark and
sunlight-blinding at the same time, pushing the beast beneath
her, racing toward what she believed to be God's truth, flush-
ing through her from the saddle up as eternity might when the
saints were called), while watching himself, on the cinescreen
of her billowing behind, kneel to it that first time like an atheist
falling squeamishly into conversion—was not instant rapture.
No, like olives, home brew, and Arab cooking, it took a little
getting used to. But she taught him how to stroke the vulva
with his tongue, where to find the nun's cap ("my little sister,"
she called it, which struck him as odd) and how to draw it out,
how to use his fingers, nose, chin, even his hair and ears, and
the more he practiced for her sake, the more he liked it for his
own, her pleasure (he could *see* it: it bloomed right under his
nose, filling his grimy life with colors he'd never even thought
of before!) augmenting his, until he found his appetite for it
almost insatiable. God, the boys on the block back in New York
would laugh their asses off to see how far he'd fallen! And though
he has tried others since, it is still the only one he really likes.
Yvonne's is terrible, bitter and pomaded (she seems to sense this,
gets no pleasure from it at all, often turns fidgety and mean
when he goes down on her, even had a kind of biting, scratching
fit once: "Don' you lak to *fuck?*" she'd screamed), which is the
main reason he's lost interest in her. That and her hairy legs.

His screen is shrinking (her knees have climbed to his

shoulders, scrunching her hips into little bumps and bringing her shoulderblades into view, down near the floor, where she is gasping and whimpering and sucking the carpet), but his vision of the past is expanding, as though her pumping cheeks were a chubby bellows, opening and closing, opening and closing, inflating his memories. Indeed, he no longer needs a screen for them, for it is not this or that conquest that he recalls now, this or that event, not what she wore or what she said, what he said, but something more profound than that, something experienced in the way that a blind man sees or an amputee touches. Texture returns to him, ambience, impressions of radiance, of coalescence, the foamy taste of the ineffable on his tongue, the downy nap of timelessness, the tooth of now. All this he finds in Ilsa's juicy bouncing cunt—and more: love's pungent illusions of consubstantiation and infinitude (oh, he knows what he lost that day in the rain in the Gare de Lyon!), the bittersweet fall into actuality, space's secret folds wherein one might lose one's ego, one's desperate sense of isolation, Paris, rediscovered here as pure aura, effervescent and allusive, La Belle Aurore as immanence's theater, sacred showplace—

Oh hell, he thinks as Ilsa's pounding hips drive him to his back on the couch, her thighs slapping against his ears (as she rises, her blood in riptide against her mounting excitement, the airport beacon touching her in its passing like bursts of inspiration, she thinks: childhood is a place apart, needing the adult world to exist at all: without Victor there could *be* no Rick!— and then she cannot think at all), La Belle Aurore! She broke his goddamn heart at La Belle Aurore. "Kiss me," she said, holding herself with both hands as though to keep the pain from spilling out down there, "one last time," and he did, for her, Henri didn't care, merde alors, the Germans were coming anyway, and the other patrons thought it was just part of the entertainment; only Sam was offended and went off to the john till it was over. And then she left him. Forever. Or anyway until she turned up here a night ago with Laszlo. God, he remembers everything about that day in the Belle Aurore, what she was wearing, what the Germans were wearing, what Henri was wearing. It was not an easy day to forget. The Germans were at the very edge of the city, they were bombing the bejesus out of the place and everything was literally falling down around their ears (she's smothering him now with her bucking arse, her scissoring thighs: he heaves her over onto her back and pushes his arms between her thighs to spread them); they'd had to crawl over rubble and dead bodies, push through barricades, just to reach the damned café. No chance to get out by car, he was lucky there was enough left in his "F.Y. Fund" to buy them all train tickets. And then the betrayal: "I can't find her, Mr. Richard. She's checked outa de hotel. But dis note come jus' after you lef'!" Oh shit, even now it makes him cry. "I cannot go with you or ever see you again." In perfect Palmer Method handwriting, as though to exult in her power over him. He kicked poor Sam's ass up and down that train all the way to Marseilles, convinced it was somehow his fault. Even a hex maybe, that day he could have believed anything. Now, with her hips bouncing frantically up against his mouth, her bush grown to an astonishing size, the lips out and flapping like flags, the trench between them awash in a fragrant ooze like oily air, he lifts his head and asks: "Why weren't you honest with me? Why did you keep your marriage a secret?"

"Oh Gott, Richard! Not *now*—!"

She's right, it doesn't seem the right moment for it, but then

nothing has seemed right since she turned up in this godfor-
saken town: it's almost as though two completely different
places, two completely different times, are being forced to mesh,
to intersect where no intersection is possible, causing a kind
of warp in the universe. In his own private universe anyway.
He gazes down on this lost love, this faithless wife, this trust-
ing child, her own hands between her legs now, her hips still
jerking out of control ("Please, Richard!" she is begging softly
through clenched teeth, tears in her eyes), thinking: It's still a
story without an ending. But more than that: the beginning and
middle bits aren't all there either. Her face is drained as though
all the blood has rushed away to other parts, but her throat
between the heaving white breasts is almost literally alight
with its vivid blush. He touches it, strokes the soft bubbles to
either side, watching the dark little nipples rise like patriots—
and suddenly the answer to all his questions seems (yet another
one, that is—answers, in the end, are easy) to suggest itself.
"Listen kid, would it be all right if I—?"

"Oh yes! yes!—*but hurry!*"

He finds the cold cream (at last! he is so slow!), lathers it on,
and slips into her cleavage, his knees over her shoulders like
a yoke. She guides his head back into that tropical explosion
between her legs, then clasps her arms around his hips, already
beginning to thump at her chest like a resuscitator, popping little
gasps from her throat. She tries to concentrate on his bouncing
buttocks, but they communicate to her such a touching blend of
cynicism and honesty, weariness and generosity, that they nearly
break her heart, making her more light-headed than ever. The
dark little hole between them bobs like a lonely survivor in a
tragically divided world. It is he! "Oh Gott!" she whimpers. And

she! The tension between her legs is almost unbearable. "I can't fight it anymore!" Everything starts to come apart. She feels herself falling as though some rift in the universe (she cannot wait for him, and anyway, where she is going he cannot follow), out of time and matter into some wondrous radiance, the wheeling beacon flashing across her stricken vision now like intermittent star bursts, the music swelling, *everything* swelling, her eyes bursting, ears popping, teeth ringing in their sockets—"Oh Richard! Oh fokk! *I luff you so much!*"

He plunges his face deep into Ilsa's ambrosial pudding, lapping at its sweet sweat, feeling her loins snap and convulse violently around him, knowing that with a little inducement she can spasm like this for minutes on end, and meanwhile pumping away between her breasts now like a madman, no longer obliged to hold back, seeking purely his own pleasure. This pleasure is tempered only by (and maybe enhanced by as well) his pity for her husband, that heroic sonuvabitch. God, Victor Laszlo is almost a father figure to him, really. And while Laszlo is off at the underground meeting in the Caverne du Roi, no doubt getting his saintly ass shot to shit, here he is—Rick Blaine, the Yankee smart aleck and general jerk-off—safely closeted off in his rooms over the town saloon, tit-fucking the hero's wife, his callous nose up her own royal grotto like an advance scout for a squad of storm troopers. Its not fair, goddamn it, he thinks, and laughs at this even as he comes, squirting jism down her sleek belly and under his own, his head locked in her clamped thighs, her arms hugging him tightly as though to squeeze to juices out.

He is lying, completely still, his face between Ilsa's flaccid thighs, knees over her shoulders, arms around her lower body, which sprawls loosely now beneath him. he can feel her hands resting lightly on his hips, her warm breath against his leg. He doesn't remember when they stopped moving. Maybe he's been sleeping. Has he dreamt it all? No, he shifts slightly and feels the spill of semen, pooled gummily between their conjoined navels. His movement wakes Ilsa: she snorts faintly, sighs, kisses the inside of his leg, strokes one buttock idly. "That soap smells nice," she murmurs. "I bet effry girl in Casablanca wishes to haff a bath here."

"Yeah, well, I run it as a kind of public service," he grunts, chewing the words around a strand or two of pubic hair. He's always told Louis—and anyone else who wanted to know—that he sticks his neck out for nobody. But in the end, shit, he thinks, I stick it out for everybody. "I'm basically a civic-minded guy."

Cynic-minded, more like, she thinks, but keeps the thought to herself. She cannot risk offending him, not just now. She is still returning from wherever it is orgasm has taken her, and it has been an experience so profound and powerful, yet so remote from its immediate cause—his muscular tongue at the other end of this morosely puckered hole in front of her nose—that it has left her feeling very insecure, unsure of who or what she is, or even where. She knows of course that her role as the well-dressed wife of a courageous underground leader is just pretense, that beneath this charade she is certainly someone— or something—else. Richard's lover, for example. Or a little orphan girl who lost her mother, father, and adoptive aunt, all before she'd even started menstruating—that's who she often is, or feels like she is, especially at moments like this. But if her life as Victor Laszlo's wife is not real, are these others any more so? Is she one person, several—or no one at all? What was

that thought she'd had about childhood? She lies there, hugging
Richard's hairy cheeks (are they Richard's? are they cheeks?),
her pale face framed by his spraddled legs, trying to puzzle it
all out. Since the moment she arrived in Casablanca, she and
Richard have been trying to tell each other stories, not very
funny stories, as Richard has remarked, but maybe not very
true ones either. Maybe memory itself is a kind of trick, something that turns illusion into reality and makes the real world
vanish before everyone's eyes like magic. One can certainly sink
away there and miss everything, she knows. Hasn't Victor, the
wise one, often warned her of that? But Victor is a hero. Maybe
the real world is too much for most people. Maybe making up
stories is a way to keep them all from going insane. A tear forms
in the corner of one eye. She blinks (and what are these unlikely
configurations called "Paris" and "Casablanca," where in all
the universe is she, and what is "where"?), and the tear trick-
les into the hollow between cheekbone and nose, then bends its
course toward the middle of her cheek. There is a line in their
song (yes, it is still there, tinkling away somewhere like mice in
the walls: is someone trying to drive her crazy?) that goes, "This
day and age we're living in gives cause for apprehension, /With
speed and new invention and things like third dimension . . ."
She always thought that was a stupid mistake of the lyricist, but
now she is not so sure. For the real mystery—she sees this now,
or *feels* it rather—is not the fourth dimension as she'd always
supposed (the tear stops halfway down her cheek, begins to
fade), or the third either for that matter . . . but the *first.*

"You never finished answering my question . . ."

There is a pause. Perhaps she is daydreaming. "What question, Richard?"

"A while ago. In the bathroom . . ." He, too, has been mulling
over recent events, wondering not only about the events themselves (wondrous in their own right, of course: he's not enjoyed
multiple orgasms like this since he hauled his broken-down
blacklisted ass out of Paris a year and a half ago, and that's just
for starters), but also about their "recentness": When did they
really happen? Is "happen" the right word, or were they more like
fleeting conjunctions with the Absolute, that *other* Other, bound-
less and immutable as number? And, if so, what now is "when"?
How much time has elapsed, for example, since he opened the
door and found her in this room? Has *any* time elapsed? "I asked
you what you meant when you said, 'Is this right?' "

"Oh, Richard, I don't know what's right any longer." She lifts
one thigh in front of his face, as though to erase his dark imaginings. He strokes it, thinking: well, what the hell, it probably
doesn't amount to a hill of beans, anyway. "Do you think I can
haff another drink now?"

"Sure, kid. Why not." He sits up beside her, shakes the butt
out of the damp towel, wipes his belly off, hands the towel to
her. "More of the same?"

"Champagne would be nice, if it is possible. It always makes
me think of Paris . . . and you . . ."

"You got it, sweetheart." He pushes himself to his feet and
thumps across the room, pausing at the humidor to light up
a fresh smoke. "If there's any left. Your old man's been going
through my stock like Vichy water." Not for the first time, he has
the impression of being watched. Laszlo? Who knows, maybe the
underground meeting was just a ruse; it certainly seemed like
a dumb thing to do on the face of it, especially with Strasser in
town. There's a bottle of champagne in his icebox, okay, but no

ice. He touches the bottle: not cold, but cool enough. It occurs to him the sonuvabitch might be out on the balcony right now, taking it all in, he and all his goddamn underground. Europeans can be pretty screwy, especially these rich stiffs with titles. As he carries the champagne and glasses over to the coffee table, the cigarette like a dart between his lips, his bare ass feels suddenly both hot and chilly at the same time. "Does your husband ever get violent?" he asks around the smoke and snaps the metal clamp off the champagne bottle, takes a grip on the cork.

"No. He has killed some people, but he is not fiolent." She is rubbing her tummy off, smiling thoughtfully. The light from the airport beacon, wheeling past, picks up a varnishlike glaze still between her breasts, a tooth's wet twinkle in her open mouth, an unwonted shine on her nose. The cork pops, champagne spews out over the table top, some of it getting into the glasses. This seems to suggest somehow a revelation. Or another memory. The tune, as though released, rides up once more around them. "Gott, Richard," she sighs, pushing irritably to her feet. "That music is getting on my nerfs!"

"Yeah, I know." It's almost as bad in its way as the German blitzkrieg hammering in around their romance in Paris— sometimes it seemed to get right between their embraces. Gave him a goddamn headache. Now the music is doing much the same thing, even trying to tell them when to kiss and when not to. He can stand it, though, he thinks, tucking the cigarette back in his lips, if she can. He picks up the two champagne glasses, offers her one. "Forget it, kid. Drown it out with this." He raises his glass. "Uh, here's lookin'—"

She gulps it down absently, not waiting for his toast. "And

that light from the airport," she goes on, batting at it as it passes as though to shoo it away. "How can you effer sleep here?"

"No one's supposed to sleep well in Casablanca," he replies with a worldly grimace. It's his best expression, he knows, but she isn't paying any attention. He stubs out the cigarette, refills her glass, blowing a melancholy whiff of smoke over it. "Hey, kid here's—"

"No, wait!" she insists, her ear cocked. "*Is* it?"

"Is what?" Ah well, forget the fancy stuff. He drinks off the champagne in his glass, reaches down for a refill.

"Time. Is it going by? Like the song is saying?"

He looks up, startled. "That's funny, I was just—!"

"What time do you haff, Richard?"

He sets the bottle down, glances at his empty wrist. "I dunno. My watch must have got torn off when we . . ."

"Mine is gone, too."

They stare at each other a moment, Rick scowling slightly in the old style, Ilsa's lips parted as though saying "story," or "glory." Then the airport beacon sweeps past like a prompter, and Rick, blinking, says: "Wait a minute—there's a clock down in the bar!" He strides purposefully over to the door in his stocking feet, pausing there a moment, one hand on the knob, to take a deep breath. "I'll be right back," he announces, then opens the door and (she seems about to call out to him) steps out on the landing. He steps right back in again. He pushes the door closed, leans against it, his face ashen. "They're all down there," he says.

"What? Who's down there?"

"Karl, Sam, Abdul, that Norwegian—"

"Fictor?!"

"Yes, everybody! Strasser, those goddamn Bulgarians, Sasha, Louis—"

"Yffonne?"

Why the hell did she ask about Yvonne? "I said everybody! They're just standing down there! Like they're waiting for something! But . . . for what?!" He can't seem to stop his goddamn voice from squeaking. He wants to remain cool and ironically detached, cynical even, because he knows it's expected of him, not least of all by himself, but he's still shaken by what he's seen down in the bar. Of course it might help if he had his pants on. At least he'd have some pockets to shove his hands into. For some reason, Ilsa is staring at his crotch, as though the real horror of it all were to be found there. Or maybe she's trying to see through to the silent crowd below. "It's, I dunno, like the place has sprung a goddamn leak or something!"

She crosses her hands to her shoulders, pinching her elbows in, hugging her breasts. She seems to have gone flat-footed, her feet splayed, her bottom, lost somewhat in the slatted shadows, drooping, her spine bent. "A leak?" she asks meaninglessly in her soft Scandinavian accent. She looks like a swimmer out of water in chilled air. Richard, slumping against the far door, stares at her as though at a total stranger. Or perhaps a mirror. He seems older somehow, tired, his chest sunken and belly out, legs bowed, his genitals shriveled up between them like dried fruit. It is not a beautiful sight. Of course Richard is not a beautiful man. He is short and bad-tempered and rather smashed up. Victor calls him riffraff. He says Richard makes him feel greasy. And it is true, there is something common about him. Around Victor she always feels crisp and white, but around Richard like a sweating pig. So how did she get mixed up with him, in the first place? Well, she was lonely, she had nothing, not even hope, and he seemed so happy when she took hold of his penis. As Victor has often said, each of us has a destiny, for good or for evil, and her destiny was Richard. Now that destiny seems confirmed—or sealed—by all those people downstairs. "They are not waiting for anything," she says, as the realization comes to her. It is over.

Richard grunts in reply. He probably hasn't heard her. She feels a terrible sense of loss. He shuffles in his black socks over to the humidor. "Shit, even the fags are gone," he mutters gloomily. "Why'd you have to come to Casablanca anyway, goddamn it; there are other places . . ." The airport beacon, sliding by, picks up an expression of intense concentration on his haggard face. She knows he is trying to understand what cannot be understood, to resolve what has no resolution. Americans are like that. In Paris he was always wondering how it was they kept getting from one place to another so quickly. "It's like everything is all speeded up," he would gasp, reaching deliriously between her legs as her apartment welled up around them. Now he is probably wondering why there seems to be no place to go and why time suddenly is just about all they have. He is an innocent man, after all; this is probably his first affair.

"I would not haff come if I haff known . . ." She releases her shoulders, picks up her ruffled blouse (the buttons are gone), pulls it on like a wrap. As the beacon wheels by, the room seems to expand with light as though it were breathing. "Do you see my skirt? It was here, but—is it getting dark or something?"

"I mean, of all the gin joints in all the towns in all the—!" He pauses, looks up. "What did you say?"

"I said, is it—?"

"Yeah, I know . . ."

They gaze about uneasily. "It seems like effry time that light goes past . . ."

"Yeah . . ." He stares at her, slumped there at the foot of the couch, working her garter belt like rosary beads, looking like somebody had just pulled her plug. "The world will always welcome lovers," the music is suggesting, not so much in mockery as in sorrow. He's thinking of all those people downstairs, so hushed, so motionless: it's almost how he feels inside. Like something dying. Or something dead revealed. Oh shit. Has this happened before? Ilsa seems almost wraithlike in the pale staticky light, as though she were wearing her own ghost on her skin. And which is it he's been in love with? he wonders. He sees she is trembling, and a tear slides down the side of her nose, or seems to, it's hard to tell. He feels like he's going blind. "Listen. Maybe if we started over . . ."

"I'm too tired, Richard . . ."

"No, I mean, go back to where you came in, see—the letters of transit and all that. Maybe we made some kinda mistake, I dunno, like when I put my hands on your jugs or something, and if—"

"A mistake? You think putting your hands on my yugs was a mistake—?"

"Don't get offended, sweetheart. I only meant—"

"Maybe my bringing my yugs *here* tonight was a mistake! Maybe my not shooting the *trigger* was a mistake!"

"Come on, don't get your tail in an uproar, goddamn it! I'm just trying to—"

"Oh, what a fool I was to fall . . . to fall . . ."

"Jesus, Ilsa, are you crying . . . ? Ilsa . . . ?" He sighs irritably.

He is never going to understand women. Her head is bowed as though in resignation: one has seen her like this often when Laszlo is near. She seems to be staring at the empty buttonholes in her blouse. Maybe she's stupider than he thought. When the dimming light swings past, tears glint in the corners of her eyes, little points of light in the gathering shadows on her face. "Hey, dry up, kid! All I want you to do is go over there by the curtains where you were when I—"

"Can I tell you a . . . story, Richard?"

"Not *now*, Ilsa! Christ! The light's almost gone and—"

"Anyway, it wouldn't work."

"What?"

"Trying to do it all again. It wouldn't work. It wouldn't be the same. I won't even haff my girdle on."

"That doesn't matter. Who's gonna know? Come on, we can at least—"

"No, Richard. It is impossible. You are different, I am different. You haff cold cream on your penis—"

"But—!"

"My makeup is gone, there are stains on the carpet. And I would need the pistol—how could we effer find it in the dark? No, it's useless, Richard. Belief me. Time goes by."

"But maybe that's just it . . ."

"Or what about your tsigarette? Eh? Can you imagine going through that without your tsigarette? Richard? I am laughing! Where are you, Richard . . . ?"

"Take it easy, I'm over here. By the balcony. Just lemme think."

"Efen the airport light has stopped."

"Yeah. I can't see a fucking thing out there."

"Well, you always said you wanted a wow finish . . . Maybe . . ."

"What?"

"What?"

"What did you say?"

"I said, maybe this is . . . you know, what we always wanted . . . Like a dream come true . . ."

"Speak up, kid. It's getting hard to hear you."

"I said, *when we are fokking*—"

"Nah, that won't do any good, sweetheart, I know that now. We gotta get back into the goddamn world somehow. If we don't we'll regret it. Maybe not today—"

"What? We'll forget it?"

"No, I said—"

"What?"

"Never mind."

"Forget what, Richard?"

"I said I think I shoulda gone fishing with Sam when I had the chance."

"I can't seem to hear you . . ."

"No, wait a minute! Maybe you're right! Maybe going back isn't the right idea . . ."

"Richard . . . ?"

"Instead, maybe we gotta think ahead . . ."

"Richard, I am afraid . . ."

"Yeah, like you could sit there on the couch, see, we've been fucking, that's all right, who cares, now we're having some champagne—"

"I think I am *already* forgetting . . ."

"And you can tell me that story you've been wanting to tell—are you listening? A good story, that may do it—anything that *moves!* And meanwhile, lemme think, I'll, let's see, I'll sit

down—no, I'll sort of lean here in the doorway and—*oof!*—
shit! I think they moved it!"

"Richard. . . ?"

"Who the hell rearranged the—*ungh!*—goddamn geography?"

"Richard, it's a crazy world . . ."

"Ah, here! this feels like it. Something like it. Now what
was I—? Right! You're telling a story, so, uh, I'll say . . ."

"But wherever you are . . . "

"*And then*—? Yeah, that's good. It's almost like I'm remembering this. You've stopped, see, but I want you to go on, I want
you to keep spilling what's on your mind, I'm filling in all the
blanks . . ."

". . . whatever happens . . ."

"So I say: *And then*—? C'mon, kid, can you hear me? Remember all those people downstairs! They're depending on us! Just
think it: if you think it, you'll do it! *And then*—?"

". . . I want you to know . . ."

"*And then* . . . ? Oh shit, Ilsa . . . ? Where are you? And then . . . ?"

". . . I luff you . . ."

"And then . . . ? Ilsa . . . ? And *then* . . . ?"

AESOP'S FOREST

(1986)

1

Deep in the gloom of the forest, the old lion lies dying in his cave. His ancient hide drapes the royal bones like a worn blanket, rheum clots his warm nose, his eyes are dimmed with cataracts. Yet, even in such decline, the familiar hungers stir in him still, rippling in tremors across his body from time to time like mice scurrying under a tattered carpet, his appetite for power outlasting his power to move, his need for raw flesh biting deeper than his decaying teeth. "I would be king!" he rumbles wheezily, his roar muddied with catarrh.

"Eh? Eh?" asks the fox insolently from the mouth of the cave.

"Damn your eyes. Bring me meat."

He does not trust the fox, of course, but on the other hand he has never trusted anyone, and the fox at least is useful. It is a wise policy, he knows, to keep potential enemies where you can either watch them or eat them. Unfortunately, that now means keeping them pretty close (even now, though the mouth of the cave seems empty of his scrawny silhouette, he cannot be sure the devil's gone) and so, fearing seditious alliances just beyond the reach of his shriveling senses, he has reduced his court to one, this fox, whose very notoriety for wiliness has isolated the wretch from any serious contenders for his power. The fox, a likely victim of any new regime, serves him because it is in the fox's own best interest to do so, though such bitter truths— and his helpless reliance on them—sadden the old lion. He has roared against them all his life, knowing that some truths are just not worth having, and now they have returned to haunt him, as though the instinct for survival were itself the ultimate disgrace. A sigh rips through him like the windy echo of some half-remembered rage: his hatred of duplicity.

There was a time when such treacherous lickspits, leading him to trapped prey, would have served him as prior savories: dispassionately he would have slit their bellies with his fierce claws, nuzzled in the hot wound as though to caress them with their own culpability, and, staring resolutely into their craven eyes already glazing over, his cool majestic gaze the last thing on this earth their fading sight would see, would have eaten their still-pulsing hearts, just appetizers for the feast to follow, juicy morals for the hunchback's fables. He who plots against another, the fabler would say then, plots his own destruction, and if this was a truth the world felt it could depend upon, it was a truth founded upon his own powerful claws and sharp white teeth, his incorruptible detachment. It is this—his sovereign independence, his lonely freedom—that he now misses most. As must all. For if he was once the source of all their truths, now, crippled, sinking into dry rot, reduced to begging from a thieving liar, he still is: it is truth itself that is changing. Yes, yes, he thinks, we take *everything* with us when we go.

"Who, *what*—?!" Ah. That dumb stag. Vainglory in the flesh. The more or less succulent flesh. The old king, tired eyes asquint, lies low, settling his jowls behind his paws. He's seen this one before, smelled him before. That funk: the poor fool must still have his stripes, and yet here he is, serving himself up again, will wonders never cease. "I tell you, when he caught hold of your ear last time," he hears the fox whispering, nudging the stag forward, "it was to give you his last advice before he died." Such big eyes he has: eyes for looking where forbidden . . . "It is you he wants as our next king: your horns scare the snakes, he told me so!" Inwardly, waiting patiently, the old lion grins. Have to admire the sly bastard: in his way, he's an artist. "You see? He's smiling! He's pleased you're here! Now lean forward and tell him that you accept your great responsibilities!"

2

Death is everywhere in Aesop's dark forest. Asses are drowning under sodden loads, vixens are being torn to pieces by maddened dogs, swans sacrificed for the sake of their songs. Cats are eating cocks. Kites frogs. "What an unexpected treat has come our way!" they cry, descending. All have butcher's work to do. Eagles and vixens devour each other's young, newborn apes are murdered by their mothers, hens by serpents they themselves have hatched. Partridges, goats, doves betray their own to preying men, nannies are butchered to doctor asses. At the request of horses, boars are slaughtered: yet happiness is elusive. Snakes are driven to suicide by the stinging of wasps, elephants by gnats in their ears, hares by their own weariness, as though it were time's way of solving difficult problems. "The moral is

that it is too late to be sorry after you have let things go wrong,"
the fabler explains, but the fact is it is always too late. Lambs
are being devoured by wolves, mice by weasels, fawns by bears,
nightingales by hawks, and all by the patient intransigent vul-
tures. Even lions. The news of the old despot's decline, spread
by the fox, stirs ambition in some (a lot of emptyheaded people rejoice over the wrong things, needless to say), but provokes
skepticism in most: with that fox things are not always what
they seem, most here in the forest know that all too well, having learned from painful experience, once bitten and all that,
no, seeing is believing. Not too close, though: there are a lot of
bones around the cave mouth, and tracks leading up but none
leading away.

3

The fabler watches the watchers watch. It is comforting to the
wretched, he knows, to see others worse off than themselves.
The victor vanquished, the mighty fallen—it's a kind of nar-
cotic, this pageant, numbing for the cowardly their common
wound of mortality. The fabler envies them this easy consolation. In him, something more fundamental is dying with
the dying lion, and just when he needs it most, his own death
approaching inexorably and apace. Not so much the courage, no,
for though his is not so lofty perhaps, being that bitter grit of the
misfit, the freak, the taunted cripple, it is no less mettlesome.
Not the fabled power either, far from it, he has often reveled in
forcing humiliating compromise upon the old tyrant, throwing
him into bad company, jamming thorns in his paws and enfee-
bling love in his heart, snatching him up in nets and cages to

spoil his appetite with a moral lesson or two, chiding him with avarice and brutality. Sour grapes? Perhaps, especially now at life's and wit's end when he could use a little last-minute clout, but political power as such has never held the fabler's fancy. Hasn't he turned his crooked back on it all his life, abandoning the court life again and again for his dark uncivil forest? Yes, freedom has been his one desire, freedom and—and this is what the old lion's death means to him, this is what he fears to lose, even as he's losing it—his ruthless solitude.

As though to dramatize his sense of loss, the fox, that cartload of mischief, emerges from the cave mouth now, swaggering presumptuously, his red tail on high, a bloody heart between his jaws. Not the lion's heart, of course—a consumptive rumble from the cave behind the charlatan attests irritably to that—yet it might as well be. That lion's kingly roar once caused havoc at three hundred miles, women miscarried, men's teeth fell out; now it flutters thinly from the cave mouth like wisps of dirty fleece. In the end, crushed by fortune, even the strongest become the playthings of cowards: this is the message of the dripping heart in the fox's grinning jaws. And it enrages him. Not the message, but the grin. It is his, the fabler's own.

4

There is a grisly tension building in the forest, he can feel it as he stalks the cave mouth, the stag's heart in his jowls like a gag, bitter foretaste of the impending disaster. Well, foretasted, forearmed, he reminds himself with a giddiness that brings a grimace to his clamped jaws—for how *does* one arm himself against the sort of nightmare about to descend here? Eyes blink and glitter behind tree trunks, clumps of grass, leaves, heavy stones: in them he sees avarice, panic, vanity, distrust, lust for glory and for flesh, hatred, hope, all the fabled terrors and appetites of the mortal condition, drawn together here now for one last demented frolic. The louring forest is literally atwinkle with that madness that attends despair.

Two eyes in particular absorb his gaze: the dark squinty lopsided orbs of the little brown humpback, come to hurl himself like a clown into the final horror—for isn't it the cripple who always wants to lead off the dance? The grotesque grotesqued. That loathsome monscrosity now huddles swarthily behind a pale boulder, hugging it as if afraid it might fly away from him, his knee-knobs stuck out like a locust's. A turnip with teeth, he's been fairly called, a misshapen pisspot. His hump rises behind his flapping ears like a second head, but one stripped of its senses as though struck mute and blind with terror. Or wisdom, same thing. What that snubnosed bandylegged piece of human garbage has never appreciated is how much they're two of a kind, and how much the fraud owes him for his bloated reputation. The fox has been the butt of too many horseshit anecdotes not to have grasped a moral the fabler seems to have missed: that we ridicule in others what we most despise in ourselves.

The humpback lets go the boulder now and hops, toadlike, behind a stunted laurel. Headed this way, it seems. Can't leave well enough alone. Or ill enough. Perhaps he dreams still of some last-minute escape from the calamity that awaits him, awaits them all in this airless stinkhole of a so-called forest. Well, if he hopes for help from the sorehead behind him, still grumbling in his tubercular senility about the missing heart

("You can stop looking, he didn't have one," he'd told the moth-eaten old geezer, talking with his mouth full, "anybody who'd come twice into a lion's den and within reach of his paws has to be ninety percent asshole, and that's what you just ate . . ."), then the fool's in for a bitter experience.

5

As the fabler advances through the penumbral forest, creeping, bounding, stumbling over roots, crouching under bushes, zigging and zagging in the general direction of the lion's den, he stirs a wide commotion. There are scurryings, flutterings, rustlings all around. Twigs pop, pebbles scatter, leaves and feathers float on the air like the tatters of muffled rumors, stifled panic, as though the forest were beset on all sides—and from within as well—by strange and unexpected dangers. Wild rumors. Hopes. Mad ambitions.

Much of this the fabler reads in all the shit he squats and tumbles in: the hard nuggets of avidity and pride, puddled funk, noisome pretense, the frantic scatter of droppings unloosed on the run in uncertainty and confusion—that eloquent text of the forest floor. He knows it well, he's had his nose in it since the day he was born. "Has he lost something?" people would ask. "He's like a hog rooting in mud." He was pretending to be studying the ground, of course, in order to pretend he could straighten up if he wanted to, an impostor twice over. But out of adversity, wisdom. Once a famous Hellenic philosopher, his master in the dark days of his enslaved youth, had asked him why it was, when we shat, we so often turned around to examine our own turds, and he'd told that great sage the story of the king's loose-living son who one day, purging his belly, passed his own wits, inducing a like fear in all men since. "But you don't have to worry, sire," he'd added, "you've no wit to shit." Well, cost him a beating, but it was worth it, even if it was all a lie. For the real reason we look back of course is to gaze for a moment in awe and wonder at what we've made—it's the closest we ever come to being at one with the gods.

Now what he reads in this analecta of turds is rampant disharmony and anxiety: it's almost suffocating. Boundaries are breaking down: eagles are shitting with serpents, monkeys with dolphins, kites with horses, fleas with crayfish, it's as though there were some mad violent effort here to link the unlinkable, cross impossible abysses. And there's some dejecta he's not sure he even recognizes. That foul mound could be the movement of a hippogriff, for example, this slime that of a basilisk or a harpy. His own bowels, convulsed by all this ripe disorder, fill suddenly with a plunging weight, as though heart, hump, and all might have just descended there: he squats hastily, breeches down (well, Zeus sent Modesty in through the asshole, so may she exit there as well), to leave his own urgent message on the forest floor. Ah! yes! a man must put his hand to his wealth and use it, example is—grunt!—better than precept. Just so . . . But quality, not quantity. Inconsistency is harmful in everything, though no forethought, of course, can prevail against destiny. Oof! Easy. Accomplishments are not judged by speed but by completeness. With what measure you mete shall it be measured to you again, and so on. That's better. He wipes himself with his soiled breeches, leaves them behind. Doesn't need them here anyway. When in Delphi, as they say . . .

6

Not all here in Aesop's troubled forest are pleased, of course, to have their miserable excrement read so explicitly. It makes many of them feel vulnerable and exposed, especially at a time when all the comforting old covenants are dissolving, and no one knows for certain who they are anymore, or who they're supposed to fuck or eat. Can one not even take a homely shit without worrying about the consequences, they ask, are there no limits? But of course that's just the point, there *are* no limits any longer, that's the message of the old king's desperate condition, this pointy-headed freak's intrusion here, his frantic bare-ass bob through these dark brambly thickets at the core. Though he talks wolfy enough at times, he rarely comes this deep, skirting the edges mostly where the shepherds keep their sheep, plummeting in here only when lust or terror overtake him. What beast here wouldn't raise its tail for the hunchback, painful as the experience can be, if that's all it would take to resume the old peaceful carnage? But, alas, it's plain to see it's not rut that's brought the fabler back—that heavy wattle he's dragging through the pine needles and dead leaves between his crooked shanks is, by itself in its gross wilt, cause enough for panic here.

So it is that birds screech, beetles scurry, moles burrow in blind desperation, as Aesop makes his way toward the lion's den. Stupidity, fear, deceit, carnality, treason break out in the forest like scabies. There is the sharpening of tusks, the popping of toads, breath-sucking, the casting of long shadows. Suicidal hares and frogs hurl themselves out of their element, elephants eat their own testicles, worms blind themselves so as not to see the approaching catastrophe. As Aesop reaches the cave mouth, the fox slinks aside, lips curled back, baring his teeth above the stag's heart cradled bloodily in his paws. He snarls. Clouds of fleas, gnats, lice, mosquitos explode from foul-smelling holes in the forest floor like a sudden pestilence. Wells clog with bewildered beasts fallen they know not where. Storms rumble and winds whistle. Flames lap at an eagle's nest. And from high in the sky, a frightened humpbacked tortoise falls.

7

The fox lies stretched out across the cave mouth, as though to define certain boundaries, or invent them, gnawing, ears perked, at the stag's heart. Inside, the fabler squats in the dirt, his hump resting against the cavewall, gazing morosely at the dying lion, a much sorrier sight than he'd anticipated. "It stinks in here," he says. The lion snorts sourly, cocks one rheumy eye above his paw. "Nothing's so perfect," he grumbles, "that it's not subject to some pisant's criticism." In the old days he'd have simply stepped on him, popped the runt like a blister. Now he's not even sure he sees him. "Misfortune stinks, crookback. Dying stinks. If you don't like it, why do you wallow in it?"

"That's not why I'm here." He stares out past the fox at the dusky forest, which seems to have brightened slightly, as seen from within this dreary cave. An illusion, like hope itself. It's darkening by the second out there. "How is it you've taken up with this miserable blot on creation?"

"Expediency."

"I expected more from you."

"Our expectations are often deceived."

He accepts this continuous mockery though it pains him. Somewhere just below the hump, in fact. What is he doing here in this shithole, taking this kind of abuse? And from an old friend once honored above all others—even his shabby new alliance with the fox is a kind of taunt, a way of rubbing the fabler's nose in his most craven cynicism, just when he needed something nobler than that. Courage, in a word. Proud example. "I've been condemned."

The fox seems to snicker at this. The lion too would appear to have a grin on his face. The floor of the cave is rough and damp, reassuring in its rude discomfort, but somewhere water is dripping, echoing cavernously as though there might be a leak in the remote recesses of his own skull. He shudders as if to shake himself out of here, but he knows he can never leave again. They'll have to come and kill him in this place. Mangy and decrepit as it's become. Sometimes in the past he has managed to stay away from his forest for days on end, imagining himself a man like any other, yet even then these creatures had a way of haunting his consciousness, lingering just beneath it like stars behind the light of the sun, visible only from the bottom of a well. That well he's always dumping them down as a cushion against his own clumsiness. His own attraction to abysses. "Which flap," the lion rumbles wheezily, "were you wagging this time?"

He shrugs his hump. "Sin against Apollo." This time the fox does snicker, standing to scratch a flea behind his ear, or pretending to. "Go have a fit and tumble in a hole," the vicious schemer once said, all too prophetically. His fate now, by decree, he the fabler become his own goat. "I told them the truth, they called it sacrilege."

"Same old story," sighs the lion.

"Same old story."

"Natures never change. You're a meddlesome foul-mouthed stiff-necked exhibitionist. You remind me of that story of yours about the wild ass and the tame ass."

"Well, but the real moral of that one was——"

"The real moral was they were *both* asses, just the same. What did you think you'd gain by taunting fools?"

"I don't know. A laugh or two?" What does he have left, if not the truth? It has shaped, shaped by his misshapen body, his entire life. One thing about being a monster, it puts you in touch with the cosmos, biggest humpback of all. "I wanted to make the truth so transparent even these pigheaded provincials could see it, that's all." He liked to think of it as a kind of remembering, as though all men were animals in some way, or had been.

"Yes, and turtles want to fly, too," the old king rumbles. "There's only one truth, my friend. If you've forgotten what it is, come a little closer and let me give you a few pointed reminders." A mere reflex. The old fellow hasn't eaten the garbage he's lying in. He laps his jowls with a tongue so dry it sounds like the spreading of sand on stone.

Anyway, it's . . . "Impossible. There's a barrier . . ." At least there was . . . Has it somehow been breached?

"If there's a moral to be had, fabler, it can be done . . ."

He'd always thought of that distance between them as ontological and absolute, but now—he stirs uncomfortably. He's rarely come this deep before. The fox seems to have let one, his own commentary on the truth no doubt. He bats the air irritably, his hump scraping the wall behind: "Filthy bastard!"

"He does that from time to time just to let me know he's still

here," the lion grumbles drowsily. "You get used to it. Familiar-
ity, as they say . . ."

Not they. He. The rich man and the tanner. Or better yet: the
fox and the lion, almost forgot that one. Yet now, these words,
too: only an echo . . . He realizes he hasn't told many fables
on the evanescence of truth, brain-rot as the universal achievement. The old lion snorts ruefully. He seems to be drifting off.
The hunchback trembles. They'll be here soon. He got away
from them once, but they'll find him. Even from inside the cave,
he can hear the turbulence out at the edge. He squeezes shut
his eyes. Sometimes it feels almost like a dream. As though he
might still be back on Samos, living with that fatheaded philosopher and his lascivious slave-fucking wife, the one who liked to
say that even her arse had eyes. Any minute, he thinks, I might
wake up to a beating or a bath . . .

8

The tortoise, tumbling through the air, wags his arms frantically. If he just works at this hard enough, he knows, he can do
it, persistence has paid off before, he's famous for it. In order to
try to free his mind from extraneous matters, such as the rising
panic which is threatening to freeze him up entirely and stop
his wings, as they should perhaps now be called, from func-
tioning at all, he tries to concentrate on the splendid view he
has from up here of the forest, a view few of its inhabitants
have been privileged to enjoy, and one he himself will probably
forego in the future, even if he does manage to get the hang of
this flying thing on this one occasion. Like he told Zeus, meaning no offense, though unfortunately that's how it was taken,

there's no place like home. If you don't get there too fast. But his effort to concentrate is frustrated somewhat by the way the forest keeps looping around him, appearing over his head one moment, beneath his tail the next: probably this has something to do with his flying problem.

Why did he want to get up here in the first place? A question he might well ponder, since the second place, rushing up at him like the moral to a foreshortened fable, is all but imponderable. He always tries to judge every situation from its outcome, not its beginning, though each, as he knows, flapping wildly, contains the other, ambition being both goal and goad. But what *was* that ambition? Was it aesthetic? Philosophical? The pursuit of some sort of absolute worldview (already slipping away from him, he notes, as the forest loops by again, losing now in structural clarity what it is rapidly gaining in detail)? A moral imperative? The spirit of rivalry? A rebellion against boundaries? The desire for travel? Who knows? Why anything? Why is the pig's belly bare or the magpie bald? Why does the crab have its eyes behind? Why does the lizard nod its head or the dying swan sing? Who gives a bloody shit? Should *he* be singing? Why are turtles dumb? Why are their heads flat and their shells hard? But not hard enough? Why has that goddamn eagle left him up here—flap! flap! flap!—*all alone?*

9

When Aesop opens his eyes, he finds himself lying under a tree in a green, peaceful field, where all kinds of flowers bloom amid the green grass and where a little stream wanders among the neighboring trees. The most savage thing in sight is a grazing cow. A gentle zephyr blows and the leaves of the trees around about are stirred and exhale a sweet and soothing breath: he draws in a deep lungful, as a great relief sweeps over him. What a terrible dream I was having, he thinks. Those shits were going to kill me! He still feels vaguely troubled (it seemed so real!), but the stream is whispering, the cicadas are humming from the branches, the song of birds of many kinds and many haunts can be heard, the nightingale prolongs her plaintive song, the branches murmur musically in a sympathetic refrain, on the slenderest branch of a pine tree the stirring of the breeze mocks the blackbird's call, and mingling with it all in harmony, Echo, the mother of mimesis, utters her answering cries, all of it resolving into a kind of rhythmic tinkle, reassuring in its simplicity like the drip of rainwater after a shower. Better a servant in safety, he reminds himself, than a master in danger, though at first this comes out, better a savory never than born a masker in a manger. Which doesn't make much sense. Is it some kind of oracle? And why is that cow standing there with her teats in the fire and plucked crows in her antlers with meat in their beaks? The trees' breath, he now notices, is not as sweet as he'd thought at first, and what the stream is whispering (how is it he fell asleep out here in this open field with his breeches off?) seems to be some suggestion about staying in line or alive, or playing the—

"What? *What*—?!" He starts up in alarm, opens his eyes a second time. Ah, it is the fox, that treacherous foulmouth, whispering something in his ear about flaying the lion and wearing his hide as a disguise. "Don't wait until danger is at hand!" He turns his head away. He must have dozed off. But it seemed so *real*! "Fuck these useless shows of strength, humpback! Remember the fable of the hunting dog! Use your wits!"

Perhaps a *third* time, he thinks, straining to pop his eyes wider open. He uses his fingers to press his lids apart. But they *are* apart. Is he dreaming that he's pressing his fingers to his lids? Alas . . . "It's been tried," he mumbles, trying his voice out.

"Only by asses. The morals of those stories are stay out of the wind and keep your mouth shut."

Would it work? Not likely. He can already hear his pursuers. "We were told to get the one in the lionskin," they'd be saying. "Why am I even listening to a doublecrossing liar like you?"

"Because we understand each other. I wouldn't even be here without you, I know that, even if the others don't. You think I'd want to shit you now? Anyway, it's impossible. Think about it."

"He'd betray himself if he could figure out how to do it and profit by it at the same time," the lion growls from inside his paws. "Get back to your post, stinkbreath, before I decide to tear that red tail off at the root and sweep out this stinking boghouse with it!" He watches the miserable beggar slink, smirking no doubt (can't see a damned thing), back to the cave mouth. The hunchback stands to piss against the wall, at least that's what it sounds like. "And don't be fooled, fabler. Wit will *not* get the better of strength. Ever. That's just a fairytale for weaklings. Helps them die easier."

"But I can't outrun them and I can't eat them," the dwarf whines from the other side of his hump as he splashes against the wall. "What am I going to *do?*"

"What you can. There's an inscription here . . ." The old lion knows, in the end, he is going to have to abide by it himself. If puffed-up toads and flying turtles are ridiculous, humble lions are worse. He shakes his mane. If he could just lift his jaws up off the floor. ". . . At the oracle . . ."

"I've seen it." The hunchback is wiping that monstrous engine of his on his shirt. "But I don't know who I am and I don't know where to start."

"You know more than you know," the lion rumbles solemnly, and the fox snarls: "There he is!"

"What—?! *Who?*" squeaks the fabler, shrinking back against the wall he's just fouled.

"It's for me," says the lion, rearing his head up at last. It sways a bit like an old drunk's, but he holds it up there. This is not going to be easy, he thinks. But had he ever supposed it would be? "My herald, as you might say. My advice to you is to take a long walk."

"But—!"

"*GET OUT!*" he roars, and the hunchback, in panic, goes lurching out on all fours, nipped mischievously in the tail by the fox as he scrambles past. "Now come here, slyboots, I want to show you something. We're going to let you play the hero."

10

A plaintive ascendant whine silences the unruly forest. Flappings, snortings, rustlings, scurryings cease. The black-hooded magpie, death's acknowledged messenger, lowers his gaping beak and from his perch above the cave mouth shrieks: "*The king is dying! The king is dying!* Scrawk! *Long live the king!*" A kind of communal gasp sweeps through the forest like a sudden brief gust of wind, then dies away. The magpie hacks raucously as though trying to spit. "*Miserable morsels—harck! tweet!—mortals who, like leaves, at one moment—whawk!— flame with life and at another weakly—*prreet! c*aw!—perish* *down the drain of Eternity in the mighty whirl of dust, the hour of*—wheep!—*equal portions has ARRIVED!"* A furtive scrabbling and fluttering ripples now through the forest like gathering applause, from the outside in, rushing toward the center as though beaters were assaulting the periphery. Though only the magpie is visible (even the fox has disappeared), the area around the cave mouth seems suddenly congested, aquiver with terror and anticipation. And appetite. *"Cree! Cree! Creatures of a day, be quiet and have patience, not even the gods fright*—purrr-wheet!—*fight against the child within us! We go our*—WARRCKK!—*ways in the same honor already for*—caw! caw!—*forfeit!"* The magpie's long bright tail drops like a falling axe. Is it over? Is the tyrant already dead? Heads peek out from behind foliage. Insects hover nervously. Monkeys swing closer, swing back again. A snake uncoils from a limb. A boar in the underbrush snorts and paws the ground. A crab sallies forth, eyes to the rear. *"Either death is a state of nothingness and utter*—kwok!—*or better never to have been born!"* the oracular magpie cries, and parrots, cats, crickets and hermaphroditic hyenas scream their assent. The entire twilit forest is alive with beasts surging furtively toward the dying lion's cave. *"Must not all things be swallowed up in*—shreek!—*a single night?* Just SO! Crrrr-*AWKK!"* As though in fear of being left behind, the animals at this signal burst from their hiding places and rush, squealing and bawling, toward the cave mouth—but just as suddenly pull up short. The old king stands there in the fading light, muscles rippling, fiery mane blowing in the breeze, eyes feverish with fury. With fierce deliberation, he steps forward, his teeth bared. Has this been a trap? *"Only one!"* shrieks the magpie. Ah. But a lion . . .

11

We found the fabulist at last in the Temple of the Muses, clearly deranged, howling about "death in the forest" and "the revenge of dungbeetles," and bounding around arse-high with his nose to the stone floor like a toad looking for water. After having abused us earlier, while still in prison, with filthy tales about the rape of widows and children ("A man put it in me with a long sinewy red thing that ran in and out," he'd leered: had he been trying to seduce us with these simpering obscenities?) as well as racist slurs, insults against our fathers, and seditious threats to revenge himself upon us, even after he was dead, this grotesque little Egyptian, or Babylonian, was now, in one of our own temples, berating us with sacrilege, shrieking something truly offensive about "God with shit in his eye!" It was almost, we thought, as though he'd come here to our city *seeking* to die.

He was not easy to catch or, once caught, to subdue. As we chased him about the temple, wrestling with him, losing him, catching him again, he kept making brutish noises, now squawking, now roaring, now barking or bleating or braying, as though he were all these beasts at once, or thought himself to be, and at times we did feel somewhat like Menelaus grappling with the inconstant and malodorous Proteus. His stunted limbs were too rubbery to hold, his pot too sleek—finally we caught him by the ears (his Achilles' heel, as it were) and, twisting them, extracted from him a more human howl.

As we dragged him toward his site of execution, his madness took on a subtler, yet no less bizarre form. He grew suddenly serene, almost flaccid in our many-handed grip, and commenced to lecture us on the evils we were presumably

bringing upon ourselves with this action. "Not much time will
be gained, O Delphians," he proclaimed shrilly, as his pointed
head bounced along on the uneven ground, "in return for the
evil name which you will get from the detractors of the city,
who will say that you killed Aesop, a wise man; for it will be
said of me, that I never did any wrong, never gave any ill advice
to any man; but that I labored all my life long to excite to virtue
those who frequented me." Such pomposities, emerging reedily
from that twisted liver-lipped mouth with its scattered teeth,
under the squashed-up nose and squinty eyes, neither of which
ever seemed to be looking at the same thing at the same time,
struck us as so ludicrous we were all driven to fits of convulsive
laughter, and nearly lost our grip on him again. "Fancy such a
warty little thing as you making such a big noise!" we hooted.

"I prophesy to you who are my murderers, that immediately
after my departure punishment far heavier than that you have
inflicted on me will surely await you!" he squealed then, and we
reminded him, laughing, that braggarts are easily silenced, as
he was about to discover. "People who brag to those who know
them must expect to be laughed at, gypsie, evil tricks don't fool
honest men! Such playacting has cost many a man his life, you
will not be the first or last to perish of it!" We hauled the droll
little monster up to the edge of the cliff and prepared to heave
him over. Some of us had his arms, some his horny feet. "Destiny is not to be interfered with, melonhead—if you had any
real wisdom you'd know that! A man should courageously face
whatever is going to happen to him and not try to be clever, for
he will—ha ha!—not escape it!"

"Wait!" he begged, gigantic tears rolling down the bumps of
his temples and off his earflaps. He seemed prepared to recant at

last and, though it wouldn't save his life, right his wrongs against us before he died. We set him on his bandy legs and stepped back, blocking any possible escape. He cocked his head impudently to one side. "Let me tell you a story," he said. Ye gods, the little freak was incorrigible. It has been wisely observed, natures remain just as they first appear. When you do a bad man a service, some sage has said, all you can hope for is that he will not add injury to ingratitude, but even this hope was to prove in vain. "There was this old farmer," he piped, "who had never seen the city and decided to hitch up the donkeys and go see it before he died. But a storm came up and they got lost among the cliffs. 'Oh God, what have I done to die like this,' he wept (and here *he* wept mockingly), in the company of these miserable jackasses?' " We rushed at him, enraged at such impiety, but he stopped us again with a wild bewitching screech, lurching forward as though stabbed from behind, and we fell back, momentarily startled. "A man once fell in love with his own daughter," he wailed as though in great pain, rolling his lopsided eyes, and pointing at all of us— what?! what was he saying? "So he shipped his old lady off to the country and forced himself on his daughter. She said, as I say to you, men of Delphi: 'This is an unholy thing you are doing! I would rather have submitted to a hundred good men than be fucked by you!' " We flung ourselves at his loathsome obscenity, but before we could reach him, he hurled himself, cackling derisively, off the cliff, flapping his stunted little arms as though the fool thought he might fall up instead of down.

12

He has just, with what dignity remains, his knees weak and threatening to buckle, stepped forth from the cave mouth to confront his erstwhile citizenry, when something whistles past his ear and explodes—*SPLAT!*—beside him, startling him just enough to tip him over. What an irony, he muses, shrugging tortoise shell out of his ear, nearly got him before he could even get started. As it is, his jaw is back on the ground again, his paws trapped under his belly. His rear legs seemed to have held, but he is not sure what overall impression this position makes. Perhaps they will think he is crouching, preparing to spring. More likely not.

Though he cannot see them, they are all out there, he knows, all the rejected, the trod-upon, the bitten and the stung, the ridiculed, the overladen, all of God's spittle, lusting now for this compensatory kill. The great equalizer that makes their own poor lives and deaths less odious. Let them come. He will have one last glorious fray, one final sinking of tooth and claw into palpating flesh and gut, a great screaming music of rage and terror, before he dies. If he can just get his feet under him again. How was it he used to do that? He can feel his rump begin to sway, can hear them start to shift and mumble in the clearing down below. His aide-de-camp has slipped out of sight, of course. He has instructed the fox on how to kill him quickly when the time comes, when he's too weak to fight on. He doesn't want to die slowly, or ignobly. Or seem to. He has appealed to the fox's own ambition: let the opposition cut itself up, and then, when he gets the nod, move in as the decisive and heroic liberator. The wily bastard actually seemed moved: perhaps there's hope for him yet.

The sullen hesitant hush is shattered suddenly by another long shrieking whine from the intransigent magpie. *"They who hesitate*—SCRAWKK!—*flourish only for an omen*—hrreet!—*MOMENT!"*

And, just as his rump tips and smacks the ground, they are on him: wolves, boars, apes, moles, toads, dancing camels, plucked daws, serpents, spiders, snails, incestuous cocks and shamming cats, hares, asses, bats, bears, swarms of tongueless gnats, fleas, flies and murderous wasps, bears, beavers, doves, martins, lice and dungbeetles, mice and weasels, owls, crabs, and goats, hedgehogs and ticks, kites, frogs, peacocks and locusts, all the fabled denizens of the forest, all intent on electing him into the great democracy of the dead. A boar wounds him with a blow from its flashing tusks as he sprawls there, paws high, a bull gores him in the belly, a mosquito stings his nose, a cowardly ass kicks him in the forehead.

But even as they convene upon his body, something stirs in the enfeebled lion, something like joy or pride or even love. The rage of. His battered head rears and roars, his pierced muscles flex, his blunted teeth and claws find flesh to rend, bones to crush. The air is thick suddenly with blood and feathers and smashed carapaces, shrieks and howls, mighty thrashings about. He even, for a splendid moment, feels young again, that renowned warrior of old, king of the beasts. He no longer knows which animals he's embracing in this final exaltation—one eye is gone, the other clouded, an ear is clogged with bees, his hide's in tatters—but it doesn't matter. It is life itself he is clutching bloodily to his breast in this, his last delicious moment on earth, and it's the most fun he's had since he sneezed a cat.

But then, through the flurry of beaks and antlers and the blood in his eye, he sees the fox skulking toward him, head ducked, an insolent smirk on his skinny face. "No, wait!" he roars. "*Not yet!*" But he should have known better, take pity on such a creature, you get what you deserve. And what he gets is, too soon, oh much too soon, the treacherous villain at his throat. "You fool!" he gasps, while he's still voice left. "I can't help it," snickers the miserable wretch, nuzzling in. "It's just my—hee hee!—nature . . ." With a final swipe of his paw (he is being invaded from below, he knows, a seeding of teeth in his plowed-up nether parts as though to found a city there, but it has ceased to matter), he slashes the fox open from heart to groin, then hugs him close, locking his jaws around his nape, their organs mingling like scrambled morals. "It's all shit any-way," he seems to hear the devil grunt as his spine snaps—one final treachery! He feels then as though he's falling, and he only wishes, hanging on as the light dies and the earth spins, that his friend the fabler were here to whisper in his ear, the one without the bees in it, one last word, not so much of wisdom, as of communion. Just so . . . What? What? "*SKWWAARRRK!*" replies the magpie, as the forest extinguishes itself around him.

CARTOON

(1987)

T he cartoon man drives his cartoon car into the cartoon
town and runs over a real man. The real man is not badly
hurt—the cartoon car is virtually weightless after all, it's hardly
any worse than getting a cut lip from licking an envelope—but
the real man feels that a wrong has nevertheless been done him,
so he goes in search of a policeman. There are no real police-
men around, so he takes his complaint to a cartoon policeman.
The cartoon policeman salutes him briskly and, almost without
turning around, darts off in the direction of the accident, but
the real man is disconcerted by the way the policeman hurries along about four inches above the pavement, taking five or
six airy steps for every one of his own and blowing his whistle
ceaselessly. It's as though they were walking side by side down
two different streets. The cartoon town, meanwhile, slides past
silently, more or less on its own.

At the scene of the accident, they find the cartoon man with
a real policeman. The cartoon car is resting on its roof, look-

ing ill and abused. "Is this the one?" demands the real policeman, pointing with his nightstick. The cartoon man jumps up
and down and makes high-pitched incriminating noises, the
car snorting and whimpering pathetically in the background.
When the cartoon policeman blows his whistle in protest, or
perhaps just out of habit, a huge cartoon dog, larger than the
cartoon car, bounds onto the scene and chases him off. "You'll
have to come with me," announces the real policeman severely,
collaring the real man, and he can hear the cartoon car snick-
ering wickedly. "There are procedural matters involved here!"

As though in enactment of this pronouncement, the huge
cartoon dog comes lumbering through again from the opposite direction, chased now by a real cat, the cat in turn chased
by a cartoon woman. The woman pulls up short upon spying
the real policeman, who has meanwhile shot the cat (this is
both probable and confounding), and, winking at the real man,
bares her breasts for the policeman. These breasts are nearly
as large as the woman herself, and they have nipples on them
that turn sequentially into pursed lips, dripping spigots, traffic
lights, beckoning fingers, then lit-up pinball bumpers. The real
policeman is not completely real, after all. He has cartoon eyes
that stretch out of their sockets like paired erections, locking
on the cartoon woman's breasts with their fanciful nipples. She
takes her breasts off and gives them to the real policeman, and
he creeps furtively away, clutching the gift closely like a fearful
secret, his eyes retracting deep into his skull as though to empty
it of its own realness, what's left of it.

"Thank you," says the real man. "You have probably saved
my life." He can hear the cartoon car sniggering and wheezing at this, but the cartoon woman simply shrugs and remarks

enigmatically: "Plenty more where those came from." She snuggles up to the huge cartoon dog, who has returned and is pawing curiously at the cadaver of the real cat. "I feel somehow," murmurs the dog, sniffing the cat's private parts, "a certain inexplicable anxiety." The cartoon car hoots and wheezes mockingly again, and the dog, annoyed, lifts its leg over it. There is a violent hissing and popping, and then the car is silent. The cartoon man is infuriated at this, squeaking and yipping and beating his fists on the cartoon dog and the cartoon woman. They ignore him, cuddling up once more, the dog panting heavily after exerting himself, both mentally and physically, the woman erotically touching the dog's huge floppy tongue with the tip of her own (she has a real mouth, the real man notices, and the touch of her tiny round tongue against the vast pink landscape of the dog's flat one for some reason makes him want to cry), so the cartoon man scurries over to beat on the real man. It is not so much painful as vaguely unnerving, as though he were being nagged to remember something he had managed to forget.

The cartoon woman drifts off with the cartoon dog ("When," the dog is musing, scratching philosophically behind his ear, "is a flea *not* a flea?"), and the cartoon man, his rage spent, walks over to pick up the dead cat. As the cartoon man walks away, he seems to grow, and when he returns, dragging the dead cat by its tail, he seems to shrink again. He gives the real man a huge cartoon knife, produced as if from nowhere, then dashes off, returning almost instantly with a cartoon table, tablecloth, napkins, plates and silverware, a candelabra, and two cartoon chairs: before these things can even be counted, they are already set in place. His voice makes shrill little speeded-up noises once more, which seem to suggest he wants the real man to cut the cat up for dinner. He zips away again, returning with cartoon salad, steak sauce, and cartoon wine, then streaks off to a cartoon bakery.

Who knows? thinks the real man, tucking in his napkin, all this may be in fulfillment of yet another local ordinance, so more out of respect than appetite, he prepares to cut up the dead cat. When he lays the cat out on the cartoon table, however, all the cartoon plates and silverware, condiments and candelabra leap off the table and run away shrieking, or else laughing, it's hard to tell, and though the table looks horizontal, the cat slides right off it. Oh well, the real man sighs to himself, dropping the knife disconsolately on the table as though paying the check, they can't say I didn't try. He goes over to the cartoon car and sets it on its wheels again and, after a puddle has formed beneath it, gets inside and starts up the motor. Or rather, the motor starts up by itself, choking and sputtering at first and making loud flatulent noises out its exhaust pipes, then clearing its throat and revving up, eventually humming along smoothly. The cartoon town meanwhile slides by as before.

When they reach the real town, or when the real town, the one where the real man lives, reaches them, the cartoon car doesn't seem to work anymore. The man finds he has to push his feet through the floor and walk it home, much to the apparent amusement of all the real or mostly real passersby. He is reminded of the time when, as a boy, he found himself looking up at his teacher, hovering over him with a humorless smile, wielding a wooden ruler (he thinks of her in retrospect as a cartoon teacher, but he could be mistaken about this—certainly the ruler was real), and accusing him, somewhat mysteriously, of "failing his interpolations." "What?" he'd asked, much to his immediate regret, a regret he strangely feels again now, as if he were suffering some kind of spontaneous reenactment, and it suddenly occurs to him, as he walks his cartoon car miserably down the middle of the street through all the roaring real ones, that, yes, the teacher was almost certainly real—but her accusation was a cartoon.

At home he shows his wife, lying listlessly on the sofa, the cartoon car, now no bigger than the palm of his hand, and tells her about his adventures. "It's like being the butt of a joke without a teller or something," he says, casting about for explanations, when, in reality, there probably are none. "I know," she replies with a certain weary bitterness. She lifts her skirts and shows him the cartoon man. "He's been there all day." The cartoon man smirks up at him over his shoulder, making exaggerated under-cranked thrusts with his tiny cartoon buttocks, powder white with red spots like a clown's cheeks. "Is he . . . he hurting you?" the real man gasps. "No, it just makes me jittery. It's sort of like cutting your lip on the edge of an envelope," she adds with a grimace, letting her skirt drop, "if you know what I mean."

"Ah . . ." He too feels a stinging somewhere, though perhaps only in his reflections. Distantly, he hears a policeman's whistle, momentarily persuasive, but he knows this is no solution, real or otherwise. It would be like scratching an itch with legislation or an analogy—something that cartoon dog might have said and perhaps did, he wasn't listening all the time. No, one tries, but it's never enough. With a heavy heart (what a universe!), he goes into the bathroom to flush the cartoon car down the toilet and

discovers, glancing in the mirror, that, above the cartoon napkin still tucked into his collar like a lolling tongue, he seems to
have grown a pair of cartoon ears. They stick out from the sides
of his head like butterfly wings. Well, well, he thinks, wagging
his new ears animatedly, or perhaps being wagged by them,
there's hope for me yet . . .

TOP HAT

(1987)

Uniformed men move in a dark choral mass at the foot of an iron tower under unlit lamps, their top hats squared, their shadowed faces anonymous and interchangeable. They suggest power without themselves possessing it, moving with ceremonial precision, otherwise silent, their secret motives concealed. They seem to want their walking sticks, carried like emblems of the elect, to speak for them.

Suddenly their decorum is shattered, as out of the vanishing point of the night a new figure emerges, strolling jauntily into their midst as though a door were being opened, light thrown, a die cast: they all fall back. At first glance, he might seem to be one of their own: he too wears top hat and tails, white tie, spats, carries a stick. But he is dressed like them and not like them: the top hat is tilted defiantly over one ear, the walking stick twirls like a vulgar unriddling of sacrament, his lapels are pulled back to show more of his snowy white breast by a hand flicking in and out of his pants pocket like a lizard's tongue. He is unmistakably (his face is lit up with an open disarming grin, he is a loner and extravagant and his grip is firm) an outsider here. And he means to offend.

The others close ranks behind him as though to seal a wound, watch him apprehensively. Perhaps he *is* one of them, as yet unformed. Is this possible? As though in reply, that frisky hand takes another dip, emerges this time with a scrap of paper: "I've just got an invitation through the mail," he crows, wagging the paper about like a press release. They lean on their sticks, studying this strutting intruder: perhaps they find heresy momentarily fascinating. Perhaps this is a weakness. "Your presence requested this evening, it's formal, top hat, white tie, and tails!" He has been slapping the paper with his walking stick as though it were a sales pitch, a sermon, a writ, but now he wads it up and impiously—the men behind him stiffen, their walking sticks gripped tightly between their legs—tosses it away. Credentials? Hey, who needs them? He twirls his stick and swaggers up and down in front of them, grinningly mocking their vestments, their rituals, their very raison d'être, as the natives might say. "And I trust you'll excuse my dust when I step on the gas!" he laughs, beating back their tentative lockstep challenge with a cocky, limbs-akimbo reply of his own.

There is an indignant bang of walking sticks bringing him to a halt. He hesitates, then shrugs as though to say, oh well, when in Rome (if that's where he is), even if they're crazy—and (maybe, deep down, this is what he truly wants, it's not much fun being a loner in this world, after all, even if you are number one) joins the others in a formal strut. But not for long. He just doesn't fit in somehow. They turn away, perhaps to lead him back where he came from, but he's in no mood to go home yet. Not like this. He follows them for a step or two, but then, as though overcoming temptation (all social forms are conspiracies in the end, are they not?), breaks away and, shoulders bobbing and hips swiveling, lets them know who he really is. He drums it out loud and clear with stick, heels, and toes, all four limbs rapping away at once, then plants the walking stick as though claiming turf. They watch impassively, their own sticks discreetly concealed. He restates his dissent, even more emphatically, elbows out and pumping as though he might be trying to take off.

He pauses. Has he won his case? He looks back over his shoulder. No, they are not even impressed. They repeat his sequence, but staidly and en masse. It's a kind of reprimand: the movement is possible, technically anyway, but unbridled egoism is not. He insists, throwing himself into ever more unorthodox convulsions, his walking stick flicking around his head like a cracked whip. He is incorrigible. A barbarian, a peacock. He does not even seem completely white. They leave him.

Or maybe I somehow wished them away, reversed them out of my life like a rejected fairytale, a shabby dream, just as, for all I knew, I might well have wished them here in the first place. I was far from home; anything seemed possible. Certainly they vanished like shadows, leaving these strange streets bathed in a fresh light that lifted my spirits. I knew time was passing because I could hear my hands and feet tick-tocking away below, but the sensation I had was of a languorous serenity, a delicious pause between clocked anxieties. My life was changing, but for a moment it was standing still.

I may have got carried away a bit by the sheer enchantment of it, for, alone now, I could feel my body shed its weight suddenly and burst into an almost uncontrollable spasm of hip-twisting exuberance. Perhaps I meant it as an affront: their tails hung down, mine had to fly! Even as I dutifully planted my walking stick, my feet—I seemed to have at least four of them, all rattling at once—kicked it away. The stick took on a life of its own, whirling me giddily round and round as it whipped at the hard ground, sliced the air. I'd never known anything quite like it. I felt like I was about to blow my doggone hat off.

I knew that I had come to this place to change my life. Or that, somehow, because my life had to change, I had come to this place. The invitation seemed to suggest this: it was a special occasion. But, even as I found myself suddenly spinning dizzily around my rooted walking stick, I could not imagine what the nature of that change could be. Perhaps it had to do with the old men (I seemed to remember old men), or perhaps with the place itself, a place that seemed to be there and not to be there at the same time, like an unwritten melody, more an aura than a place, barren and seductive and overhung with melancholic storm clouds. And growing ominously dark. . .

Wait! I stopped, staggered drunkenly, spread my legs to keep from falling. What place *was* this? What exactly was I *doing* here? I tucked my elbows in. I'd taken that invitation for granted: but who had sent it? I couldn't remember. Perhaps I'd never known. I looked up at the louring sky, gripping my walking stick with both hands, feeling bereft, forgotten. Yet liking the feel of the stick. The streetlamps had come on. And under them, a girl stood. "I suppose," she said, staring at my feet, which were, though I had little to do with it, still on the move, "it's some kind of affliction."

"Yes, yes," I stammered, "it's—it's an affliction . . ." I lowered my walking stick. Her caustic twang, so far from home, had startled me. She had genuine melting-pot lard in her cheeks and hips, her negligee was swank, but it was also vulgar, straight off Main Street, and she had the crusty don't-number-two-me worldliness of the girl-next-door. I felt I had seen her somewhere before. I began to perceive the nature of my trial.

I was in a foreign place. The light was bad but I could see plain enough this guy was not one of the locals. The fancy duds were right but they fit him funny, like he was growing into them and out of them at the same time. He was playing with that swagger stick of his like he was trying to jerk it off, and I had the impression from the way he gaped at me that about all he could register for the moment was two tits and a tongue. Right away he starts mooning about his nursies, by which I supposed he meant his old lady, this john being strictly backwater, soup and fish notwithstanding—I mean, he had some pretty fancy moves, but all that nimble-footedness looked to me like something he mighta learned tippytoeing through the cowshit. It was my guess that the nearest he'd had to a nursemaid was some old Gran out on the prairie who'd spooned him baked squash, rhubarb pie, and get-up-and-go marketplace fairytales, but bull's wool or no, the message was clear: this guy wanted his mommy.

The weird thing was how he couldn't stop jiggering about. It was like somebody had wound him up, then thrown away the key. Was it those old guys up in the balcony? I'd come on him spinning round and round his planted stick like he was in love with it. His dick, sure, I thought, but more than that: it was like some hole in the middle that he could circle round all day but never get inside of, and it was driving him crazy. "I'm free, that's me," he was hollering, and it was scaring him spitless. When he finally tucked his stick back in his clothes, he was staggering so he could hardly stand up—yet his feet kept ticky-tocking away under him like he had the St. Vitus dance or something. So I spoke up. I said I supposed it was some kind of affliction, and he said it was and in fact he really shouldn't be left alone. I could see that, and suggested a couple of guards. I had to admit there was something attractive about him, though, in spite of his being a wanker and a loony. Maybe I was just homesick. Or tired of trying to get by in these hard times as a rich dressmaker's whore: there's a side to this kind of glamour that most people don't see. And it ain't the front side. Whatever the reason, when he launched into a little birds-and-bees number about "a clumsy cloud and a fluffy little cloud" (was he kidding? maybe all he'd had to shag till now were sheep . . .), I found myself thinking, oh well, what the hell, though I don't know the yokel from Adam, I just might let him scud up to a pap if it'd make him feel any better. If only he'd stop weewawing around like that.

And that was when these guys showed up.

Don't ask me who they were. I'm not even sure *what* they were. They came rising up out of the ground like from you-know-where. And you could tell these greasers meant business. Fluffy little clouds, my fanny, I thought, that boy shoulda stayed home on the farm! He looked like he was about to poop marbles, hunkered down there with his willow between his legs and his hat squashing his big ears out. Even his twitchy feet had gone dead on him. I figured the rube was done for and was just starting to feel sorry for him, when whaddaya know! he suddenly rears up, turns that little white-tipped stick of his into some kind of magical popgun, and starts mowing down the lot of them! Rappy-tappy-tap, down they go, blood and brains blowing everywhere, it's a fantastic rub-out! Hey, I thought, this guy is *good!*

They return as they left: as though compelled. Arising like plants from the soil. Have they been called back because of the girl? To present her perhaps with a moral alternative? Or to recall *him* to the world of men? They bring with them, certainly, the aura of purpose, of culture, law, of subjection of the will to the greater beauty of the whole, but this aura rests upon them more like an affliction than a promise. Or perhaps it's just those preposterous squared-off hats.

They pause, standing in a row like soldiers at ease, their walking sticks planted between their legs, their white-gloved hands clasped at the heads as though protecting their genitals. Or pointing to them. They seem ready to serve, yet uncertain as to the nature of their service. Is he to join their ranks? Is she to embellish them? Or are they mere witnesses to a drama from which they are—ontologically, as it were—excluded? He provides an answer of sorts: he raises his walking stick and, pointing it like a fairground rifle, shoots one of their number: p-*tang!* The man crumples and falls, clutching at the sky.

Nothing changes. And everything changes. The outsider, it seems, is here to kill. And they his hosts, are here to die. Possessed suddenly of an amazing and exemplary grace, he executes them one by one, but after the first surprise, there is no other: p-*tang!* p-*tang!*—down they go, grabbing at their breasts, their faces, reaching desperately for the darkening sky.

The girl meanwhile is falling madly in love—or perhaps is at last being rejoined with her true love—her face lit up now with a kind of mystical ecstasy. She falls into step with him, moving in adoring concert, yet never touching, discovering—or rediscovering—an essential affinity, a zest for life and art— p-*tang!* p-*tang!*—innately shared. He fires from over his head, drops them two at a time from the hip, even lifts his leg and shoots from under it, as though to deepen the humiliation of their ineluctable and spellbound deaths. She moves among the victims, her heels rapping out a pitter-patter of termination, flouncing her skirts like the dropping of final curtains.

He knocks another one down, shooting blindly over his shoulder, then, holding the stick at his belly—*ruckety-tackety-tuckety-tack!*—impatiently machine-guns the lot. The dying men whirl and writhe, blood jetting from their bodies like the release of some inner effervescence. Their executioner, grown tall, staggers momentarily as though drunk with pleasure, turns wide-eyed toward the girl. She draws near to complete their final figure, which would seem, by the expression on her face, to be nothing short of orgasm (perhaps it is already over-taking her, as his arms reach out she is rolling to her back, her eyes closed, mouth agape)—

But wait! there's one still standing! This one seems smaller somehow, or else more remote, planted at the foot of the iron tower like a flaw in the visitor's own character, hands clasped soberly at the head of his stick. The visitor drops the girl (she gasps, grabbing herself as she falls), draws himself erect, and, his boyish grin frozen on his face, fires: the man leans to one side, ducking the shot, and says: I know what you're trying to do my friend, and I don't want to take the wind out of your sails, but perhaps, in your pursuit of untrammeled happiness, you have been a little imprudent. For there are dates that cannot be broken, and words, you know, that cannot be spoken. This is more than a clash of taste, a bit of a tiff. You are seeking, through murder—"

His executioner, sweating now though still grinning widely, teeth clamped in what is either manly determination or unbridled terror (the girl, groaning, convulses ambivalently at his feet), fires again: the man calmly leans the other way and continues, "You are seeking, as I say, through murder, to overcome that ambivalence at the heart of your quest, but what you are killing is merely something in yourself. Indeed, it is unlikely that, when the killing is done, there can possibly be anything left. You cannot celebrate, my friend, what does not exist. There is no Adam, for all your wishful thinking, and there never was; those treacherous brothers just made that up to account for their discontent. Yours is a grave misapprehension, with consequences far beyond your hasty actions here. Believe me, a few technical skills, gutsiness, and a silly smile will not resolve—"

Enraged, the newcomer bounces his swagger stick off the street and, as though to argue the case for personal ingenuity and pluck (it's *not* just technology, blast it, it's a whole new *spirit*—!), grabs it on the rebound and raises it like an Indian's bow. "Wait!" cries the man at the foot of the tower. The overhanging globes are so aligned as to seem to be pointing to his chest. "Hear me out!" The girl can be seen crawling away into the shadows in her glossy negligee, perhaps to sleep awhile, and dream. "I admit your instincts are sound, but your methods are ingenuous! It's not *whose* hats, but who's—!" His opponent draws the bow—or seems to: there is a mystery about the arrow—and lets it go. There is a crack like a rifle shot, the man at the tower cries out: "*No, no, damn it! SHOOT THE OLD ME-e-e-e-ennn—!*" and, flinging an arm in the air, crumples, his face falling into shadows.

The intruder is alone now on the street, except for all the bodies, those bitten apples, heaped about like cairns, like gates for a dance routine. The night has deepened. He tucks the stick under his arm, straightens his white tie, brushes off his tails, as though recollecting an old code. He looks at his feet: they are quiet at last. He grins at this, and shrugs, waggles his hips. In the heavy silence (he will never, never change), he doffs his hat and takes his spidery bow.

INSIDE THE FRAME

(1987)

Dry weeds tumble across a dusty tarred street, lined by low ramshackle wooden buildings. A loosely hinged screen door bangs repetitiously; nearby a sign creaks in the wind. A thin dog passes, sniffing idly at the borders of the street. More tumbleweeds. More dull banging. Finally, a bus pulls up, its windows opaqued with dust and grease. The creaking sign is heard now but not seen. Down the street, a young woman opens a door and peers out, framed by the darkness within. There is a furtive movement on a store roof, martial music in the distance. The door of the bus opens and two men step down. After a brief discussion, one of them shoots the other. Meanwhile, a matriarchal figure waits at the gate of her house like a mediating presence, somber yet hopeful. The sound of a cash register suggests a purchase. In the distance, a rider-less horse can be seen, its flanks trembling and glistening with sweat. More martial music, steadily approaching. The figure on the roof is an Indian. A tall man is holding a limp woman in his arms before a window. A couple swirl past, arms linked, singing at the tops of their voices. There is something startling about this. The sky darkens as though before a storm. A richly dressed lady exits the bus, followed by her Negro servant. The Indian leaps, a knife between his teeth. Someone is crying. It is a man, seated at a dinner table with his family, seen through an open doorway. The martial music augments as a marching band comes down the street, trumpets blaring. The Negro servant lifts down several valises, trunks, and hatboxes. Watched by the gunslinger, four men stride vigorously out of one building, the door banging behind them, and enter another. Beneath the back wheel of the bus, the pinned dog lifts its head plaintively, as though searching for someone who is not present and perhaps could never be. A boy with a slingshot takes aim at an old man delivering an unheard graveside soliloquy. Before this, the distant horse was seen to neigh and shake its mane. And then the martial music abruptly ended. Now, the rich lady enters the dilapidated hotel, surrounded by attentive bellhops and followed by her Negro servant, struggling comically with the baggage. A card-player, angry, throws his cards in the dealer's face: trouble seems to be brewing. Somewhere a garbage lid rattles menacingly in an alleyway. All of this is surrounded by darkness. The singing couple swing past again, going the other way, dressed now in identical white tuxedos, crisply edged. Thunder and lightning. The surviving member of the marching band retrieves his battered trumpet and puts it defiantly to his crushed lips. The gunslinger turns to reboard the bus, but is held back by the grizzled old sheriff. What occurs between them is partly hidden behind six young women who, flouncing by, turn their backs in unison and flip their skirts over their

heads as though to suggest in this display the terrible vulnerability of thresholds. Is there laughter in the brightly lit hotel
lobby? Perhaps it's only the rain beating on tin roofs. The sheriff has shot the Indian. Or an Indian. The bus has departed and
several of the doors along the street have closed. Behind one of
them a tear glistens in an upturned eye. A strange-looking person walks woodenly past, crossing the rain-slicked tar, staring
straight ahead, his arms held out stiffly before him. Down the
street, the door opens again and a young woman peers out: the
same door as before, the same dark space within, a reassurance
that is not one. Beneath the creaking sign, visible once more, a
man now pulls a hat brim over his eyes and steps provisionally
down off a wooden porch. There is the sound somewhere of
suddenly splintering glass, a piano playing. The dog with the
broken back, its search forsaken, lowers its thin head in the
pounding rain. And the banging door? The banging door?

THE PHANTOM OF THE MOVIE PALACE

(1987)

"We are doomed, Professor! The planet is rushing madly toward Earth and no human power can stop it!" "Why are you telling me this?" asks the professor petulantly and sniffs his armpits. "Hmm. Excuse me, gentlemen," he adds, switching off his scientific instruments and, to their evident chagrin, turning away, "I must take my bath." But there is already an evil emperor from outer space in his bathtub. Even here then! He sits on the stool and chews his beard despondently, rubbing his fingers between his old white toes. The alien emperor, whose head looks like an overturned mop bucket, splashes water on the professor with his iron claw and emits a squeaky yet sinister cackle. "You're going to rust in there," grumbles the professor in his mounting exasperation.

The squat gangster in his derby and three-piece suit with boutonniere and pointed pocket handkerchief waddles impassively through a roomful of hard-boiled wisecracking bottle-blond floozies, dropping ashes on them from his enormous stogie and gazing from time to time at the plump bubble of fob-watch in his hand. He wears a quizzical self-absorbed expression on his face, as though to say: Ah, the miracle of it all! the mystery! the eternal illusion! And yet . . . It's understood he's a dead man, so the girls forgive him his nasty habits, blowing at their décolletages and making such vulgar remarks and noises as befit their frolicsome lot. They are less patient with the little bugger's longing for the ineffable, however, and are likely, before he's rubbed out (will he even make it across the room? no one expects this), to break into a few old party songs just to clear the air. "How about 'The Sterilized Heiress'?" someone whispers even now. "Or, 'The Angle of the Dangle!' " " 'Roll Your Buns Over!' " "Girls, girls . . . !" sighs the gangster indulgently, his stogie bobbing. " 'Blow the Candle Out!' "

The husband and wife, in response to some powerful code from the dreamtime of the race, crawl into separate beds, their only visible concession to marital passion being a tender exchange of pajamas from behind a folding screen. Beneath the snow-white sheets and chenille spreads, they stroke their strange pajamas and sing each other to sleep with songs of faith and expediency and victory in war. "My cup," the wife gasps in her chirrupy soprano as the camera closes in on her trembling lips, the luminescent gleam in her eye, "runneth over!" and her husband, eyelids fluttering as though in prayer, or perhaps the onset of sleep, replies: "Your precious voice, my love, here and yet not here, evokes for me the sweet diaphanous adjacency of presence"— (here, his voice breaks, his cheeks puff out)—"and loss!"

The handsome young priest with the boyish smile kneels against the partition and croons a song of a different sort to the nun sitting on the toilet in the next stall. A low unpleasant sound is heard; it could be anything really, even prayer. The hidden agenda here is not so much religious expression as the filmic manipulation of ingenues: the nun's only line is not one, strictly speaking, and even her faint smile seems to do her violence.

The man with the axe in his forehead steps into the flickering light. His eyes, pooled in blood, cross as though trying to see what it is that is cleaving his brain in two. His chest is pierced with a spear, his groin with a sword. He stumbles, falls into a soft plash of laughter and applause. His audience, still laughing and applauding as the light in the film flows from viewed to viewer, rises now and turns toward the exits. Which are locked. Panic ensues. Perhaps there's a fire. Up on the rippling velour, the man with the split skull is still staggering and falling, "*Oh my God! Get that axe!*" someone screams, clawing at the door, and another replies: "*It's no use! It's only a rhetorical figure!*" "*What—?!*" This is worse than anyone thought. "*I only came for the selected short subjects!*" someone cries irrationally. They press their tear-streaked faces against the intractable doors, listening in horror to their own laughter and applause, rising now to fill the majestic old movie palace until their chests ache with it, their hands burn.

Ah, well, those were the days, the projectionist thinks, changing reels in his empty palace. The age of gold, to phrase a coin. Now the doors are always open and no one enters. His films play to a silence so profound it is not even ghostly. He still sweeps out the vast auditorium, the grand foyer and the mezzanine with their plaster statues and refreshment stands, the marble staircase, the terraced swoop of balcony, even the orchestra pit, library, rest rooms and phone booths, but all he's ever turned up is the odd candy wrapper or popcorn tub he's dropped himself. The projectionist does this intentionally, hoping one day to forget and so surprise himself with the illusion of company, but so far his memory has been discouragingly precise. All that human garbage—the chocolate mashed into the thick carpets, the kiddy-pee on the front-row seats and the gum stuck under them, sticky condoms in the balcony, the used tissues and crushed cups and toothless combs, sprung hairpins, stools clogged with sanitary napkins and water fountains with chewing gum and spittle and soggy butts—used to enrage him, but now he longs for the least sign of another's presence. Even excrement in the Bridal Fountain or black hair grease on the plush upholstery. He feels like one of those visitors to an alien planet, stumbling through endless wastelands in the vain search for life's telltale scum. A cast-out orphan in pursuit of a lost inheritance. A detective without a clue, unable even to find a crime.

Or, apropos, there's that dying hero in the old foreign legion movie (and where is that masterpiece? he should look for it, run it again some lonely night for consolation) crawling inch by inch through the infinite emptiness of the desert, turning the sand over in his fingers in the desperate hope of sifting out something—a dead weed perhaps, a mollusk shell, even a bottle cap—that might reassure him that relief, if not near at hand, at least once existed. Suddenly, off on the horizon, he sees, or seems to see, a huge luxury liner parked among the rolling dunes. He crawls aboard and finds his way to the first-class lounge, where tuxedoed gentlemen clink frosted glasses and mill about with ladies dressed in evening gowns and glittering jewels. "Water—!" he gasps hoarsely from the floor, which unexpectedly makes everyone laugh. "All right, whiskey then!" he wheezes, but the men are busy gallantly helping the ladies into lifeboats. The liner, it seems, is sinking. The men gather on the deck and sing lusty folk ballads about psychologically disturbed bandits. As the ship goes down, the foreign legionnaire, even while drowning, dies at last of thirst, a fool of sorts, a butt of his own forlorn hopes, thereby illustrating his commanding officer's earlier directive back at the post on the life of the mercenary soldier: "One must not confuse honor, gentlemen, with bloody paradox!"

The mischievous children on the screen now, utterly free of such confusions, have stolen a cooling pie, glued their teacher to her seat, burned a cat, and let an old bull loose in church. Now they are up in a barn loft, hiding from the law and plotting their next great adventure. "Why don't we set the school on fire?" suggests one of them, grinning his little freckle-faced gap-toothed grin. "Or else the truant officer?" "Or stick a hornets' nest in his helmet?" "Or in his *pants*!" They all giggle and snicker at this. "That's great! But who'll get us the hornets' nest?" They turn, smiling, toward the littlest one, squatting in the corner, smeared ear to ear with hot pie. "Kith my ath," she says around the thumb in her mouth. The gap-toothed kid claps one hand to his forehead in mock shock, rolls his eyes, and falls backwards out the loft door.

Meanwhile, or perhaps in another film, the little orphan girl, who loves them all dearly, is crawling up into the hayloft on the rickety wooden ladder. No doubt some cruel fate awaits her. This is suggested by the position of the camera, which is following close behind her, as though examining the holes in her underwear. Or perhaps those are just water spots—it's an old film. He

reverses it, bringing the orphan girl's behind back down the ladder for a closer look. But it's no good. It's forever blurred, forever
enigmatic. There's always this unbridgeable distance between
the eye and its object. Even on the big screen.

Well, and if I *were* to bridge it, the projectionist thinks, what
then? It would probably be about as definitive an experience
as hugging a black hole—like all those old detective movies
in which the private eye, peering ever closer, only discovers,
greatly magnified, his own cankerous guilt. No, no, be happy
with your foggy takes, your painted backdrops and bobbing
ship models, your dying heroes spitting blood capsules, your
faded ingenues in nunnery loos or up loft ladders. Or wherever
she might be. In a plane crash or a chorus line or a mob at
the movies, or carried off by giant apes or ants, or nuzzled by
grizzlies in the white wastes of the Klondike. The miracle of
artifice is miracle enough. Here she is, for example, tied to the
railroad tracks, her mouth gagged, her bosom heaving as the
huge engine bears down upon her. Her muffled scream blends
with the train's shrieking whistle, as sound effects, lighting,
motion, acting, and even set decor—the gleaming ribbons of
steel rails paralleling the wet gag in her mouth, her billowing
skirts echoing the distant hills—come together for a moment
in one conceptual and aesthetic whole. It takes one's breath
away, just as men's glimpses of the alleged divine once did, projections much less convincing than these, less inspiring of true
awe and trembling.

Sometimes these flickerings on his big screen, these Purviews
of Cunning Abstractions, as he likes to bill them, actually set
his teeth to chattering. Maybe it's just all this lonely space with
its sepulchral room presence room presence more dreadful than

mere silence, but as the footage rolls by, music swelling, guns blazing, and reels rattling, he seems to see angels up there, or something like angels, bandannas on their faces and bustles in their skirts, aglow with an eery light not of this world. Or of any other, for that matter—no, it's scarier than that. It's as though their bones (as if they had bones!) were burning from within. They seem then, no matter how randomly he's thrown the clips together, to be caught up in some terrible enchantment of continuity, as though meaning itself were pursuing them (and him! and him!), lunging and snorting at the edge of the frame, fangs bared and dripping gore.

At such times, his own projections and the monumental emptiness of the auditorium spooking him, he switches everything off, throws all the houselights on, and wanders the abandoned movie palace, investing its ornate and gilded spaces with signs of life, even if only his own. He sets the ventilators and generators humming, works the grinding lift mechanisms, opens all the fountain cocks, stirs the wisps of clouds on the dome and turns on the stars. What there are left of them. To chase the shadows, he sends the heavy ornamented curtains with their tassels and fringes and all the accompanying travelers swooping and sliding, pops on the floods and footlights, flies the screen and drops the scrim, rings the tower chimes up in the proscenium, toots the ancient ushers' bugle. There's enough power in this place to light up a small town and he uses it all, bouncing it through the palace as though blowing up a balloon. Just puzzling out the vast switchboard helps dispel those troublesome apparitions: as they fade away, his mind spreading out over the board as if being rewired—*s-pop!* flash! *whirr!*—it feels to the back of his neck like the release of an iron claw. He goes then to the mezzanine and sets the popcorn machine thupping, the cash register ringing, the ornamental fountain gurgling. He throws the big double doors open. He lets down the velvet ropes. He leans on the showtime buzzer.

There are secret rooms, too, walled off or buried under concrete during the palace's periodic transformations, and sometimes, fleeing the grander spaces, he ducks down through the low-ceilinged maze of subterranean tunnels, snapping green and purple sugar wafers between his teeth, the crisp translucent wrapper crackling in his fist like the sound of fire on radio, to visit them: old dressing rooms, kennels and stables, billiard parlors, shower rooms, clinics, gymnasiums, hairdressing salons, garages and practice rooms, scene shops and prop rooms, all long disused, mirrors cracked and walls crumbling, and littered with torn posters, the nibbled tatters of old theatrical costumes, mildewed movie magazines. A ghost town within a ghost town. He raids it for souvenirs to decorate his lonely projection booth: an usherette's brass button, some child-star's paperdolls, old programs and ticket rolls and colored gelatin slides, gigantic letters for the outdoor marquee. A STORY OF PASSION BLOODSHED DESIRE & DEATH! was the last appeal he posted out there. Years ago. THE STRANGEST LOVE A MAN HAS EVER KNOWN! DON'T GIVE AWAY THE ENDING! The only reason he remembers is because he ran out of D's and had to change BLOODSHED to BLOOSHED. Maybe that's why nobody came.

He doesn't stay down here long. It's said that, beneath this labyrinth from the remote past, there are even deeper levels, stair-stepped linkages to all the underground burrowings of the city, but if so, he's never found them, nor tried to. It's a kind of Last Frontier he chooses not to explore, in spite of his compulsive romanticism, and, sooner or later, the dark anxiety which this reluctance gives rise to drives him back up into the well-lit rooms above. Red lines, painted in bygone times on the tunnel floors and still visible, point the way back, and as he goes, nose down and mufflered in clinging shadows, he finds himself longing once more for the homely comforts of his little projection booth. His cot and coffeepot and the friendly pinned-up stills. His stuffed peacock from some demolished Rivoli or Tivoli and his favorite gold ticket chopper with the silver filigree. His bags of hard-boiled eggs and nuts. The wonderful old slides for projecting blizzards and sandstorms, or descending clouds for imaginary ascensions (those were the days!), or falling roses, rising bubbles or flying fairies, and the one that says simply (he always shouts it aloud in the echoey auditorium): "PLEASE READ THE TITLES TO YOURSELF. LOUD READING ANNOYS YOUR NEIGH-BORS." Also his stacked collections of gossip columns and animation cels and Mighty Wurlitzer scores. His tattered old poster for *Hearts and Pearls: or, The Lounge-Lizard's Lost Love*, with its immemorial tag line: "The picture that could change your life!" (And it has! It has!) And all his spools and tins and bins and snippets and reels of film. Film!

Oh yes! *Adventure!* he thinks, taking the last of the stairs up to the elevator lobby two at a time and—*kfthwump!*—into the bright lights. *Comedy!* He is running through the grand foyer now, switching things off as he goes, dragging the darkness along behind him like a fluttering cape. Is everything still there? How could he have left it all behind? He clambers breathlessly up the marble staircase, his heels clocking hollowly as though chasing him, and on into the projection room tunnel, terror and excitement unfolding in his chest like a crescendo of luminous titles, rolling credits—*Romance!*

"Excuse me," the cat woman moans huskily, peering at him over her shoulder as she unzippers her skin, "while I slip into something more comfortable . . ." The superhero, his underwear bagging at the seat and knees, is just a country boy at heart, tutored to perceive all human action as good or bad, orderly or dynamic, and so doesn't know whether to shit or fly. What good is his famous X-ray vision *now*? "But—but all self-gratification only leads to tragedy!" he gasps as she presses her hot organs up against him. "Yeah? Well, hell," she whispers, blowing in his ear, "what doesn't?" Jumpin' gee-whillikers! Why does he suddenly feel like crying?

"Love!" sings the ingenue. It's her only line. She sings it again: "Love!" The film is packed edge to edge with matings or implied matings, it's hard to find her in the crowd. "Love!" There is a battle cry, a war, perhaps an invasion. Sudden explosions. Ricocheting bullets. Mob panic. "Love!" She's like a stuck record. "Love!" "*Stop!*" Bodies are tumbling off of ramparts, horses are galloping through the gates. "Love!" "*Everything's different now!*" someone screams, maybe he does. "Love!" She's incorrigible. "*Stop her, for god's sake!*" They're all shouting and shooting at *her* now with whatever they've got: arrows, cannon, death rays, blowguns, torpedoes—"Love . . . !"

The apeman, waking from a wet dream about a spider monkey and an anteater, finds himself in a strange place, protected only by a sticky breechcloth the size of a luncheon napkin, and confronted with a beautiful High Priestess, who lights up two cigarettes at once, hands him one, and murmurs: "Tell me, lard-ass, did you ever have the feeling that you wanted to go, and still have the feeling that you wanted to stay?" He is at a loss for words, having few to start with, so he steps out on the balcony to eat his cigarette. He seems to have been transported to a vast city. The little lights far below (he thinks, touching his burned tongue gingerly: Holy ancestors! The stars have fallen!) tremble as though menaced by the darkness that encases them. The High Priestess steps up behind him and runs her hand under his breechcloth. "Feeling moody, jungle boy?" World attachment, he knows, is the fruit of the tree of passion, which is the provoker of wrath as well as of desire, but he doesn't really know what to do with this knowledge, not with the exploitative hand of civilization abusing his noble innocence like this. Except maybe to yell for the elephants.

"Get away from that lever!" screams the scientist, rushing into his laboratory. But there's no one in there, he's all alone. He and all these bits and pieces of human flesh he's been stitching together over the years. There's not even a lever. That, like everything else in his mad, misguided life, is just wishful thinking. He's a complete failure and a presumptuous ass to boot. Who's he to be creating life when he can't even remember to brush his own teeth? This thing he's made is a mess. It doesn't even smell good. Probably it's all the innovations that have done him in. All these sex organs! Well, they were easier to find than brains, it's not entirely his fault, and no one can deny he did it for love. He remembers a film (or seems to: there is a montage effect) in which the mad scientist, succeeding where he in his depressing sanity has failed, lectures his creation on the facts of life, starting with the shinbone. "The way I see it, kid, it's forget the honors, and go for the bucks." "Alas, I perceive now that the world has no meaning for those who are obliged to pass through it," replies the monster melancholically, tearing off the

shinbone and crushing his creator's skull with it, "but one must act as though it might."

Perhaps it's this, he thinks, stringing up a pair of projectors at the same time, that accounts for his own stubborn romanticism—not a search for meaning, just a wistful toying with the idea of it, because: what else are you going to do with that damned bone in your hand? Sometimes, when one picture does not seem enough, he projects two, three, even several at a time, creating his own split-screen effects, montages, superimpositions. Or he uses multiple projectors to produce a flow of improbable dissolves, startling sequences of abrupt cuts and freeze frames like the stopping of a heart, disturbing juxtapositions of slow and fast speeds, fades in and out like labored breathing. Sometimes he builds thick collages of crashing vehicles or mating lovers or gun-toting soldiers, cowboys, and gangsters all banging away in unison, until the effect is like time-lapse photography of passing clouds, waves washing the shore. He'll run a hero through all the episodes of a serial at once, letting him be burned, blasted, buried, drowned, shot, run down, hung up, splashed with acid or sliced in two, all at the same time, or he'll select a favorite ingenue and assault her with a thick impasto of pirates, sailors, bandits, gypsies, mummies, Nazis, vampires, Martians, and college boys, until the terrified expressions on their respective faces pale to a kind of blurred, mystical affirmation of the universe. Which, not unexpectedly, looks a lot like stupidity. And sometimes he leaves the projector lamps off altogether, just listens in the dark to the sounds of blobs and ghouls, robots, galloping hooves and screeching tires, creaking doors, screams, gasps of pleasure and fear, hoots and snarls and blown noses, fists hitting faces and bodies pavements, arrows targets, rockets moons.

Some of these stratagems are his own inventions, others come to him through accident—a blown fuse, the keystoning rake of a tipped projector, a mislabeled film, a fly on the lens. One night he's playing with a collage of stacked-up disaster movies, for example, when the layering gets so dense the images get stuck together. When he's finally able to peel one of them loose, he finds it stripped of its cracking dam, but littered with airliner debris, molten lava, tumbling masonry, ice chunks, bowing palm trees, and a whey-faced Captain from other clips. This leads him to the idea ("What seems to be the trouble, Captain?" someone was asking, her voice hushed with dread and earnestness, as the frames slipped apart, and maybe he should have considered this question before rushing on) of sliding two or more projected images across each other like brushstrokes, painting each with the other, so to speak, such that a galloping cowboy gets in the way of some slapstick comedians and, as the films separate out, arrives at the shootout with custard on his face; or the dying heroine, emerging from montage with a circus feature, finds herself swinging by her stricken limbs from a trapeze, the arms of her weeping lover in the other frame now hugging an elephant's leg; or the young soldier, leaping bravely from his foxhole, is creamed by a college football team, while the cheerleaders, caught out in no-man's-land, get their pom-poms shot away.

He too feels suddenly like he's caught out in no-man's-land on a high trapeze with pie on his face, but he can't stop. It's too much fun. Or something like fun He drives stampedes through upper-story hotel rooms and out the windows, moves a monster's hideous scar to a dinner plate and breaks it, beards a breast, clothes a hurricane in a tutu. He knows there's something corrupt, maybe even dangerous, about this collapsing of boundaries, but it's also liberating, augmenting his film library exponentially. And it is also necessary. The projectionist understands perfectly well that when the cocky test pilot, stunt-flying a biplane, leans out to wave to his girlfriend and discovers himself unexpectedly a mile underwater in the clutches of a giant squid, the crew from the submarine meanwhile frantically treading air a mile up the other way, the crisis they suffer—*must* suffer—is merely the elemental crisis in his own heart. It's this or nothing, guys: sink or fly!

So it is with a certain rueful yet giddy fatalism that he sweeps a cops-and-robbers film across a domestic comedy in which the goofy rattle-brained housewife is yattering away in the kitchen while serving her family breakfast. As the frames congeal, the baby gets blown right out of its highchair, the police chief, ducking a flipped pancake, gets his hand stuck in the garbage disposal, and the housewife, leaning forward to kiss her husband while telling him about her uncle's amazing cure for potato warts, drops through an open manhole. She can be heard still, carrying on her sad screwball monologue down in the city sewers somewhere, when the two films separate, the gangster, left behind in the kitchen, receiving now the husband's sleepy good-bye kiss on his way out the door to work. The hood, disgusted, whips out his gat to drill the mug (where the hell is Lefty? what happened to that goddamn bank?), but all he comes out with is a dripping eggbeater.

Lefty (if it is Lefty) is making his getaway in a hot-wired Daimler, chased through the streets of the crowded metropolis by screaming police cars, guns blazing in all directions, citizens flopping and tumbling as though the pavement were being jerked out from under them. Adjacently, cast adrift in an open boat, the glassy-eyed heroine is about to surrender her tattered virtue to the last of her fellow castaways, a bald-headed sailor with an eye-patch and a peg leg. The others watch from outside the frame, seeing what the camera sees, as the sailor leans forward to take possession of her. "Calamity is the normal circumstance of the universe," he whispers tenderly, licking the salt from her ear, as the boat bobs sensuously, "so you can't blame these poor jack-shites for having a reassuring peep at the old run-in." As her lips part in anguished submission, filling the screen, the other camera pulls back for a dramatic overview of the squealing car chase through the congested city streets: he merges the frames, sending Lefty crashing violently into the beautiful cave of her mouth, knocking out a molar and setting her gums on fire, while the sailor suddenly finds himself tonguing the side of a skyscraper, with his social finger up the city storm drains. "Shiver me timbers and strike me blind!" he cries, jerking his finger out, and the lifeboat sinks.

He recognizes in all these dislocations, of course, his lonely quest for the impossible mating, the crazy embrace of polarities, as though the distance between the terror and the comedy of the void were somehow erotic—it's a kind of pornography. No wonder the sailor asked that his eyes be plucked out! He overlays frenzy with freeze frames, the flight of rockets with the staking of the vampire's heart, Death's face with thrusting buttocks, cheesecake with chaingangs, and all just to prove to himself over and over again that nothing and everything is true. Slapstick *is* romance, heroism a dance number. Kisses kill. Back projections are the last adequate measure of freedom and great stars are clocks: no time like the presence. Nothing, like a nun

with a switchblade, is happening faster and faster, and cause
(that indefinable something) is a happy ending. Or maybe not.

And then . . .

THE NEXT DAY

. . . as the old title would say, back when time wore a white hat,
galloping along heroically from horizon to horizon, it happens.
The realization of his worst desires. Probably he shouldn't have
turned the Western on its side. A reckless practice at best, for
though these creatures of the light may be free from gravity, his
projectors are not: bits and pieces rattle out every time he tries it,
and often as not, he ends up with a roomful of unspooled film,
looping around his ears like killer ivy. But he's just begun sliding a Broadway girlie show through a barroom brawl (ah, love,
he's musing, that thing of anxious fear, as the great demonic
wasteland of masculine space receives the idealized thrust of
feminine time), when it occurs to him in a whimsical moment
to try to merge the choreography of fist and foot against face
and floor by tipping the saloon scene over.

Whereupon the chorus-line ingenue, going on for the ailing star, dances out into the spotlight, all aglow with the first
sweet flush of imminent stardom, only to find herself dropping
goggle-eyed through a bottomless tumult of knuckles, chairs
and flying bottles, sliding—*whoosh!*—down the wet bar, and
disappearing feet-first through a pair of swinging doors at the
bottom of the frame. Wonderful! laughs the projectionist. Worth
it after all! The grizzled old prospector who's started the brawl
in the first place, then passed out drunk, wakes up onstage now
as the frames begin to separate in the ingenue's glossy briefs and

pink ankle-strap shoes, struggling with the peculiar sensation that gravity might not know which way it wants him to fall. Thus, his knees buckle, suggesting a curtsy, even as his testicles, dangling out of the legbands of the showgirl's briefs like empty saddlebags, seem to float upward toward his ears. He opens his mouth, perhaps to sing, or else to yelp or cadge a drink, and his dentures float out like ballooned speech. "Thith ith dithgrathe-ful!" he squawks, snatching at air as he falls in two directions at once to a standing ovation. *"Damn your eyeth!"*

Over in the saloon, meanwhile, the brawl seems to have died down. All eyes not closed by fist or drink are on the swinging doors. He rights the projector to relieve the crick in his neck from trying to watch the film sideways, noting gloomily the clunk and tinkle of tumbling parts within, wishing he might see once more that goofy bug-eyed look on the startled ingenue's face as the floor dropped out from under her. There is a brief clawed snaggle as the film rips erratically through the gate, but an expert touch of his finger on a sprocket soon restores time's main illusion. Of which there is little. The swinging doors hang motionless. Jaws gape. Eyes stare. Not much moves at all except the grinding projector reels behind him. Then slowly the cam-era tracks forward, the doors parting before it. The eye is met by a barren expanse of foreground mud and distant dunes, undis-turbed and utterly lifeless. The ingenue is gone.

He twists the knob to reverse, but something inside the machine is jammed. The image turns dark. Hastily, his hands trembling, he switches off, slaps the reels onto a spare projector, then reverses both films, sweeps them back across each other. Already changes seem to have been setting in: someone thrown out of the saloon window has been thrown back in, mouth crammed with an extra set of teeth, the stage is listing in the musical. Has he lost too much time? When the frames have separated, the old prospector has ended up back in the town saloon all right, though still in the ingenue's costume and with egg on his face, but the ingenue herself is nowhere to be seen. The ailing star, in fact, is no longer ailing, but is back in the spotlight again, belting out an old cowboy song about the saddleback image of now: *"Phantom Ri-i-i-ider!"* she bawls, switching her hips as though flicking away flies. "When stars are *bright* on a frothy *night*—"

He shuts both films down, strings up the mean gang movie with the little orphan girl in it: the water spots are there, but the loft ladder is empty! She's not in the nunnery either, the priest croons to an empty stall, as though confessing to the enthroned void—nor is she in the plummeting plane or the panicking mob or the arms, so to speak, of the blob! The train runs over a ribbon tied in a bow! The vampire sucks wind!

He turns off the projectors, listens intently. Silence, except for the faint crackle of cooling film, his heart thumping in his ears. He is afraid at first to leave his booth. What's happening out there? He heats up cold coffee on his hot plate, studies his pinned-up publicity stills. He can't find her, but maybe she was never in any of them in the first place. He's not even sure he would recognize her, a mere ingenue, if she were there—her legs maybe, but not her face. But in this cannibal picture, for example, wasn't there a girl being turned on the spit? He can't remember. And whose ripped-off heat-shield is that winged intergalactic emperor, his eyes glazed with lust and perplexity, clutching in his taloned fist? The coffee is boiling over, sizzling and popping on the burners like snapped fingers. He jerks the plug and rushes out, caroming clumsily off the doorjamb, feeling as dizzy and unhinged as that old prospector in the tights and pink pumps, not knowing which way to fall.

The cavernous auditorium, awhisper with its own echoey room presence, seems to have shrunk and expanded at the same time: the pocked dome presses down on him with its terrible finitude, even as the aisles appear to stretch away, pushing the screen toward which he stumbles further and further into the distance. "Wait!" he cries, and the stage rushes forward and slams him in the chest, knocking him back into the first row of seats. He lies there for a moment, staring up into what would be, if he could reach the switchboard, a starlit sky, recalling an old Bible epic in which the elders of a city condemned by the archangels were pleading with their unruly citizens to curb their iniquity (which looked something like a street fair with dancing girls) before it was too late. "Can't you just be friends?" they'd cried, and he wonders now: Why not? Is it possible? He's been so lonely . . .

He struggles to his feet, this archaic wish glimmering in the dark pit of his mind like a candle in an old magic lantern, and makes his way foggily up the backstage steps, doom hanging heavy over his head like the little orphan girl's water-spotted behind. He pokes around in the wings with a kind of lustful terror, hoping to find what he most fears to find. He kicks at the tassels and furbelows of the grand drapery, flounces the house curtains and travelers, examines the screen: is there a hole in it? No, it's a bit discolored here and there, threadbare in places, but much as it's always been. As are the switchboard, the banks of lights, the borders, drops, swags and tracks above. Everything seems completely normal, which the projectionist knows from

his years in the trade is just about the worst situation he could
be in. He tests out the house phone, pokes his nose in the empty
trash barrels, braves the dusky alleyway behind the screen. And
now our story takes us down this shadowed path, he murmurs
to himself, feeling like a rookie cop, walking his first beat and
trying to keep his chin up, danger at every strangely familiar
turn, were there any in this narrow canyon. Old lines return
to him like recalled catechism: She was the sort of girl who . . .
Little did he know what fate . . . A few of the characters are
still alive . . . He's aware of silhouettes flickering ominously just
above his head—clutching hands, hatted villains, spread legs—
but when he looks, they are not there. It's all in your mind, he
whispers, and laughs crazily to himself. This seems to loosen
him up. He relaxes. He commences to whistle a little tune.

And then he sees it. Right at nose level in the middle of his
precious screen: a mad vicious scatter of little holes! His untuned
whistle escapes his puckered lips like air from a punctured tire.
He shrinks back. Bullet holes—?! No, not so clean as that, and
the wall behind it is unmarked. It's more like someone has been
standing on the other side just now, kicking at it with stiletto
heels. He's almost unable to breathe. He staggers around to the
front, afraid of what he'll find or see. But the stage is bare. Or
maybe that *is* what he was afraid of. Uneasily, watched by all
the empty seats, he approaches the holes punched out in the
screen. They form crude block letters, not unlike those used on
theater marquees, and what they spell out is: BEWARE THE MID-
NIGHT MAN!

He gasps, and his gasp echoes whisperingly throughout the
auditorium, as though the palace itself were shuddering. Its
irreplaceable picture sheet is ruined. His projections will always

bear this terrible signature, as though time itself were branded. He steps back, repelled—just as the huge asbestos fire curtain comes crashing down. *Wha*—*?!* He ducks, falls into the path of the travelers sweeping across him like silken whips. The lights are flaring and vanishing, flaring again, colors changing kaleidoscopically. He seems to see rivers ascending, clouds dropping like leaded weights. He fights his way through the swoop and swat of rippling curtains toward the switchboard, but when he arrives there's no one there. The fire curtain has been flown, the travelers are tucked decorously back in the wings like gowns in a closet. The dream cloth with its frayed metallic threads has been dropped before the screen. The house curtains are parting, the lights have dimmed. Oh no . . . !

Even as he leaps down into the auditorium and charges up the aisle, the music has begun. If it is music. It seems to be running backwards, and there are screams and honkings and wild laughter mixed in. He struggles against a rising tide of garish light, bearing down upon him from the projection booth, alive with flickering shades, beating against his body like gamma rays. "I don't need that spear, it's only a young lion!" someone rumbles through the dome, a bomb whistles, and there's a crash behind him like a huge mirror falling. "Look out! It's— *aaarrghh!*" "Sorry, ma'am!" "Great Scott, whaddaya call *that?!*" "Romance aflame through dangerous days and—" "You don't mean—?!" The uproar intensifies—"*What* awful *truth?*"—and his movements thicken as in a dream. He knows if he can reach the overhanging balcony lip, he can escape the projector's rake, but even as he leans against this storm of light—"I'm afraid you made one fatal mistake!" —he can feel his body, as though penetrated by an alien being from outer space, lose its will to resist. "No! No!" he cries, marveling at his own performance, and presses on through, falling momentarily blinded, into the musky shelter of the back rows.

He sprawls there in the dark, gripping a cold bolted foot, as the tempest rages on behind him, wondering: *now* what? Which calls to mind an old war film in which the two surviving crew-members of a downed plane, finding themselves in enemy ter-ritory, disguise themselves as the front and back end of a cow to make their escape. They get caught by an enemy farmer and locked in a barn with the village bull, the old farmer muttering, "Calves or steaks! Calves or steaks!" "*Now* what?" the airman in back cries as the bull mounts them, and the one up front, sniff-ing the fodder, says: "Well, old buddy, I reckon that depends on whether or not you get pregnant." Such, roughly, are his own options: he can't leave, and staying may mean more than he can take. Already the thundering light is licking at his heels like an oncoming train, and he feels much like she must have felt, gagged and tied to the humming track: "Not all of us are going to come back alive, men, and before we go out there, I—" "Oh, John! Don't!" "Mad? I, who have solved the secret of life, you call me mad?" *WheeeeeooOOOOoo-ooo!* "Please! Is *nothing* sacred?" He drags himself up the aisle, clawing desperately—"Catch me if you can, coppers!"—at the carpet, and then, driven by some-thing like the downed airmen's craving for friendly pastures, clambers—"We accept him, one of us, one of us . . ."—to his feet. If I can just secure the projection booth, he thinks, lumber-ing forward like a second-string heavy, maybe . . .

But he's too late. It's a disaster area. He can't even get in the door, his way blocked by gleaming thickets of tangled film spooling out at him like some monstrous birth. He hacks his way through to cut off the projectors, but they're not even there any more, nothing left but the odd takeup reel, a Maltese cross or two like dropped coins, a lens blotted with a lipsticked kiss. His stuffed peacock, he sees through the rustling underbrush of film, has been plucked. Gelatin slides are cooking in his coffeepot. He stares dumbly at all this wreckage, unable to move. It's as though his mind has got outside itself somehow, leaving his skull full of empty room presence. Ripped-up publicity stills and organ scores, film tins, shattered glass slides, rolls of punched tickets lie strewn about like colossal endings. All over his pinned-up poster for *Hearts and Pearls*, she has scribbled: FIRST THE HUNT, THEN THE REVELS! The only publicity photo still up on the wall is the one of the cannibals, only now someone *is* on the spit. *He* is. The spit begins to turn. He flees, one hand clapped over his burning eyes, the other clawing through the chattery tentacles of film that now seem to be trying to strangle him.

He staggers into the mezzanine, stripping scraps of clinging celluloid from his throat, his mind locked into the simplistic essentials of movement and murder. He throws the light switch. Nothing happens. The alcove lights are also dead, the newel post lamps on the marble staircase, the chandeliers in the grand foyer. Darkness envelops him like swirling fog, teeming with menace. Turning to run, he slaps up against a tall column. At least, he thinks, hanging on, it didn't fall over. The marble feels warm to his touch and he hugs it to him as the ingenue's insane giggle rattles hollowly through the darkened palace, sweeping high over his head like a passing wind or a plague of twittering locusts. The column seems almost to be moving, as though the whole room, like a cyclorama, were slowly pivoting. He recalls an old movie in which the killer finds himself trapped on a merry-go-round spinning out of control, sparking and shrieking and hurling wooden horses into the gaping crowd like terrorists on suicide missions. The killer, too: he lets go, understanding at last as he slides helplessly across the polished terrazzo floor the eloquent implications of pratfalls. What he slams into, however, is not a gaping crowd, but the drinking fountain near the elevator lobby, its sleek ceramic skin as cold to the touch as synthetic flesh. He can hear the cavernous gurgle and splatter of water as though the fountains throughout the movie palace might be overflowing. Yes, his pants are wet and his toes feel squishy inside their shoes.

He's not far, he realizes, from the stairwell down to the rooms below, and it occurs to him, splashing over on his hands and knees (perhaps he's thinking of the bomb shelters in war movies or the motherly belly of the whale), that he might be able to hide out down there for a while. Think things out. But at the head of the stairs he feels a cold draft: he leans over and sweeps the space with his hand: The stairs are gone, he would have plummeted directly into the unchartered regions below! It's not completely dark down there, for he seems to see a dim roiling mass of ballroom dancers, drill sergeants, cartoon cats, and restless natives, like projections on smoke, vanishing even as they billow silently up toward him. Is that the ingenue among them? The one in the grass skirt, her eyes starting from their sockets? Too late. Gone, as though sucked away into the impossible chasms below.

He blinks and backs away. The room has come to a stop, a hush has descended. The water fountains are silent. The floor is dry, his pants, his shoes. Is it over? Is she gone? He finds a twist of licorice in his pocket and, without thinking, slips it between his chattering teeth. Whereupon, with a creaking noise like the opening of a closet door, a plaster statue leans out of its niche and, as he throws himself back against the wall, smashes at his feet. The licorice has disappeared. Perhaps he swallowed it whole. Perhaps it was never there. He's reminded of a film he once saw about an alien conspiracy which held its nefarious meetings in an old carnival fun house, long disused and rigged now ("now" in the film) for much nastier surprises than rolling floors and booing ghosts. The hero, trying simply to save the world, enters the fun house, only to be subjected to everything from death rays and falling masonry to iron maidens, time traps, and diabolical life-restoring machines, as though to problematize his very identity through what the chortling fun-house operators call in their otherworldly tongue "the stylistics of absence." In such a maze of probable improbability, the hero can be sure of nothing except his own inconsolable desires and his mad faith, as firm as it is burlesque, in the prevalence of secret passages. There is always, somewhere, another door. Thus, he is not surprised when, hip-deep in killer lizards and blue Mercurians, he spies dimly, far across the columned and chandeliered pit into which he's been thrown, what appears to be a rustic wooden ladder, leaning radiantly against a shadowed wall. Only the vicious gnawing at his ankles surprises him as he struggles toward it, the Mercurians' mildewed breath, the glimpse of water-spotted underwear on the ladder above him as he starts to climb. Or are those holes? He clambers upward, reaching for them, devoted as always to this passionate seizure of reality, only to have them vanish in his grasp, the ladder as well: he discovers he's about thirty feet up the grand foyer wall, holding nothing but a torn ticket stub. It's a long way back down, but he gets there right away.

He lies there on the hard terrazzo floor, crumpled up like a lounge-lizard in a gilded cage (are his legs broken? his head? *something* hurts), listening to the whisperings and twitterings high above him in the coffered ceiling, the phantasmal tinkling of the chandelier crystals, knowing that to look up there is to be lost. It's like the dockside detective put it in that misty old film about the notorious Iron Claw and the sentimental configurations of mass murder: "What's frightening is not so much being able to see only what you want to see, see, but discovering that what you think you see only because *you* want to see *it . . . sees you . . .*" As he stands there on the damp shabby waterfront in the shadow of a silent boom, watching the night fog coil in around the tugboats and barges like erotic ribbons of dream, the detective seems to see or want to see tall ghostly galleons drift in, with one-eyed pirates hanging motionless from the yardarms like pale Christmas tree decorations, and he is stabbed by a longing for danger and adventure—another door, as it were, a different dome—even as he is overswept by a paralyzing fear of the unknown. "I am menaced," he whispers, glancing up at the swaying streetlamp (but hasn't he just warned himself?), "by a darkness beyond darkness . . ." The pirates, cutlasses in hand and knives between their teeth, drop from the rigging as though to startle the indifferent barges, but even as they fall they curl into wispy shapes of dead cops and skulking pickpockets, derelicts and streetwalkers. One of them looks familiar somehow, something about the way her cigarette dances between her spectral lips like a firefly (or perhaps that *is* a firefly, the lips his perverse dream of lips) or the way her nun's habit is pasted wetly against her thighs as she fades away down a dark alley, so he follows her. She leads him, as he knew she would, into a smoky dive filled with slumming debutantes and sailors in striped shirts, where he's stopped at the door by a scarred and brooding Moroccan. "The Claw . . . ?" he murmurs gruffly into his cupped hands, lighting up. The Moroccan nods him toward the bar, a gesture not unlike that of absolution, and he drifts over, feeling a bit airy as he floats through the weary revelers, as though he might have left part of himself lying back on the docks, curled up under the swaying lamp like a piece of unspooled trailer. When he sets his revolver on the bar, he notices he can see right through it. "If it's the Claw you're after," mutters the bartender, wiping a glass nervously with a dirty rag, then falls across the bar, a knife in his back. He notices he can also see through the bartender. The barroom is empty. He's dropped his smoke somewhere. Maybe the bartender fell on it. The lights are brightening. There's a cold metallic hand in his pants. He screams. Then he realizes it's his own.

He's lying, curled up still, under the chandelier. But not in the grand foyer of his movie palace as he might have hoped. It seems to be some sort of eighteenth-century French ball-room. People in gaiters, frocks, and periwigs are dancing min-uets around him, as oblivious to his presence as to the distant thup and pop of musket fire in the street. He glances up past the chandelier at the mirrored ceiling and is surprised to see, not himself, but the ingenue smiling down at him with softly parted lips, an eery light glinting magically off her snow-white teeth and glowing in the corners of her eyes like small coals, smoldering there with the fire of strange yearnings. "She is the thoroughly modern type of girl," he seems to hear someone say, "equally at home with tennis and tango, table talk and tea. Her pearly teeth, when she smiles, are marvelous. And she smiles often, for life to her seems a continuous film of enjoyment." Her smile widens even as her eyes glaze over, the glow in them burning now like twin projectors. "Wait!" he cries, but the room tips and, to the clunk and tinkle of tumbling parts, all the people in the ballroom slide out into the public square, where the Terror nets them like flopping fish.

Nor are aristocrats and mad projectionists their only catch. Other milieus slide by like dream cloths, dropping swashbucklers, cowboys, little tramps, singing families, train conductors and comedy teams, a paperboy on a bicycle, gypsies, mummies, leather-hatted pilots and wonder dogs, neglected wives, Roman soldiers in gleaming breastplates, bandits and gold diggers, and a talking jackass, all falling, together with soggy cigarette butts, publicity stills, and flattened popcorn tubs, into a soft plash of laughter and applause that he seems to have heard before. "Another fine mess!" the jackass can be heard to bray mournfully, as the mobs, jammed up behind police barricades in the dark but festive Opera House square, cry out for blood and brains. "The public is never wrong!" they scream. "Let the revels begin!"

Arc lights sweep the sky and somewhere, distantly, and ancient bugles blows, a buzzer sounds. He is pulled to his feet and prodded into line between a drunken countess and an animated pig, marching along to the thunderous piping of an unseen organ. The aisle to the guillotine, thickly carpeted, is lined with red velvet ropes and leads to a marble staircase where, on a raised platform high as a marquee, a hooded executioner awaits like a patient usher beside his gigantic ticket chopper. A voice on the public address system is recounting, above the booming organ and electrical chimes, their crimes (hauteur is mentioned, glamour, dash and daring), describing them all as "creatures of the night, a collection of the world's most astounding horrors, these abominable parvenus of iconic transactions, the shame of a nation, three centuries in the making, brought to you now in the mightiest dramatic spectacle of all the ages!" He can hear the guillotine blade rising and dropping, rising and dropping, like a link-and-claw mechanism in slow motion, the screams and cheers of the spectators cresting with each closing of the gate. "There's been some mistake!" he whimpers. If he could just reach the switchboard! Where's the EXIT sign? Isn't there always . . . ? "I don't belong here!" "Ja, zo, it iss der vages off cinema," mutters the drunken countess behind him, peeling off a garter to throw to the crowd. Spots appear on his clothing, then get left behind as he's shoved along, as though the air itself might be threadbare and discolored, and there are blinding flashes at his feet like punctures where bright light is leaking through.

"It's all in your mind," he seems to hear the usherette at the foot of the stairs whisper, as she points him up the stairs with her little flashlight, "so we're cutting it off."

"What—?!" he cries, but she is gone, a bit player to the end. The animated pig has made his stuttering farewell and the executioner is holding his head aloft like a winning lottery ticket or a bingo ball. The projectionist climbs the high marble stairs, searching for his own closing lines, but he doesn't seem to have a speaking part. "You're leaving too soon," remarks the hooded executioner without a trace of irony, as he kicks his legs out from under him. "You're going to miss the main feature." "I thought

I was it," he mumbles, but the executioner, pitilessly, chooses not to hear him. He leans forward, all hopes dashed, to grip the cold bolted foot of the guillotine, and as he does so, he notices the gum stuck under it, the dropped candy wrapper, the aroma of fresh pee in plush upholstery. Company at last! he remarks wryly to himself as the blade drops, surrendering himself finally (it's a last-minute rescue of sorts) to that great stream of image-activity that characterizes the mortal condition, recalling for some reason a film he once saw (*The Revenge of Something-or-Other*, or *The Return of, The Curse of*...), in which—

LAP DISSOLVES

(1987)

S he clings to the edge of the cliff, her feet kicking in the wind, the earth breaking away beneath her fingertips. There is a faint roar, as of crashing waves, far below. He struggles against his bonds, chewing at the ropes, throwing himself against the cabin door. She screams as the cliff edge crumbles, a scream swept away by the rushing wind. At last the door splinters and he smashes through, tumbling forward in his bonds, rolling and pitching toward the edge of the cliff. Her hand disappears, then reappears, snatching desperately for a fresh purchase. He staggers to his knees, his feet, plunges ahead, the ropes slipping away like a discarded newspaper as he hails the approaching bus. She lets go, takes the empty seat. Their eyes meet. "Hey, ain't I seen you somewhere before?" he says.

She smiles up at him. "Perhaps."

"I got it." He takes the cigar butt out of his mouth. "You're a hoofer over at Mike's joint."

"Hoofer?"

"Yeah—the gams was familiar, but I couldn't place the face."

She smiles again, a smile that seems to melt his knees. He grabs the leather strap overhead. "I help out over at *Father* Michael's 'joint,' as you'd say, Lefty, but—"

"Father—? *Lefty!* Wait a minute, don't tell me! You ain't that skinny little brat who useta—?" It's her stop. She rises, smiling, to leave the bus. "Hey, where ya goin'? How'm I gonna see you again?"

She pauses at the door. "I guess you'll have to catch my act at Mike's joint, Lefty." She steps down, her skirts filling with the sudden breeze of the street, and, one hand at her knees, the other holding down her fluttering wide-brimmed hat, walks quickly toward the church, glancing up at him with a mischievous smile as the bus, starting up again, overtakes and passes her. Her body seems to slide backwards, past the bus windows, slipping from frame to frame as though out of his memory—or at least out of his grasp. *"Wait!"* The driver hesitates: he jams his gat to the mug's ear—she's like his last chance (he doesn't know exactly what he means by that, but he's thinking foggily of his mother, or else of his mother in the fog), and she's gone! The feeling of inexpressible longing she has aroused gives way to something more like fear, or grief, frustration (why is it that some things in the world are so hard, while others just turn to jelly?), anger, a penetrating loathing—how could she *do* this to him? He squeezes, his eyes narrowing. Everything stops. Even, for a moment, time itself. Then, in the distance, a police whistle is heard. He takes his hands away from her throat, lets her drop, and, with a cold embittered snarl, slips away into the foggy night streets, his cape fluttering behind him with the illusory suggestion of glamour.

There is a scream, the discovery of the body, the intent expression on the detective's face as, kneeling over her, he peers out into the swirling fog: who could have done such a heinous thing? The deeper recesses of the human heart never fail to astound him. "Looks like the Strangler again, sir—a dreadful business." "Yes . . ." "Never find the bastard on a night like this, he just dissolves right into it." "We'll find him, Sergeant. And don't swear." People speak of the heart as the seat of love, but in his profession he knows better. It is a most dark and mysterious labyrinth, where cruelty, suspicion, depravity, lewdness lurk like shadowy fiends, love being merely one of their more ruthless and morbid disguises. To prowl these sewers of the heart is to crawl through hell itself. At every turning, another dismaying surprise, another ghastly atrocity. One reaches out to help and finds one's arms plunged, up to the elbows, in viscous unspeakable filth. One cries out—even a friendly "Hello!"—and is met with ghoulish laughter, the terrifying flutter of unseen wings. Yet, when all seems lost, there is always the faint glimmer of light in the distance, at first the merest pinprick, but soon a glow reflecting off the damp walls, an opening mouth, then out into sunshine and green fields, a song in his heart, indeed on his lips, and on hers, answering him across the hills, as they run toward each other, arms outspread, clothing flowing loosely in the summery breeze.

They run through fields of clover, fields of sprouting wheat, fields of waist-high grasses that brush at their bodies, through reeds, thick rushes, hanging vines. He is running through a sequoia forest, a golden desert, glittering city streets, she down mountainsides, up subway stairs, across spotlit stages and six-lane highways. Faster and faster they run, their song welling as though racing, elsewhere, toward its own destination, the back-grounds meanwhile streaking by, becoming a blur of flickering images, as if he and she in their terrible outstretched urgency were running in place, and time were blowing past them like the wind, causing her long skirts to billow, his tie to lift and flutter past his shoulder, as they stare out on the vast rolling sea from the ship's bow, arms around each other's waists, lost for a moment in their thoughts, their dreams, the prospect of a new life in the New World, or *a* new world (where exactly are they going?). "We're going home," he says, as though in reply to her unspoken (or perhaps spoken) question. "We'll never have to run again."

"It hardly seems possible," she sighs, gazing wistfully at the deepening sunset toward which they seem to be sailing.

Their reverie is rudely interrupted when pirates leap aboard, rape the woman, kill the man, and plunder and sink the ship—but not before the woman, resisting the violent advances of the peg-legged pirate captain, bites his nose off. "Whud have you dud?!" he screams, clutching the hole in his face and staggering about the sinking ship on his wooden peg. The woman, her fate sealed (already the cutlass that will decapitate her is whistling through the briny air), chews grimly, grinding the nose between her jaws like a cow chewing its cud, the sort of cow she might—in the New World and in a better, if perhaps less adventurous, life—have had, a fat old spotted cow with swollen udder and long white teats, teats to be milked much like a man is milked, though less abundantly. Of course, what does she know about all that, stuck out on this desolate windblown ranch (listen to it whistle, it's enough to take your head off) with her drunken old father and dimwit brothers, who slap her around for her milkmaid's hands, saying they'd rather fuck a knothole in an unplaned board—what's "fuck"? How will she ever know? How *can* she, cut off from all the higher things of life like finishing schools and sidewalks and floodlit movie palaces and world's fairs with sky-rides and bubble dancers and futuramas? But just wait, one day . . . ! she promises herself, tugging tearfully on the teats. She leans against Old Bossy's spotted flank and seems to see there before her nose a handsome young knight in shining armor, or anyway a clean suit, galloping across the shaggy prairie, dust popping at his horse's hooves, coming to swoop her up and take her away from all this, off to dazzling cities and exotic islands and gay soirees. She sees herself suddenly, as a ripple courses like music through Bossy's flank, aswirl in palatial ballrooms (the dance is in her honor!) or perhaps getting out of shining automobiles and going into restaurants with tuxedoed waiters who bend low and call her "Madame" (the milk squirting into the bucket between her legs echoes her excitement, or perhaps in some weird way *is* her excitement), or else she's at gambling tables or lawn parties, at fashion shows and horse races, or, best of all, stretched out in vast canopied beds where servants, rushing in and out, bring her all her heart's desires.

But no, no, she sees nothing at all there, all that's just wishful thinking—some things in this world are as hard and abiding as the land itself, and nothing more so than Bossy's mangy old rump, even its stink is like some foul stubborn barrier locking her forever out here on this airless prairie, a kind of thick muddy wall with rubbery teats, a putrid dike holding back the real world (of light! she thinks, of music!), a barricade of bone, a vast immovable shithouse, doorless and forlorn, an unscalable rampart humped up into the louring sky, a briary hedgerow, farting citadel, trench and fleabitten earthworks all in one, a glutinous miasma (oh! what an aching heart!), a no-man's-land, a loathsome impenetrable forest, an uncrossable torrent, a bottomless abyss, a swamp infested with the living dead, their hands clawing blindly at the hovering gloom, the air pungent with rot. He staggers through them, gasping, terrified, the quicksand sucking at his feet, toothless gums gnawing at his elbows, trying to remember how it is he ended up out here—some sort of fall, an airplane crash, an anthropological expedition gone sour, shipwreck, a wrong turn on the way to the bank? Certainly he is carrying a lot of money, a whole bucketful of it—he throws it at them and they snatch it up, stuffing it in their purulent jaws like salad, chewing raucously, the bills fluttering obscenely from their mouths and the holes in their flaking cheeks.

The money distracts them long enough for him to drag himself out of the swamp and onto higher ground, where he finds an old ramshackle clapboard house, its windows dark, door banging in the wind. He stumbles inside, slams the door shut, leans against it. He can hear them out there, scratching and belching and shedding bits and pieces of their disintegrating bodies as though appetite itself were pure abstraction, made visible in but fettered by flesh. A hand smashes through a window—he swings at it with a broom handle and it splatters apart like a clay pigeon, the wrist continuing to poke about as though in blind search of its vanished fingers. He shoves furniture up against the door and nearest windows, locates hammer and nails, rips away cupboard doors and shelves and table tops, nails them higgledy-piggledy across every opening he finds, his heart pounding. When he's done, the woman frying up pancakes and bacon at the stove says, "I *know* how you feel about traveling salesman, dear, but wouldn't it be cheaper just to buy one of their silly little back-scratchers and forget it?" He sighs. The air seems polluted somehow, as though with artifice or laughter. Is it those people outside?

"Gee, Dad," his son pipes up, ironically admiring his handiwork, "does that mean I don't have to go to school today?"

"I'm sure you can find your usual way out of the attic window and down the drainpipe, Billy, just as though it were Saturday," replies his mother, and again there is a disturbing rattle in the air.

"Hey, come on," the father complains, "it's not funny," but he seems to be alone in this opinion. He has the terrible feeling that his marriage is collapsing, even though the bacon's as crisp as ever. Or, if not his marriage, something . . .

"Hey, Dad, that's terrific!" exclaims his daughter, coming down for breakfast. "It looks like a giant tic-tac-toe board. What's it supposed to be, some kind of tribute to hurricanes or something?"

"That's right," says the mother, "it's called 'Three Sheets to the Wind.' Now, why don't you take it down, dear, and let the dog in. She's been scratching out there for an hour."

"Wow, speaking of sheets, I had the weirdest dream last night," says the daughter, ignoring the hollow static in the air. Her father shrinks into his chair, wondering whether the problem is that no one's listening—or that everyone is. "I was in this crazy city where everything kept changing into something else all the time. A house would turn into a horse just as you walked out of it or a golf course would take off and fly or a street would become a dinner table right under your feet. You might lean against a wall and find yourself out on the edge of a cliff, or

climb into a car that turned out to be the lobby of a movie theater. Some guy would walk up to you and change into a pizza or
a parking meter in front of your very eyes. Billy was in it, only
he was sort of like a pinball machine and to shoot a ball you had
to give a jerk on his peewee."

"That's stupid! Pinball machines are *girls*!"

"Maybe that explains the bed-wetting," sighs his mother.

"You were in it, too, Mom. You were in a chorus line in a
kind of scary burlesque show, in which all the dancers were collapsing into blobs and freaks. One of your breasts seemed to
slip down and slide out between your legs and you kept yelling
something like 'Get a bucket! Get a bucket!' Dad wasn't in the
dream, at least I didn't recognize him, but somebody who was
pretending to be him kept hammering on the door and saying
he was 'the loving dad' and please let him in. But I knew it was
just a werewolf who was trying desperately to change back into
a human and couldn't. See, everything kept changing except
the things that were *supposed* to change."

"Speaking of your father, where is he? Wasn't he here just a
minute ago?"

"I don't know. He wasn't looking very good. Sort of vague or
something."

"Oh boy! Can I have his pancakes, Mom?"

"Well, I hope he paid the mortgage this month."

"Anyway, there were these midget league baseball players
who turned out to be prehistoric monsters, and all of a sudden
they attacked the city, only even as they went on eating up the
people, the whole thing turned into a song-and-dance act in
which the leading monster did a kind of ballet with the Virgin
Mary who just a minute before had been a lawn chair. The

two of them got into a fight and started zapping each other with ray guns and screaming about subversion on the boundaries, but just then the ship sank and everybody fell into the sea. You could see them all floating down past these enormous buttocks that turned out to belong to a dead man in a bathtub. Don't ask me who *he* was! Well, it occurred to me suddenly that if everything else was changing I must be changing, too. I looked in a mirror and saw I could flatten my nose or pull it out to a point, push my chin up to my forehead, stretch my cheeks out like wings. Still, I felt like there was something that *wasn't* changing, I couldn't put my finger on it exactly, but it was something down inside, something I could only call *me*. In fact there *had* to be this something, I thought, or nothing else made sense. But what was it? Who was down there? I was curious, so I asked the woman I was with to tell me what she thought of when she thought of me. I told her it couldn't be anything physical, my scars or my cock or the shit-streaks in my underwear, it had to be something you couldn't touch or see. And what she said was, 'Well, I think of you as a straight shooter, Sheriff, but one who can't stop lustin' after the goddamn ineffable.' "

"She said that, hunh?"

"Yup."

"Shitfire, Sheriff, what'd you do?"

"Well, I shot her." He hacks up a gob and aims it at the spittoon. "When a woman starts askin' me to change my ways— *ptooey!*—I change women." He tosses down his drink, leans away from the bar, cocks a wary eye on the swinging doors. "But now tell me somethin', podnuh—is that just my bowels movin' or is this saloon *goin'* somewhere?!"

"I'm afraid nothing stands still for long. So, just buckle up and enjoy the ride, ma'am."

"Ma'am?!"

"Yes, we'll be there soon."

"*There*—?"

THE EARLY LIFE OF THE ARTIST

(1991)

For Benet Rossell

He was born in the thunderous and calamitous year of the aborted comet halfway between the letter Aleph and the seductively duplicitous alto clef (the village was otherwise nameless) under the astral sign of the Spilt Ink (in more modern times known as the Black-Hearted Hole), notorious for its disorderly influence on otherwise virtuous and economical lives.

His father was the inventor of radical mathematical formulae and was himself the walking double of the symbol for the square root (thus: rootless roots, a key to the artist's buoyant gravity and his tendency, not so much to float, as to bounce, lightly). His father's propositions, in the form of kaleidoscopic satires, bestial and beautiful at the same time, once caused the earth to turn inside out, but the only creatures awake at the time were drunks, bats, ogresses, and a scattering of poets and dungbeetles, and only the bats took notice and changed their habits. Fortunately, history was spared a nasty conversion, the members of the select committee for the

Nobel Prize for Mathematics being among those sleeping, though his son, a bat and yet not a bat, alas, was not. Later, he was to fix the blame for his lifetime of visual servitude upon the way his father's terrible calculations that fateful night spun his eyes inward and made his ears pop.

His mother, who was either an exquisitely beautiful parallelogram with tufts of feathers and insect wings at the corners or else a muddy mythological river, dark with carob pods, depending on her disposition, was, in spite of shifting appearances, the family anchor. It was she who emptied the brainpans and swept the tortured beds, prepared the daily stew of catastrophe and frolic, tolled the hours, cast the shadows, shielding them from death by illumination, washed out all their humble preshrunk anxieties, hanging them on her farflung limbs and curing them in the violent sun like mountain hams. When asked, much later, to describe his earliest memories, the artist replied: "Salty."

It was also his mother who first observed that words were stones and thus not only indigestible but also poor coin at the market, good only (like the rest of us) for landfill. This was her public observation; her private observation, made only to her family, was that everything was a stone, even air, love, and dreams. This brought great stability to her son's life, and great despair, making it hard, among other things, to breathe (always that caustic rattle, like a shingle beach raked by storm waves), but freeing his art from the illusion of permutability.

The village where he was born never acknowledged the family's presence or the artist's birth there, but this was nothing strange, for acknowledgment, like traffic lights and uncertainty, was utterly foreign to it. The village's fame indeed rested upon its stubborn and silent insouciance, which was, except for a certain ingenuous hylomorphism expressed by orchestrated wind-breaking in the village square and the occasional burst of spontaneous sky-writing, all it knew or knows of civic and religious procedure.

When he was young, the village was not strange. The world was strange. Now it is the village that is strange. The world, too.

For all that the artist came to know the world, if something so opaque and ephemeral can be said to be knowable, he was never able to leave the village of his birth behind. It clung to him like rumor, like wet underwear, like a swarm of sick flies, lovingly tenacious as athlete's foot. It hobbled his gait on city pavements, tripping him up on his way into subways and revolving doors. It caused the peas to roll off his knife in fashionable restaurants. Nor did his art escape, for the village got in his inks and paints like cowdung in honey and tracked up his canvases with ineradicable clawings and scratchings and turned his paper as fragrant and crumbly as hot country bread.

Much light might be thrown on this symbiosis of village and artist had the artist's earliest works, scratchings with a stick in the dust of his village streets completed at the age of three, been preserved for posterity, but in the village posterity had been over for some time, gone the way of the wooden whistle, immaculate conceptions, and the comforting orthodoxy of the garrote. His father had a mathematical formula about it, his mother a sobering aphorism. As for the artworks themselves, the village livestock had a more explicit comment, one artist speaking, so to speak, to another. "What you might call the natural reaction of invisible forces at work in the theater of the brain," one villager put it bluntly in his rude tongue, twitching his long ears, "and other bodily parts . . ."

The artist, too, precursor to both the action-painting ecstatics and the disposable art fundamentalists of a later age, could accept the obscuring of elemental vision by the anarchical graffiti of even more elemental sheep turds and mule tracks—who was he to insist on orderly alphabets when there were none?—yet it might be said that everything he has ever drawn, written, painted, fractured, composed, filmed, fondled, or sculpted since has been nothing more than an attempt to recover those first scratchings in the village dust all those years ago.

Thus, on the one hand, the village created the artist, providing him with implements and canvas and a palette enriched with the primary pigments of alienation and suffering (there was nettle-rash and hogbite, for example) and festive despair, together with song and murder and the spatialization of time with its saffron yellows and olive greens and mauves and ochers and cerulean blues, and, on the other hand, it made his art impossible, all art in fact, not just his, art being excluded from the village's available categories. Only when the village moved away one day and left him, alone as a crack in the sidewalk in the world's urban maze, did his life as an artist suddenly begin.

It began with little animated stitchings as though to suture a wound, or open one. Then color emerged and flowed from unseen sources, pushing the margins out until now the artist's drawings and paintings are as large as the village itself, which was probably not so large as the artist remembers it. What is he trying to do? Reinvent the lost village? Paper the void? Use up the world's forests in case the village might be hidden there? The artist will not say. He will only remark enigmatically to his circle of disbelieving admirers, while turning over and over in his paint-stained hands the luminous stones of his loves and dreams, that "there *was* no early life, only this mockery of a prolonged and bitter afterlife . . ."

THE NEW THING

(1994)

She attempted, he urging her on, the new thing. The old thing had served them well, but they were tired of it, more than tired. Had the old thing ever been new? Perhaps, but not in their experience of it. For them, it was always the old thing, sometimes the good old thing, other times just the old thing, there like air or stones, part (so to speak) of the furniture of the world into which they had moved and from which, sooner or later, they would move out. It was not at first obvious to them that this world had room for a new thing, it being the nature of old things to display themselves or to be displayed in timeless immutable patterns. Later, they would ask themselves why this was so, the question not occurring to them until she had attempted the new thing, but for now the only question that they asked (he asked it, actually), when she suggested it, was: Why not? A fateful choice, though not so lightly taken as his reply may make it seem, for both had come to view the old thing as not merely old or even dead but as a kind of, alive or dead, ancestral curse, inhibitory and perverse and ripe for challenge, impossible or even unimaginable though the new thing seemed until she tried it. And then, when with such success she did, her novelty responding to his appetite for it, the new thing displaced the old thing overnight. Not literally, of course, the old thing remained, but cast now into shadow, as the furniture of the world, shifting without shifting, lost its familiar arrangements. The old thing was still the old thing, the world was still the world, its furniture its furniture, yet nothing was the same, nor would it ever be, they knew, again. It felt—though as in a dream, so transformed was everything—like waking up. This was exhilarating (his word), liberating (hers), and greatly enhanced their delight—she whooped, he giggled, this was fun!—in the new thing, which they both enjoyed as much and as often as they could. Indeed, for a time, it filled their lives, deliciously altering perception, dissolving habit, bringing them ever closer together, illuminating what was once obscure, while making what before was ordinary now seem dark and alien. This was the power of the new thing, and also (they knew this from the outset) its inherent peril. The new thing, being truly new, not merely a rearrangement of the old, removed the ground upon which even the new thing itself might stand. The old things' preclusive patterns were like those frail stilts that flood-plains housing was erected on; the new thing joined forces with the cleansing flood. As did they in their unbound joy, having anticipated all this from the start, though perhaps not guessing then how close together delight and terror lay, nor back then considering, as she, he urging, made the new thing happen, how indifferent to their new creation would be both world and thing. Indifferent, but not untouched. All shook and they, the shakers, were not themselves unshaken. This, too, even trembling, they ardently embraced, though perhaps they whooped and giggled less. Scary! she laughed, reaching for him, and he, clinging to her and thinking as he fell that some principle must be at stake, something to do with time, cause, and motion perhaps: So much the better! Thus, even if somewhat apprehensively in such an altered yet indifferent world, they found pleasure in what might in others inspire dread, their own apprehension mitigated by their shared delight in this new thing, their delight dampened less by antique fears of being swept away in metaphoric floods than by their awareness that the new thing did not, could not know them, nor would or could the world in which they had brought it into being. The new thing, which was theirs, was, alas, not really theirs at all, nor could it ever be. Moreover (her logic, this), they had chosen the new thing, chose it still, but with the old thing lost from view, what choice was theirs in truth? Were they not in fact the chosen? And his reply: Let's go back to the old thing, just for fun, and see. And did they, could they? Of course! The old thing was waiting there for them as though neither they nor it had ever gone away, like an old shirt left in the closet, a lost friend discovered in a crowd, and they found new pleasure in returning to it, or at least comfort, and something like reconciliation with the entrenched and patterned ways of the world. The old thing reminds me of my childhood, he acknowledged gratefully, and she: Why this appetite for novelty anyway, when we are here so briefly we don't even have time enough to exhaust the old? Thus, they enjoyed the old thing anew and in ways they had not done before, chiefly by way of ceasing all resistance, and they told themselves that they were pleased. Of course, they had to admit, after knowing the new thing, it was not quite the same, the old thing. Sort of like dried fruit, she said, sweet and chewy now but not so juicy as before. He agreed: More like body than person, you might say, more carcass than body. They experimented, giving the old thing a new wrinkle or two, but could not sustain their revived interest in it: it was still the old thing and it still oppressed them. Back to the new thing. Which was still there and was delightful and exhilarating, as before. They were pleased and did not have to tell themselves they were. What fun! Truly! But the new thing, like the old thing, no matter how at first they denied this to each other, was also not the same as it had been before, he the first to admit it when regret, batlike, flickered briefly across her brow. No, she objected, falsely brightening, it is not it but we who have changed. By going back. To the old thing. Yes, you were right in the first place, he said, we were not free to choose. But we cannot go back to the new thing either. No, she agreed, we must try a new new thing. And so they did, and again, beginning to get the hang of this new thing thing, they found joy and satisfaction and close accord with one another. Out with old things and old new things, too! they laughed, falling about in their world-shaking pleasure. But was this delight in the new new thing as intense as that they'd felt when they'd first tried the old new thing? No (they couldn't fool themselves), far from it. So when the new new thing bumped up provocatively against the old new thing they were filled with doubt and confusion and no longer knew which of the two they most desired or should desire, if either. Out of their uncertainties came another new thing (his handiwork this time), momentarily delightful and distracting, but soon enough this too was replaced by yet another (now hers), itself as soon displaced (both now were separately busy at what had become more task than pleasure), the devising of new things now mostly what they did. By now, even the new thing's newness was in question. I am lost, she gasped, falling to her knees. He called out from across the room: I felt oppressed by the old thing, now I feel oppressed by the new. This is probably, she said, speaking to him by telephone, just the way of the insensate world. We were fooled yet again. No, no, I can't accept that, he replied by mail, else no new thing is a new thing at all. His letter crossed with hers: My unquenchable appetite for novelty is matched only by my unquenchable appetite for understanding. What a clown! I am deeply sorry. Adding: I have now become a collector of old things. There is not much fun in them, but there is satisfaction. But wait, he wrote in his diary. Does not the invention of one new thing insist by definition upon a second? And a third, a fourth, and indeed is this not in fact, this sequential generation of new things, the *real* new thing that we have made? And is that not delightful? He thought, if he tore this diary entry out and sent it to her, he might well see her again and they could have fun in their old new things way, but the time for all that was itself an old thing now and, anyway, he no longer knew, now after the flood, where in the world she was.

PUNCH

(2000)

Here comes Judy. Popping up. Mad about the baby. If you'd been walking by, I say, you could've caught him. My bitter half carries on in the grand style. Oh my poor child, my poor child, and so on. What a peach! I kill her with my stick. It's what I do best. I'm laughing. Roo-tee-too-ee-too-it. That's the rusty sound I make. They say it's not natural. They're right. It's not natural. Now here comes the law. I don't get a minute's rest. No respect for a poor widower. Doesn't take long. Bop. He's gone, too. More to follow. I can't help it. It's this big finger in my head. It points and says: Kill. I don't hesitate. If I did, they'd knock my hooter off and use me for the hangman. Anyway, it's fun. Something like fun. Biff, boff, another corpse. Roo-tee-to-to-toot. The baker: Roo-tee-too. A lawyer. That's the way to do it. A yapping dog: shut him up. Root-to-too-it. He's now the dog that everyone's as dead as. Joey comes to help me count the bodies. Too many. We lose track. Who cares. Stack 'em up. Joey's my pal. He's a brainless wall-eyed knockabout but a pal. Not big on the ladies, but it takes all kinds. My werry merry companion, as they say in the trade. I don't kill him. Probably couldn't if I tried. In fact, I have tried, but he's too quick. Straight out of the circus, that peckerless greaseball, and no hump or belly to slow him down. Let's forgive and forget, Joey, I say, and aim a blow at him, but he's behind me suddenly with a stick of his own. Ow, Joey, ow! I give up! Come on, let's go drown our sorrows. Is that like drowning cats, Mister Punch? Like enough, Joey. Well, here, put 'em in this bag, then. All right, Joey, here they are. Very good, Mister Punch. Now give 'em a widdle and they're gone to glory. The finger's out of my head and sticking out below and, after I wag it around a bit just to give it an airing, it's in the bag. Pssshh! Is the sound it makes. That did it, Mister Punch, says Joey, your sorrows have gone out with the tide, they've crossed over the waters, they're on the other side, and he snaps the bag shut around my psshher. Help, Joey, I'm caught! We have to get rid of those dead sorrows, Mister Punch, says Joey, and throws the bag out the window. I nearly follow it out but I don't. My arse is well-anchored. The bag dangles out there on my psshher, swinging back and forth like a pendulum, making a watery tick-tock sound. You shouldn't have done that, Joey. Why not, Mister Punch? I'll be arrested for deceitful exposure. They'll say I was inflaming the masses. Inflaming them whats? Come here, Joey, you scoundrel. Just look at that mob out there! Shaking their bellies and gapping their jaws! You think they want to eat my sorrows? Joey comes over to the window. I stiffen up and hit him with the bag, send him flying. Got him at last. Or maybe not. He bobs up again with another stick. Maybe it's mine. We fence in the heroic style, Joey with his stick, me with my stiffened psshher and bag of sorrows. The bag flies off and Joey's gone. I'm a happy man again. Free and frolicsome. Sorrows gone and psshher tucked safely away between my ears. But I miss Joey. Killing's no fun without a pal, and before I know it my head's getting diddled and I'm at it again. Roo-tee-toot, and so on, what I do best, down they go. Corpses everywhere. And now it's the hangman. You've broken the laws of the country, he says. I never touched them, says I. Just the same, your time is up, he says. Up whose? I ask. Ask the devil, he says. I just did. Enough of this impertinence! It's back to the woodpile for you, blockhead. Sawdust thou art and unto sawdust shalt thou return. And he sets up the gallows, the sanctimonious blowhard. Looks very like a puppet booth, I remark. That's right, Mister Punch, and you're going to dance in it, says he. Do you have any last words? Yes. I'm off. Good-bye. But police have popped up and are holding me. It's not that easy, you villain, says the hangman with a cruel laugh. Prepare to meet your Maker. I already know him, says I. He's a drunken wanker. That's enough now, Mister Punch, just put your head in here. I've never done this before, I say. I don't know how. Show me. He does and I jerk the rope and hang him. There's nothing to it. He's dancing on air. I whistle a little tune. The mob loves me for it. I'm a fucking hero.

Oh oh. It's Judy again. Thought I did her already. Must be her ghost. Probably. I killed her too soon, she wasn't done with her nagging, she has to come back and finish it. Can't be sure, though. She's as hard as ever. Take that, she says. And that. It's a real thumping I'm getting. Can you hit a ghost? Where's my stick? Somebody took my stick! She's got the baby. Or the ghost of the baby. The one I threw out the window. She hits me with it. Blow after blow. It's yowling fit to be tied. I'm yowling, too. Like a stuck pig. You can hear me for miles around. I'm a real crybaby when it comes to it. The dead brat and I're into a bawling duet that is sort of like roo-tee-too-it and sort of like boo-hoo and tee-hee. No, the tee-hees are Judy's. She's having a party. Her beak is lit up like a lantern, she's grinning ear to ear, her skirts are flying. Always one to give the mob a glim at her underparts, such as they are. But finally she poops herself out with so much strenuous haunting and, with a final whack that knocks me right off my pegs, she flits off with her squalling cudgel. It's all right. My hump's sorely blistered and I'm not likely to rise soon, but I'm not dead yet. Not quite. I've apparently got more killing to do. Who's next? It's the doctor. We know how this is going to turn out. Well, well, it's my old friend Punch, he says. Looks to have paid the debt to nature at last, and high time, too, he owed it a potful. Are you dead, Punch? Dead as a stone, I say. Well, that's good news, but you're a terrible liar, why should I believe you? Feel my pulse, I say. He gropes about and my knuckled gap-stopper pops out. Zounds! What's that? cries the doctor with some consternation. It's my brains oozing out, I say. I always supposed yours were down there in the dreck, Punch. It stiffens up. Great snakes! Now what's happening? exclaims the learned man, aghast at the dreadful sight. Rigor mortis, says I, and I bat his spectacles off with it. I think all you need, Punch old boy, is a sturdy dose of medicine. I prescribe a rum punch with extract of shillalagh, he declares, and he takes a swing at the offending digit with his cane. But it's already buried away again, so in remedy he cracks my nose instead. It honks like a goosed gander. I give him a taste of his own medicine with my stick, but it's evidently not a strong enough dose, for his condition worsens, I must improve on it. He tries to run away but I catch him with that clever thing between my legs and, holding him with it, chin in my chest, apply my therapeutics until he's physicked to a lifeless pulp. Roo-tee-too-it. Way to do it. The police are back. There's a law against killing doctors in broad daylight, they tell me. My watch must have stopped, I say. They take me to the judge. You're incorrigible, Punch, he says. A vile pestiferous reprobate, a murderer, a heartless foul-mouthed bully, a course loathsome unrepentant knave with-out a single redeeming feature. The mob is eating this up. How do you plead? Innocent, Your Honor! The mob boos and laughs. Innocent? Of all what you say, Your Honor, and lots more besides! The mob's cheering, he's banging his gavel. I'm feeling eloquent. I'm going to kill him, it's all I can do in this world except fall down, but I feel a spell of rhetoric coming on, so I rear back and let fly. By my oath, Your Worship, I am but as my Maker made me. His hand is in my head. By the smell, I think it's the same hand the sodden letch wipes his ass with. So what can I do? Whomsoever he hates, I hate, and he hates everybody. Even me, I think, that's why he takes it out on me from time to time. And whomsoever he hates, we dispatch. It's as much a law of nature, Your Honor, as that for which we need boghouses. The judge is immovable. Is that your final plea? Not quite, I say. Here it is. And I let a loud blattering fart that causes my shirttails to ripple out behind. The guards fall back, fanning their faces. The mob howls and I peer out at them and grin my rigid grin. Then I take the judge's gavel away from him and club him with it until he's a bag of mushy robes. That might have been Joey wearing a wig, but if so, too bad. I kill the guards before they can recover their senses and all the jury and it's time for a rest. Maybe I can find Polly.

And here comes Polly, popping up. No sooner maybe'd than here she is in all her silks and satins. Life's like that. A miraculous sequence of joys and sorrows. Punch, says the beautiful pink-cheeked strumpet, you're looking a touch woebegone. What's the trouble, my darling? Hemorrhoids again? No, Polly, love of my life, the pain's not in my arse but in my heart. Didn't know you had one, Punch, my precious knob, I'm gratified to hear of it. Maybe we can boil it up and have it for supper. Do not make light, Polly, of my little inquietudes. Oh dear, are they swoll up again? No, Polly dear, I speak of my mortified soul. My vexation of spirit. On the subject of spirits, she says, and she reaches into her skirts and pulls out a bottle. This should make you feel better, she says, or if not better, less, and in her loving way she drinks most of it off and hands the dregs to me. Now lie back and pull out that fidgety widget of yours, my dearest darling, she says with a tender burp, and let us dance our dance before your Judy comes round with her vengeful stick again. A sweet innocent child, Polly, still given to euphemisms. It's out and she's on it, doing her little gavotte, as one might call it. Perhaps there is music playing. A panpipe. Lovely. But I feel emptied out in heart and head. It's sad. You know me, Polly, as a happy bawdy fellow without a care in the world. I get to do a lot of killing, it's great fun, and the mob loves me for it, especially the ladies, whom as you know I never disappoint. I'm immortal and handsome and find the wherewithal for all my daily needs in the pockets of the recently deceased. I should be a most satisfied gent. But something's missing, I add with a tremulous sigh, my hands clapped to her bouncing bum, and I don't know what it is. Polly has got carried away with her dance and has nothing to say except: Oh! Oh! Oh! Some pleasure I'm missing out on? If I don't know what it is, I reply, conversing with myself, I'm not missing it. A reason for being? A tautology, dear heart, if you'll pardon the French. Meaning, am I missing? Pah! I don't even know what meaning means. Love? I'm drowning in it. Polly lets out a wild shriek, quivers all over as if caught by a sudden fever, then collapses over the mound of my belly, conking her head on my nose but seeming not to notice. Her little bum contin- ues to rise and fall gently as if trying to remember something. Maybe, I say as her dance dies away, it's just that everything seems to happen as it must. Even what I'm saying now. Polly grunts in sympathetic understanding and tweedles a pretty fart out between my fingers, perhaps an answer of sorts. Yes, I can always count on wise Polly.

But no time to contemplate it Her flatus raises the dead. Here comes Judy's ghost again, mad as ever, swinging the howling baby. The kid's had a tough life. Or death. I maybe should have been a better father. Judy, bellowing in her termagant fashion, rain blows on the both of us with the poor brat, intent, it would seem, on belting us both into her own domain of the dead. What rage! She's a real beauty! My sweet duck! For a moment I love her all over again and am sorry I killed her. Maybe I can take it back. Pretty Polly, though, just a wisp of a thing and drained by her dance, unable even to get disconnected from my digit, squeezed up tight in terror as she is, is no match for my Judy, and I worry for her health. She is not part of our little circle and does not understand why she is being walloped by a dead baby. Some things are best kept inside the family. Grateful still

for her fragrant little whiffle of wisdom, I ease her off me, and
cover her with my hump until she can drop out of sight, being
myself somewhat inured to the baby's blows. More than to its
cries. It's a maddening din. If I could, I'd throw it out the window again and the yowping mother with it. But they're ghosts.
They'd just fly back in again. In the pandemonium, I have forgotten to put Polly's dancing partner back where it belongs and
now dead Judy clamps her jaws on it, trying to bite it off. It's my
tenderest part. It hurts so much I can't think. Even though she's
got no teeth. All I can do is try to pull her off. She bites down
the harder, her nose and chin joining like the pincers of a crab.
Having her head there, for all the excruciating pain of it (if I
could cry, there'd be tears in my eyes, maybe there are tears in
my eyes), reminds me of happier times, though I can recall none
specifically. All the melting moments. There must have been
some. Where did we go wrong? Better not to ask. Finally, in desperation, I yank so hard, I rip her body away from her head. The
body, silent at last, flies away with the baby, but her head, still
wearing the Georgian mobcap, remains clamped on my suffering instrument of mercy and thanksgiving, my great anima-
tor. Without it in prime and proud condition, I'd be disgraced,
unable to hold my head up in public. I'll have to call for a doctor,
if there are any left, or else a carpenter, and have her sawn off.
Then I'll have to kill the doctor or carpenter, roo-tee-too-it, how
you do it, et cetera. Because I must. And then I'll do it all again.
As maybe I've done it all before. So much happens in this world.
I can hardly keep up with it from minute to minute. But then
it's gone. There's no residue. Ah. Well. Maybe, dear Polly, that's
what's missing. The price of immortality. When nothing ends,
nothing remains.

THE INVISIBLE MAN

(2002)

The Invisible Man gave up his life as a crime fighter, it was too hard and no one cared enough, and became a voyeur, a thief, a bugaboo, a prowler and pickpocket, a manipulator of events. It was more fun and people paid more attention to him. He began inhabiting horse tracks, women's locker rooms, extravagant festivities, bank vaults, public parks, schoolyards, and centers of power. He emptied tills, altered votes, made off with purses and address books, leaked secrets, started up fights in subway cars and boardrooms, took any empty seat he wanted on planes and trains, blew on the necks of naked women, moved pieces on gameboards and gambling tables, made strange noises in dark bedrooms, tripped up politicians and pop stars on stage, and whispered perverse temptations in the ears of the pious.

Theft was particularly easy except for the problem of what to do with what he took. To be invisible he had to be naked, and there were not too many places on or in his body where he could hide things which themselves were not invisible. And these places (notably, his mouth and his rectum, which served as his overnight bag, so to speak) were often filled with other necessities. So, except for small jewelry store heists which could be slipped in, he was generally limited to what he could hold in his closed fists or squeeze under his armpits or between his buttocks, his daily spoils comparable then to those of a common panhandler, from whom on bad days he also sometimes stole. Still, there was not much on which to spend his wealth, whatever he wanted he could simply take and he could travel and live as and where he pleased, so he soon amassed a small fortune and, privy to all the inside information he needed, became a successful day trader on the side.

Though drawn into a life of crime without remorse, and tempted like anyone else to kill a few people while he was at it, he had no place to conceal a suitable weapon, indeed it would be dangerous if he tried, so his new career was necessarily limited to lesser felonies. Of course, he could discreetly misdirect the aim of others, but in fact he steered clear of armed persons, as well as reckless drivers, busy kitchens, operating rooms. He could still be hurt. Stray bullets could wound him, knives could prick. He was only invisible, not immortal. And his insides were not invisible, his excretions weren't, his blood. What a sight, a wound in view and no wounded! Moreover, if wounded, who would heal him? Perhaps he could find a blind doctor, though probably there weren't many. And if he died, who would mourn him? Who would even see him there to bury him? He'd become a kind of odd speed bump in the road for a month or two. Such were the handicaps of an invisible person, no matter how rich they were or how much secret mischief they enjoyed.

He was also obliged to stay away from cold places. Though

his nakedness was apparent to no one and he himself was accustomed to it, it was a reality he could not ignore. Cold winds drove him inside, air conditioning out. Sometimes, to warm himself or to conduct some business or other such as fencing his stolen goods, or perhaps simply in response to a deep longing, he made himself visible with masks, wigs, and costumes. So as not to have to steal these things over and over, he bought a house to store them in, and took up stamp and coin collecting and growing orchids on the side. There were many choices amongst his costumes, many characters he could be, and this added to his existential angst: who was he really? Without a costume, he was invisible even to himself. In the mirror he could see no more than anyone else could see: a blurry nothingness where something should be. "You are a beautiful person," he would say to it, more as an instruction than a comment.

When costuming himself, he had to dress carefully from head to toe. One day he forgot his socks and caused something of a sensation when taking his seat on the subway. "Sorry, a . . . a kind of cancer," he explained to the people staring aghast at his missing ankles, fully aware (he exited hastily at the next stop) that the mouth on the mask was not moving. On another day in a crowded elevator (when visible, he loved to mingle with the human masses, feel the body contact, something that usually had to be avoided when invisible), his scarf fell off, which was even worse. A woman fainted and the other passengers all shrank back. "It's just a trick," he chuckled behind the deadpan mask, which no doubt appeared to them to be floating in mid-air. He riffled a deck of cards enigmatically in his gloved hands, and when the door opened, he turned his empty eyes upon them to mesmerize them long enough to make his escape. After that, he took to wearing body suits as the first layer, a kind of under-coat, much as he hated getting in and out of them.

Mostly, though, he went naked and unseen, committing his crimes, indulging himself in his manipulative and voyeuristic pleasures. Women fascinated him, and he loved watching them do their private things, frustrating as it was at times not to par-ticipate. Even when they were most exposed, they remained unfathomably mysterious to him, and an unending delight. And it was one day while hanging out in the ladies' room of a grand hotel during a hairdressers' convention that, when things were slow, he stepped into a stall and raised the seat to relieve himself, only to have the door open behind him and the seat lower itself again, and he knew then that he was not alone in his invisibility. Was she (he assumed "she") sitting on the seat or was this merely a gender signal and a warning? Taking no chances, he backed out silently, hoping he wasn't dripping, the opening and closing of the stall door no doubt telling her all she needed to know.

After that, he began to feel pursued. Perhaps she had been following him for some time and he hadn't noticed. Now he seemed to sense her there whether she was or not, and whether or not, he had to consider his every move as if she were. She might still be an active crime fighter, just waiting to appre-hend him or to avenge some crime that he'd committed in the past. He retreated from more than one burglary, sensing her presence in the room, and sometimes it seemed there was another hand in the pocket he was trying to pick. He watched the women on the street carefully in case she, like he, occasion-ally made herself visible, and they all appeared to him to be wearing masks. He was jostled by absences, felt a hot breath often on his neck. His income dropped off sharply and he was even inhibited from acquiring his daily necessities. Her possible proximity made him self-conscious about his personal hygiene and interfered with his voyeuristic routines. He felt especially vulnerable inside his own house and went there less often, with the consequence that the food in his refrigerator spoiled and his orchids died.

How did she know where he was if she couldn't see him? By following the clues the invisible always leave behind: footprints in the mud, snow (of course he never walked in snow), and sand, bodily excretions, fingerprints (he couldn't wear gloves, nor carry them without getting them messy), discarded costumes and toothbrushes, mattress indentations, floating objects, swirling dust, fogged windows. She could watch for places where the rain did not fall and listen for the noises his body made. He had always stumbled over things; now he could not be sure she was not placing those things in his path to expose him, so just moving about was like negotiating a mine field. He had to eat more surreptitiously, not to exhibit the food flying about before vanishing, and so ate too fast, giving himself heartburn. But when he started to steal a packet of antacids, he thought he saw it move as he reached for it.

Then it occurred to him one day that she might not be a crime fighter after all, merely another lonely invisible person seeking company, and as soon as he had that thought, she disappeared, or seemed to. He should have felt relieved, but he did not. He found that he missed her. Though she had not been exactly friendly, she was the nearest thing to a friend he'd ever had. He went back to where they'd first met and raised and lowered the toilet seat, but there was no response. He should have spoken up that day. He did now: "Are you there?" he whispered. No reply, though the lady in the next stall asked: "Did you say something?" "No, dear, just a frog in the throat," he wheezed in a cracking falsetto, then flushed quickly and swung the door open and closed before the woman could get up from where she was sitting and peek in. But he remained in the stall for a time, reflecting on how something so ordinary as a toilet seat can be transformed suddenly into something extraordinary and, well, beautiful . . .

Now he left clues everywhere and committed crimes more daring than before. If she was a crime fighter he wanted to be arrested by her. If she was not, well, they could be partners. She even had more room to hide things, they could tackle bigger jobs. As he moved about, he swung his arms freely, hoping to knock into something that did not seem to be there, but caused only unfortunate accidents and misdirected anger. Twice he got shot at in the dark. He figured it was a small price to pay. Perhaps if he were hurt she'd feel pity for him and make herself known. He began to see her, even in her invisibility, as unutterably beautiful, and he realized that he was hopelessly in love. He thought of his adoration of her as pure and noble, utterly unlike his life in crime, but he also imagined making mad impetuous love to her. Rolling about ecstatically in their indentations. Nothing he'd seen in his invisible powder-room prowls excited him more than these imaginings.

Still, for all his hopes, she gave no further evidence of her existence. In his house, he left messages on the mirrors: "Take me, I'm yours!" But the messages sat there, unanswered, unaltered. When he looked in the mirrors, past the lettering, he could not see his cheeks but he could see the tears sliding down them. His love life, once frivolous, had turned tragic, and it was all his fault. Why had he never *touched* her? A fool, a fool! He was in despair. He hung out in bars more often, drinking other people's drinks. He got sick once and threw up beside a singing drunk peeing against a wall, sobering the poor man up instantly. He knew that rumors about him were beginning to spread, but what did it matter? Without her, his life was meaningless. It had not been very meaningful before she came into it, but now it was completely empty. Even crime bored him. Voyeurism did: what did he care about visible bodies when he was obsessed by an invisible one?

He tried to find some reason for going on. Over the years, he'd been collecting a set of antique silverware from one family, a piece at a time. He decided to finish the set. He didn't really want the silverware, but it gave him something to do. He successfully picked up another couple of pieces, operating recklessly in broad daylight, but then went back one time too many and, with a soup spoon up his ass, got bit on the shins by a watchdog the family had bought to try to catch the silverware thief. He got away, doing rather serious damage to the dog (in effect, it ate the soup spoon), but he bled all the way home. He supposed they'd follow the trail, didn't care if they did, but they didn't. Maybe they were satisfied not to lose the spoon.

But the wound was slow to heal and he couldn't go about with it or the bandage on it exposed, so he donned the costume of an old man (he *was* an old man!) and spent his days in cheap coffee shops feeling sorry for himself and mooning over his lost love. He went on doing this even after the dog bite had healed, drawn to coffee shops with sad songs on their sound systems. He no longer stole but bought most of what he needed, which was little, but now included reading materials for his coffee shop life. He avoided newspapers and magazines, preferring old novels from vanished times, mostly those written by women, all of whom he tended to think of as beautiful and invisible. He would sometimes sit all day over a single page, letting his mind drift, muttering softly to himself, or more or less to himself, all the things he should have said when she was still in his life.

Then one day he saw, sitting at another table, also greatly aged, an old police captain he used to work with back in his crime-fighting days. He made himself known to him (the captain did not look surprised; perhaps he'd been tailing him) and asked him how things were going down at the station. "Since you left, Invisible Man," said the officer, "things have gone from bad to worse. You became something of a nuisance to us when you took up your new career, but it was a decision we could understand and make allowances for. Now there are gangs of invisible people out there committing heinous crimes that threaten to destroy the very fabric of our civilization." The Invisible Man stroked his false beard thoughtfully. "And since I stopped being a crime fighter, have you had help from any other . . . person like myself?" "No. Until these new gangs came along, you were unique in my experience, Invisible Man." So, he thought, she might be among them. "It's why we're turning to you now. We're asking you to come back to the force, Invisible Man. We need you to infiltrate these gangs and help us stop them before it's too late." "You're asking me to turn against my own people," he said, somewhat pretentiously, for in truth he never thought of himself as having people. "These aren't your people, Invisible Man, it's a whole new breed. They create fields of invisibility so even their clothing and weapons and everything they steal is made invisible when it enters it. And now they're into bomb-making." This was serious, all right; but he was thinking about his beloved. His former beloved. He understood now that she might have been trying to recruit him for her gang, but had found him unworthy, and he felt hurt by that. "They think of you as old-fashioned, Invisible Man, and have said some very unflattering things about you. In particular, about your personal habits, of which of course I know nothing. But they also look up to you as a kind of pioneer. And though their power is greater than yours, their technology is less reliable. They've suffered catastrophic system crashes, and we want them to suffer a few more. It's a dangerous job, Invisible Man, but you're the only one we know who can handle it."

So once again he took up his old life as a crime fighter, but under cover of renewed criminality, drifting somewhat cynically through the city in his old invisible skin, targeting the city fathers for his burglaries and vandalisms, dropping inflammatory notes to draw attention to himself, and even, with help from the captain, blowing up the captain's own car, which he said was anyway in need of extensive clutch and transmission repairs, so he was glad to get rid of it—in short, making himself available, waiting to be contacted. Would she be among them? He felt misunderstood by her, undervalued, and in some odd way misused. A victim of love. Which he no longer believed in, even while still in the grip of its unseen power. And if he found her again, would he crash her system? Or would she succeed in seducing him into the gangs' nefarious activities? Who knows? He decided to keep an open mind about it. The future was no easier to see than he was.

THE RETURN OF THE DARK CHILDREN

(2002)

When the first black rats reappeared, scurrying shadowily along the river's edge and through the back alleyways, many thought the missing children would soon follow. Some believed the rats might *be* the children under a spell, so they were not at first killed, but were fed and pampered, not so much out of parental affection, as out of fear. For, many legends had grown up around the lost generation of children, siphoned from the town by the piper so many years ago. Some thought that the children had, like the rats, been drowned by the piper, and that they now returned from time to time to haunt the town that would not, for parsimony, pay their ransom. Others believed that the children had been bewitched, transformed into elves or werewolves or a kind of living dead. When the wife of one of the town councilors hanged herself, it was rumored it was because she'd been made pregnant by her own small son, appearing to her one night in her sleep as a toothless hollow-eyed incubus. Indeed, all deaths, even those by the most natural of causes,

were treated by the citizenry with suspicion, for what could be
a more likely cause of heart failure or malfunction of the inner
organs than an encounter with one's child as a member of the
living dead?

At first, such sinister speculations were rare, heard only
among the resentful childless. When the itinerant rat-killer
seduced the youngsters away that day with his demonic flute, all
the other townsfolk could think about was rescue and revenge.
Mothers wept and cried out the names of their children, calling
them back, while fathers and grandfathers armed themselves
and rushed off into the hills, chasing trills and the echoes of
trills. But nothing more substantial was ever found, not even
a scrap of clothing or a dropped toy, it was as though they had
never been, and as the weeks became months and the months
years, hope faded and turned to resentment—so much love
misspent!—and then eventually to dread. New children meanwhile were born, replacing the old, it was indeed a time of great
fertility for there was a vacuum to be filled, and as these new
children grew, a soberer generation than that which preceded
it, there was no longer any place, in homes or hearts, for the
old ones, nor for their lightsome ways. The new children were,
like their predecessors and their elders, plump and happy, much
loved, well fed, and overly indulged in all things, but they were
more closely watched and there was no singing or dancing. The
piper had instilled in the townsfolk a terror of all music, and
it was banned forever by decree. All musical instruments had
been destroyed. Humming a tune in public was an imprison-
able offense and children, rarely spanked, were spanked for it.
Always, it was associated with the children who had left and
the chilling ungrateful manner of their leaving: they did not

even look back. But it was as though they had not really quite gone away after all, for as the new children came along the old ones seemed to return as omnipresent shadows of the new ones, clouding the nursery and playground, stifling laughter and spoiling play, and they became known then, the lost ones, the shadowy ones, as the dark children.

In time, all ills were blamed on them. If an animal sickened and died, if milk soured or a house burned, if a child woke screaming from a nightmare, if the river overflowed its banks, if money went missing from the till or the beer went flat or one's appetite fell off, it was always the curse of the dark children. The new children were warned: Be good or the dark children will get you! They were not always good, and sometimes, as it seemed, the dark children did get them. And now the newest menace: the return of the rats. The diffident pampering of these rapacious creatures soon ceased. As they multiplied, disease broke out, as it had so many years before. The promenade along-side the river that ran through the town, once so popular, now was utterly forsaken except for the infestation of rats, the flower gardens lining the promenade trampled by their little feet and left filthy and untended, for those who loitered there ran the risk of being eaten alive, as happened to the occasional pet gone astray. Their little pellets were everywhere and in everything. Even in one's shoes and bed and tobacco tin. Once again the city fathers gathered in emergency council and declared their deter-mination to exterminate the rats, whether they were bewitched dark children or not; and once again the rats proved too much for them. They were hunted down with guns and poisons and burned in mountainous heaps, their sour ashes blanketing the town, graying the laundry and spoiling the sauces, but their

numbers seemed not to diminish. If anything, there were more
of them than ever seen before, and they just kept coming. But
when one rash councilor joked that it was maybe time to pay the
piper, he was beaten and hounded out of town.

For, if the dark children were a curse upon the town, they
were still their own, whereas that sorcerer who had lured them
away had been like a mysterious force from another world, a
diabolical intruder who had forever disturbed the peace of the
little community. He was not something to laugh about. The
piper, lean and swarthy, had been dressed patchily in too many
colors, wore chains and bracelets and earrings, painted his bony
face with ghoulish designs, smiled too much and too wickedly
and with teeth too white. His language, not of this town, was
blunt and uncivil and seemed to come, not from his throat, but
from some hollow place inside. Some seemed to remember that
he had no eyes, others that he did have eyes but the pupils were
golden. He ate sparely, if at all (some claimed to have seen him
nibbling at the rats), and, most telling of all, he was never seen
to relieve himself. All this in retrospect, of course, for at the
time, the townsfolk, vastly comforted by the swift and entertaining eradication of the rats, saw him as merely an amusing
street musician to be tolerated and, if not paid all that he imper-
tinently demanded (there had been nothing illegal about this,
no contracts had been signed), at least applauded——the elders,
like the children, in short, fatally beguiled by the fiend. No,
should he return, he would be attacked by all means available,
and if possible torn apart, limb from limb, his flute rammed
down his throat, the plague of rats be damned. He who placed
himself beyond the law would be spared by none.

Left to their own resources, however, the townsfolk were no

match for the rats. For all their heroic dedication, the vermin continued to multiply, the disease spread and grew more virulent, and the sky darkened with the sickening ash, now no longer of rats only, but sometimes of one's neighbors as well, and now and then a child or two. Having lost one generation of children, the citizenry were determined not to lose another, and did all they could to protect the children, their own and others, not only from the rats but also from the rumored dark children, for there had been reported sightings of late, mostly by night, of strange naked creatures with piebald flesh moving on all fours through the hills around. They had the form of children, those who claimed to have seen them said, but they were not children. Some said they had gray fleshy wings and could hover and fly with the dating speed a dragonfly. Parents now boiled their children's food and sterilized their drink, policed their bedrooms and bathrooms and classrooms, never let them for a single minute be alone. Even so, now and then, one of them would disappear, spreading fear and consternation throughout the town. But now, when a child vanished, no search parties went out looking for it as they'd done the first time, for the child was known to be gone as were the dead gone, all children gone or perished spoken of, not as dead, but taken.

The city elders, meeting in continuous emergency session, debated the building of an impregnable wall around the town to keep the dark children out and hopefully to dam the tide of invading rats as well. This had a certain popular appeal, especially among the parents, but objections were raised. If every able-bodied person in town worked day and night at this task, it was argued, it would still take so long that the children might all be gone before it could be finished: then, they'd just be wall-ing themselves in with the rats. And who knew what made a wall impregnable to the likes of the dark children? Weren't they, if they existed, more like phantoms than real creatures for whom brick and stone were no obstruction? Moreover, the building of such a wall would drain the town of all its energy and resources and close it off to trade, it would be the end of the era of prosperity, if what they were suffering now could still be called prosperity, and not only the children could be lost, but also the battle against the rats, which was already proving very taxing for the community. But what else can we do? We must be more vigilant!

And so special volunteer units were created to maintain a twenty-four-hour watch on all children. The playgrounds were walled off and sealed with doubled locks, a compromise with the proponents of the wall-building, and all the children's spaces were kept brightly lit to chase away the shadows, even as they slept at night. Shadows that seemed to move by themselves were shot at. Some observed that whenever a child disappeared a pipe could be heard, faintly, just before. Whether this was true or not, all rumors of such flaunting of the music laws were pursued with full vigor, and after many false alarms one piper was at last chased down: a little boy of six, one of the new children, blowing on a wooden recorder. He was a charming and dutiful boy, much loved by all, but he had to be treated as the demon he now was, and so, like any diseased animal, he and his pipe were destroyed. His distraught parents admitted to having hidden away the childish recorder as a souvenir at the time of outlawing musical instruments, and the child somehow, inexplicably, found it. The judges did not think it was inexplicable. There were calls for the death penalty, but the city fathers were not cruel or vindictive and understood that the parents had been severely punished by the loss of their child, so they were given lengthy prison sentences instead. No one protested. The prison itself was so rat-infested that even short sentences amounted to the death penalty anyway.

The dark children now were everywhere, or seemed to be. If the reports of the frightened citizenry were to be believed, the hills about now swarmed with the little batlike phantoms and there was daily evidence of their presence in the town itself. Pantries were raided, flour spilled, eggs broken, there was salt in the sugar, urine in the teapot, obscene scribblings on the school chalkboard and on the doors of closed shops whose owners had taken ill or died. Weary parents returned from work and rat-hunting to find all the pictures on their walls tipped at odd angles, bird cages opened, door handles missing. That these sometimes turned out to be pranks by their own mischievous children was not reassuring for one had to assume they'd fallen under the spell of the dark children, something they could not even tell anyone about for fear of losing their children to the severity of the laws of vigilance now in place. Whenever they attempted to punish them, their children would cry: It's not my fault! The dark children made me do it! All right, all right, but shush now, no talk of that!

There were terrible accidents which were not accidents. A man, socializing with friends, left the bar one night to return home and made a wrong turn, stumbled instead into the ruined gardens along the promenade. One who had seen him passing by said it was as if his arm were being tugged by someone or something unseen, and he looked stricken with terror. His raw carcass was found the next morning at the edge of the river.

One rat-hunter vanished as though consumed entirely. Another was shot dead by a fellow hunter, and in two different cases, rat poison, though kept under lock and key, turned up in food; in both instances, a spouse died, but the partners were miraculously spared. When asked if the killing was an accident, the hunter who had shot his companion said it certainly was not, a mysterious force had gripped his rifle barrel and moved it just as he was firing it. And things didn't seem to be where they once were any more. Especially at night. Furniture slid about and knocked one over, walls seemed to swing out and strike one, stair steps dropped away halfway down. Of course, people were drinking a lot more than usual, reports may have been exaggerated, but once-reliable certainties were dissolving.

The dark children remained largely invisible for all that the town felt itself swarming with them, though some people claimed to have seen them running with the rats, swinging on the belfry rope, squatting behind chimney pots on rooftops. With each reported sighting, they acquired new features. They were said to be child-sized but adult in proportions, with long arms they sometimes used while running; they could scramble up walls and hug the ground and disappear right into it. They were gaudily colored and often had luminous eyes. Wings were frequently mentioned, and occasionally tails. Sometimes these were short and furry, other times more long and ratlike. Money from the town treasury disappeared and one of the councilors as well, and his wife, though hysterical with grief and terror, was able to describe in startling detail the bizarre horned and winged creatures who came to rob the town and carry him off. Ah! We didn't know they had horns. Oh yes! With little rings on the tips! Or bells! They were glittery all over as if dressed in jewels! She said she was certain that one of them was her own missing son, stolen away by the piper all those many years ago. I looked into his eyes and pleaded with him not to take his poor father away, she wept, but his eyes had no pupils, only tiny flickering flames where the pupils should be! They asked her to write out a complete profile of the dark children, but then she disappeared, too. When one of the volunteer guards watching children was charged with fondling a little five-year-old girl, he insisted that, no, she was being sexually assaulted by one of the dark children and he was only doing all he could to get the hellish creature off her. The child was confused but seemed to agree with this. But what happened to the dark child? I don't know. The little girl screamed, a crowd came running, the dark child faded away in my grasp. All I managed to hold on to was this, he said, holding up a small gold earring. A common ornament. Most children wear them and lose them daily. I tore it out of his nose, he said. He was found innocent but removed from the unit and put on probation. In his affidavit, he also mentioned horns, and was able to provide a rough sketch of the dark child's genitalia, which resembled those of a goat.

The new children pretended not to see the dark children, or perhaps in their innocence, they didn't see them, yet overheard conversations among them suggested they knew more than they were telling, and when they were silent, they sometimes seemed to be listening intently, smiling faintly. The dark children turned up in their rope-skipping rhymes and childish riddles (When is water not wet? When a dark child's shadow makes it . . .), and when they chose up sides or games of ball or tag, they tended always to call one of their teams the dark children. The other was usually the hunters. The small children cried if they couldn't be on the dark children's team. When a child was taken, his or her name was whispered among the children like a kind of incantation, which they said was for good luck. The church organist, unemployed since the piper went through and reduced to gravetending, a task that had somewhat maddened him, retained enough presence of mind to notice that the familiar racket of the children's playground games, though still composed of the usual running feet and high-pitched squealing, was beginning to evolve into a peculiar musical pattern, reminiscent of the piper's songs. He transcribed some of this onto paper, which was studied in private chambers by the city council, where, for the first time in many years, surreptitious humming was heard. And at home, in their rooms, when the children played with their dolls and soldiers and toy castles, the dark children with their mysterious ways now always played a part in their little dramas. One could hear them talking to the dark children, the dark children speaking back in funny squeaky voices that quavered like a ghost's. Even if it was entirely invented, an imaginary world made out of scraps overheard from parents and teachers, it was the world they chose to live in now, rather than the one provided by their loving families, which was, their parents often felt, a kind of betrayal, lack of gratitude, lost trust. And, well, just not fair.

One day, one of the rat-hunters, leaning on his rifle after a long day's work and smoking his old black pipe, peered down into the infested river and allowed that it seemed to him that whenever a child vanished or died, the rat population decreased. Those with him stared down into that same river and wondered: Was this possible? A rat census was out of the question, but certain patterns in their movements could be monitored. There was a wooden footbridge, for example, which the rats used for crossing back and forth or just for cavorting on, and one could at any moment make a rough count of the rats on it. At the urging of the hunters, these tabulations were taken by the town clerk at dawn, midday, and twilight for several days, and the figures were found to be quite similar from day to day, no matter how many were killed. Then, a little girl failed to return from a game of hide-and-seek (the law banning this game or any game having to do with concealment was passing through the chambers that very day), and the next day the rat numbers were found to have dropped. Not substantially perhaps, one would not have noticed the change at a glance, but it was enough to make the bridge count mandatory by law. A child, chasing a runaway puppy, fell into the turbulent river and was taken and the numbers dropped again, then or about then. Likewise when another child disappeared (he left a note, saying he was going where the dark children were to ask if they could all be friends) and a fourth died from the diseases brought by the rats.

Another emergency session of the council was called which all adult members of the community were invited to attend. No one stayed away. The choice before them was stark but, being all but unthinkable, was not at first enunciated. The parents, everyone knew, were adamant in not wanting it spoken aloud at all. There were lengthy prolegomena, outlining the history of the troubles from the time of the piper's visit to the present, including reports from the health and hospital services, captains of the rat-hunting teams, the business community, the volunteer vigilance units, school and toiler monitors, the town clerk, and artists who provided composite sketches of the dark children based on reported sightings. They did not look all that much like children of any kind, but that was to be expected. A mathematician was brought in to explain in precise technical detail the ratio between the disappearance or death of children and the decrease in the rat population. He was convincing, though not well understood. Someone suggested a break for tea, but this was voted down. There was a brief flurry of heated discussion when a few parents expressed their doubts as to the dark children's actual existence, suggesting they might merely be the fantasy of an understandably hysterical community. This argument rose and faded quickly, as it had few adherents. Finally, there was nothing to do but confront it: their choice was between letting the children go, or living—and dying—with the rats.

Of course it was unconscionable that the children should be sacrificed to save their elders, or even one another. That was the opinion vehemently expressed by parents, teachers, clergy, and many of the other ordinary townsfolk. This was not a decision one could make for others, and the children were not yet of an age to make it for themselves. The elders nodded solemnly. All had to acknowledge the rightness of this view. Furthermore, the outcome, based on speculative projections from these preliminary observations, was just too uncertain, the admirable mathematics notwithstanding, for measures so merciless and irreversible. A more thorough study was required. As for the bridge counts themselves, seasonal weather changes were proposed as a more likely explanation of the decline in the rat population—if in fact there had been such a decline. The numbers themselves were disputed, and alternative, unofficial, less decisive tabulations made by others, worried parents mostly, were presented to the assembly and duly considered. And even if the official counts were true, a teacher at the school argued, the vermin population was probably decreasing normally, for all such plagues have their tides and ebbs. With patience, it will all be over.

The data, however, did not support this view. Even those sympathetic with them understood that the parents and teachers were not trying to engage in a reasoned search for truth, but were desperately seeking to persuade. The simple facts were that the town was slowly dying from its infestation of rats, and whenever a child was taken the infestation diminished; everyone knew this, even the parents. The data was admittedly sketchy, but time was short. A prolonged study might be a fatal misjudgment. A doctor described in uncompromising detail the current crisis in the hospitals, their staffs disease-riddled, patients sleeping on the floors, medications depleted, the buildings themselves aswarm with rats, and the hunters reminded the assembly that their own untiring efforts had not been enough alone to get the upper hand against the beasts, though many of them were parents, too, and clearly ambivalent about their testimony. Those who had lost family members to the sickness and risked losing more, their own lives included, spoke bluntly: If the children stay, they will all die of the plague like the rest of us, so it's not as though we would be sacrificing them to a fate worse than they'd suffer here. But if they go, some of us might be saved. A compromise was proposed: Lots could be drawn and the children could be released one by one until the rats disappeared. That way, some might be spared. But that would not be fair, others argued, for why should some parents be deprived of their children when others were not? Wouldn't that divide the community irreparably forever? Anyway, the question might be purely academic. Everyone had noticed during the mathematician's presentation the disconcerting relationship between the rate of decrease of the rat population and the number of children remaining in the town. They want the children, shouted a fierce old man from the back of the hall, so let them have them! We can always make more!

Pandemonium broke out. Shouts and accusations. You think it's so easy! cried one. Where are your own? It's not the making, cried others, it's the raising! They were shouted down and they shouted back. People were called murderers and cowards and egoists, ghouls and nihilists. Parents screamed that if their children had to die they would die with them, and their neighbors yelled: Good riddance! Through it all, there was the steady pounding of the gavel, and finally, when order was restored, the oldest member of the council who was also judged to be the wisest, silent until now, was asked to give his opinion. His chair was wheeled to the illumined center of the little platform at the front of the hall whereon, behind him, the elders sat. He gazed out upon the muttering crowd, his old hands trembling, but his expression calm and benign. Slowly, a hush descended.

There is nothing we can do, he said at last in his feeble old voice. It is the revenge of the dark children. Years ago, we committed a terrible wrong against them and this is their justified reply. He paused, sitting motionlessly in the pale light. We thought that we could simply replace them, he said. But we were wrong. He seemed to be dribbling slightly and he raised one trembling hand to wipe his mouth. I do not know if the dark children really exist, he went on. I myself have never seen them. But, even if they do not, it is the revenge of the dark children just the same. He paused again as if wanting his words to be thoroughly understood before proceeding, or perhaps because his thoughts came slowly to him. I have, however, seen the rats, and even with my failing eyesight, I know that they are real. I also know that the counting of them is real, whether accurate or not, and that your responses to this counting, while contradictory, are also real. Perhaps they are the most real thing of all. He seemed to go adrift for a moment, his head nodding slightly, before continuing: It may be that the diminishing number of rats is due to the day-by-day loss of our children or it may be due to nature's rhythms or to the weather or the success at last of our hunters. It may even be that the numbers are not diminishing, that we are mistaken. It does not matter. The children must go. There was a soft gasp throughout the hall. Because, he said as the gasp died away, we are who we are. The old man gazed out at them for a short time, and each felt singled out, though it was unlikely he could see past the edge of the platform. The children will not go one by one, he went on. They will go all at once and immediately. That is both fair and practical. And, I might add, inevitable. He nodded his head as though agreeing with himself, or perhaps for emphasis. They themselves will be happier together than alone. And if we who remain cannot avoid grief, we can at least share it and comfort one another. Even now, if our humble suggestions are being followed, the children are being gathered together and told to put on their favorite clothes and bring their favorite toys and they are then being brought to the town square outside this building. As parents, turning pale, rose slowly from their seats, he again wiped his mouth with the back of his hand and his expression took on a more sorrowful aspect. I foresee a rather sad future for our town, he said. The rats will finally disappear, for whatever reason, though others of us will yet perish of their loathsome diseases, and our promenade will reopen and trade will resume. Even should we repeal the music laws, however, there will still be little if any singing or dancing here, for there will be no children, only the memory of children. It has not been easy for the town's mothers and fathers to suffer so, twice over, and I feel sorry for them, as I am sure we all do. We must not ask them to go through all that again. He cocked his old head slightly. Ah. I can hear the children outside now. They are being told they are going off to play with the dark children. They will leave happily. You will all have an opportunity to wave goodbye, but they will probably not even look back. Nor of course will they ever return. In the shocked pause before the rush to the exits, he added, speaking up slightly: And now will we at last be free of the dark children? He sighed and, as his head dipped to his chest, raised one trembling finger, wagging it slowly as though in solemn admonishment. No. No. No, my friends. We will not.

RIDDLE

(2005)

I t is the lieutenant's first execution. Five men are to die by firing squad, and his company has drawn the assignment. He
does not look forward to it, but he will not falter in his duty. He
is a hunter and has killed often, creatures large and small. Nor
will these five be the first men he has killed, though they will
be the first he has put away in this manner, tied helplessly to
a post and shot on command. At least, he believes, they should
be allowed to run free and be chased down as fair game. He is
a sportsman and a soldier, not a butcher. Still, what's to be done
will be done. The five—a priest, a truck driver, a labor organizer,
a student, and a farm worker—will not see the morrow. Their
fate is a harsh one, but it is not an undeserved one. Directly or
indirectly, with arms or with words, they have brought about
the deaths and injuries of many, have sown the seeds of law-
lessness, and have even threatened the downfall of the state.
They have their reasons, their causes, but they do not justify
the havoc they have unleashed on orderly society. Which is, at

best and by necessity, as all know well, an unsatisfactory compromise. Not all rules are good rules, but they must be obeyed
until better ones are found, else all collapses into anarchy and
humankind returns to that condition from which it has so labo-
riously emerged, one ruled by blood, not by mind.

That is anyway what the lieutenant, dedicated keeper of law
and order, believes: that civilization such as that he serves is
hard-won over many centuries and all too easily lost in a day,
man being the capricious undisciplined animal that he is. He
understands, as the student Lázaro Luján would say, his own
weaknesses and urges, and fears them in others, the law their
safe container. Lázaro Luján, known to his comrades as the
Reader, also believes in civilized society but does not believe
that he lives in one. Moreover, civilization is not a condition or
an achievement or even an ideal, but a process, demanding constant renewal, its good health dependent upon periodic upheav-
als, such as this one he is presently guilty of fostering. He
does agree with the lieutenant that civilization does not come
without hard work and sacrifice. There is always a price to be
paid, and in his case that price is high. He has suffered expul-
sion from the university, rejection by his family, the deaths of
friends and loss of lovers, injustice, incarceration, and torture,
and now must pay with his life. His remote austere father, a
judge with high connections, might have saved him but did not.
As Lázaro Luján himself fiercely demanded: Hands off, this
choice is mine! Thus, he feels at once respected and abandoned.
When the lieutenant asked him if he had any final request, he
asked that he be allowed to say in what order they will stand for
their executions, placing himself at one end.

Which is why Carlos Timoteo faces the firing squad with

the labor organizer on his right. The lieutenant understands the student's choice. He knows that Carlos Timoteo has no ideology at all unless it be that of a primitive and superstitious religion which even the priest would scorn. He seems confused by life, speaks only in incoherent mutters. The labor organizer beside him is a brave man, brazen even, devoted to his dangerous politics, ambitious, well spoken, proud. He has lived a life of confrontation, this thus its natural conclusion, whereas Carlos Timoteo is a man who finds himself on history's stage without quite knowing, though his crimes were many, how he got there. The lieutenant therefore supposes that the student wanted the least committed of the condemned to stand alongside someone who might give him courage and a sense at the end, however illusory, of purpose. Actually, however, Carlos Timoteo's purpose is clear and free of illusions. His has been a long life of humiliation and abuse. He has been beaten, chained, mocked, knifed, used as a human mule, kicked, branded, tied to a tree and whipped. Even now, his gnarled calloused hands are suppurating at the fingertips where, until yesterday, his nails were. They laughed, who tore them out, as many have laughed before. Carlos Timoteo was not born to wealth or power, nor has he even dreamed of it; all he has sought his whole life through is dignity. Which at last today he has found. For once, he signifies. He will face his executioners with his head held high.

It's true, the populist creed of Carlos Timoteo is not that of the priest, but he would not scorn it. In fact, simple as it is, it is more reliable and steadfastly held than his own. All the poverty, injustice, corruption, cruelty that he has witnessed have taken their toll. Suffering humankind has won his love at the expense of his lost love of God. Which is an idea he no longer trusts,

any more than he trusts the church which propagates it, hand-
maiden to the venal state. The priest's logic is simple: If God is
good, He cannot exist. If He is not, He should not. All but the
student have asked him for spiritual guidance at this moment
of extremity, even the anarchist. He has told all of them that in
the eyes of the church they are saints and will be blessed by the
best the afterlife has to offer. Which, he knows but does not say,
is nothing; he could provide the lieutenant and his soldiers the
same consolation, or even the corrupt and ruthless leaders they
have struggled against, the lascivious bishop who denounced
him. The soldiers will raise their rifles, silhouetted against the
blank whiteness of the overcast sky, and the door will close. The
priest, unlike Carlos Timoteo, has no one on his right to give
him company and strength. I am merely one of the thieves, he
thinks bitterly, and what's more, I will it so.

The anarchist, Umberto Iglesias, sees no conflict between
anarchism and religion. Indeed, he thinks of God, in His absolute freedom and cosmic violence, as the ultimate anarchist.
Order stifles and is the devil's realm. Look only at the devils
who maintain it. He's not as smart maybe as the Reader beside
him, but he's not stupid. He knows that violence is the natural
state of things, the universe a boiling pot of ceaseless eruption,
destruction, and renewal, life itself a mere fleeting aberration,
the nation-state life's mad invention. Destroy it, Umberto Iglesias figures, you're doing the universe a favor. The labor leader
cries out now for justice, and the others mutter their assent,
poor fools. They just don't get the joke. They're like a comedian's nightmare audience, probably they deserve to die for that
reason alone. But, then, who doesn't, and for whatever reason?
Umberto Iglesias has never actually blown anything up, but he's

trucked the explosives around for those who have. He's dreamed
of hitting the floorboard one day and driving his loaded truck
at top speed into the capitol or the stock exchange or even the
casino where over the years he has been robbed of all he's ever
earned, but much as he disdains life, he's been reluctant to give
it up, having too much fun in it. Especially with the women,
fucking being the best thing about being alive, maybe the only
good thing, and at the same time the weirdest thing of all. Now,
it's too late for revolutionary glory (fuck glory of any kind, history is a farcical delusion), too late for anything short of shitting
himself. Already, he is shackled to the post, the firing squad is
standing at attention, the lieutenant is giving the soldiers their
final instructions. Umberto Iglesias has had his eye on the lieutenant, that jaunty bastard, recognizing in him a kindred spirit,
but one warped by fear and ambition into its contrary, that sickness men, suckered by reason, call sanity. The lieutenant is calling out their names. So how is Umberto Iglesias going to meet
the end of things? By thinking about the open road and about
all the women he's had. See if he can remember them all in
order and how they smelled and what they did.

The lieutenant has also been aware of Umberto Iglesias—
while being bound to the post, the condemned man winked at
him and grinned—and he too recognizes that there is something that they have in common, though the lieutenant supposes this simply to be the love of women. Umberto Iglesias is a
handsome man with dark eyes and sensuous lips and a dissolute
air, no doubt a favorite with the ladies. Perhaps he should have
had the insolent wretch emasculated before executing him, but,
though this has on occasion happened under the lieutenant's
command, he has never himself ordered it, being respectful of

the authority of love as of all authority. He has never even neutered animals, his own possible neutering in warfare his worst and most persistent nightmare. The lieutenant is not a superstitious man—even his gambling is grounded in a mathematical logic—yet he fears (irrationally, he knows, and reconsiders the truck driver's wink) love's reprisal should he in any way interfere with its sweet mechanics. He could at least have blindfolded Umberto Iglesias, but he, like the other prisoners, chose as his final request to face his executioners with open eyes, and this, because it suited him, he granted them. He too, as with the animals that he hunted, wished to gaze into their eyes before killing them, watching them as they watched death's advent. Noting Hugo Urbano standing to the right of Amadeo Fernández while calling out the names of the condemned, the lieutenant realizes that there was a purpose after all to the student's lineup, an unexpectedly ironic one, and that consequently he will have a riddle tonight for his riddle-loving lover. He raises his hand as a signal.

As the members of the firing squad raise and cock their rifles, the lieutenant having turned toward him with a bemused gaze, his hand in the air, Lázaro Luján suddenly, with deep chagrin, realizes his mistake. His last chance to raise a word against the gun, and he has, yet again, written, not for his audience, but for himself. Trapped as always in his own ego, just as his mentors and peers have so often said. What a pity at such a moment as this to feel their scorn. His comrades have fallen silent. In the distance, he sees a lone black bird, scribbling its riddles on the white sky. Its message is obscure but, Lázaro Luján realizes with a sudden flash of insight, it is not completely illegible. If only . . .

Later that night, the lieutenant describes the day's events to his lover while she works aromatic oils into his chest and abdomen. He does not tell her about his personally giving each of the condemned the coup de grâce with his pistol while they were still hanging from their posts, nor about the stripping of the bodies of their possessions by his soldiers, but he has left in the truck driver's knowing wink. I think my men found too much pleasure in the killing, he says. Pleasure? Well, excitement. Thrills. One is never so aware of consciousness as at the moment of annihilating it in another. They are probably all with their lovers tonight, as am I, and no less rampant and awake. I'm afraid I don't understand such excitement, she says. Is that the riddle you spoke of? No. From what I have told you, can you tell me who were each of the condemned and in what order they were standing? And what was the message the student wished to leave behind? I had supposed he might have been given to some jejeune romantic gesture, and so I was surprised by its bitter irony. I have already solved it, his lover said with a smile, and told him the names and occupations of each and where in the line they stood. And as for the message, she added, spreading the oils between his thighs, perhaps you yourself have not entirely puzzled out the riddle left you.

GRANDMOTHER'S NOSE

(2005)

S he had only just begun to think about the world around her. Until this summer, she and the world had been much the same thing, a sweet seamless blur of life in life. But now it had broken away from her and become, not herself, but the place her self resided in, a sometimes strange and ominous other that must for one's own sake be studied, be read like a book, like the books she'd begun to read at the same time the world receded. Or maybe it was her reading that had made the world step back. Things that had once been alive and talked to her because part of her—doll, house, cloud, well—were silent now, and apart, and things that lived still on their own—flower, butterfly, mother, grandmother—she now knew also died, another kind of distance.

This dying saddened her, though she understood it but dimly (it had little to do with her, only with the inconstant world she lived in), and it caused her to feel sorry for these ill-fated things. She used to think it was funny when her mother chopped the head off a chicken and it ran crazily around the garden; now she didn't. She no longer squashed ants and beetles under foot or pulled the wings off flies and butterflies, and she watched old things precious to her, like her mother, with some anxiety, frightened by the possibility of their sudden absence. Since dying was a bad thing, she associated it with being bad, and so was good, at least as good as she could be: she wanted to keep her mother with her. If her mother asked her to do something, she did it. Which was why she was here.

She also associated dying with silence, for that was what it seemed to come to. So she chattered and sang the day through to chase the silence away. A futile endeavor, she knew (she somehow had this knowledge, perhaps it was something her grandmother taught her or showed her in a book), but she kept it up, doing her small part to hold back the end of things, cheerfully conversing with any creature who would stop to talk with her. This brought smiles to most faces (she was their little heroine), though her mother sometimes scolded her: Don't speak with strangers, she would say. Well, the whole world was somewhat strange to her, even her mother sometimes, it was talk to it or let the fearful stillness reign.

Though the world was less easy to live in than before, it was more intriguing. She looked at things more closely than she had when looking at the world was like looking in at herself, her eyes, then liquid mirrors in a liquid world, now more like windows, she poised behind them, staring out, big with purpose. To be at one with things was once enough, sameness then a comfort like a fragrant kitchen or a warm bath. Now, it was difference that gave her pleasure: feathers (she had no feathers), petals, wrinkles, shells, brook water's murmuring trickle over stones, not one alike, her mother's teeth (she hadn't even seen them there in her mouth before), the way a door is made, and steps, and shoes. She thought about words like dog, log, and fog, and how unalike these things were that sounded so like cousins, and she peered intensely at everything, seeking out the mystery in the busyness of ants, the odd veiny shape of leaves, the way fire burned, the skins of things.

And now it was her grandmother's nose. It was a hideous thing to see, but for that reason alone aroused her curiosity. It was much longer and darker than she remembered, creased and hairy and swollen with her illness. She knew she ought not stare at it—poor Grandma!—but fascination gripped her. Such a nose! It was as if some creature had got inside her grandmother's face and was trying to get out. She wished to touch the nose to see if it were hot or cold (Grandma lay so still! it was frightening); she touched her own instead. Yes, dying, she thought (though her own nose reassured her), must be a horrid thing.

The rest of Grandma had been affected, too. Though she was mostly covered up under nightcap, gown, and heaped-up bedclothes as though perhaps to hide the shame of her disease, it was clear from what could be glimpsed that the dark hairy swelling had spread to other parts, and she longed—not without a little shudder of dread—to see them, to know better what dying was like. But what could not be hidden was the nose: a dark bristly outcropping, poking out of the downy bedding like the toe of a dirty black boot from a cloud bank, or from snow. Plain, as her grandmother liked to say, as the nose on your face. Only a soft snort betrayed the life still in it. Grandma also liked to say that the nose was invented for old people to hang their spectacles on (Grandma's spectacles were on the table beside her bed, perched on a closed book), but the truth was, eyes were probably invented to show the nose where to go. The nose sat in the very middle of one's face for all to see, no matter how old one was, and it led the way, first to go wherever the rest went, pointing the direction. When she'd complained that she'd forgotten the way to Grandma's house, her mother had said: Oh, just follow your nose. And she had done that and here she was. Nose to nose with Grandma.

Her grandmother opened one rheumy eye under the frill of her nightcap and stared gloomily at her as though not quite recognizing her. She backed away. She really didn't know what to do. It was very quiet. Perhaps she should sing a song. I've brought you some biscuits and butter, Grandma, she said at last, her voice a timid whisper. Her grandmother closed her eye again and from under her nose let loose a deep growly burp. A nose was also for smelling things. And Grandma did not smell very nice. On the way I also picked some herbs for tea. Shall I put some on? Tea might do you good.

No, just set those things on the table, little girl, her grandmother said without opening her lidded eye, and come get into bed with me. Her voice was hoarse and raw. Maybe it was a bad cold she was dying of.

I'd rather not, Grandma. She didn't want to hurt her grandmother's feelings, but she did not want to get close to her either, not the way she looked and smelled. She seemed to be scratching herself under the bedding. It's . . . not time for bed.

Her grandmother opened her near eye again and studied her a moment before emitting a mournful grunt and closing it again. All right then, she mumbled. Forget it. Do as you damned well please. Oh dear, she'd hurt her feelings anyway. Her grandmother burped sourly again and a big red tongue flopped out below her swollen nose and dangled like a dry rag on a line, or her own cap hanging there.

I'm sorry, Grandma. It's just that it scares me the way you look now.

However I look, she groaned, it can't be half so bad as how I feel. Her grandmother gaped her mouth hugely and ran her long dry tongue around the edges. It must have been—*fooshh!*—something I ate.

She felt an urge to remark on her grandmother's big toothy mouth which was quite shocking to see when it opened all the way (so unlike her mother's mouth), but thought better of it. It would just make her grandmother even sadder. She'd said too much already, and once she started to ask questions, the list could get pretty long, not even counting the parts she couldn't see. Her big ears for example, not quite hidden by the nightcap. She remembered a story her grandmother told her about a little boy who was born with donkey ears. And all the rest was donkey, too. It was a sad story that ended happily when the donkey boy got into bed with a princess. She began to regret not having crawled into bed with her poor grandmother when she begged it of her. If she asked again, she would do it. Hold her breath and do it. Isn't there some way I can help, Grandma?

The only thing you're good for, child, would just make things worse. Her grandmother lapped at her nose with her long tongue, making an ominous scratchy sound. Woof. I'm really not feeling well.

I'm sorry . . .

And so you should be. It's your fault, you know.

Oh! Was it something I brought you that made you sick?

No, she snapped crossly, but you led me to it.

Did I? I didn't mean to.

Bah. Innocence. I eat up innocence. Grandma gnashed her teeth and another rumble rolled up from deep inside and escaped her. When I'm able to eat anything at all . . . foo. . . She opened her eye and squinted it at her. What big eyes you have, young lady. What are you staring at?

Your. . . your nose, Grandma.

What's the matter with it? Her grandmother reached one hand out from under the bedding to touch it. Her hand was black and hairy like her nose and her fingernails had curled to ugly claws.

Oh, it's a very *nice* nose, but . . . it's so . . . Are you dying, Grandma? she blurted out at last.

There was a grumpy pause, filled only with a snort or two. Then her grandmother sighed morosely and grunted. Looks like it. Worse luck. Not what I had in mind at all. She turned her head to scowl at her with both dark eyes, the frill of the nightcap down over her thick brows giving her a clownish cross-eyed look. She had to smile, she couldn't stop herself. Hey, smartypants, what's funny? You're going to die, too, you know, you're not getting out of this.

I suppose so. But not now.

Her grandmother glared at her for a moment, quite ferociously, then turned her head away and closed her eyes once more. No, she said. Not now. And she lapped scratchily at her nose again. In a story she'd read in a book, there was a woman whose nose got turned into a long blood sausage because of a bad wish, and the way her grandmother tongued her black nose made her think of it. Did her grandmother wish for something she shouldn't have?

I sort of know what dying is, Grandma. I had a bird with a broken wing and it died and turned cold and didn't do anything after that. And living, well, that's like every day. Mostly I like it. But what's the point if you just have to die and not be and forget everything?

How should I know what the damned point is, her grandmother growled. She lay there in the heaped bedding, nose high, her red tongue dangling once more below it. She didn't move. It was very quiet. Was she already dead? Or just thinking? Appetite, her grandmother said finally, breaking the silence. And the end of appetite. That's it.

That was more like the Grandma she knew. She had lots of stories about being hungry or about eating too much or the wrong things. Like the one about the little girl whose father ate her brother. He liked it so much he sucked every bone (now every time she ate a chicken wing, she thought of that father). The little girl gathered all the bones he threw under the table and put them together and her brother became a boy again. Grandma often told stories about naughty boys and cruel fathers, but the little boy in this story was nice and the father was quite nice, too, even if he did sometimes eat children.

Her grandmother popped her eye open suddenly and barked in her deep raspy voice: Don't look too closely! It scared her and made her jump back. She'd been leaning in, trying to see the color of the skin under the black hairs. It was a color something like that of old driftwood. Look too closely at anything, her grandmother said, letting the dark lid fall over her eye once more and tilting her nose toward the ceiling, and what you'll see is nothing. And then you'll see it everywhere, you won't be able to see anything else. She gaped her jaws and burped grandly. Big mistake, she growled.

The thing about her grandmother's nose, so different from her own, or from anyone's she knew, she thought as she put the kettle on for tea, was that it seemed to say so much more to her than her grandmother did. Her nose was big and rough, but at the same time it looked so naked and sad and kind of embarrassing. She couldn't figure out exactly *what* she thought about it. Grandma's talk was blunt and plain and meant just what it said, no more. The nose was more mysterious and seemed to be saying several things to her at once. It was like reading a story about putting a brother back together with his licked bones and discovering later it was really about squashing bad ladies, one meaning hidden under another one, like bugs under a stone. With a pestle, she ground some of the herbs she'd brought in a mortar, then climbed up on a chair to get a cup down from the cupboard. Her grandmother's nose was both funny and frightening at the same time, and hinted at worlds beyond her imagination. Worlds, maybe, she didn't really want to live in. If you die, Grandma, she said, crawling down from the chair, I'll save all your bones.

To chew on, I hope, her grandmother snapped, sinking deeper into the bedding. Which reminds me, she added, somewhat more lugubriously. One thing your grandmother said, as I now recall, was: Don't bite off more than you can chew.

Yes. But *you're* my grandmother.

That's right. Well—*wuurpp!*—don't forget it. Now go away. Leave me alone. Before I bite your head off just to shut you up.

This dying was surely a hard thing that her grandmother was going through, one had to expect a little bad temper. Even her grandmother's nose seemed grayer than it had been before, her tongue more rag-like in its lifeless dangle, her stomach rumblings more dangerously eruptive. It was like she had some wild angry beast inside her. It made her shudder. Dying was definitely not something to look forward to. The kettle was boiling so she scraped the mortar grindings into the cup and filled it full of hot water, set the cup on the table beside the bed. Here, Grandma. This will make you feel better. Her grandmother only snarled peevishly.

Later, when she got home, her mother asked her how Grandma was feeling. Not very well, she said. A wolf had eaten her and got into bed in Grandma's nightclothes and he asked me to get in bed with him. Did you do that? No, I sort of wanted to. But then some men came in and chopped the wolf's head off and cut his tummy open to get Grandma out again. I didn't stay but I think Grandma was pretty upset. Her mother smiled, showing her teeth, and told her it was time for bed.

Was that what really happened? Maybe, maybe not, she wasn't sure. But it was a way of remembering it, even if it was perhaps not the best way to remember poor Grandma (that nose!), though Grandma was dying or was already dead, so it didn't really matter. She crawled into her bed, a place not so friendly as once it was, but first she touched her bedstead, the book beside it (Grandma gave it to her), her pillow, doll, felt the floorboards under her feet, convincing herself of the reality of all that, because some things today had caused her doubt. No sooner had her feet left the floor, however, than there was nothing left of that sensation except her memory of it, and that, she knew, would soon be gone, and the memory of her grandmother, too, and some day the memory of her, and she knew then that her grandmother's warning about the way she looked at things had come too late.

STICK MAN

(2005)

The Stick Man is gazing out upon the horizon. Wistfully perhaps, it's hard to be certain. Even he is not sure what he is feeling or ought to be feeling. The horizon is a mere line, but as always he fills it in with a landscape of his imagination. He does this simply by announcing it: e.g., the Stick Man is standing in the Garden of Paradise. And, with that, so he is. This is usually rewarding and satisfies him. He lives a rich and complex life and is rarely not satisfied. Today, however, the Garden of Paradise seems a bit tatty. Trampled. Gone to seed.

Perhaps he has been too long inactive. Standing limbs akimbo in the same place inventing landscapes. Straightening up from time to time when pleased or displeased with his mental transformations of the horizon line, otherwise motionless. So he puts himself through some exercises. He lifts his stick hands above his head. He bends over and touches the ends of his stick feet. He squats. He sits. He lies down. That's better. He lies there for awhile on the featureless plain, inventing activities appropriate to this position. The Stick Man meditates on the ontology of being. The Stick Man digests. The Stick Man gazes at the stars (it is night now). The Stick Man watches the clouds roll by, changing their shapes (it is day). The Stick Man waits in vain for a revelation to descend. The Stick Man wonders if he can get up again. The Stick Man attempts a sit-up. Abandons it. The Stick Man rests.

It is in the prone position that he has his best ideas, and his idea now is to make love to the Stick Woman. He often does this when he's feeling a bit low or his imagination goes flat. To have the idea is to bring her to his side. She is identical to him in every way—the same empty circle for a head, the same straight spine, crossed by a shoulder bar and a hip bar at the base, with the four trisected limbs hanging off the bar ends—except that she has a notch in the bottom of the hip bar where he has a tab, which is something like a comma except when making love. Even then, actually. A thing of naught. The Stick Woman calls it his tendril. Always hopeful. When their sticks are heaped together, they make a pretty picture, as of secret hieroglyphs.

After making love, he does feel better and he thanks the Stick Woman for it, but his creative appetite remains unaroused. The Stick Man reinvents the universe, he announces. But in fact he continues to lie there in the inert postcoital position. Perhaps he should visit the human world again. The Stick Woman reminds him that in the past these visits have not been very successful. That's right, he had forgotten. Or, rather, he had not forgotten, but he had not wanted to remember. No, he tells the Stick Woman, they have not, but they give me fresh ideas. Help me get up.

The horizon line has vanished and all visible space in all

possible directions is filled with human activity. The Stick Man is standing in the middle of it, more or less erect, his limbs slightly akimbo: he wants to appear relaxed. But he is not relaxed and anyone can see that. He looks desperately out of place and all too aware that he looks out of place. These humans would look out of place in his stick world, too, he knows that, but they are not in his world, nor are they likely to go there; he is in their world. Where he is unwanted. He remembers now that the last time he was here they tried to dismantle him and use his head for a manhole cover. People are uncomfortable around someone without facial features of any kind. Not to mention someone without clothing, however simple and innocent may be his poor figure. On this occasion, a crowd gathers around him, pointing and staring. They do not seem hostile. Or merely hostile. They seem prepared to give him a chance. But a chance at what? Perhaps they think he is a street performer. In order to try to please them, he does a little dance. It is a very elaborate dance, as he thinks of it, balletic and energetic (e.g., the Stick Man attempts a flying *pas de chat*), but to the humans it probably appears that he is standing still. At most, twitching slightly. They grow restless. Someone speaks of building a bonfire and cigarette lighters are produced. Humans are a hard lot. The Stick Man is standing in the Garden of Paradise, he announces resolutely; it worked before, more or less, but it doesn't work now. He's in the wrong world. And it's closing in on him. The Stick Man runs like a bat out of hell, he announces, but that doesn't work either. His knees bend slightly. More in dismay probably than in flight.

Just when all seems lost, a Cartoon Man flies in from overhead and the humans fall back. Leave him alone, you racist assholes, the Cartoon Man shouts, or prepare to die! He looks rather out of place, too, with his bright colored body suit and sketchy features, and he seems anything but threatening, even somewhat undersized, they could probably tear him apart, but they do as they are told. Maybe it's the surprise factor. Or maybe it's the intimidating way the Cartoon Man speaks, as if in capitals and bold type like a billboard. It's okay now, he says to the Stick Man, lowering his booming voice. Let's go throw back a snort.

In the bar, they are drinking and telling each other their life stories. The Cartoon Man is soaking up glass after glass of whiskey, with beer chasers. I can't get enough of this swill, he says, pouring another glassful down his cartoon gullet. Not that it does much for me, he adds with a belch so powerful it makes the bottles tinkle on the shelves behind the bar. I seem to have a hard time getting a buzz on, but when I do, boy, watch out! The Stick Man is not actually having a drink in human terms, because they won't serve him. The Cartoon Man made a loud fuss about this, springing up and down so he could see over the bar, banging his fist on it as he leapt and speaking in huge jagged capitals, but the Stick Man told him not to bother, he prefers having a drink his own Stick Man way. To demonstrate this, he bends one arm at the elbow and holds his stick hand near his tipped "O" of a head, and announces: The Stick Man tastes a glass of wine. He makes a scuffing noise, which might be the sound of him sniffing or that of his knees brushing together. Hmm, he says. Complex bouquet of black currant, green olive, and cedarwood, faintly herbaceous, reminiscent of bell peppers. Promising. He tips his head back; the movement is almost imperceptible. Harmonious flavors, deep and long-lasting, with a noble balance of fruit, alcohol, tannin, and acid. It's a classic from the best vintage of the decade. Beautiful. And it's opening up nicely. I think I'll have another. And he does.

That's pretty good, says the Cartoon Man. Me, I couldn't tell a bell pepper from a stale armpit. We're not very big on taste and smell in the cartoon world. Mostly we're into low comedy and killing people. A lot of people. Fighting evil, man, it's fucking endless. He shakes his cartoon head sadly, his eyes and nose seeming to move about on his face as he does so, and throws down another tumbler of whiskey. The Stick Man thinks about evil. Perhaps for the first time. He realizes it has caused him to bend over slightly as if he has taken up a sack of potatoes. But tell me, Stick Man, what brings you to this shapeless shithole? These humans'll snuff you, you know. You're a fucking insult to their world.

I come to watch them, and when I see them do something interesting, I remember it and take it back to my stick world and do it there. In truth, I can't imagine my own world except in relation to theirs, though of course mine's superior. To walk on water or fall off a building is not the same in my world as it is here. There's so little in my world, there's room for everything, all I have to do is think of it, but theirs is so cluttered and congested, and, well, so obvious. In your face, as they like to say. If you have one, that is.

Yeah, I know what you mean, Stick Man, this bloated meat farm dumps a streamlined heavy action guy like me straight into snore mode. Five minutes and out come the Z's. A bore to the core, show me the door. Don't know why they love it so. Just goddamn stupid, I guess. It's not like where I come from. We got the best of their world in ours, all the sex and violence, tears and laughter, but speeded up with none of the dull sweaty bits. The Stick Man disagrees with this, the cartoon world just makes the obvious more obvious, painting it, as one might say, in primary colors, but out of politeness does not say so. He tilts his shoulder bar in sympathy, though perhaps a little too far. The Stick Man expresses empathy should perhaps read: The Stick Man expresses inebriation. Shouldn't have had that second one. No tolerance. Delicious, though. Listen, come on back with me to my strip, Stick Man. We'll go on a toot, tear up the fucking frame. I got a set of wheels you won't believe. We'll pick up some hot dames. I know a couple of doozies who'll blow your pants off. Loosely speaking, I mean.

Thanks. But I've been there. I get treated as a handicapped person. Or else I'm just laughed at.

I know, it's that kind of place, they'll laugh at anything, they can't help themselves. But, hey, this time you'll be with me, man. I'm a superhero, they don't mess with me. I catch anyone even smirking, he's a dead man. Or woman. I'm evenhanded on that score. Whaddaya say?

It's very kind. But, well, I have a doozie back in the stick world, and I miss her. Maybe that's what he's expressing in his drunken tilt: the Stick Man remembers his absent lover. The tilt deepens. But you could come with me to the stick world.

Nah. Too square for me. So goddamn flat and colorless. Whaddaya got? A straight line and a few sticks to play with. No wonder you come slumming here. Mix it up with a little push and shove, get your feet in the paint, pick up the tempo for a change. Must be a drag to hang out in all that emptiness for long.

No. Not for stick people. It's exciting, really. It's got everything. For it's always just what we imagine it to be.

Yeah? Listen, tell me, do you really get your rocks off with your little doozie, Stick Man, or do you just imagine that, too?

Well. I guess in my world, it's sort of the same thing.

That's what I thought, says the Cartoon Man, throwing down another tumblerful. I'll stick with what I got. I don't want to have to think it up. I love to get hit by surprises. Even bad ones. Especially bad ones. I love the danger, the speed, the contact, the whole wild toot and scramble. Bif! Boff! He drives his free fist into the bar. I need adversaries!

As if on cue, a group of humans come in, shoulders squared, looking threatening. There he is! The Stick Man! The Cartoon Man tosses his empty glass over the bar, causing an explosive crash that makes the humans stagger back a step, and prepares to defend them both. They'll never take us alive, Stick Man!

No, wait, says one of the humans. We are here on a peaceful diplomatic mission.

Bullshit! Take another step, you treacherous scumbags, and I'll peaceful mission your ass! His head's down and his legs are churning. He seems about to fly forward and head-butt them all. Don't trust those shifty meatsacks, Stick Man! You know what they're like! Let's kill them!

Tell him to calm down, Stick Man. And to stop using such appalling language. We are here to speak about large and serious matters.

And we do quite a lot of killing in the human world, too, Cartoon Man, so you better cool it!

The Stick Man assumes a posture of conciliation, something he learned on previous visits here. We should hear what they have to say, he says, but be prepared. Also something learned. Not sure what it means, but it's effective.

Stick Man, we realize that—excuse me, but am I looking at your face or—? never mind, I shouldn't have asked—we realize

that, as a people, we have not always received you here with the
dignity and respect properly due you and, well, your kind. But
now, on behalf of the entire human world, or at least that part of
it which is empowered to establish committees such as ours, we
are calling upon you henceforth to represent officially for us the
human condition, as we understand it. We feel somehow you
can encapsulate it in economical ways difficult to achieve for
those of us with a, what can one say, a more complex personal
architecture.

The Stick Man's posture of conciliation shifts slightly to
express the humility he feels in the face of such an unexpected
honor and, at the same time, the anxiety aroused by its implicit
obligations which may include having to remain in the human
world, and he knows that he is already, in exhibiting this struggle with ambivalence, exercising his new office.

We have prepared a stage, Stick Man, that captures the
essence of your world, which is to say, imitates it exactly, for you
have nothing but essence there. We will provide the text each
day; you will, so to speak, illustrate it.

I have always made my own announcements, he says, letting
his turned-out elbows suggest modesty and apology.

We know that, but that's in the stick world. This is the human
world. We do things differently here.

We hope you'll accept our offer, Stick Man.

And anyway you have no alternative. We always get what
we want.

You going along with this horseshit? the Cartoon Man asks
at his elbow.

It appears I have no choice.

I could kill them all if you want me to. Wham! Ker-splat!

No. I'll do as they ask. It should be fun. He expresses this with a lighthearted disposition of his limbs and tilt of his head, though he recognizes (and probably reveals this to a careful observer) that a certain dissimulating artifice has crept into his demeanor, for he does not feel at all lighthearted, and he wonders if he has caught some baneful human infection. The Stick Woman was probably right. He shouldn't have come here.

Well then, I'm popping back to the strip to get in a few frames of the old down-and-dirty. Pow! Whop! Blam! I can use a workout. But if you need me, pal, just blow your horn.

Wait a minute, says the bartender. Who's paying for all this broken glass?

Do not complain, says the leader of the humans. History has been made in here today. By next week, this will be a famous tourist attraction. You can sell the broken glass as souvenirs. In fact, you'd be doing yourself a favor to smash a few more things.

When the Stick Man takes the oath of office on his little stage, he bends one of his stick arms at the elbow and raises his stick hand. It is the wrong arm, the left one, but no one objects, given the solemnity of the occasion. There are vast multitudes gathered to witness this oath and his premier performance, which can begin only after elaborate ceremonies and a great many lengthy orations of the sort that humans seem to require. Perhaps because their other means of expression are so limited and so occluded by their clumsy fragile integument. Or perhaps because they can never say one thing alone or directly, but must always, as if by nature, flesh out the bare bones of their simple little thoughts. He warms up for his new role by acting out the successive lines of the orations, but he is all too aware of what his posture really expresses: The Stick Man is bored to tears.

Commingled with: the Stick Man is homesick. He hopes that no one perceives this, but that they all assume instead that he is responding dutifully to the text provided by the committee for the occasion: the Stick Man receives with a mixture of pride and humility the adulation of the masses.

They do seem to have warmed to him. The speeches are flattering and enthusiastically applauded, and his every gesture brings on wild cheering. Here you see him in all his suchness, in all his plenitude! declares one speaker, and everyone claps and huzzahs. His more or less rectilinear, geniculate, and symmetrical frame is utterly without habiliment, and yet it cannot be said the Stick Man is standing here before us in the buff, for he has no buff either! Whistles and applause. He has no pelt or epidermis, no casing, sheath, or rind, no fell, fur, leather, fleece, husk, or pericarp! No *flesh*! Cheers and whoops of friendly laughter. Which is why his expression of our existential situation is so vivid! So transparent! He shows us the naked truth! He continues to receive the feverish adulation of the masses. He has nothing extraneous! Not even a face! Just a head that says "O!" A head wide open to all experience! What is his age? He can be—and is—a baby, child, adult, and ancient, all at once, or in any order as he pleases! Most persons are less within than they seem on the surface, the Stick Man is more! Watch him now as he ponders infinity! As he demonstrates that it is better to sit still than to rise and fall! As he counts his blessings! As he decries disorder! As he admires the perfect beauty of the human world!

And so, at the inauguration ceremony and during the weeks that follow, he does these things and to great acclaim, not only from the crowds who gather daily before his stage, but also from the vast television audiences throughout the human world, for his every move and position are captured by the cameras and shown live every hour on the news and each evening on prime time in an edited version. He is, as the humans say, hot. A celebrity. Presidents, kings, and movie stars send their greetings and felicitations, ordinary people their gratitude and suggestions for further aspects of the human condition he might take on, professors critical disquisitions for him to comment upon by word or gesture, human women love letters. Though he would be hard pressed to respond to the latter in the ordinary way, even his ordinary way which is not theirs. The committee members who appointed him to this office were greatly disturbed by his tab, feeling that it marred the purity of his representations, sprouting there on the stick between his legs like an unruly twig, a kind of obscene error of punctuation, as one of them said, and they considered shaving it off, but they were a bit queasy about handling it, so they accepted the idea that it could be taped to the back of his hip bar with black electrical tape, provided the Stick Man kept it taped and out of sight at all times, though they do, being realists, permit him, as an official act, to meditate from time to time upon the mind-body paradox, to the delight, as with all else, of his fans.

The committee is well pleased with his success, and on the whole they treat him kindly and with consideration, but they turn a deaf ear to his expressed wish to return home, if only for a visit, believing that their world is so vastly superior to his, he should be grateful to be allowed to live in it and should desire no other. And so he goes on, though with increasing sorrow in his heart, performing in his Stick Man way the texts that they provide: The Stick Man demonstrates that good service is a great enchantment. The Stick Man recalls the joys of childhood. The Stick Man bears with equanimity the malice of others, while anticipating always their kindness. The Stick Man laughs at adversity. The Stick Man goes shopping. He takes up positions reflecting grand themes like good and evil, illusion and reality, money (his illustration of the ancient human proverb that a man without money is like a bow without an arrow, is particularly successful), religion, politics, work, and the arts of success, but also lesser elements of the human condition like desire, knowledge, manners, the digestive processes, the fine arts, and so on, as well as certain negative aspects thought to be exemplary: The Stick Man wrestles with his guilty conscience. The Stick Man is embarrassed by his bodily parts. The Stick Man is envious of the success of others. The Stick Man is obsessed by the memory of his mother. The Stick Man is afraid of heights. The Stick Man fails to understand the meaning of the universe. Of course, he's just acting. He is not embarrassed, envious, or afraid, and he does understand the meaning of the universe, at least in Stick Man terms. It's quite simple, but not really relevant to the human world. But he understands why they are asking him to do this. He is not illustrating their condition merely, he is also absorbing it. Sucking it up into his rectilinear and geniculate frame. The Stick Man fully recognizes that the humans hope that his taking on the human condition will free them from it. And he knows that they will be frustrated in their hope.

As happens. After he represents the human condition, it is still theirs, not his, and the crowds begin to drift away, burdened as before. The hourly news dispatches end and The Stick Man Show moves out of prime time into the latenight comedy

and extended news hour. There are no more love letters. Many
do still come to see him, especially groups on package tours
sold during the height of his popularity, but the expressions of
excitement and delight which had previously confronted him
now give way to ones of disappointment, perplexity, and even
revulsion. Which he reads, of course, as self-revulsion and disappointment, for he is only reminding them of their own condition. The Stick Man contemplates the sadness of the human
enterprise: a position he takes up on his own without informing
the committee, his posture in effect imitating that of most of
his audience, a posture appropriate as well to his stick condition,
for he longs only to be back in his stick world again and with
his Stick Woman and his tab untaped. He has often imagined
her, when making love, in a shape the human world would call
voluptuous, but he realizes, far from her, he loves her just as she
is, her simple notched frame now dearer to him than anything
in this world or any other.

The committee, for its part, works hard to revive interest in
him, evidently having considerable personal investment in the
success of his office, as created by them. Aware that illustrated
texts of edifying moral uplift are failing to attract audiences,
they impose upon him the darker aspects of the human condition: The Stick Man suffers from an inferiority complex. The
Stick Man tells a lie and is empowered by it. The Stick Man
shows the ill effect of trying to live on hope alone. The Stick
Man feels like a worm and behaves like one. The Stick Man
emits a bad odor. The Stick Man fears death. Now he no longer
suffers neglect. He suffers rejection. Hostility. The Stick Man
is shunned as the bearer of ill tidings. Those who come to his
performances do so only to insult him (Sick Sticks, they call

him) and throw things at him. Their enmity worries him less than the possibility that he might be acquiring the fears and complexes that he is asked to represent. If left alone, these ideas might never have occurred to him, and he is afraid that he will contaminate the stick world with them, should he ever be able to return. The Stick Man peers into an open grave, displaying a distasteful morbidity. The Stick Man lusts after a small child. The Stick Man considers poisoning his neighbor's dog. The Stick Man ridicules the human condition. The Stick Man betrays his best friend. He remains a celebrity, but in the way that serial killers are celebrities. There are protests and The Stick Man Show is taken off the air.

Desperate, the committee decides to untape his tab and let it, as they say in their world, all hang out. They run electric billboard advertisements of his forthcoming texts: The Stick Man exposes his private parts, heretofore concealed. The Stick Man admires his backside in the mirror. The Stick Man goes to the bathroom standing up. The Stick Man goes to the bathroom sitting down. The Stick Man wishes someone would lick his tab. He becomes fair game for the human comedians and his ratings rise, but this is not his office as originally defined. The Stick Man laments his unhappy fate: this is the position he would assume were he not obliged to assume so many others, mostly related to his tab. The Stick Man, stroking himself, thinks of his beloved. The Stick Man attempts an act of autofellatio. The Stick Man suffers from castration anxiety. He is a celebrity again, but the committee members themselves are wrangling about ends and means. The Stick Man suggests it might be time for him to return quietly to the stick world. They don't listen. It's as though he's not even there. When he timidly repeats his suggestion, they throw up a new text—the Stick Man scratches his hemorrhoids—and tell him to get to it, while they continue their deliberations.

In the end, though some of the more sober and idealistic committee members resign in disgust, the decision of those remaining (they speak vaguely of the educational aspect) is to introduce the Stick Woman into the act, and an expedition is mounted to capture her and bring her back to the human world. The Stick Man is both elated and fearful, for the Stick Woman has never been to the human world, nor ever wished to be. Far less restless than he, she has always been happy in the stick world and unhappy whenever he left it. She arrives, chained and manacled, desperately relieved to see him again but terrified by her ordeal (she resisted her captors and now has a second elbow on her right arm), his worst fears realized. The Stick Man tenderly embraces his loved one. As officially announced. She melts into his arms. Also. The crowds have returned. Some of the delight. The cameras. She does not see them. She sees only him. She clings to him. He was not really afraid before, but now, for her, he is. They are encouraged to enjoy each other in the classical manner, and they do, though more in a consolatory fashion than a passionate one, for they are well aware that their trials are not concluded. After the initial surprise of this newest innovation has worn off, they are obliged to perform all the positions known to the human world, which they do, but, by unspoken agreement, they do not reveal those intimacies peculiar to their stick world. The Stick Man Show returns to the networks during the afternoon hours of the soap operas.

Stick person sex is different and has a certain appeal of the sort described by the orator on the day of the Stick Man's inauguration, namely, its naked and exemplary transparency, but in the end it cannot compete in the human world with fleshy sex. Even the simple stroking of human skin—a knee, say, or a fat bottom, a tear-stained cheek—seems to have more appeal to humans than the Stick Man and Stick Woman attempting exotic positions like the wheelbarrow or the triple X, especially given the subdued nature of their performances. The show's ratings, at first promising, drop off again. The committee, what's left of it, feels the act has to be more extreme, there's no other way. Animals are ruled out. There are no available stick animals. Likewise, third or fourth parties. They decide on violence. Rape. Whips. Bondage. Torture. Disfigurement. Hammers and nails.

The Stick Man refuses. His imagination is vast, but hurting the Stick Woman is beyond it. They have reached a point of no return. The committee meets in emergency session. It is clear to them that the show must end. But it is still in their power to decide how it will end and what they can extract from it. They consider the possibility of destroying the Stick Woman, reducing her to a heap of broken sticks, her facial platter shattered as a mirror might be, all of her remains dumped on the stage in front of the Stick Man to see what he will do. Text: The Stick Man throws up. The Stick Man mourns his beloved. The Stick Man goes berserk. But then what would they do with the Stick Man? He'd be useless but still here. He'd probably have to be destroyed, too. So they decide to get rid of them both at the same time. A lovers' tragedy. But it makes for better television if they can create a plot around the killings and delay over a few weeks the final denouement to lure the audiences back. They find the perfect solution: Let the audience kill them.

First, they must begin a rumor campaign against them. They must be utterly reviled. Later, it will be seen that they were only misunderstood, but only after they no longer exist. Then it will be a sad story. Songs will be written and so on. There will edited reruns. For now, by way of letters to the editor, graffiti, anonymous advertisements, phone calls pretending to be from poll takers, dirty jokes, leaked "disclosures," they are decried as deserters, traitors, perverts, racketeers, revolutionary anarchists, scofflaws, thieves, sex fiends, mercenaries, atheists, dangerous aliens. The crowds begin to gather once more. They are increasingly hostile. Weapons appear. Guns and knives are temptingly displayed in shop windows. The gathered multitudes shout out positions the Stick Man and Stick Woman are to take, but they have stopped performing and simply cling to one another. It is not clear whether their circle heads are looking out upon the crowd or at each other. Either way, they make a good target. Down on your knees! the mob shouts. Eat shit, Stick Man! Say your prayers! It is happening faster than the committee has expected but it is too dangerous to try to do anything about it. They watch the proceedings from the safety of a television studio. It becomes apparent to them that many in the crowd must have hankered to do this since the day of the Stick Man's inauguration. They have not aroused them so much as released them, a lesson to be learned. Thus, they tell themselves they are not responsible for what happens next.

What happens next, however, could not have been anticipated. The Cartoon Man swoops down, snatches up the Stick Man and Stick Woman, and flies them back to their stick world. They are shot at as they lift away, but without consequence; tragedies only happen in the human world and they are soon out of it. How did you know we were in trouble? I saw it on television. In the cartoon world? We get the same programs. The Stick Man feels like weeping when he sees the stick world again, though he never wept before; something the humans taught him. Many things will be different now. Expressing his gratitude, he remarks that the Cartoon Man has served as a kind of miraculous deus ex machina. I'm not a fucking deus of any kind, man, replies the Cartoon Man. I'm just a super- hero. It's what I do. It gives me a surge. They invite the Cartoon Man to stay for supper in the stick world, but the Cartoon Man declines, saying the place makes him itchy. I need a place I can sink my teeth into, as you might say. Let me know, though, the next time you're back in the neighborhood. Not soon, says the Stick Woman, having locked her double-elbowed arm around the Stick Man.

When the Cartoon Man has gone and the Stick Man and Stick Woman are embracing once more, tab to slot, in the old stick world way, the Stick Man sighs and says: A little while ago I decided to imagine the Garden of Paradise. Just to feel like I was home again. And I did, but it was darker than I remem- bered, and I saw that dangers lurked there, and I was afraid. In the past I have, whenever I wished, imagined fear, but now it's inside me without my imagining it and I know it will never go away. It is the darkness of the human world, says the Stick Woman. We have brought it back with us like a kind of shadow. We never had shadows before. Yes, but I don't think that's what I'm afraid of. I've always known the human world was a sad place where lives are short and meaningless and mostly wasted, and where the fear of death drives humans either to madness or despair unless they find some means of distracting themselves, which, if it's not lethal, is a kind of benign madness. That's what they call the human comedy. In fact, it's their gentle crazed distractions that I have mostly taken pleasure in expressing here in the stick world, and it has often made it beautiful. The humans really only asked me to do what I've been doing all along, though they made me take up many aspects of their lives I had never imagined before. Some of them left me very sore at heart. And the trouble is, now that I have lived in their world, truly lived there, I don't really like it any more. And if I don't like it, how can I find pleasure in imagining it? The darkness I saw in the Garden of Paradise was an omen of an absolute darkness setting in. And when it does, then what? That's what I'm afraid of. The Stick Woman grips his hip bar tenderly, her round head on his shoulder bar. We need another world, she says. Yes. But there is no other.

GOING FOR A BEER

(2011)

He finds himself sitting in the neighborhood bar drinking a beer at about the same time that he began to think about going there for one. In fact, he has finished it. Perhaps he'll have a second one, he thinks, as he downs it and asks for a third. There is a young woman sitting not far from him who is not exactly good-looking, but good-looking enough, and probably good in bed, as indeed she is. Did he finish his beer? Can't remember. What really matters is: Did he enjoy his orgasm? Or even have one? This he is wondering on his way home through the foggy night streets from the young woman's apartment. Which was full of Kewpie dolls, the sort won at carnivals, and they made a date, as he recalls, to go to one. Where she wins another—she has a knack for it. Whereupon, they're in her apartment again, taking their clothes off, she excitedly cuddling her new doll in a bed heaped with them. He can't remember when he last slept, and he's no longer sure, as he staggers through the night streets, still foggy, where his own apartment is, his orgasm, if he had one, already fading from memory. Maybe he should take her back to the carnival, he thinks, where she wins another Kewpie doll (this is at least their second date, maybe their fourth), and this time they go for a romantic nightcap at the bar where they first met. Where a brawny dude starts hassling her. He intervenes and she turns up at his hospital bed, bringing him one of her Kewpie dolls to keep him company. Which is her way of expressing the bond between them, or so he supposes, as he leaves the hospital on crutches, uncertain what part of town he is in. Or what part of the year. He decides that it's time to call the affair off—she's driving him crazy—but then the brawny dude turns up at their wedding and apologizes for the pounding he gave him. He didn't realize, he says, how serious they were. The guy's wedding present is a gift certificate for two free drinks at the bar where they met and a pair of white satin ribbons for his crutches. During the ceremony, they both carry Kewpie dolls that probably have some barely hidden significance, and indeed do. The child she bears him, his or another's, reminds him, as if he needed reminding, that time is fast moving on. He has responsibilities now and he decides to check whether he still has the job that he had when he first met her. He does. His absence, if he has been absent, is not remarked on, but he is not congratulated on his marriage, either, no doubt because—it comes back to him now—before he met his wife he was engaged to one of his colleagues and their coworkers had already thrown them an engagement party, so they must resent the money they spent on gifts. It's embarrassing and the atmosphere is somewhat hostile, but he has a child in kindergarten and another on the way, so what can he do? Well, he still hasn't cashed in the gift certificate, so, for one thing, what the hell, he can go for a beer, two, in fact, and he can afford a third. There's a young woman sitting near him who looks like she's probably good in bed, but she's not his wife and he has no desire to commit adultery, or so he tells himself, as he sits on the edge of her bed with his pants around his ankles. Is he taking them off or putting them on? He's not sure, but now he pulls them on and limps home, having left his beribboned crutches somewhere. On arrival, he finds all the Kewpie dolls, which were put on a shelf when the babies started coming, now scattered about the apartment, beheaded and with their limbs amputated. One of the babies is crying, so, while he warms up a bottle of milk on the stove, he goes into its room to give it a pacifier and discovers a note from his wife pinned to its pajamas, which says that she has gone off to the hospital to have another baby and she'd better not find him here when she gets back, because if she does she'll kill him. He believes her, so he's soon out on the streets again, wondering if he ever gave that bottle to the baby, or if it's still boiling away on the stove. He passes the old neighborhood bar and is tempted but decides that he has had enough trouble for one lifetime and is about to walk on when he is stopped by that hulk who beat him up and who now gives him a cigar because he's just become a father and drags him into the bar for a cel-ebratory drink, or, rather, several, he has lost count. The cele-brations are already over, however, and the new father, who has married the same woman who threw him out, is crying in his beer about the miseries of married life and congratulating him on being well out of it, a lucky man. But he doesn't feel lucky, especially when he sees a young woman sitting near them who looks like she's probably good in bed and decides to suggest that they go to her place, but too late—she's already out the door with the guy who beat him up and stole his wife. So he has another beer, wondering where he's supposed to live now, and realizing—it's the bartender who so remarks while offering him another on the house—that life is short and brutal and before he knows it he'll be dead. He's right. After a few more beers and orgasms, some vaguely remembered, most not, one of his sons, now a racecar driver and the president of the company he used to work for, comes to visit him on his deathbed and, apologizing for arriving so late (I went for a beer, Dad, things happened), says he's going to miss him but it's probably for the best. For the best what? he asks, but his son is gone, if he was ever there in the first place. Well . . . you know . . . life, he says to the nurse who has come to pull the sheet over his face and wheel him away.

THE GOLDILOCKS VARIATIONS

(2013)

Aria

G enters the unoccupied cottage. Porridge, chairs, beds. Too hot, too cold, too high, too wide, too hard, too soft. Just right. G eats, breaks, crawls in. The owners return. *An intruder!*

G, wildflower picker, enters the snug little cottage in the woods, knowing or not knowing whose it is, the owners absent as if by arrangement. Three pots of porridge, three chairs, three beds. Too hot, too cold, too high, too wide, too hard, too soft. Just right. The rule of three. G eats, breaks, crawls in. The owners return. *There has been an intruder!*

G, restless by nature, is picking wildflowers and chasing butterflies in the woods when, in a particularly lonely spot, she comes upon a snug little cottage. She may or may not know whose it is (there are stories). She peeps through the keyhole. The owners seem conveniently to be away, so she enters. There are three pots of porridge on the table, set out to cool. She tastes them: too hot, too cold, just right (she eats it up). There are three chairs. She sits on them: too high, too wide, just right (she breaks it). She is sleepy. Upstairs, there are three beds. She tries them: too hard, too soft, just right (she crawls in). The owners return. *There has been an intruder!* They have expected this.

G, restless butterfly chaser, enters the little cottage in the woods, probably knowing whose it is (there are stories), the owners absent as if by arrangement. Pots of porridge, chairs, beds. Too hot, too cold, too high, too wide, too hard, too soft. Just right. The rule of three. G eats, breaks, crawls in. The owners return. The intruder they have anticipated has arrived.

G enters the unoccupied cottage. Porridge, chairs, beds. Too hot, cold, high, wide, hard, soft. Just right. G eats, breaks, crawls in. The owners return. An intruder. But where is she now?

First variation

She is in the kitchen of the snug little cottage she has come upon in the woods, lifting the lids of the three porridge pots on the table, each in a primary color as if there were some rule about it. She does not know whose cottage it is, but while picking flowers she has seen a family of wild things and supposes it must be theirs. Was it improper to intrude upon their home while they are away? Or are they away so that she might intrude? G has read and been read stories about such cottages and their beastly occupants and has been guided by them, and is guided by them now as she tastes the pots of porridge with wooden spoons to test their temperature. One too hot, the next too cold, the little one just right. She probes the meaning of this and believes she sees it, and she knows now what will follow. There will be chairs—there *are* chairs!—and beds and rude awakenings. She picks up the smallest chair, excited by the wild things' smell, and dances with it, imagining other dances yet to come.

Second variation

The B family are also dancing, B1 and B2 slowly rising and falling from foot to foot, B3 leaping with abandon, exhibiting his youthful virtuosity. They have seen G passing by, her eyes lit with exhilarated anticipation, wildflowers in her golden hair, and they, too, have felt the exhilaration. While the other two chatter excitedly about what they will find and do when they return, B1 ruminates about past intrusions, other little butterfly chasers and thieving old crones and, in the storied days when there were only bears and foxes in the world, the mischievous vixens. Mostly, though, he thinks about the restless golden-haired girls, and he lifts one foot and then the other. B2 also remembers them. Indeed, the cottage is haunted by their fleeting presences. *Somebody has been sleeping in my bed*: something she will say and hear again today. B3 says he wants to eat this one. It is against the rules, B2 says. All the more reason, B3 says, and bounces about, gleefully trampling wildflowers and scattering butterflies. Watching him, B1 supposes he himself must have been like that once upon a time, and hops a wistful hop.

Third variation

Someone has been tasting my porridge! . . . tasting my porridge! . . . my porridge! Someone has been sitting in my chair! . . . sitting in my chair! . . . in my chair! G, tucked in, listens to the

wild things recite their lines as they emerge from the brambly
woods and march three times around the cottage (the rule of
three!), repeating the words precisely, though in their different
voices, each just a step behind the other as in a childish round.
The leader has a rumbly old voice, deep and growly, and the
followers, too, have growly voices, though not so deep. *Someone has been lying in my bed! . . . lying in my bed! . . . in my
bed!* She is that someone, curled up under the coverlet in the
smallest one, the one just right, knowing what ought to happen
next, not knowing if it will. It is very exciting and she is determined not to fall asleep, but she does, as if overtaken suddenly
by a spell. *Someone has been tasting my porridge! . . . tasting my
porridge! . . . my porridge!* B3 knows he is the unlucky one, his
porridge will be eaten, his chair broken, his bed invaded, but
though the grip of the past on the present is fierce, variations
can happen. It would earn him a fearful cuffing, but new endings can be imagined, old rhythms broken. He has seen her. A
tidbit, but succulent. *Someone has been sitting in my chair! . . . in
my chair! . . . my chair!* B3, B2 believes, is suffering from the delu-
sions of the young, unable to see that change itself is changeless,
new rhythms mere resortings of the old. For what has *not* been
imagined and, imagined, done? She has no sympathy, however,
for the intruder. In the past, such creatures were impaled on
church steeples, and she would not mind if they did that now.
B1, leading them around the cottage on their final turn with
his deep rumble, would agree with B2 about change, but he
knows that the illusion of changeability generates desire, and
the tender agitation of desire is what makes life possible. See B3
now, bouncing about, gleefully leaping and laughing. Of course,
there is also the inescapable conflict of desires . . . *Someone has*

been lying in my bed!... in my bed!... in my bed! Their ceremonial march completed, they enter the cottage.

Fourth variation

Lying sound asleep in the little cottage's littlest bed, the one just right, G has a dream of dancing with the wild things. She is wearing no clothes because she is also a wild thing. They recognize her as one of their own, and they love her and share their porridge with her, and she loves them. She dances with each of them in turn and, one by one, laughing joyfully, they lift her high and set her gently down again. She feels like a beautiful princess, princess of the wild things, lifted up to be adored. And then one of them does not lower her, but continues to hold her high, so high she can see the roof of the cottage and the tops of the trees, and she is suddenly frightened and begs to be let down, but they are only laughing in their rude barking way somewhere far below. *She is falling!* She wakes. Where is she?

Fifth variation

The intruder's exciting smell is everywhere, but they know where to find her. B3, hopping about like his tail is on fire, wants to leap straight to the finale, but B1 insists on adherence to form, starting with the telltale wooden spoons standing in the porridge pots, though he agrees to hurry along, his ponderous obduracy scarcely concealing his own agitation. They rush trillingly through the porridge tasting and chair sitting, B3 bouncing back and forth impatiently, B2 standing stolidly in the middle, performing as obliged, but minimally, without ornament, and then B3 sings out (he is already bounding up the stairs, B1 and B2 on his heels): *Somebody has been sitting in my chair, and has broken it all to pieces!* In their bedroom, they sniff briefly at their coverlets (arousing! dangerous! delicious!) but skip the recitations to gather around the bed of the sleeping golden-haired intruder. Slowly, as her eyes open, their faces break into broad toothy smiles.

Sixth variation

She wakes. Where is she? She remembers entering the cottage of the wild things, as if invited, and sampling porridge, chairs, beds—but was it all a dream? No, there they are, leaning hugely over her, showing all their teeth. *Someone has been lying . . . lying . . . lying . . .* , they growl, *. . . in my bed! . . . bed! . . . bed!* The biggest one with the deep gruff voice has been leading them, but now it is the smallest who goes first. *And here she IS! . . . IS! . . . IS!* Then they all laugh uproariously, but it is not a very nice laugh, more like ferocious barking. She smiles hopefully, pulling the coverlet up to her chin, and the wild things commence to shuffle slowly, ceremonially, around the bed. She would be encouraged by this dance, if that is what it is, were it not for the savage glitter in their eyes. She recalls now her dream of dancing with them. Something bad happened. Does she have any clothes on?

Seventh variation

They have heard the stories about girls with golden hair, about their divine resplendence, their demonic powers. These stories and their embodiments haunt their lives. B2 is particularly afflicted by such creatures and wants to see this one impaled on the church steeple like the thieving old crones of the past. Bygone tales also haunt B3, who wishes to be free of them, by whatever means, once and for all. B1, more comfortable with tradition, prefers to welcome the intruder into the family circle, each member free to use her in turn as they please, he leading, they following. He plucks her out from under the coverlet, lifts her high. She is still wearing her clothes, but he removes them with a swipe of his paw to make her more like one of the family and then dances a cheerful little jig with her. She is making a noise that might be laughing, or else screaming, one can't be sure.

Eighth variation

G was so happy when she discovered the wild things' cottage. It was like a story coming true. After the obligatory peek through the keyhole, she had entered and found everything just as she had imagined: porridge, chairs, and beds, three of each, following the rule. So, joyfully—G is the very essence of joy—she did all she was supposed to do, eagerly awaiting the adventure to follow. It was very exciting, even their *smell* was exciting. To crawl into their beds was like crawling into a warm cave in the forest. What a surprise when they lift the coverlet! She knew of course what usually happens. She has seen the open window. But this time, she believed, would be different. This time she would stay to see what happens next. Perhaps, however, she thinks now, soaring naked through the pungent air, the stories misled her. She believed the wild things would be just like her. They are not.

Ninth variation

The intruder is passed from hand to hand, sometimes pinched, sometimes caressed, sometimes tossed or swung by her ankles, each gesture repeated three times (the rule), B1 leading, the others following. She is making an undefinable squealing sound—of joy perhaps, or terror—that adds to their pleasure. Even B3 agrees this is better than eating her, though that option is still on the table, so to speak. We should fatten her up first, B2 says. *Fatten her up, fatten her up*, the others say. She is such a thin hairless little thing, there is scarcely a bite each. *Scarcely a bite, scarcely a bite.* Hairless, yes, except for her golden strands which weave beautiful patterns in the air as she is flung about, patterns that express the family's delight in having an intruder to play with. And there are many more games they can play. B3 will not be allowed to spoil their fun with too hasty a finale.

Tenth variation

G enters the unoccupied cottage. Porridge, chairs, beds. Too hot, cold, high, wide, hard, soft. Just right. G eats, breaks, crawls in. The owners return. An intruder. But where is she now?

She is hanging by her feet from a rafter above the B family's beds, where they lie resting after their joyful exertions, eating their cold porridge and reflecting upon the games they have played thus far and imagining those to follow. Above them, her golden strands waft silkily in the breeze from the open window, the last of the entangled wildflowers dropping decoratively upon their coverlets. When the intruder pulls herself up to look around (there is no place to go, she drops back down), B1 watches her with delight, B2 dismissively, B3 with conflicting desires.

G, inverted, looks out upon a world turned upside down. The wild things lie stretched out on their beds below her, watching her, growling amiably from time to time. The burly one has finished his porridge, the middle one is eating hers, but the littlest one, who seems the most dangerous (while she was being thrown about, he pinched her all over, as if testing the amount of meat on her bones), has had to do without. Just look at the little bushytailed vixen, the big one says. Takes me back to the old days. I will save her hair and make something nice with it, says the middle one. With garlic, wild thyme, and forest mushrooms, the littlest one mutters ominously to himself, licking his hairy chops.

Eleventh variation

The rules of "Bouncing the Intruder" are that she must be kept aloft by passing her rapidly from hand to hand without catching her or palming her or letting any part of her touch the floor. As she falls, each of them in turn slaps her up in the air again, with the consequence that the pale little thing is turning quite rosy, augmenting their delight. B3 adds further zest to the game by challenging them to hit the ceiling with her, so the smacks get louder and the intruder rosier, as she bounces higher and higher into the air, singing again that loud squealing song of hers. It is B2 who finally succeeds, using both hands to pop her all the way up, and when she falls back she gives her another loud percussive whop and up she goes again,

fluttering like a butterfly and knocking the dust from the rafters, and then all the way up a third time (the rule of three).
This time when she falls, B1 catches her by her ankles and,
twirling her around his head, announces that the next game
will be "Sweeping the Floor."

Twelfth variation

G again has an inverted view of the world, as the wild things
joyfully sweep the cottage with her golden locks, passing her
rhythmically from hand to hand, her head wheeling dizzyingly
within a hair, as one might say, of the floor. *Cleaning house is
our great delight! . . . delight! . . . delight!* they chant, led by the
largest of them as they whisk her about, the others following. G
is too terrified even to scream, she can only grit her teeth and
stare straight ahead as the floor flies by, thinking, not for the first
time, that perhaps it was a mistake to come here. *We searched for
a broom and this one is just right! . . . just right! . . . just right!* The
middle one sweeps her under the table and dusts off the top, and
the little one deftly brushes spider webs out of the corners with
her. The big one flicks her locks at the bats in the rafters, then
gives her a little shake to make the dust fly. G sneezes, causing
her head to bounce off the floor, and the wild things laugh their
growly laugh. *Just right! . . . just right! . . . just right!*

Thirteenth variation

G is slowly rising and falling, rising and falling, as if caught
in some endless loop, one no longer wholly related to the wild
things who, except for their hands, may not even be there. Her

motion is not entirely continuous, but momentarily stops at the bottom of each fall when she is caught and held in those hairy hands (it feels like a kind of punctuation), before she slowly floats up toward the rafters again. So precise are the repetitions of this stuttery cycle that it feels fixed and static even in its constant motion, and it provokes a curious feeling in her not unlike panic. Let me out! she is screaming, or believes herself to be screaming, though she rises and falls in silence. Yet someone must have heard her, for suddenly she is flying across the room toward the open window. Escape! Her head passes through it but she feels a pull from behind, and she flies back into the hairy hands. Again and again she flies toward and through the window and is sucked back. It is as if the house has been tipped on its side and she is still rising and falling. Faster and faster she flies back and forth (or up and down) until, just as she leaves the cottage altogether (at last!), all illusion of motion ceases and she awakes to find herself stretched out on the kitchen tabletop where the porridge pots once stood, an apple in her mouth, the grinning wild things hovering menacingly above her.

Fourteenth variation

The intruder, recovering from the blow she took when she sneezed her head against the floor, sits up on the edge of the table, still biting the apple and staring in terror at the three of them crowding around her in their large friendly way. Perhaps she will try to run away and they can have a game of chase, B3 is thinking with pleasure, flexing his claws. The pallor of her hairless body is now besmudged and her golden hair is full of spiders, an improvement in B3's opinion, though she still has a strange alien smell, which he likens to that of pond water. Though their games are a great delight for the whole family, B3 believes they belong to a bygone time and wants an end of them. He is already imagining a supper of roast intruder with a honey glaze. But B1 insists on more games. Several are proposed such as "Golden Cat's Cradle" and "Pin the Tail on the Intruder," but B1 says he was thinking of something more traditional like "Bears and Vixens." B2 picks up a porridge pot and smashes it furiously against the wall.

Fifteenth variation

G, restless butterfly chaser . . . *chaser!* . . . *chaser!* . . . *chaser!* enters the little cottage in the lonely woods . . . *woods!* . . . *woods!* . . . *woods!* Too big, too small, too rigorous, too frivolous, too hairless, too hairy . . . *hairy!* . . . *hairy!* . . . *hairy!* Too empty, too full, too sharp, too dull, too funny, too scary— . . . *scary!* . . . *scary!* . . . *scary!*

The cottage kitchen has fallen silent with the shattering of the porridge pot. They stare down melancholically at the scattered shards. It is as though some of the fun they were having was in that pot, and now it lies in ruins. And was it really fun, or only a desperate effort to stave off the emptiness? The pale intruder, sitting on the table's edge, takes the apple out of her mouth and says timidly: I want to go home. B1 can only shake his head and grin his sad toothy grin. B3 angrily smashes his pot against the wall. B2 and B3 have led, but B1 does not follow. He announces solemnly that the intruder must be washed and dressed for the games yet to be played.

The littlest wild thing, in punishment for breaking his porridge pot, is given the task of bathing and dressing her. G hates his hairy hands and beady eyes, but she has no choice but to submit. They will do with her as they please; she fears she may even be their dinner. The middle one sews together her ripped pinafore and combs the spiders out of her golden hair, seeming to relish pulling on the snarls. G came here hoping for so much. Well, maybe that was her mistake. Hoping. The wild things harness her in a cat's cradle of silken cords and hook her skirt with fishing line. The burly one announces that the prelude to "Bears and Vixens" will be "The Dance of the Naughty Marionette."

G, restless wildflower picker . . . *restless!* . . . *restless!* . . . *restless!* enters the cottage in the lonely woods . . . *lonely!* . . . *lonely!* . . . *lonely!* Too big, too small, too happy, too sad, too dark, too bright . . . *bright!* . . . *bright!* . . . *bright!* Too empty, too full, too sharp, too dull, too wild . . . *just right!* . . . *just right!* . . . *just right!*

Sixteenth variation

With an overture blast from B3's toy trumpet, the intruder glides over the table, her feet grazing the surface. When she stops, her feet swing. She wears a pinafore and cape and carries a basket of wildflowers. Her knees dip and, though her free hand hangs loosely at her side, her skirt rises in a discreet curtsy. Her audience growls and hisses. *Too nice!*

When the intruder next appears, heralded again by the tin trumpet, her face has been garishly painted, her golden locks stand spikily, her pinafore halter is filled out with apples. She kicks her legs high and shakes her little hips, then pivots, bends over, and, though her hands dangle, her skirt flips up. What is revealed is brightly rouged. Barking laughter, growling. *Too naughty!*

Again heralded, the golden-haired intruder, carrying a basket of wildflowers, glides over the kitchen table, her feet swinging. Her face paint is smeared with tears. She wears only the cape and under it a bushy red tail, which she swishes back and forth with a discreet shaking of her pale hairless hips. B2 and B3 bump their paws together in jubilant applause. *Just right!*

Seventeenth variation

The pale vixen with golden locks glides over the table in a crouch, head between her front paws, elbows grazing the surface, bushy red tail high. The puppeteer causes the foxy creature's hind legs to rise and her tail to swish back and forth provocatively; the spectators bark and thud their paws together. The little vixen rolls over onto her back and waves her limbs in the air like four dancing figures on the stage of her pallid torso, crossing and crisscrossing in a sinuous pattern, then jumps up on her hind legs to perform a nimble decorative movement with vigorous tail wagging, which she repeats inversely on her front paws, then on her elbows, her golden head, her toes again. She resumes her bushytailed crouch, peering at them through teary eyes. Then she launches into a manic replication of her previous performances, only much faster and with limbs flying in all directions. The spectators pound the table and bark wildly. Faster and faster she shakes and twists until the tail flies off. More paw thumping as she rises to dangle limply above the table. The puppeteer announces the finale: "Restlessness Punished."

Eighteenth variation

While the largest one dresses her again in her tattered resewn pinafore, tugs her stockings on, and reattaches all her silken cords, he leads the others in another round of exuberant chanting. In overlapping voices, they describe a restless girl with golden hair picking wildflowers and chasing butterflies, who enters a lonely cottage without permission, eats someone's porridge, breaks a chair, crawls into someone's bed, and has a rude awakening. With each phrase's repetition, decorated with their toothy grins and punctuated by cruel barking laughter, the chant grows ever more frightening. Whatever happened to that open window? She wishes she were back in her own house again, but doubts she is in a story where wishes are granted. *Someone has been ... has been ... has been ... sleeping in my ... in my ... in my ... bed and here she ... here she ... here she ... IS! ... IS! ... IS!* A basket of wildflowers is attached to her wrist and she is lifted by her strings to be suspended over the kitchen table. Her audience's eyes glitter with anticipation. To stay at home is too dull. To dance with the wild things is too terrifying. Is anything just right?

Nineteenth variation

Announced by the tin trumpet, the girl in the pinafore glides over the table, feet swinging, basket of wildflowers on her arm. She is the very expression of innocence. But she is not innocent. She is the restless intruder. She appears to pick up a bowl of porridge with her hands and knees. She lifts it to her mouth, leans back, knees high: she is bathed in porridge. There are muttered accusations, but also rude barks of laughter. The smallest one jumps on the table to lick her clean but is swatted away by the puppeteer. A chair appears. She is seated upon it. Nothing happens. She is lifted and dropped back onto it. Nothing happens. She is lifted toward the rafters. She screams. They laugh. She drops, hammering it hard enough this time to splinter it. More ritual mutterings, barks. Strings are pulled and her clothing flies away, leaving her dressed in her golden hair. Traces of rouge remain, but no sign now of divine resplendence or demonic powers. The puppeteer gathers her up and moves toward the stairs. When the others follow, he turns and snarls at them. Resentful grumblings.

Twentieth variation

G dreamt of dancing with the wild things. She has done so. It has not been as she imagined. In another story, they might all have been beautiful princes in animal skins. But she is in this one, on her way up the stairs in the hairy arms of a huge wheezing beast, bound in a tangle of silken cords. She has been soundly punished, but there is evidently more to come. The rule of three. He calls her his bushytailed little vixen. Somewhere in the cottage can be heard the explosive smashing of porridge pots.

In the kitchen, B3 is preparing a sauce robert, which he says is the perfect accompaniment for roast intruder—chopped onions cooked in butter with a reduction of white wine and pepper, an addition of demi-glace, finished with mustard—but he cannot find the mustard. She who daily boils the porridge, keeps the sitting room clean, and makes their beds, resentfully kicks the pot shards aside and shows him where it can be found. She has already prepared the demi-glace, a honey glaze as well. She will teach the wicked little intruder what is just right.

Twenty-first variation

B1, in bed with the golden-haired intruder, muses melancholically upon time's signature betrayal: It promises and it withdraws its promises. He dreams of happy endings, but the story he is in, which is every creature's story, must do without. Raising voices against it is of no avail. The consequence is a despair that invites the very ending one is seeking in vain to avoid.

G, too, lying in the wild thing's densely fragrant bed, once dreamt of happy endings. Now, however, a dismaying aroma of cooking onions rises from below, where, in the kitchen, B3 stirs in the demi-glace, his only interest in time's passage being that required for his sauce's preparation. B2 does think about time and its betrayals, but only as something not worth thinking about.

B1 believes that life, to be lived at all, must first be invented. He therefore attempted every imaginable variation of the puppeteer's art, a veritable compendium—firmly based in tradition—of innovative virtuosities. He thought of it as a brave attempt to hold despair at bay by, if not staying time, at least stretching it. But time's burly motions, alas, are singular and implacable.

To hold the intruder's pond-water smell at bay, B3 stretches his sauce robert with honeyed milk, richly spiced, which B2 recognizes as an innovative touch. She herself is more traditional in her cooking, uninterested in innovation or in virtuosity either, though she respects B3's youthful appetite for the new. An appetite that G once shared, though—having been well punished for it—no longer.

B1's final puppet act was an abject failure. He attempted, pulling on her silken cords, to settle the little marionette into a useful position on the bed—namely, that of the pinned butterfly—but the strings were hopelessly entangled, his fingers too clumsy to undo the knots. In the end, he had to abandon his loftier ambitions and resort to a pair of scissors.

B2 keeps scissors handy, intending to make something useful from the intruder's locks. Silken doilies for their chairs maybe, her own area of virtuosity and invention. Those locks' owner, though her bonds have been cut, still feels hopelessly pinned. Is there no escape? Perhaps. B1 may have enjoyed his maniacal finale, B3 is thinking, but his own ambition is to play one game more.

B1, drowsily, considers the pretensions of beauty and invention, their melancholic limits, the yawning emptiness beyond both. There is, after all, a certain desperation to the games they have been playing, futile attempts to stave off despondency by making something delightful out of nothing . . . *out of nothing . . . out of nothing . . .* The other two have gathered at his bed, peering down upon him and the sad hairless creature trembling beside him, casting judgment. They are disappointed. He is disappointed. To raise one's voice is to shout impotently at the void . . . *at the void . . . at the void . . .* Yet what else can they do? They will use this one up and then wait hopefully for the next.

He will rest a moment and start again . . . *start again . . . start again . . . . . . start again . . .*

Twenty-second variation

G's punishment for being a restless intruder is over. She is herself a wild thing now; she is even beginning to smell like one. The puppeteer has fallen asleep. From below: the clatter of pans, cooking aromas. She has been left alone, unwatched. Is she brave enough to jump from up here? She is. The wild thing's thunderous snore will cover any move she makes. She slips out of his bed, uncertain hope returning. But the window is tightly shut. She has been crying, she is crying again. The littlest wild thing, who is nonetheless much larger than she, enters stealthily and opens the window. He has knotted some sheets together so that she need not jump. She has misjudged him and is grateful and would say so, but his hairy hands are pushing her out the window. She descends hastily and sets off running through the woods. The rocks and roots hurt her bare feet, the brambles tear at her skin, but she is too exhilarated to care. Free at last! She pauses to catch her breath. She can hear footsteps crashing through the undergrowth. Oh no! Someone is chasing her!

Twenty-third variation

B3, much faster than the barefoot intruder and knowing the woods as she does not, is able to bound ahead of her or race from one side or the other, thus forcing her to change directions over and over until she is lost and crying out. He is tempted to do with her as B1 did, but is enjoying too much the overlapping chase.

B1 is watching this madcap frolic from the upstairs window. When he woke to find the little vixen missing and the window open, he felt at first alarm, then wistfully happy. She had helped him rebound from the onset of despair. Let her go. Now he sees the game that B3 is playing. If he brings her back, that will also make him happy.

As G runs frantically through the woods, now in one direction, now another, she feels pursued by a dozen wild things, coming at her from all sides. Her feelings of exhilaration have evaporated. She has had strange nightmares of being treed by baying dogs. Perhaps this is another, she thinks, tears streaming down her cheeks. Perhaps she is still in the big one's bed.

Bounding joyfully, B3 is in effect encircling her, driving her back toward their cottage. She is getting scratched as she races through the brambly woods, appetizing crimson droplets appearing on her hairless flanks. Sometimes he lets her run awhile, imagining escape, before closing in on her again. Making the panicky creature run before cooking her, he knows, will add to her wild spicy flavor.

B2 watches B3's extravaganza from the kitchen window, admiring his leaps and bounds and laughing at the intruder's distant cries. B1 let her go, obeying tradition; B3 is changing it. She chops up nuts and dried fruits for dessert, stirs the sauce with a wooden spoon. A spider falls from the rafters into the sauce like a kind of punctuation. She stirs it in.

G can run no more. She crouches in the hollow of a tree, stinging all over, her breath coming in sobbing gasps. The littlest one, laughing, picks her up by the nape and holds her high, swats her just for fun. He has been toying with her as a cat toys with a crippled mouse. G feels like the punchline of a bad joke.

Twenty-fourth variation

With playful pokes and pinches, B3, wishing the chasing game could have gone on longer, prods the forlorn intruder toward the cottage where the others await with forks and knives, old B1 in his nightcap, B2 in her apron. *Someone has been tasting my porridge!... tasting my porridge!* they sing, dancing a rocking cadence from foot to foot, rising and falling. *Someone has been sitting in my chair!... sitting in my chair!* B3 proudly lifts his trophy by her hair. The others show their teeth and clack their forks and knives together, continuing their stately round. *Someone has been lying in my bed!... lying in my bed!* B3 lowers the intruder to the ground where she collapses like an unstrung marionette, then lifts her high by her ankles. B1 sets one of his big porridge pots beneath her dangling head. *Too long!... too long!... too long!* they chant, led by B3. B2 steps forward with a pair of scissors. *Snip! snip! snip!* The locks are gone, become a potful of golden threads for B2's art, the intruder's head now as hairless as the rest of her. *Just right! Just right! Just right!*

Twenty-fifth variation

G, sheared, listens to the mocking barks of the wild things as they carry her into the cottage, wondering if it always ended this way. Maybe there never was an open window, but no one wanted to say so. A kind of gentle lie meant to ease fears of the inevitable. If so, she is learning about it rather late, though maybe that is always true: A long sleep, then—briefly, too late—a rude awakening. They lay her on the kitchen table, which has been set, she sees, for three. Above her, bats flutter in the rafters. It is warm. The oven must be on. She recalls the porridge, chairs, beds, and feels a wistful nostalgia for those comforting lies, but anger, too, that she had been so misled, haunted lifelong by corrupted tales told by tellers long dead. There was also of course her dangerous desire to dance with the wild things, maybe even, in some manner, to be one, which desire she thought of as entirely her own. But was that desire also a haunting of sorts? Is anything truly her own except the fate that now awaits her?

The pale intruder lies limply on their kitchen table like a plucked chicken, her clipped head now the whitest part of her. They have suffered such annoyances for as long as B2 can remember, and although the others are sorry this day's games are over, she is not. The foxes and crones of olden times were bad enough, but these naughty towheads have made criminal behavior frivolous, even permissible, at the expense of her family's privacy and reputation. The big bad Bs. Well, watch out, they shall be so. B1, whose cheerful mood is giving way to melancholy, his roars of laughter increasingly hollow, is less inclined to dismiss the restless golden-haired girls as mere nuisances. Admittedly, he has enjoyed their visits in ways the others have not, but they bring, if nothing else, consoling illusions, pretty markers to decorate the passing days, otherwise leaden and meaningless. His leadership usurped, he watches B3 bound about the kitchen, full of himself, devoted, not to harmony, but to its disruption. Perhaps, B1 thinks, he shall yet find an open window, disrupt the disruption. B3, grinning toothily, dips a basting brush in the honey glaze.

They are painting something sticky on her as though to mask her nakedness. Or put a gloss on it. Those brightly colored porridge pots they smashed were beautiful, as once was she. But broken shards are beautiful too, and they can hurt. Perhaps they have done her a favor. Her golden locks defined her; now she is free to seek new definitions. Maybe she can even, with what time remains, realize her old desire. She sits up on the table, crosses her legs under her, peers into their beady eyes. The wild things. They seem to be laughing at her. They shouldn't do that. She springs into a crouch, snatches up a scalpel and a carving knife, bares her teeth and snarls. Ruff! huff! huff! they bark, bumping their paws together. They think she is entertaining them. She uses her hind paws, as she thinks of them, to kick the dishes off the table, sends the pot of sticky stuff flying, and with an audacious swing of the scalpel knocks the saucepan off the stove. Their laughter ends. The littlest one, growling menacingly, reaches for her with his paw; she stabs it.

Twenty-sixth variation

Q. Ecstatic moment. G has become a wild thing. Why? The mere desire to be weird?

A. It was weird to come here, but she has no choice now, nothing to lose.

Q. B3, bleeding, roars in pain and fury. The bald intruder smirks. Will no one retaliate?

A. B2 retaliates, leaps upon the table, lashes out at the intruder, who dances away, laughing.

Q. G is such a scrawny sprite. What chance has she against three big wild things?

A. She supposes, though she is nimble, none at all. Unless she finds an open window.

Q. G clings thus to the myth of the open window. Can anyone save her now?

A. B1, reality inventor, can, but at the cost of losing forever his traditional family role.

Q. B3, loathing tradition, has disrupted the family patterns, seeking fundamental change. What is his desire?

A. Freedom. Power. But someone must lose theirs if he gains his. Way of the wild.

Q. B2 meanwhile, swinging wildly, takes a tumble, landing below in shattered dinnerware. Who avenges her?

A. B1, stifling his laughter, should, but hesitates. He has lost his appetite for roast intruder.

Q. With his newfound ambivalence, has B1 also lost his credibility as the wild things' leader?

A. In the eyes of B2 and B3, he has, but G still fears him most.

Q. The wild things are in disarray, their feast disrupted, the feisty intruder trapped. What next?

A. Perhaps G is eaten. Perhaps B1 invents an open window. Only inexorable time will tell.

Twenty-seventh variation

Something is ending. The ecstatic moment has passed. The biggest wild thing has absented himself. The other two, growling menacingly, approach the table whereon she crouches. *Someone has been tasting my porridge*, declares the middle one solemnly, and the other, following some beats behind, repeats the line in an icy monotone, holding up his bandaged paw in remonstrance. G, no longer restless, can only wait for them amid the tabletop ruins of the disrupted feast, scalpel and carving knife in her fists. *Someone has been sitting . . . . . . been sitting in my chair!* They crawl upon the table, their huge claws unsheathed. *Someone has been lying*— She bangs her weapons down, interrupting their canonic litany, scoops her clipped hairs out of the porridge pot, and applies them to her sticky body, transforming herself into a golden wild thing. They snarl, back off. She grabs up more golden hairs and flings them at them. They duck and fall from the table, landing heavily, but soon climb up again, grinning their chilling grins. A faint breeze tells her that, somewhere, there is now an open window, but she also knows, alas, she could never reach it.

Twenty-eighth variation

B1 is lying in his bed upstairs, musing wistfully upon the world's restless golden-haired girls, assuagers of time's betrayals, key to their happiness, and musing most immediately upon the feisty but doomed intruder, misled by hope, in the kitchen below. He has opened a window for her, but surely too late. There will be other wildflower pickers and butterfly chasers, but he is saddened to lose this one: his virtuosic marionette, his mischievous little vixen. He rises, heavy of heart, and descends the stairs. She is trapped on one corner of the table, B3 closing in, B2 posted on the floor below, blocking her escape. The intruder's audacious transformation makes him smile. From the rear she is still a pale inconsequential hairless thing, but her fuzzy chest and belly are resplendently golden. Her unnatural desire to transcend her kind has provoked, however, not a familial embrace, but murderous rage. She moves nimbly but not nimbly enough: B3 has her in his claws. B1 hoists himself upon the table, delivers a blow that sends B3 flying. *Somebody has been tasting my porridge*, he bellows thunderously. No reply, except for a low fierce growl.

Twenty-ninth variation

The big wild thing's roar is met with rebellious rumbles. The others, grinning humorlessly, push him off the table: he hits the floor with a heavy grunt. G braces for the worst.

B2 and B3, wielding forks, stalk the intruder. She has torn B2's family apart and must be punished. B1 returns, sweeps them both off the table. Mad clatter of pans and dishes.

G, weaponless, discovers the scissors used to shear her head. She crouches, gripping them fiercely, ready to strike, thinking of herself as a golden wild thing to keep her sinking spirits up.

B3 is back, teeth clenched, growling savagely. He claws at the armed intruder, who, ducking, falls into the waiting arms of B2. B1 snatches her away before a bite can be taken.

The puppeteer's tabletop stage is now the platform for a nightmarish dance of punching, kicking, clawing wild things, G caught in the middle. This is fun! she tells her disbelieving self, weeping.

B1, astraddle the frightened intruder, beats off her attackers. B3, standing heroically against the tyrant, takes blow after blow. B2 brains B1 with a skillet. Agitated bats flutter through the kitchen, screaming.

G's scissors have been batted away. She grabs up a wooden porridge spoon, swings it wildly, misses her attackers, hits the big one instead, surprising an angry roar from him. Oh oh.

A window is open. The oven is lit. The intruder may flee or be their dinner. Or perhaps (three) they will simply, fighting over her, tear her apart. Way of the wild.

Thirtieth variation: Quodlibet

After dinner, the B family takes nostalgic delight in singing some of the old songs—sad songs, inspiring songs, indecently comic ones—about life's ecstasies and time's betrayals, about unavoidable endings, unchanging change, and the tender agitation of desire, about skinning vixens for their fur and impaling old crones on church steeples and about shearing towheaded sprites of their golden locks. They clack wooden spoons and dance ponderously yet exuberantly, belching and snorting, around the table. It is hot in the kitchen, but somewhere a window is open and a breeze is blowing. B2 is wearing a raggedy restitched pinafore on her head like a nightcap, making everybody laugh, and B3 makes rude noises with his toy trumpet. They sing about luring intruders into their cottage—"Come closer, come closer," they growl seductively and laugh—while at the same time feeling a certain wistful nostalgia for the stories as they used to be told, the lies that made life easier.

Aria da capo

G enters the unoccupied cottage. Porridge, chairs, beds. Too hot, too cold, too high, too wide, too hard, too soft. Just right. G eats, breaks, crawls in. The owners return. *An intruder!*

G, wildflower picker, enters the snug little cottage in the woods, knowing or not knowing whose it is, the owners absent as if by arrangement. Three bowls of porridge, three chairs, three beds. Too hot, too cold, too high, too wide, too hard, too soft. Just right. The rule of three. G eats, breaks, crawls in. The owners return. *There has been an intruder!*

G, restless by nature, is picking wildflowers and chasing butterflies in the woods when, in a particularly lonely spot, she comes upon a snug little cottage. She may or may not know whose it is (there are stories). She peeps through the keyhole. The owners seem conveniently to be away, so she enters. There are three pots of porridge on the table, set out to cool. She tastes them: too hot, too cold, just right (she eats it up). There are three chairs. She sits on them: too high, too wide, just right (she breaks it). She is sleepy. Upstairs, there are three beds. She tries them: too hard, too soft, just right (she crawls in). The owners return. *There has been an intruder!* They have expected this.

G, restless butterfly chaser, enters the little cottage in the woods, probably knowing whose it is (there are stories), the owners absent as if by arrangement. Bowls of porridge, chairs, beds. Too hot, too cold, too high, too wide, too hard, too soft. Just right. The rule of three. G eats, breaks, crawls in. The owners return. The intruder they have anticipated has arrived.

G enters the unoccupied cottage. Porridge, chairs, beds. Too hot, cold, high, wide, hard, soft. Just right. G eats, breaks, crawls in. The owners return. An intruder. But where is she now?

INVASION OF THE MARTIANS

(2016)

The handsome Senator from Texas, the Capitol's leading
heartthrob, a former astronaut, and a likely future President, was in bed with two ladies, a young intern and the more
mature Secretary of the Interior (the Senator called her the
Secretary of the Posterior, about which he had just made several charming off-color but complimentary remarks about hers,
bringing an embarrassed flush to all four of her cheeks, and
giggles from the intern who was playing with two of them),
when his private security phone chimed with the news: "The
Martians have landed! In Texas!" He kissed the ladies, donned
his space suit and helmet, and sprang into action.

The Senator flew his private jet directly from his ranch to the
Martians' landing site, not at all surprised that they had chosen the great state of Texas for this historic occasion. There, in
an internationally televised address, he welcomed them to the
once-sovereign Republic of Texas, the last best place on earth,
and the heartland of the American nation, to which it also

presently owed allegiance. The Martians poured out of their pear-shaped spaceship like spilled soup. They were pea-green, as anticipated, but with fluid bodies and multiple limbs that appeared and disappeared in the sticky flow. A random scattering of startled eyes blinked like tree lights. It wasn't easy to see what separated one Martian from another.

Texans, the Senator declared, are a warm and friendly people, always ready to provide true Southern hospitality, with a Texas twist, to all self-supporting and well-behaved guests—and all the more so to distinguished visitors from outer space. He invited the Martians to a barbecue with live country music at his ranch, and offered stables full of horses and motorcycles for their enjoyment. Together, he said, we can knock out some trade agreements and cultural exchanges of benefit to both our planets, and have a grand old time while we're at it. We'll go see a rodeo, a Longhorns football game, maybe take in some clay shoots, an old-fashioned chili cook-off, and some stock-car races. Yo! Hot damn! Whaddaya say, fellas? Being fluently bilingual, he told them all this in both American and Tex-Mex, but, as it turned out, they didn't speak any civilized languages, and instead pointed their weapons at him. Couldn't they have taken a few elementary lessons before dropping in on strangers? They also seemed to have arrived without passports. He explained to them, politely, that there were certain obligatory regulations, and they shot him.

He staggered back in surprise, though in fact he felt nothing. It was like being shot with a whooshing flashlight. As soon as they had raised their soft lumpy weapons, his security people had opened fire on them with their assault rifles and submachine guns, but the bullets passed right through them. The Martians made frantic squeaky noises, their unpaired eyes wheeling about in the green muck, and whooshed him again, and the Senator's people, by now a bit panicky, shot futilely back. The Martians withdrew in a roiling green turbulence into their spaceship, one of them dropping the weapon that he—if they were divided into hes and shes—was carrying. The weapon looked like a potato with leafy ears, but it was as heavy as an armored tank. A size-XL, born-in-Texas backhoe was urgently helicoptered to the site, watched now by all the world's news media, and the potato was lifted and trucked away for scientific analysis.

The Senator, though shot, carried on gamely in his heroic West Texas manner. Reporters pressed round, shoving cameras and microphones in his face. What did it feel like, Senator? they wanted to know. Did it hurt? He smiled enigmatically. What do we do now, Senator? Does this mean interplanetary war?

First, we have to wait for the lab reports on the captured weapon, he said, solemnly removing his space helmet. Our guests seem to have a different molecular structure, and as they may be only the first of many, we need to know more about them. The security of our planet depends upon it!

The reporters said they understood that, but they were frightened. The whole *world* was frightened!

Trust me, the Senator said in his soothing western drawl, we are ready for this. We have planned for it. Even as he said so, he was himself convinced of it. Meanwhile, as the Martians are not in the way, he added, they might as well stay where we can watch them. There may be a few loose beeves wandering around out here on the open range, but it's mostly unpopulated. If the Martians give us any trouble, we'll just—he winked reassuringly—nuke the damn things. He was generously applauded by everyone, as he strode away, limping slightly for the cameras.

The ladies will be gone by now, he supposed, so he texted two or three more before jetting back and invited them over. He loved all women, and they loved him. He found, upon landing at the ranch, that the Secretary of the Interior had indeed departed, evidently flying straight back to Washington. On television, primly dressed and bespectacled, she was holding her own news conference in her office, acknowledging the internal-security threat posed by the intruders, while praising the Senator's manly intervention and proud resilience.

The young intern, however, was still squatting there in his living room, bobbing dreamily, eyes closed, in front of the news reports. She had not yet dressed, so the Senator took her hand and led her into his bedroom with its swings and toys and giant bed, which he and his guests called the Back Acre. The intern was bright and fun-loving, one of his favorites, though at the moment he couldn't remember her name. She helped him strip off his spacesuit and dropped to her knees. *Oh!* she exclaimed, and began to giggle.

What—? Holy moley! *What she was looking for wasn't there!*

In a confused rage, the Senator tossed the giggling girl out of his ranch house, locked the door against incoming traffic, and called Washington. Science be damned, those goddamn lizards must be *exterminated*, he shouted at the President. He was mad as hell. We have to *atomize* the slimy bastards! *All* of them! *Now!*

He hit the networks with a message of alarm, his white Stetson set defiantly on his brow. He watched himself on his giant television screen as he spoke, square-jawed and determined. It seems the Martians may be bringing viruses that could wipe out the entire human species, he announced gravely. They must and *will* be utterly destroyed! It is, finally, the only solution! This was what everyone wanted to hear.

Almost everyone. The breaking news report that followed was interrupted by an interview with a prominent scientist who argued that Martians might not be born the way humans are, but may be made or grown. Attempting to eradicate them, especially with nuclear weapons, as the Senator was proposing, might actually cause them to replicate. The scientist suggested spraying them with herbicides instead. This idea was not popular with the viewing audience. For the Senator, it was the next thing to treason, and he returned to the news channels to say so, accusing the scientist of intellectual bullying, and questioning his loyalty for having even suggested that the nation's weaponry might not be up to the task.

The Senator was aware, however, that, as famously cool in a crunch as he was, it might have been a serious mistake not to tell the intern, when he threw her out, to keep her mouth shut. He clicked apprehensively through the social-media websites and TV news channels, and, as he had feared, there she was, dressed in a gauzy white frock, answering a brassy interviewer's impertinent questions about the Senator's missing manhood. Nothing but a pimple! the stupid child squealed, lifting her skirt and pointing. No, he didn't give me *time* to pop it!

He went on social media to ridicule the intern's mischievous claims, accusing the opposition of cynically exploiting the child for its own dirty tricks. Never laid eyes on that poor deluded girl, he posted. And, if she is not deluded, then she is a malicious, scheming little liar, bought and paid for by my unscrupulous opponents. She needs to have her fantasies popped, he tweeted. His righteous anger convinced the people. Nevertheless, they remained curious. They wanted him to show his member on TV.

"The Yellow Rose of Texas" was binging on his top-security phone. It was the Chairman of the Joint Chiefs of Staff, an Air Force general who was a frequent overnight visitor to the ranch and its Back Acre. The President had ordered him, the General said, on the Senator's recommendation and owing to the failure of conventional weapons, to strike the Martians with a nuclear missile. The deployment of atomic weapons was an international no-no, the General said, though that wasn't really an issue, as we'd be bombing our own country. But the Secretary of Health and Human Services had bought into that dissident scientist's horse poop that atomic bombs might cause the weird creatures to proliferate, and now the President has turned chicken and left it up to the General to nuke or not to nuke. You've met them, he said. What do you think?

The Senator replied that the aliens were indeed dangerous and had to be neutralized. If it was a targeted strike, there shouldn't be a problem. Add in firebombs and a few chemical warheads, just to cover the bases. Also, that scientist's background needed to be checked, not to mention his decidedly sickly color.

The General said they'd had the wacko under surveillance for some time. He was ideologically suspect, having whined too much in public about the recent wars, but he wasn't a Martian mole, just a dipshit eastern egghead. The General was more worried about the relentless pressure from the big networks and the pesky online bloggers to provide a public and verifiable extermination of the invaders that the whole world could witness. How could he do that without irradiating a lot of people?

Mark out a hundred-mile-radius no-go zone and use hovering camera drones to watch the strike, the Senator suggested, wondering if there were some way that a drone could be useful in his own predicament with the intern.

That might work once, the General said, but what if the goddam Martians just keep coming? If they got through our early-warning system this time, they can probably do it again. What if they land next in an urban center? People are saying that, since we have no border to seal, we should cover the homeland in vast overhead nets. At a stretch, I suppose we could do that, but—

Hide under a damn blanket and give up our freedom to come and go wherever the hell we want? the Senator snapped. Never! Free exploration of the universe is our God-given constitutional right! We have to face the enemy square on! You guys had better start preparing now for a preventive war!

The Chairman of the Joint Chiefs of Staff sighed. Okeydokey, he said, assuming a more convivial manner. By the way, that supposed weapon of theirs turned out to be just what it looked like, a potato. It was apparently injected with some kind of artificial gravity that evaporated when they cut it open at the lab. A decoy to keep us distracted for a while. They're not completely stupid. Which seemed to remind him of something, and he abruptly asked about the Senator's wound. There were rumors . . .

The Senator winced, but brushed off the General's sniggering insinuations with a dry laugh. Party politics, he said. They'll say any damn thing. You know that.

The General grunted to acknowledge he did know that. Nevertheless, the Senator should be aware, he warned, that out on the Internet those rumors were spreading. Ducking them was going to get harder. He figured the best way to stop them might be to get a certification of anatomical wholeness from somebody like the Army Surgeon General. He said he could arrange a private physical. The Senator promised to take his suggestion under advisement, and hung up. Damn that kid!

He'd been treating his crisis as a kind of extraterrestrial political issue for which he was only an interested consultant, but the pimple, as she called it, was beginning to itch, and could no longer be ignored. He was afraid to touch the thing, even to look at it, much less scratch it, but it had a sharp worrying bite worse than jock itch, and finally he couldn't stop himself.

Meanwhile, plague fears and conspiracy theories were erupting everywhere. Are we assuming they're from Mars only because they're green? a news pundit asked. Maybe they were made in China in a plot to rule the world! Others feared that the Martians were offspring of the devil and had cannibalized all the angels, fulfilling an ancient Biblical prophecy. Next come the locusts and the man-eating toads! Then, a veteran newscaster at the landing site sickened suddenly and died. A doctor explained the illness, but he seemed evasive. People were convinced that the doctor was covering up the truth so as not to cause panic, which then did cause panic. We're all going to die! they cried.

A small group of noisy ill-dressed university students gathered at the state capital for a Save the Martians protest. Greenness is not a crime, they chanted. They were met by a large, patriotic Snuff the Martians anti-protest. Fights broke out. It would feel good to hit somebody, the Senator thought, watching them go at it on TV, while he scratched his itch. The Save the Martians protesters were arrested as rioters and alien sympathizers, but other subversive peace groups were said to be forming.

The opposition party, meanwhile, accused the Senator of moral weakness and catastrophically poor judgment. Why did the damn showboat go and meet with them in the first place? It compromised him and compromised the nation. Now those freaks were here, and there seemed to be no clean way to get rid of them. And what had really happened when the Martians shot him? Why wouldn't he show his member to the nation to end the disquiet? What was he hiding? The Senator wondered if the conspiracy theories about China could somehow be used to deflect the mounting curiosity. Then the Chinese started asking the same questions.

Back at the ranch, "The Yellow Rose of Texas" was chiming like a circusy call to arms. It was the Chairman of the Joint Chiefs of Staff again, calling to say that the Martians had been taken care of. Had he used nuclear weapons on them? Well, sort of, the General said. They made themselves an easy target for us, massing suicidally into a wobbly green blob. It was hard to tell whether they were wobbly with fear or laughing at us, the General added, but, after we dropped the bomb, they weren't there anymore. Our report says that we obliterated them, but the only kills we could be sure of were a few illegals sneaking North.

The Senator was feeling a bit wobbly himself, and finally, he made an appointment with his home-town family doctor, a fellow Texan whose discretion he could trust. He submitted to X-rays, brain and bone scans, blood tests, an endoscopy, cardiograms, throat swabs. During the hands-on physical examination, the doctor fingered the pimple thoughtfully, his mustache twitching slightly. Probably trying not to laugh. He sighed, applied an ointment against the itchiness, only making it worse, and admitted that he was baffled. And, no, the Senator's member wasn't likely to grow back on its own.

·

But the nation and the media are demanding to see it, the Senator said, his voice breaking. His mother had once read him a story about a prince who forgot who he was and became a poor flea-infested beggar for the rest of his life, and he'd cried and cried in his mother's arms, just as he was crying now. How could a person *not* know who he was? I've got to show them something, Doc. How about surgery?

X-rays suggest that we'd somehow have to replace the whole apparatus, the doctor said, inside and out. Potency afterward could not be guaranteed, needless to say, and I don't know if an implant is even possible. Nothing much to anchor it on. Things have got rerouted in there. I couldn't even *find* your prostate, and I'm not sure where your water goes. There might be something growing in there, though it looks more vegetal than cancerous. There were anomalies with the blood tests, too, so if you needed a transfusion during the operation we might not be able to find a donor. The doctor said he might, however, be able to provide a temporary silicone prosthesis with inflatable testes and real pubic hair, affixed with a reliable medical adhesive. Packers, he explained, have more or less worked for thousands of emasculated war veterans, and they look and feel to others almost like the real thing. It wouldn't solve your problem, any more than it solves theirs, but it should look OK on TV.

The Senator tried one on. It had the sensitivity of a dead mouse, but, with a little hidden switch under the fake testicles, it could be moved through seven degrees of flexibility and stiffness. At the seventh level, it pointed straight up and was bigger than his own had been. He felt oddly proud of it, playing with the switch.

He called the host of a popular late-night television talk show, a fellow Texan and golfer with whom he sometimes enjoyed a friendly all-day mixed-doubles nineteen-holer, and offered to expose himself on the show to satisfy the public demand. Should at least be good for the ratings, the Senator said. The talk show host har-harred. It'll be the biggest damn thing since the Creation, he said. I missed that whoop-de-doo, so I definitely want to grab hold of this one, so to speak. Shall I book you for the next show?

I'll be there, said the Senator.

There was rapturous applause, loud whistling, when the Senator, a national hero, came onstage that night in his leather vest, string tie, jeans, cowboy boots, and silver spurs. He lifted his white Stetson and waved it at the audience, while the studio band played his college spirit song, "The Eyes of Texas," and everyone clapped and cheered some more.

When prompted by the show's host, the Senator, his thumbs hooked in his holster belt, trying not to scratch, described in detail his engagement with the Martians, whom he called vicious little bug-eyed creeps. I offered them the hand of friendship, he told the audience, and in thanks they shot me—and when they shot *me*, they shot the *nation*! God created mankind, like you and me—like all of us here tonight—in His own image, but He sure as heck wasn't a model for those squeaky little green things. They don't even smell good. A muddle of laughter and cheering and booing at the same time.

The talk-show host reached under his table and came out with a green rubber mask. He pulled it over his face, hunched his shoulders, rolled his eyes, stood with bowed legs and wagged a dill pickle, drawing more hooting laughter. Then, peeling off the mask and taking a bite out of the pickle, he asked the Senator what had happened when the Martians shot him. A young woman appeared recently on a colleague's show and claimed to have had intimate relations with you shortly after you were shot, he said. Here is what she said. He played a tape of the interview. Was that how it happened, Senator?

I'm afraid she's an opportunistic little liar, the Senator said. I've never seen her before.

Can you *prove* she's lying? the host asked.

The Senator looked uncomfortable. The house was hushed. Well, I'm a conservative Christian, he said solemnly, and I reckon you are, too, sir, being a Texan. We conservatives have nothing against normal sexual behavior. In fact we're pretty good at it. But we don't like to see private intimacies turned into public pornography. To provide the only real proof I have, I'd have to expose myself to this audience and to all those watching your show around the world. As I'm sure you understand, that's fundamentally against my religion. But don't worry. I can personally assure you that everything's just fine.

I'm afraid the world needs more than your assurances, Senator, the talk-show host said. This is not pornography we're talking about, but a substantive response to an alarming human crisis. As a species, we are facing an unknown threat, perhaps extinction. In a word, we're scared spitless. And only you can give us our spit back.

The Senator shook his head and stood, tall and manly, tipped his Stetson at the audience, and prepared to leave the stage. The murmur of disappointment billowing up seemed to give him pause. He gazed thoughtfully out upon the auditorium, then removed his hat, held it reverently to his chest, pressed his hands together at the brim, and bowed his head to pray. An expectant silence fell. Perhaps others were joining him in prayer. Then he tossed his hat where he'd been sitting, unbuckled his holster belt, and dropped his jeans and boxer shorts. There were gasps and nervous titters as the prosthesis flopped out. He'd set the switch at semi-tumescent, but it was still impressive.

Amen! exclaimed the talk show host. *I believe!* The audience broke into wild cheers and thunderous applause. The Senator moved the switch to the seventh position as a kind of triumphant salute, and melancholically left the stage to a standing ovation.

ACKNOWLEDGMENTS

Stories in this volume first appeared in the following publications:

American Reader: "The Goldilocks Variations," 2013
Cavalier: "The Elevator," 1966
A Child Again (McSweeney's): "Stick Man," 2005
Conjunctions: "The Early Life of the Artist," 1991
   "Punch," 2000
Daedalus: "Grandmother's Nose," 2005
Elements of Fiction: "The Tinkerer," 1981
Esquire: "The Magic Poker," 1969
Evergreen: "The Brother," 1962
Frank: "Top Hat," 1987
Harper's: "Beginnings," 1972
Harvard Review: "The Return of the Dark Children," 2002
Iowa Review: "Aesop's Forest," 1986
   "The New Thing," 1994

Kenyon Review: "Riddle," 2005

New American Review: "The Wayfarer," 1968
"The Gingerbread House," 1969

The New Yorker: "Going for a Beer," 2011
"Invasion of the Martians," 2016

A Night at the Movies (Linden Press/Simon & Schuster):
"Inside the Frame," 1987
"Lap Dissolves," 1987
"The Phantom of the Movie Palace," 1987

Playboy: "The Hat Act," 1968
"In Bed One Night," 1980
"You Must Remember This," 1985
"The Invisible Man," 2002

Pricksongs & Descants (E. P. Dutton): "The Babysitter," 1969

Quarterly Review of Literature: "The Dead Queen," 1973

TriQuarterly: "The Fallguy's Faith," 1976
"Cartoon," 1987